DEPTH OF DECEPTION
(A Titanic Murder Mystery)

ALEXANDER GALANT

Published by Alexander Galant Entertainment

Library of Congress Cataloging in Publication Data
ISBN: 978-0-9879835-1-0

http://www.DepthOfDeception.com

Cover illustration by Carmen Gillespie, Copyright © 2012

DEDICATION

This book is dedicated to my daughter, Cynthia.
'You inspired me.'

Also, in memory of the 1,517 souls who perished with Titanic
on the night of April 15, 1912.

And to Marion. Sadly, her real killers were
never brought to justice.

.

ACKNOWLEDGMENTS

To the 3-Day Novel Writing Contest which first gave me the opportunity to write this story (77 pages) in 72 hours.

My former agent Michele Rubin, for her notes on how to expand my short novella into a full-length novel.

Lana Winter for her 'nitpickery and playful snarkeries' and Theresa Barrett for the helpful suggestions during the final process of this book.

To my friends Kirk Teeple, JP Gedeon, Denise Brady, and Paul Nadeau for sharing their professional knowledge and experiences for details.

Malcolm Anderson for taking the time to answer my questions about INTERPOL and international policing.

Also, Sara Dymond for the historical layout of Cobh Cove in 1982.

Special thanks to the Titanic International Society and its members for their assistance in some research questions.

As well as Edward Kamuda and Karen Kamuda of Titanic Historical Society, Inc.

I would take this opportunity to thank Mike Scott, Brian Chenault and Ingrid Jurek. As a writer I had their help in the past but didn't have the chance to properly acknowledge them before.

To my Oma (grandmother), who used to read a book a day, thank you for introducing me to your love of books and the power they have to travel through history or take you to faraway places. I wish you were still here to read this one.

My wife Carmen, not only for her love, support and unending patience... but for her illustration on the front cover and her dreaded red pen and her ruthless feedback.

NOTES FROM THE AUTHOR

After much thought and deliberation, I have decided, wherever possible, that
chapters set in the USA and characters who are American will use American
expressions and spellings (i.e. gasoline, gray & color), but chapters set in, and
with characters from the United Kingdom will use British expressions and
spellings (i.e. petrol, grey & colour). Being Canadian, I wanted to
accommodate all my readers on both sides of The Pond.
Thank you for your understanding.

APRIL 1, 1982

CHAPTER 1

. . . _ _ _ . . .

(dit dit dit daah daah daah dit dit dit!)

Then the radio went dead. Three dots, three dashes, three dots: Morse Code for SOS, the international distress call. Searchlights sliced frantically through the darkness of the North Atlantic, looking for the sinking ship. Nothing. Captain Sadler frowned as he peered through his binoculars into the night. The waxing crescent moon carved through the clouds of the windless night. The Atlantic water was unusually still: not a ripple, as smooth as polished glass.

He looked to the starboard side. On a frigid night like tonight, the seaman wished he were anywhere else but standing outside the bridge blasted by the cold sea air as they patrolled.

"Still no sign of life," the lookout called, his breath billowing into the frosty air.

Sadler glanced over to James, the port lookout, who announced, "Nothing on port side."

Sadler cursed under his breath. If this was an April Fool's joke, then he was not amused. Emergencies at sea were serious matters, especially in this region. The harsh North Atlantic Ocean could be cruel and powerful, demanding of mankind's respect, and merciless against human ignorance.

Less than a month and a half ago, The Ocean Ranger off-shore drilling unit had incurred the wrath of the ocean's storms and sank off the coast of Newfoundland, resulting in the deaths of eighty-four rig workers. Captain Sadler's ship, the HMS *McKinley*, had been investigating a possible illegal whaling ship and couldn't reach The Ocean Ranger soon enough. This time, however, they were close. The *McKinley* had quickly arrived at the co-ordinates given in a previous message: Latitude: 41° 46' North and Longitude: 50° 14' West.

He turned to the Lieutenant, "Any sign of a ship?"

"Nothing on the radar, sir," replied the Lieutenant, never taking his eyes off the green glowing radar screen.

The GIUK listening line had first picked up the call at 00:05 hundred hours. The Greenland, Iceland, United Kingdom (GIUK) line's purpose was to detect any Soviet submarines trying to pass through the North Atlantic. Captain Sadler sighed as he looked at his watch. He was about to give the order to turn about when a voice in the darkness called out sharply: "Man overboard! Man overboard! Off the starboard bow!"

"All ahead slow!" roared Sadler, then picked up the microphone and barked into it, "Rescue Stations!"

. . .

Able Seaman Donaldson had been at the ready in his neoprene wetsuit, prepared to dive into the icy waters for a search and rescue.

His seaboat was lowered into the ocean and bounced across the surface, speeding towards the solitary body of a woman floating on what appeared to be an old fashioned wooden deck chair. He was disappointed that there was only one possible survivor to retrieve. The chance of survival was slim in these conditions. No one could survive these icy waters for any length of time, especially sprawled out the way she was. Donaldson had been trained to survive in extreme climates. He knew how to prevent hypothermia by keeping his limbs tucked in and as close to his chest as possible. Most civilians panic and try treading water or swimming to keep their limbs moving, thinking the movement would keep them warm. The exact opposite was true: the movement pumps warm blood to the limbs, where it cools quickly, cutting survival by fifty percent. Swimming can also cause debilitating cramps, not to mention uncontrollable shivering.

Though he knew it was pointless, Donaldson plunged himself into the water as the boat neared the woman. In the winter moonlight, this victim had an eerie, almost ghostlike, appearance. She clenched a soggy teddy bear in one hand and a book of some sort in the other. The diver turned the woman's face towards him. Her dark wet hair, framing her lovely face, contrasted sharply against her alabaster skin. She appeared to be dead. Donaldson had encountered death at sea before but it never got...

She suddenly gasped for air, nearly shocking Donaldson out of his wetsuit.

"She's breathing!" he hollered, and frantically tried to place the Kisbie ring around the woman. He soon discovered it would be no simple task, as she was wearing a cumbersome, multi-layered dress. Donaldson tried to remove the bear and the book from the woman's grasp, but her fingers would not loosen. He gave up quickly. It was more urgent to get her out of the biting water. The three other crewmen in the seaboat helped to hoist the woman out of the frigid ocean. With every second counting, Donaldson wasted no time by getting into the boat himself. He grabbed the wooden deck chair in one hand and the side of the seaboat with the other, and called out "Let's go!" to the crewmen behind the wheel.

— — —

The night was bitingly cold despite the many layers he was wearing; Sadler could feel the wind created by the moving ship ripping through him and rattling his bones. With a renewed admiration for the lookouts, he tried not to blink as his eyelashes seemed to freeze together, and he felt icicles forming on his greying moustache. He could hear them crunch in his eyebrows as he scowled while the mysterious woman was hoisted on-board. Sadler was hoping that the discovery of this survivor would bring answers to some questions, but her surprising attire and her unconscious state only served to deepen the mystery.

Even as she fell upon the deck, her vice-like fists did not relax to drop their contents. It was as if rigor mortis was setting in.

"Quick, get her below to sickbay!"

"Aye sir," responded two crewmen as they hauled her out of the night air. Sadler turned to Ordinary Seaman Cartier, one of the few female crewmembers on board, who was stamping her feet on the deck to keep warm. Sadler signaled for her to follow. "Get her into dry clothes as quickly as possible!"

"Aye sir."

As the HMS *McKinley* sailed onward, its searchlights continued to scan the ocean. There *had* to be a ship nearby. The woman couldn't have been in the icy waters for long and had to have come from somewhere. Sadler had already given the order to commence a grid search from this point to try to locate the ship, or any other survivors. He looked at the beech wood folding deck chair that had acted as her floatation device. He recognized the style — his grandfather had had the same design on his yacht. Sadler bent down to take a closer look at the mark emblazoned onto the headboard . A five-point star was carved perfectly into the wood. There was something familiar about it. Suddenly a voice called from the bridge.

"I'm picking something up on the radar, sir!"

"A ship?" Sadler hoped.

"No, sir."

Before the Lieutenant could respond, Sadler already knew the answer. Suddenly he could see it, glowing in the night.

"Iceberg! Dead ahead, sir!"

"Sound the collision alarm!" cried out Sadler as he raced back into the bridge.

The familiar cry of the action alarm pierced the night air, spurring the crew to the ready. From the bosun's mate station, the officer grabbed the microphone and roared, "All hands brace for impact! All hands brace for impact!"

As his crew readied themselves, Sadler needed to quickly decide the best course of action. Starboard or Port? What were the better odds?

He flicked the switch to keep the microphone active while he barked the evasive maneuvers, "Hard to starboard!"

"Hard to starboard!" echoed the voice of the helmsman, who was two decks below closer to the stern of the ship.

"Starboard engine back *full!*"

"Starboard engine back full!" repeated Helm. Sadler detected a hint of nervousness in the helmsman's voice. The use of the word 'full' for engines was only used in a state of emergency. The helmsman was in a windowless room away from the bridge with only a compass and two engine repeaters. He had no way of knowing what lay before them. This odd placement is traced back to the old wartime days when the possibility of ramming an enemy ship might have been necessary. The Helm Officer might have been less likely to follow such an order if he could see what the bridge saw; hence Helm was stationed where it was.

"Wheel hard to starboard, starboard engine back full, sir," stated Helm.

Sadler's eyes were drawn to the ghostly specter looming before them. It was a very large pinnacle iceberg.

"Wheel hard to starboard," Helm began to repeat. "Starboard engine..."

"Very good," huffed Sadler curtly. Even though Sadler already knew from the compass and seeing the arrow on the engine repeater settings, the Helmsman was following standard protocol. Sadler, who was in no mood for pleasantries, held his breath as he could feel the ship struggling against inertia to slow down and turn. The Lieutenant and two other officers rushed over to the port wing to gauge their status.

As his hands gripped the rail in front of the console, Sadler realized he was unconsciously sucking in his gut, as he did in his youth as he tried to squeeze through a broken fence to a scrap yard, as if he were willing the ship's girth to do the same as it edged past the enormous glacial menace.

The Lieutenant turned back to Sadler and with a nod called out, "All clear."

Everyone on the bridge sighed collectively as the ship moved past the icy monolith, unscathed. The Action Alarm was turned off.

"Midships, both engines ahead slow," ordered the Captain.

"Midships, both engines ahead slow," echoed the voice of the Helm Officer. Sadler awaited the confirmation that they were now putting the ship back on course. "Rudder amidships, both engines ahead slow, sir."

"Very good," replied Sadler into the microphone, his eyes still drawn to the iceberg that caught them all off guard. Sadler scowled. *How did it suddenly appear out of nowhere?* His eyes drifted to the lookouts. They were not looking at him but rather continuing to scan the sea for any further sign of danger. He couldn't blame them for missing it. Over a dozen crewmembers, including himself, had been staring into the endless horizon looking out for a ship in distress. It might have been a windless night, making the sea a flat calm, but despite the absence of waves breaking on icebergs to aid the visual, the radar should have picked up the iceberg before it was upon them. Strange.

As they moved safely away from the iceberg, Sadler needed some answers. Any answers. "Lieutenant, you have the bridge."

The captain's boots echoed on the metal ladder as he descended below deck. In sickbay, the mysterious woman had been stripped of the multiple layers of clothing and was covered by warm blankets and hot water bottles. A stocking cap had been put on her head to retain her body temperature. Her odd costume was dripping from a hook on the nearby bulkhead, the waterlogged teddy bear she had gripped so tightly was resting in a metal bedpan, and the soggy book lay on the table nearby.

"How is our patient?" asked Sadler as he neared the woman.

The ship's doctor didn't look up as he shone a light into the woman's sapphire blue eyes, "She's suffered stage-three hypothermia. Her body temperature was so low that I can only assume that her cellular metabolic process had shut down."

"In layman's terms, please." Sadler asked.

The doctor peered over his glasses at Sadler, "I'm sorry, Sir. At that point internal organs usually fail. I can't be sure if she'll ever regain consciousness."

After all this, they still might lose their only survivor. Sadler couldn't bear to think about it. Sadler turned his attention to Cartier who was still trying to wring the water out of the woman's cumbersome underdress. "Did you find any I.D.?"

"Not quite, Sir. But she was wearing this," Cartier said as she handed Sadler a gold locket on a chain. Sadler held the locket up to the light to examine it closely. It was quite elegant. On the back was an ornate inscription. Sadler tilted it past the light to make the engraving more legible,

To Myra,
Happy Anniversary!
Archie
December 31.

Myra? Was this woman Myra? Sadler looked again at the locket. As he hoped, there was a small hinge on the one side. He tried to open it. It was stuck. He reached into the pocket of his trousers, taking out his pocketknife. He flicked it open and then proceeded to carefully pry the tip of the blade along the seam. He felt himself sigh in relief as it popped open. Setting the knife down, he parted the two halves delicately. There he saw two pictures inside: one was of a young man with the mysterious woman—presumably Myra—dressed in turn-of-the-century costumes. The other photo was of a small baby boy dressed in a cheesy old-fashioned navy suit. Both photos had a sepia tone to them—*no doubt created at some novelty booth at a carnival,* he thought.

"And Captain, there might also be something here," Cartier said, pointing to the book on the nearby table. "Looks like a piece of paper used as a makeshift bookmark."

Sadler set the locket down carefully as Cartier held the small hardcover up for him to see. It looked antiquated, like the kind found in old used bookstores. Quite small in size, on first glance it appeared to be about five or six inches by eight inches and quite thin. The grey cloth cover was water damaged but as Cartier gingerly opened the book, Sadler could make out the single title on the spine: *Futility*.

Futility? The title was somehow oddly familiar to Sadler, but he could not recollect having read it. Cartier carefully pried the pages open to the marked section. The wet mysterious bookmark was stuck into the page. Cartier gently set the book down as she looked about and then grabbed the tweezers from the nearby metal pan. She carefully began to pry up a corner. Sadler was getting impatient but he could see that Cartier had to move ever-so-slowly so as not to rip it.

She turned it over and gingerly unfolded it, carefully smoothed it out and moved it into the light to take a look. A confused frown crossed her brow. She looked up at Captain Sadler, opened her mouth as if to say something, then looked back down at the paper and continued to stare at it, as if waiting for something to happen.

"Well? What is it?"

Cartier said nothing, but backed away so Sadler could inspect the piece of paper. Sadler recognized it immediately; it was an old style ticket for a steamship. In curved text at the top were the bold letters:

WHITE STAR LINE

That was where Sadler had seen that five-point star. It was the old logo of the prominent British shipping company. This was a 'Cabin Passenger's

Contract Ticket', which meant 'First Class' but the names that were written in ink were smudged by water damage. He could barely make out: "A__G."

Beneath the illustrated image of a four-funneled 'Cunard Class' Steamer was the name of the passenger ship typed in bold letters. Captain Sadler felt an odd chill as he read the impossible:

British Steamship: R.M.S. TITANIC

CHAPTER 2

Callum Toughill looked at his wristwatch as he sat in the uncomfortable chair outside of Percy Winthrope's office. Quarter to nine. Mr. Winthrope was uncharacteristically late to his own meeting. As one of the senior brokers at the head office of Lloyd's of London, Winthrope was always very punctual.

"Can I get you a tea while you wait?" asked Mr. Winthrope's new assistant. Callum had met her only once before and was now too embarrassed to ask her name again. She then corrected herself, "No wait... you prefer coffee, correct?"

Callum smiled as he waved his hand dismissively. "No, thank you. I've had too much already."

"Now then, I'll be *gain-hand...* nearby, if you change your mind," she said with a smile as she sat back down behind her typewriter. Callum noticed that her accent had strong traces of Yorkshire in it. Callum smiled back. He hated lying to her but he didn't have the heart to tell her that he didn't like the coffee at the Lloyd's head office. This was ironic considering that Lloyd's of London began in the 1700's as a coffee house catering to sailors, merchants and ship owners. To make ends meet, the founding Lloyd would set up business meetings and keep up on the latest shipping news. Now the insurance and brokering company not only had offices all over the world but their head office was overcrowded and designs for a new head office down the street were being reviewed.

Callum rose from the back-numbing guest chair as he looked at his watch again. He hated to sit still and started to pace about the underwriter's bullpen's puke-green carpet. He smirked. He hoped that Winthrope would update the new building's décor. Its 1960's styling was twenty years out of date. *Hope they get rid of that ship too,* he thought as he looked at the framed picture of the *Titanic* sinking. Callum winced at the sight. Like hanging a horseshoe upside down, surely it must be bad luck to have a sinking ship on display. Still, as a freelance investigator Callum understood why Winthrope wanted it there. It was a little-known fact that in 1912, a New York client sent a desperate telegraph in the middle of the night to a broker here in London to insure the RMS *Titanic* for £1 million. Respecting the urgency of an established client, the request was processed quickly. Later the next day, that broker learned that the *Titanic* had perished and that the insurance request was made as it was sinking. The portrait was there as a reminder of their folly. Callum remembered that whenever something out of the ordinary came into the office, Percy Winthrope always reminded his brokers to *'look for icebergs.'*

As he continued to pace, Callum Toughill caught his reflection in the mirror near the coat rack. He grimaced. *Time for another haircut.* He liked it shaved military-style. He was still in good shape for a man in his forties, and liked wearing fitted tailored suits to show off that fact just enough. The whole appearance made him look intimidating to the people he was investigating, but deep down he took extra pride in having come a long way from the mining town in Scotland where he'd grown up. He had all but lost the brogue in his accent. Unless he got angry. Or drunk.

"Sorry to keep you waiting, mate," Percy said in his familiar Northern Irish accent as he entered the bullpen briskly. Percy Winthrope was one of the few men who could wear a bow tie on a regular basis and not look like a dolt. As usual his suits were as grey as his demeanor. Callum grabbed his briefcase from the floor next to the uncomfortable chair and followed Winthrope into his office. As he dropped some papers next to the ashtray on his desk, Winthrope grumbled, "Things have been chaotic around here."

"Don't fret it, Mr. Winthrope," Callum said as he held out a file folder.

"What's that?" Winthrope asked.

"My preliminaries on the Bolshar art claim," replied Callum. Then, noticing the confusion in Winthrope's face he quickly asked, "Isn't that why you called me in this morning?"

"My apologies," huffed Winthrope. "I had no time to go into details over the phone. I need to pull you off that case."

"Have I done something wrong?"

"Good heavens, no!" retorted Winthrope. "You're one of the best investigators I know... which is why I need to reassign you to another case."

"What of the Bolshar art claim?"

"Someone else can take over. Have a seat, Callum." Winthrope gestured to the chair across from his desk. "Can I offer you some coffee?"

"No!" Callum paused and cleared his throat. "No, thank you. I'm eager to know about this new case."

Winthrope peered over his glasses at Callum, then took out a handkerchief and began polishing them as he spoke. It was a nervous habit that Callum had observed over the years. It was something Winthrope did when he was trying to choose his words carefully.

"Have you heard of the murder of…" Winthrope paused. *Was it nerves or dramatic effect?* Winthrope put on his glasses before he continued, "The murder of Agatha Gilcrest?"

Callum arched his back and felt the muscles tighten in his jaw. He needed to be sure he heard correctly. "Did you say Agatha Gilcrest?"

Winthrope nodded.

"As in the old woman murdered in Scotland seventy-five years ago?"

"Precisely."

Did he know about it? He knew of the case but it was forbidden to utter the name 'Agatha Gilcrest' in Toughill's home. The case was the very reason Callum Toughill was unable to pursue his true dream of becoming a police officer like his grandfather who had been a police detective at the time of the murder. He was later disgraced and forced to resign.

Once, as a young boy, Callum could see that his grandfather was miserable and asked about it. The usually cheery old man became cross and snarled, *"Not something I care to discuss in this lifetime, I shall take the burden to my grave."* And that was the end of the discussion. It was a moment Callum never forgot, and he never dared to mention it again.

When Callum announced that he was going to pursue a career in law enforcement, his grandfather forbade it. All of his relatives, even ones he only saw at baptisms and funerals, felt the need to contact him and chastise him for opening such horrible wounds in his dear, sweet 'granda'.

Callum eventually relented, but not because of family pressure. He would have gladly proven them wrong; however, when the 'truth' of the past reared its hideous fangs, along with the sneers of his would-be superior officers, Callum came to a sobering realization. It was clear the police force he so wanted to join was not going to be fair. The sins of the father are inherited by the sons. Being an insurance investigator was the closest vocation he could find without carrying a badge that would be forever tarnished through no fault of his own.

"Yes I know of it," sighed Callum.

"Forgive me," replied Winthrope. "It was a rhetorical question. I'm well aware of your family's history…. And your grandfather… Jack?"

"John. My grandfather John," added Callum dryly. He then leaned in. "What is it about this case that interests you?"

"The infamous brooch that was stolen," Winthrope said as he retrieved a photo from a nearby folder and held it up for Callum to see. It was a crescent-shaped silver brooch with twenty-two diamonds. Some were notably large ones at the thickest curve of the jewelry. It was elegant and stunning. Winthrope continued, "As you know it was never recovered."

Callum nodded.

"What you don't know is that it may have been on the *Titanic* when it sank."

Callum looked at Winthrope with confusion. He knew Winthrope had a mild... no, *severe* obsession with the *Titanic*, but this seemed preposterous. "Are you serious?"

"Very much so."

"And how do we come to this revelation seventy-odd years after the fact?"

"We, here at Lloyd's, have been privy to the possibility for some time," Winthrope said as his hand patted the thick file folder. "Some years ago, a lost claim turned up with an original date of 1912 and a description of this very brooch. The name on the slip was smeared with water and we were never able to make it out."

"Why does Lloyd's care about it now after all these years?"

"As we speak, there is a court battle raging on over the salvage rights for the wreck of the *Lusitania*. We have received word that Dr. Ballard, a renowned oceanographer, has received more funding and the support of several countries to locate the wreck of the *Titanic*. We need to ascertain if that brooch really was on the *Titanic* and how it got there. This may even help prove your grandfather's case."

Callum sighed. Any clues were long gone. The trail was cold... seventy-five years cold. He had little reason to believe this would work. "Aw Percy, I wouldn't know where to start."

"You can start by reading through this file. Look for icebergs."

CHAPTER 3

RING!

Edward Hoffman ignored his phone, as well as the arthritic pain in his joints, as he dipped the fine-tipped brush into the oil paint and mixed it into the other hue on the palette, trying to get the right shade of blue. He carefully applied it onto the canvas. *It's not quite right yet. Needs a touch more white to lighten it.*

RING!

Who would be calling this early? The copper rays of morning were just starting to burst through the east window, caressing the rustic room with a sun-kissed glow. Shadows of the cedar trees danced on the wooden wall. Watching the sun rising over the lake enraptured his soul. Perhaps he was getting melancholy in his old age but each day meant a fresh beginning. In summertime he would sit in the Gazebo for hours, painting until the sun went down… or the mosquitoes came out to feast.

RING!

Over the last twenty years Edward would drive out to spend a few days per month at the old family lake house on the New England coast. The 'main room' was once the entire structure of the ancient log cabin, but over the years additional rooms, plumbing and other such modern amenities were added. Still, it maintained its charm, decorated with elegant yet simple furniture from various decades past. Over the years, the cabin had been host to such gadgets such as the radio, icebox, television and now the mammoth-sized C-Band satellite dish, which allowed Edward to receive cable channels and news in this remote area of New England.

RING!

The sound shattered the tranquility of his thoughts. *What idiot is calling me here?* Everyone knew not to disturb him while he retreated into creative solitude. He finally heard the click of the answering machine as it began to whirl into action. Not very many people could afford an answering machine but, like the television, Edward believed it would only be a matter of time before everyone had one in their home.

BEEP!

"Edward. It's me, I know you're there." It was Roger Zisholm, a lawyer and colleague. Roger was originally an in-house council for Hoffman International, the family's company, and when he left to set up his own practice, he'd become Edward's personal attorney.

His voice called out from the machine's speaker, "Turn on the news. Any channel. You'll thank me later."

What could be so important? Edward wondered. Still, Roger knew better than to bother him here. Wiping the paint off his hands, his eyes darted about the room looking for another one of the latest gadgets: the television remote control. Edward caught a glimpse of his reflection in the dark glass screen. For a man of his advanced years he still looked healthier than men half his age. He found the remote upon the TV itself and harrumphed. *Defeats the purpose of having a remote control.* Moments later, the TV sparked to life, showing an image of a staunch British navy captain on the screen. The name 'Captain Sadler of the HMS *McKinley*' was superimposed over his chest. Edward was familiar with the crisp tone of the captain. The accent reminded him of his own commanding officer, a good man who had died too young.

"This is obviously an elaborate hoax, and this unfortunate woman will most likely die as a result of this caper," Sadler snarled from the television.

Edward picked up a nearby videotape, remembering that he had used it to record the Oscars three nights earlier. No loss there if he recorded over it, though he had been happy to see Henry Fonda win. At age 76, Fonda was only a couple of years older than Edward. *Chariots of Fire* won 'Best Picture', which was a disappointment. Secretly, Edward was rooting for *Raiders of the Lost Ark* as it reminded him of the old movie serials from his youth. Any movie that had Nazis seared by the hand of God deserved merit. The machine whirred as Edward popped the tape in and turned his attention back to the news.

"When did you first receive the distress call?" asked a reporter.

"Zero-zero, zero-five hours. Um…five minutes after midnight. It led us to where the woman's body was discovered."

The image on the screen changed to a map of the North Atlantic. An X was drawn at a specific latitude and longitude. Sadler's voice seemed miles away as Edward felt his blood turn cold. He knew that location very well. His hand flew to the buttons on the VCR and pressed 'record'. Edward stood back and continued to watch as the news segment unfolded on the television. A mysterious woman, found floating on a wooden deck chair...

"This was one of the items she was carrying," said the Captain on the television screen, as he quickly held up a hardcover book. The familiar sight shocked Edward so much that he made an audible gasp. "As you can see, the perpetrators of this prank added this... prop... as a way of misleading us. This hoax may have some dire consequences, however: this civilian was obviously in the freezing waters longer than they might have expected and she may die as a result."

"Thank you Captain Sadler," interjected the young male reporter. He then turned to the camera. "Anyone with information is asked to contact..."

Edward's finger hit 'stop' on the recorder, then he pressed 'play'. The image flickered and jumped as he saw what he had taped over for a moment, then he hit rewind and watched as the image of the newscast he had just recorded flickered in reverse. Edward released the rewind button, winced as the gears made a labored grinding sound, then jabbed the 'pause' button the instant the book cover appeared on the screen.

There was no denying it. The book was the 1898 original printing of the novel *Futility* by Morgan Robertson. There were only a handful of first prints left in the world, and Edward owned two of them. The last one had cost him $10,000 in an auction sale. It seemed ludicrous to think someone had put something so rare into seawater for a prank. He strolled over to the glass-covered bookshelf where he kept his most precious books and opened the door to retrieve one of his copies for comparison. The 1898 edition was sitting next to the 1912 edition. The latter had the title changed on the cover to "*Futility or the Wreck of the Titan*" to capitalize on the infamous tragedy that same year.

Pulling the first edition out, he turned and walked back to the jittery, paused image on the television set. Same grey cloth cover, same solitary title '*Futility*' in bright red letters centered in a black lined box. There was a crude, hand-drawn illustration of a large ocean liner with three visible smoke stacks sinking into wavy waters next to a mammoth iceberg. Anyone looking at this drawing would immediately suspect that the artist was depicting the sinking of the *Titanic*. It is astonishing to think that the artist drew this image 14 years *before* the *Titanic* existed.

Furthermore, the story itself had more startling similarities. The fictional ship from 1898 was called the *Titan* and, like its real life counterpart from 1912, was the largest luxury craft in the world. They were both roughly the same size, with the *Titan* only 82 ft shorter than *Titanic's* 882 ft. The fictional ship was traveling at 25 knots one night during the month of April and struck an iceberg. The RMS *Titanic* was breaking speed records at 23 knots and on the night of April 14, 1912, struck an iceberg. Neither ship had enough lifeboats for the number of passengers aboard and as a result there was a tremendous loss of life. The bitter irony was that both ships had been described as 'unsinkable'.

Edward glanced over to the opposite end of the room where the 1/144 scale model of the *Titanic* sat under glass. The RMS *Titanic* had been an obsession of his for most of his life. Most considered it unhealthy, but it was quite understandable since seventy years ago this month he and his family barely escaped from the sinking of the *Titanic*. While most survivors tried to forget the events of that horrendous night, Edward knew the truth: *Those who survived the sinking of Titanic… never really escaped from it.*

Edward felt himself shiver and glanced about. All warmth was drained from the room as clouds drowned out the rising sun. Edward's gaze drifted to the television set. *A prank? To what end? What purpose would the death of this poor woman serve?* Edward turned back to the model of the ship. *How ironic that this is happening now.*

. . .

Three hundred miles away, on a different television screen, the image of the mysterious woman being wheeled on a gurney through the double doors of a hospital's Emergency entrance was shown. From the television speaker, the voice of the reporter talked over the image on the screen, "The woman was found alone adrift on a wooden deck chair of a ship. She had no identification and only had a book and a child's teddy bear clutched in her hands…"

The unsteady camera zoomed into the unconscious face of the woman.

His glass of brandy smashed on the hardwood floor. *It couldn't be!*

CHAPTER 4

BLEEP BLEEP BLEEP

The heart-tracking electrocardiogram (ECG) machine bleeped very slowly. There was little hope for the woman who was found in the middle of the ocean: death was inevitable and there were no medical miracles. That was the one certainty that Denise had learned from years of being a nurse.

Denise had come a long way from her early candy-striper days in Nebraska. Being a nurse in Manhattan was drastically different from being one in her hometown. Every time she thought that the weirdest medical case ever had crossed her path, an even stranger incident would occur to trump the one before. Such was the variety that she liked about her job. The lack of routine kept her going. Every day was potentially different. She also really enjoyed helping people, and even though some situations were heartbreaking, knowing at the end of the day that she helped heal or ease pain made the long hours worthwhile. Even when encountering the direst of circumstances, she knew she had made the end of a life a little bit easier, both for the patient and their families.

On the other hand, she loathed the situations when some families were unwilling to accept that this may just be the end for their loved one. Allowing them to linger on ventilators with no neurological function, or with an end-stage disease hoping for a 'miracle' that would never come was a waste of time. As harsh as it sounded to her friends and family, Denise was forced to become a realist in her profession. There were no medical miracles.

It was odd, then, when a patient had no family at all at their bedside. This case of Jane Doe, also known as 'Myra Doe' amongst the staff, was certainly perplexing. Who was she? Did her family know where she was? How did she end up in the middle of the ocean? Denise had heard a rumor that it was some sort of stunt or prank. It would certainly explain the costume hanging in the closet. Not the craziest stunt Denise had ever seen: when the Superman movie came out a couple of years ago, there was an influx of admissions who had mixed stupidity with drugs and alcohol — a deadly combination. In most cases the dead ones were the most fortunate, for those who ended up immobilized from the neck down in the NICU would have the rest of their lives to contemplate their actions. This was not going to be the case with 'Myra Doe'. Denise sighed. She would be surprised if 'Myra' lasted the night. She looked down at her patient. Although brain death does take longer in stage-three hypothermia due to the cell degradation, the major organs most likely have failed at this point. However, the 3-lead ECG still registered a low heartbeat. Denise looked at the mysterious woman lying motionless with the olive-green oxygen mask over her face. In the dim light it appeared as if the bluish complexion was getting warmer. Denise knew that was impossible. The rhythmic sound of the bellows in her ventilator gave the illusion of life, but it was mechanically induced. This woman would never regain consciousness and she would eventually die, taking the secret of how she ended up in the middle of the ocean with her to the grave.

Denise turned to leave but a change of sound stopped her in mid-step. The tones from the ECG seemed to increase in speed. Denise furrowed her brow. *That's impossible!* She checked the individual connections to the machine and found everything working as it should. She turned back to observe the patient, even though she was convinced that her mind was playing tricks on her. If she didn't know any better, Denise could have sworn the woman's eyes were fluttering beneath her eyelids. Denise leaned closer to take a look.

The patient suddenly sat bolt upright and screamed! Denise's scream echoed it down the hospital halls.

Confused and disoriented, the patient struggled desperately to rip the oxygen mask from her face. The elasticized strap snapped it right back, causing her to scream in terror once again. Denise needed to take control of the situation.

"Myra? Is your name Myra?" asked Denise, trying to calm her own nerves as well as the patient's. The woman stopped screaming, and a blank look fell across her face.

"Myra?" Denise whispered hoarsely. There was a spark of recognition in her eyes as the woman nodded slightly. Suddenly panic fell across 'Myra's' face as she wheezed beneath the mask, "I can't remember anything."

"You were found in the ocean. Do you remember how you got there?"

"I can't remember anything! Nothing before waking up!" she wailed. Then she began to claw at the medical paraphernalia all over her body, knocking over the IV drip and tearing at the oxygen mask like a wild animal. The beeps from the ECG began to speed up at an alarming rate.

"Myra! I need you to calm down," Denise said soothingly while seizing and squeezing her hand. It was no use. Myra was in a state of panic.

"She's hyperventilating!" Denise called out to a passing nurse, trying to be urgent yet trying to use a calm voice. "Get Doctor Rowland!"

A look of terror crossed the patient's face as an odd gurgling sound emanated from her cracked lips. She fell back onto the bed as, the ECG became erratic.

BLEEP-BLEEP-BLEEPBLEEPBLEEPBLEEPBLEEP!

"She's going into cardiac arrest!" screamed Denise, knocking over the ECG as she commenced CPR, "Code Blue!"

As the shrill alarm rang out in the hallway, Denise continued alternating giving her mysterious patient breaths and pushing on her chest to simulate the heart's own pumping action. Within seconds, the Code Blue Team arrived. Many hands flew into action. 'Myra' Doe's hospital gown was ripped open as Denise continued to administer CPR. *Odd looking scar on her body*, thought Denise. It was a fleeting thought in itself amidst the chaos and the continuous chest compressions Denise was administering.

A flurry of hands, tubes, lines and overlapping voices worked expertly around Denise as she continued her work. Then when the ECG sprang back to life, Denise found herself praying. Praying for a miracle. She had never seen someone so alert after suffering severe hypothermia. Denise didn't want her to die. She didn't want the mystery to die with her.

"Clear!" yelled Doctor Rowland, the attending physician.

Denise pulled her hands away from her CPR duties, as everyone stepped away from the bed to allow the doctor to apply the defibrillator paddles. It only takes one bad experience to teach emergency personnel to take a step away from any part of the bed as 300-plus volts of electricity surges through a patient.

Every muscle in the woman's body contracted with the jolt.

BEEP-BEEP-BEEP BLEEEEEEEEEEEEEEP

CHAPTER 5

Like an archeologist trying to piece together the history of a lost civilization, Callum Toughill had the ruins of his family's name spread out on the wood-tiled floor of his modest London flat. Stacks of letters, journals, and newspaper clippings were placed in chronological order. Percy Winthrope had lulled Callum into a false sense of complacency when he showed him the file. It was only after Callum agreed to take on the case that Percy placed the little file folder in the hidden banker's box stuffed with the rest of the files.

Taking a sip of his coffee, Callum surveyed those very files surrounding him. *Where to start?* Logically, with the crime itself. Setting his cup down as far away from the rare documents as he could, he walked over to the furthest pile of papers. He carefully picked it up as to not drop a single precious page. After setting them down gingerly on his kitchen table, he stole a glance to the label on the top: **"1909 Homicide Report – Victim: Agatha Gilcrest"**

Flipping open the folder, Callum's eyes fell upon a sepia photo of the victim. He picked it up, noted the fur stole and large sparkling jewel on her hat, then stopped and studied her face. She was elderly, her features care-worn, silver hair parted in the middle, large intelligent dark eyes surrounded by laugh-lines that had deepened with age. Callum couldn't tell if it was a smudge on the picture or if she perhaps had a mole on the left side of her chin. Regardless, the wrinkles around her mouth seemed to indicate they were used to sitting in a smiling position. The expression on the old woman's face reminded him of his own grandmother when she was concentrating on baking chocolate chip biscuits. Callum smiled to himself as he thought of his own grandmother. He hadn't thought of her in years. Now looking at this old woman's picture, he felt guilty that he hadn't. After all, his grandmother practically raised him and he was away when she died. *He never got a chance to say good-bye… or even thank you.* He suddenly had a craving for chocolate chip biscuits. He carried the picture with him as he walked across the room and then grimaced as he took a sip from his coffee. It didn't quell the craving.

Turning the picture over, the photographer's mark was A. McArthur, Glasgow 1907. Callum glanced to the next page at the short paragraph of her life summarized by some officer. There was very little to tell. She was a spinster in failing health. According to her doctor she was dying from chronic kidney failure. She had inherited her fortune, valued at an estimated £80,000 in 1909, from her father. Using the calculator on his wrist watch, Callum estimated that to be equal to £8,000,000 today. Her only servant, Heather Langlea, had said in a statement:

'Miss Gilcrest didn't have many visitors. Sometimes there were some businessmen that came to the house…I think to appraise her jewels…she wore jewels every day about the house, usually a ring and her brooch… oh, and when she went out to dine she wore more jewels.'

After 82 years, there were no other details about her life. What was her favourite colour? Why did she never marry? Did someone break her heart? Who were these gentlemen visiting an old woman so often? How frequently do jewels need to be appraised? Eight decades of her life so completely eclipsed by her murder that no other detail survived.

He continued to sift through the pages of the police report, now yellowed with age. There were a few photographs of her large flat at 13 Queens Terrace in Glasgow, Scotland. *Not far from St George's Cross subway station,* thought Callum as he recalled his hometown. That particular station was one of the oldest, built in the 1890's, so it would have been operational in 1909.

The exterior photograph showed an unassuming townhome building with a waist-level wrought-iron fence surrounding it. Several gas lamps had been generously placed along the street. *Anyone entering or leaving the building would have been noticed.*

The interior of her flat was cozy. For a woman of her wealthy stature, it was quite a modestly-sized dwelling, with ornate fabric wall coverings. Callum looked up at his own gaudy wallpaper. It wasn't his style, but it had been there from the previous owners. He never planned on staying here that long; this was supposed to be temporary lodgings after his divorce five years ago. Living alone, he hadn't the time or the need to replace the wall decor. Looking back at the photo he thought to himself, *They don't make it like that anymore. At least not affordably.* Callum looked at the rest of the décor in the photo: large framed paintings surrounding the room, someone's portrait over the fireplace. Was that her father? The elegant furniture was typically Victorian in style, which would have been the height of home fashion when this photograph was taken.

At first glance there appeared to be piles of snow blanketing the floor of the room. On closer inspection of the photo, Callum determined that the effect was from pieces of paper that were scattered about. Had someone been looking for something?

Callum continued to scribble in his notepad as he read over the testimonies of eyewitness accounts from that night.

Four nights before Christmas around 7 o'clock, Heather Langlea, the sole servant and companion of Agatha Gilcrest, had stepped out to fetch a newspaper. *Odd time of day to get a paper*, thought Callum.

During that time, Adam McArthur, who lived in the apartment directly below Miss Gilcrest, stated that he and his family heard three loud knocks on the ceiling. Believing that Miss Gilcrest needed some assistance, McArthur went upstairs to investigate.

He apparently went to Miss Gilcrest's door and rang the bell. Even though no one answered, he was certain he heard noises inside the apartment.

Thinking nothing was wrong, Adam McArthur returned to his flat downstairs. After recounting what he had heard, his young daughter urged him to check on Miss Gilcrest one more time. Reluctantly he plodded back up the stairs. As he passed the front entrance of the building, he saw Heather Langlea returning from her errand. Together they glimpsed a man in the building's hallway, but neither found his presence unusual, as it could have been another tenant or a visitor. At any rate, Mr. McArthur told Miss Langlea what had transpired in her short absence and together they entered the apartment.

To their horror, they found the body of Agatha Gilcrest lying in a pool of blood by the dining room fireplace, with her head smashed in. Mr. McArthur said he bolted back down the stairway, but the mysterious man seen earlier in the hall had already vanished into the gloom of that rainy night. The only person he saw was another resident returning to the building: a 14-year-old messenger girl named Molly Wheelman.

Callum's fingers rifled through the old pages. He finally found what he was looking for: the medical statement by Dr. Hugh Glaister.

Callum's eyes meandered over the gruesome details, down to the conclusion: "Cause of death: Extensive wounds and fractures of the skull, and broken ribs, together with internal bleeding there from. Injuries were produced by violent blows with a blunt weapon, which had been applied with excessive force."

Looking again at the photo of Agatha Gilcrest, he still couldn't help thinking of his own grandmother. He wondered what kind of person would beat a sweet old woman to death. She was sickly, already dying. What possible motive was there?

He turned his attention back to the police report: "Miss Gilcrest had obviously known her attacker, as there was no sign of forced entry to her flat, and he was presumably aware of her routine. The motive appears to have been robbery."

Callum wrote the word 'robbery' in his notepad and circled it. It was already established that the victim had kept a large collection of diamond jewelry in the flat. What exactly had been stolen? He then rifled through the papers and found what he was looking for: the list of insurable assets, file number JC34-1-32-8. Callum started reading the detailed list consisting of glasses frames of 18 carat gold, 3-diamond star brooch, gold onyx pearl diamond bracelet, emerald diamond ring, ruby diamond ring, gold bangle with pearl and turquoise, even a scent bottle with a pure silver top. Using his finger he counted the pieces on the two-page list. There were 58 pieces of jewelry in all with a total value listed as £1,875 6 shillings and 3 pence. This would have been in 1909 so today they would have a value of almost £2Million, a sure-fire motive for murder.

Callum was about to get up to go take another sip from his coffee when a faint scribbled note nabbed his attention. 'Only one item missing – crescent brooch with 22 diamonds.'

There it was. Something so important was just a side note in the margin.

There was also a sketch of the brooch, which matched the photo that Percy had given to him for this investigation.

Callum glanced back at his notepad where he had circled 'robbery' for motive. He then looked at the photograph of the small jewelry box that had housed the victim's collection. If the motive had been robbery, why didn't the killer take the entire box?

"Perhaps it would have looked too suspicious to be carrying a jewelry box in the hallway," Callum said aloud to himself. Then, why just steal the one piece? What was so special about that brooch? Why not take a whole handful and stuff it in his coat pocket? It was December, so it would have been cold enough to wear an overcoat.

It didn't add up. Callum looked back at the eye witness report. Mr. McArthur and Miss Langlea described the man they saw as "about 5'6", young, fair haired, wearing a light grey overcoat and a black cap."

There was also young Molly Wheelman, who told the police that she had bumped into a man "hurriedly leaving the Gilcrest address." From the time that she quoted, and running into Mr. McArthur, it would have undoubtedly been the same man that Mr. McArthur and Miss Langlea saw. However, Wheelman described the man as "very tall, young, with a fawn cloak and a round hat."

"Eyewitness accounts," sighed Callum. When he was studying criminology, a man had suddenly stormed into the lecture hall, knocked down the professor, grabbed her purse from her desk, then darted out of the room. The professor calmly stood up and asked each person in the class to quickly write down a full description of her attacker. Callum Toughill vividly recalled the man and described him in great detail. Once everyone was finished, the professor opened the door and called out, "You can come back in."

Her attacker returned and casually handed her purse back. Callum was shocked to see that he had some details correct but many were drastically inaccurate. How could he have been so sure and yet so wrong? As it turned out, he was not the only one. His fellow classmates had done the same with varying different details.

The lesson that the professor wanted to emphasize was that eyewitness accounts and human memory are flawed. Such was the case with the man seen fleeing Miss Gilcrest's flat.

Callum was about to close the file when a statement from Molly Wheelman caught his eye.

Hours later, Molly is reported to have told Miss Cleaver that: "Miss Gilcrest had been murdered. I think I saw the man who did it... I am sure it was AG. He was walking with Miss Langlea that very night."

Callum looked at that for a moment. Callum knew from history and the file folders in the room that the police suspected and arrested a man by the name of Otto Slade. Who the blazes was AG? Was she confusing it with the initials of the victim? He looked through the alphabetic file folders, but there was nothing else resembling a man with the initials 'AG'. Why wasn't this lead pursued? What idiot didn't follow up on all these unanswered questions?

Callum flipped the pages back to look at the top of the report, and there saw the name of the investigating officer: Inspector John Toughill, Callum's own grandfather.

CHAPTER 6

"She's gone," a voice said solemnly. Denise had already known it was hopeless and stopped doing the chest compressions. The ECG was turned off and the Respiratory Nurse began to remove the tube from the patient's mouth.

"Note T.O.D..." started Dr. Rowland.

"Hold on," interrupted Denise as she grabbed the clipboard and clicked the pen to write. She then repeated, "Time of death..."

Dr. Rowland looked back at the clock on the wall. "Time of death occurred at..."

His words were quickly cut off as the patient opened her eyes, gasped and screamed. Denise dropped the clipboard and pen as much from surprise as from a sense of duty, and she rushed to her patient's side. Without another word, the woman fell back on the bed. The ECG bleeped back to life, as Dr. Rowland came out of a moment of shock and moved to open the patient's eyelids and shine a light into the pupils. Denise noted on her chart: patient was PERRL, pupils are equal, round, and reactive to light, which was a surprising but good sign.

"She's breathing on her own," remarked the Respiratory Nurse.

"Pulse is strong."

Dr. Rowland looked at the monitor screen, and then grabbed the scroll of paper that curled to the floor. His eyebrows tightened.

"Is there a cardiologist on duty?" he asked as he stretched the paper out.

"I think Dr. Morales is," replied Denise.

He handed the printout to the Respiratory Nurse, "Have him take a look at this."

"Yes, Doctor."

"Should we get her to the Critical Care Unit?" asked Denise. The doctor didn't respond. "Doctor?"

"Sorry, um...no," replied the Doctor as he looked at 'Myra' Doe breathing on her own. "She does not appear to need to go on life support. Her vitals are strong now... as though..."

He paused and looked about at the others in the room. Denise knew what he was going to say but was afraid to do so. It was as though she had never gone into cardiac arrest. There were seven people in this room who knew otherwise, but they all looked at the patient and knew the unbelievable truth. Denise wondered how she was going to write this in a report without sounding crazy. "Page me immediately when she regains consciousness. Hopefully she'll have some answers."

"Yes, Doctor," replied Denise as she picked the clipboard up off the floor. She was trying to wrap her brain around what just happened. She kept looking at the patient. How was this possible? That's twice in one night that this woman has defied the laws of physiology. In all the Code Blues that Denise had seen, only a small fraction 'come back' and most of those who do, don't last much longer on life support.

She looked up to see Dr. Rowland also looking at the patient as he waited for the medical team to file out. As he was about to leave, another nurse poked her head in, "Dr. Rowland? Here is the toxicology report you requested."

He thanked her absently as he snatched the file so quickly that the nurse looked at her hands to ensure that all her digits were still there.

Denise watched a look of confusion fall across the doctor's face as he whispered, "That can't be right."

He looked up at their mysterious patient and then looked back down at the report, his expression never changing.

"What is it?" Denise asked. The suspense was killing her.

"I fully expected to find some sort of narcotic in her system but this is... odd." He took out his pen and scribbled on the sheet. He then handed it to Denise, "I need to run some new blood work on our Jane... er 'Myra' Doe."

Denise looked down at the page and saw what he meant. It was odd. She also found herself looking at the patient, wishing she would regain consciousness. There were so many unanswered questions. She no longer knew what to believe.

CHAPTER 7

"*Titanic II?*" bellowed Edward Hoffman as he stormed into his father's Manhattan office. Edward threw down the current issue of *USA Today*. He had seen the newspaper on the waiting area's guest table outside his own office at Hoffman International Headquarters, as he popped in to pick up the messages he had received while he was out of town. Dropping his coat and scooping up the newspaper, he stomped directly across the executive floor and barged through the company president's door.

His elderly father, Archibald Hoffman, steered his antique wheelchair away as if he hadn't heard him. For a man in his early 70's, Edward took pride in his health and appearance. By contrast, his father, only 20 years his senior, looked well over a hundred and smelled like he had been dead for a decade but was too stubborn to accept it.

Archibald maneuvered through the antiquated furniture to the other side of the carved, wooden desk. Whereas Edward embraced new technologies such as fax machines, multiline phones and even a word processor, his father clung to his manual typewriter, rotary phone, and even still had a Ticker Tape machine. Edward wasn't even sure if anyone had used the Ticker Tape to send financial information in over ten years. He had told his father many times of his certainty that computers would be the wave of the future. In a short time, just like the television set, there would be a personal computer in everyone's home, and in theory it could eliminate all paper waste. After all, Edward could now review a business letter and correct any error before putting it on the page. His father considered the entire notion to be science fiction fantasy. He was also one of those who believed Neil Armstrong's moon landing was done in a Hollywood studio. Even his wheelchair was an old fashioned model made of heavy wood, brass handles and wicker inlay.

Ten years ago, Edward had bought his father a new motorized one but the old man refused to even sit in it. Edward was grateful that electricity had already been available when he was born or his father would likely have refused to buy a lamp.

Edward yelled after him, "I thought we made it clear that we weren't going to name it that!"

Archibald waved his attending nurse away, who was glaring at the younger Edward. As soon as the nurse left, Archibald retorted, "The *Titan* does not have the same impact, nor does it make the front page of any newspaper." His bony, gnarled finger trembled as it pointed at the newspaper Edward had thrown down on the desk. "You yourself brought the proof of that, Sonnyboy."

Edward bit his tongue as his elderly father launched into a coughing fit. His father knew how much he despised the 'Sonnyboy' nickname, but Edward was careful to choose his battles. He would not be baited into changing the subject.

"This Time It Really Is Unsinkable?" read Edward aloud. Even though it was there with the headline on the front page, Edward found it difficult to believe. "How could you print something so abhorrent without consulting with me first?"

Archibald spun his wheelchair around and opened his mouth... and coughed again. As Edward waited, he studied his father for a moment. Pushing a hundred, Archibald still had control of his faculties. He was living proof that money could buy everything... even longer life. Over the last few decades he had been the recipient of a kidney, a cornea, and had somehow successfully placed himself at the top of a heart transplant list last year. At this rate, Edward suspected that Archibald would Frankenstein himself into a new man by the end of the decade. If only the good die young, Archibald Hoffman would live forever. He definitely showed no signs of slowing down, and had been down to South America last week to meet with *El Consorcio*, their Latin American counterpart. Archibald felt that their staff needed motivation and went personally to meet with them.

Over the years Edward had witnessed the ruthless, cutthroat actions of his father. Archibald lived by the Sun Tzu's *Art of War* and read it several times a year, treating family and colleagues alike as the enemy, using their weaknesses to his advantage. Even now, Edward was acutely aware of the recorded music playing on the old record player. Was it a coincidence that the familiar tune of *The Last Rose of Summer* was now haunting the room? It was taking him back to a painful time. Edward would never forgive his father for what he did to him... to Dolanna... poor Dolanna. The only woman Edward had ever loved. The coughing stopped. Edward had to re-focus. He would not fall prey to his father's mind-games.

"Aside from the poor taste," Edward continued, trying to ignore the music. "It's bad luck to name a ship after a doomed one."

"Isn't it also bad luck to change the name of a ship?" asked Archie as he wheeled himself in front of the west-facing window. It was a tactical positioning that he often did, forcing his opponent to squint into the afternoon sun, putting them at a disadvantage. Edward was not going to fall prey to his father's tactics and casually strode over to one side. Without the sun in his eyes, he turned to his father, "Only after it's been christened on its maiden voyage." His father had some gall debating nautical superstition with him. He needed to get back to the heart of the issue. "If you don't retract that statement..."

"If I do that it will look like I gave into that hag's petition."

"Hag?" Edward asked.

"Eva Hart. Didn't you see that interview with Eva Hart?" His finger stabbed towards the blueprints of the new ship. "She called it 'macabre' and whined that it would bring back a nightmare of memories."

Edward shook his head in dismay. He could never understand, as a fellow survivor, how his father could be so callous with such a tragedy. As unfathomable as it might seem, Archie Hoffman always seemed 'glad' that the *Titanic* sank.

Choosing his words carefully, Edward calmly said, "Like me, she was a child when *Titanic* went down. But she wasn't as fortunate: she lost her father."

Archibald replied in some incomprehensible grumble.

"Do you recall what her mother said that night at dinner, the night before the ship struck the iceberg?" Edward asked, but Archibald made no attempt to answer. "She said, 'To boast that a ship was unsinkable was a slap in the face of God.'"

"I was there, I remember better than you do. I'm not senile you know."

"Did I say you were?" Edward asked, "You didn't answer when I asked."

"Did you see the story of the woman found in the North Atlantic?" asked Archibald, obviously changing the subject.

"Yes, I did," replied Edward. "Intriguing wouldn't you say?"

"Rubbish!" wheezed the old man without missing a beat. "That's all that is, sheer rubbish."

Archibald turned and trolled through a cabinet, hunched over the stuff, hunting, "Someone organized that hoax to steal my thunder."

"Now, who would do that?" asked Edward.

"Could be any number of past rivals. It wouldn't surprise me if Eva Hart or someone like that Dr. Alpo put that woman in the ocean to draw attention away from our moment of glory."

"Alpo?... You mean Dr. *Ballard*. He's a respected scientist."

"Who's spent the last five years looking for the wreck of the *Titanic*. I imagine he would have trouble getting funding for his dives once our *Titanic II* launches next week."

"There isn't going to be a launch of a ship called *Titanic II*. The company spent a considerable amount of money on market research and focus groups and the response was that no one would travel on a ship named *Titanic*. The common consensus was that it was 'tempting fate.' If we don't change the name we're already sunk."

"If we do that after this press release that old hag will believe it was because of her and her damned petition. I'll never live it down."

"We can spin it to your favor, that out of respect to those who perished on that fateful night you have magnanimously decided to call it the *Titan*."

It was clear that he would have more luck reasoning with a statue, but Edward still had another ace up his sleeve. He shuffled through the messages that he had picked up earlier and held out a fax page for his father to see. "Perhaps this will change your mind."

"What's this?" grumbled Archibald as he tore the page from his hand. Edward watched with anticipation as his father's gray eyes read the words on the page. He could see defeat drain the fight from the old man.

"You win," whispered Archibald. His trembling fingers opened and the page just floated down to the desk.

"We will issue a correction from our media office. We can spin it to your favor, that out of respect to those who perished on that fateful night..."

"Yes, yes," Archibald nodded as he wheeled away, stopping to impatiently pull the needle from the record player.

Edward almost felt sorry for him. Almost.

. . .

Denise noticed how out of place the greasy, leather-clad man appeared as he emerged from the elevator. Most people entering this area of the hospital looked either lost or concerned or both. This individual looked like a man on a mission and judging by the camera around his neck, Denise suspected he was a reporter. Her hand reached out to the phone to call security when a page broke over the PA system, "Anesthetist please report to maternity. Anesthetist to maternity, please."

As the voice was speaking through the speaker a terrifying scream erupted from behind Denise. She turned to see 'Myra', wrapped in her blanket, screaming, while looking about as if trying to see where the disembodied voice was coming from. Denise dropped the phone and instinctively ran to her patient. "Ma'am. You shouldn't be up. If you need something you can buzz us."

The shivering woman looked at Denise as if she didn't understand a single word. Through chattering teeth the poor woman asked, "Am I dead?"

Denise was about to answer when a flash of light distracted her. She turned to look where the greasy man with the camera had been but he was gone. An uneasy feeling came over Denise. She had to get her patient away from prying eyes and into the protection of her own private room. "Let me take you back to your room."

She took 'Myra's' trembling hand and was startled to find how cold it was. Myra opened her mouth to speak but only gibberish chattered out. Denise felt the patient go limp as she was once again losing consciousness. Denise called to a nearby orderly, "Can I have some help over here?"

– – –

Later, while Myra slept, someone sneaked into her room. A gloved hand reached towards her neck. *Nothing there.*

From a nearby closet door, a piece of embroidered fabric peeked out from below the knob, too thick to be contained. The gloved hand opened the door to find a shelf above the ornate dress. A small lidless cardboard box sat atop the shelf. The hand froze as voices passing approached the door. The other hand reached for the gun. The voices continued to move away. The gloved hands carefully pulled the box down and tilted it for a better look. The light seeping in from the hall reflected off something metal. The gloved hand held the locket up. *Yes, this is it.*

Looking back into the box, there was nothing else except a smelly old book. The box was carefully placed back onto the shelf and the door was closed. The dress pushed the door ajar.

A moment later the stranger was gone.

April 2, 1982

CHAPTER 8

"How can she be gone?!" Captain Sadler demanded of the young nurse who identified herself only as Denise. He was so furious he had almost forgotten he was holding the teddy bear in the hand he was gesturing with. The crewman who had gathered the woman's belongings from sickbay had failed to notice it and had left it there. Sadler took the opportunity of returning it to follow up on the mystery. Now the mystery thickened.

"I came in early for my shift this morning," began Denise, "and discovered that some 'benefactor' had her transferred to some private clinic and even settled the bill...in cash."

"Cash?" Sadler didn't like the sound of it. It was likely that whoever had placed her in the middle of the ocean was now trying to cover their tracks. They were not only playing with lives, but had also wasted Military resources.

"I'm sorry, Mr... er... Captain," stammered Denise. "I only found out when I went in to see if she had regained consciousness again."

"AGAIN?" bellowed Sadler. "Did anyone question her? Did she say how she got out into the middle of the bloody Atlantic?"

"There wasn't time..."

"Time! Do have any idea how much time...?"

"Captain," interrupted a middle-aged doctor in a rumpled lab coat. "My name is Dr. Rowland. I'll have to ask you to keep your voice down. This is a hospital, not a military base."

"Forgive me," simmered Sadler. "I was just informed that the mysterious woman had regained consciousness. Why did no one think to question her?"

"Because she went into cardiac arrest," replied the doctor. "We thought it better to keep her alive rather than play '20 questions'."

Sadler ignored the sarcasm and took a deep breath. He knew they were only doing their jobs and that whoever released the patient was just following orders. In a calmer voice Sadler asked, "Is there any way we can find the location of this clinic?"

"I will do my best to find out," replied the doctor.

"Well when you do…" Captain Sadler was suddenly distracted by the image on the television in the waiting lounge. On the screen were the words "*Argentina Invades Falkland Islands.*"

"Crap!" Sadler now had to get back to his ship; he knew he would soon be deployed to South America, as every available ship in Her Majesty's fleet would be required to defend the Falkland Islands. He turned to the doctor and nurse and with a sharp nod, thanked them both for their time.

With that, Sadler turned with bear in hand and marched to the exit. His involvement in the current investigation had just ended. If there were any casualties directly related to this stunt, it was too late for them.

· · ·

In a nearby hotel, a man approached the front desk. The concierge looked up from his paperwork and smiled.

"Good morning," said the concierge, he recognized the man who checked in yesterday afternoon by his leather jacket, but couldn't remember his name. "What can I do for you?"

The man handed the concierge two 8X10 photographs. "Could you fax these two pictures to the number on the back?"

"Of course, sir." The concierge flipped over the first and looked at the fax number scribbled in ink. "This is an overseas call. Shall I charge this to your room?"

The man nodded and held up his hotel key. The concierge jotted down the room number on the tag: 319. He would add this to the man's hotel bill.

As he flipped the photo over to place it in the fax machine, the concierge couldn't help but notice the strikingly beautiful woman in the picture. Though there was a look of confusion on her face it was still gentle. The second was a close up photo of a locket, housing two small photographs. In one was the same woman with a young man, and the other was a young boy in a cute sailor uniform.

Beneath the photo of the locket was a very cryptic hand written message:
No Teddy Bear found in her room!

CHAPTER 9

Beep! Beep! Beep!

Dr. Natalie Lindsay wanted to ignore her pager: this was her day off and she wasn't on call. She tried to pretend she couldn't hear it as she poured her morning coffee.

Beep! Beep! Beep!

Each time it seemed to have a more urgent tone. With reluctance, she picked it up and looked at the display. She immediately recognized the phone number of the clinic where she worked, and cursed modern technology. It was only a year ago that the clinic purchased the new state-of-the-art pagers with numeric display. Gone were the days of having to use a telephone to call in to retrieve messages. Gone were the days of excuses: *Sorry I couldn't find a phone.* Or, *Sorry I didn't have a quarter for the payphone.* Natalie sighed. She could still try to fake having misplaced her pager, or say she was in the shower. After all, she did have plans on her day off: she had tickets to see the new play, *Agnes of God*, that had opened earlier in the week at the Music Box Theatre. One of the ladies at the gym told her about the show, and its theme depicting a struggle between psychology and faith intrigued Natalie.

Beep! Beep! Beep!

Natalie's pager started up again. She sighed as she looked at her theater tickets. Her sense of duty as a psychiatrist made her pick up the phone. If they were calling on her day off it had to be important. She'd have to see the show another time.

Natalie soon had a feeling this was going to be an interesting day. She mulled over the facts that Dr. Marcus had given to her over the phone about her mysterious new patient while she rode the subway from her apartment

33

west of Central Park. Vaguely aware that some of the male riders were stealing glances at her legs, she smiled to herself about her morning choices. After fighting with her contact lenses and wrestling to put her uncooperative long blonde hair up, she had changed into her favorite business suit: a tweed jacket and matching skirt. When she first started practicing she purposely dressed in a less feminine fashion, even had shorter hair and frumpy glasses. Though women had been contributing to psychoanalysis for most of the century, the 'doctor's club' still had a 'men-only' stigma attached to it. As a career woman in her mid... well, early thirties she didn't have much time to get out and socialize, which is why she felt a twinge of regret as she gave up an evening at the theatre. Still, she now understood that she didn't have to deny being a woman in order to be taken seriously as a doctor. Thankfully, not only did subway passengers appreciate it, but her colleagues agreed.

The Clinic, sitting in the Midtown East district overlooking the East River, was unassuming from the outside. The clinic covered various addiction treatments for drugs, alcohol, gambling, eating disorders, and the newly-defined post-traumatic stress disorder.

The building had a doorman, like a private club, which was how it was supposed to appear. Patients were often people of power: politicians, celebrities, all fearing the label of 'nuts' when seeking psychiatric help. *Archaic Victorian mentality.* No one had such issues with going to dentists, or optometrists or any other kind of medical specialists. *Why was the mind any different?* It was an organ in the human body prone to fatigue, stress and illness like any other part of the body, yet admitting it was somehow weak was frowned upon. As a result, many who needed treatment were afraid to ask for it.

Natalie stopped by her office and quickly reviewed the hard copy notes on her new patient. There wasn't much to go on. *You would think the hospital would have at least given me her medical charts.* When she had spoken to Dr. Marcus this morning, he had informed her that her task was to ascertain the identity of this 'new guest'. Natalie was getting a reputation for doing so with other cases, most recently with an old man who was convinced he was the Lindbergh's kidnapped baby all grown up. He was, of course, not the son of the famed 1930's aviator, Charles Lindbergh, but someone who had been abandoned by his parents when he was a small child. The emotional scars had never healed and stayed with him his entire life. It was easier for him to believe that he was forcibly 'taken' from loving parents, willing to pay any price to get their child back, than to face the harsh reality that he was not wanted... not loved as a child. It was a heart-wrenching ordeal but Natalie was able to break through and finally helped him to accept the truth.

By contrast, Natalie didn't have any background information on her new patient at all and they would be making this journey into the unknown together. She was eager to commence, but her excitement faded as she entered the mysterious woman's room. This new patient was shivering uncontrollably and was deathly pale. Her lips seemed to have a blue hue to them. Natalie became concerned about the patient's basic health. Without the medical charts, Natalie would have to ascertain the patient's condition during this preliminary interview.

"Hello?" Natalie began softly. "My name is Dr. Lindsay. Can you tell me your name?"

The woman made no reply, as if she hadn't heard. Natalie was going to repeat herself but was taken aback by the odd expression on the patient's face. Her eyes were distracting, piercingly blue.

Those eyes were staring at Natalie as if they had seen a spider crawl up her skirt. Natalie tore herself away from them and looked down to see if there was a run in her stocking. There was nothing out of the ordinary. She looked up at the shivering woman, "Is there something wrong?"

"Your legs," the patient whispered through clattering teeth.

"What about them?"

"I can see them. It's hardly appropriate," the woman said as she tried to wrap the blankets tighter around herself.

Yes, this is going to be a very interesting day. Natalie took a moment to adjust the room's thermostat and turned back to the woman in as friendly a way as she could muster, "Let's start again. I'm Doctor Natalie Lindsay. You were transferred…"

"What kind of doctor?"

"I'm a psychiatrist," replied Dr. Lindsay, trying not to let the interruption bother her.

The woman suddenly laughed. It was a sweet laugh. Almost melodic.

"What's so funny?" asked Natalie.

"You said you were a psychiatrist."

"I am. I received my PhD in…"

She started to laugh again. Natalie could not imagine what could possibly be so damn hilarious.

"What's so funny about me being a psychiatrist?"

"You're a woman."

"I know. So?"

"So," the patient said as she tried to regain her breath. "I know of very few women studying psychology and they haven't been allowed to have a PhD."

Natalie studied her face to see if she could ascertain if this woman truly believed her statement. It was jarring for Natalie who, just after high school, protested for women's equality. As their eyes made contact, the woman mumbled that she must be dreaming about short skirted women at medical school, started to laugh again and continued to do so until fatigue took over and she started to drift.

After the woman had fallen asleep, Natalie crept out to the hallway, walked over to her assistant and asked whether they had the new patient's belongings.

"Yes. We do," replied her assistant, as she rose from her desk. Moments later she returned with an armload of tapestry and lace. Natalie couldn't help but touch the fabric. It was a heavy, yet beautiful gown, and the beading seemed to have been stitched by hand.

"Take it to our patient when she wakes up. Help her dress if she needs it."

Her assistant nodded and started down the hall.

"One other thing!" Natalie called out.

Her assistant stopped and turned back towards her. "Can you tell me where I can buy a long skirt these days?"

CHAPTER 10

Otto Slade was sentenced to be hanged for the murder of Agatha Gilcrest —the problem was, he was innocent. Callum peered out the window, giving his eyes a rest from trying to decipher handwritten notes from eighty years ago.

The grey English countryside sped past his train window, barren trees in the fields reaching up to the sky like skeletal hands. He imagined that the view in the late spring or summer might be picturesque, but not so much now with the snow melting into a muddy mess. It had been the coldest winter in recent history with record-breaking snowfall in January. Callum was glad to see winter was finally retreating. He looked at his wristwatch to find that only two hours had gone by. Another two and a half hours before the train pulled into Glasgow Central station. He was aware that flying would have only taken an hour, but he knew from experience that he wouldn't get his airfare reimbursed, so he'd decided to make good use of his travel time by piecing together the past.

In 1909 Glasgow, the murder of an elderly rich woman was not a common event, so there was a great deal of public pressure to apprehend the culprit so the good citizens would be able to sleep without locking their doors.

The police seemed to have set their sights on a man that did not match the description the eyewitnesses had given. Otto Slade was arrested and charged with murder: police claimed that he was trying to pawn the stolen brooch. Callum picked up a photocopy of the pawn receipt and read: *One brooch, oval shaped with 7 diamonds.*

The brooch that was stolen from Agatha Gilcrest was crescent-mooned shaped with 22 diamonds. These were not the same pieces of jewelry. Yet, this was the damning evidence that convicted Otto Slade — how was this possible?

During the trial, Heather Langlea had changed her testimony and identified Otto Slade as the man she had seen leaving Mrs. Gilcrest's apartment. Callum looked back at her original statement to his grandfather: *"He was about 5'6", young, fair haired, wearing a light grey overcoat and a black cap."*

According to the arresting police file on Otto Slade, he was 6'1" with black hair. Next to 'complexion' he is listed as: 'Jewish'. *Interesting adjective for skin appearance,* thought Callum. *Still,* he supposed, *prejudice knows no boundaries.* There was no denying Otto Slade did not match the description given on the night of the murder. Did Heather Langlea lie and point her finger at an innocent man in a court of law? If so, *why?*

Callum looked through the court transcripts, trying to find Adam McArthur's statement. He had also given the police a full description of the man seen leaving the scene of the crime, but there was no court statement to be found. Mr. McArthur did not testify. Again, Callum wondered, *why?*

The more answers Callum tried to find, the more questions he unearthed. Granted, looking at Slade's background, he wasn't exactly an upstanding citizen. He had an ex-wife that he tried to avoid and kept the company of prostitutes and gamblers, but was not a gambler himself. The need for money did not seem to be a concern for Otto Slade.

When the police had issued a warrant for his arrest, Otto Slade was on the *Lusitania* bound for New York. After several months of deliberation, the American Tribunal rejected the British government's extradition application on the grounds of a lack of evidence: they were prepared to grant Otto Slade political asylum, and he could have remained the rest of his days in America, but instead he decided to return to Scotland to clear his name. *Hardly the actions of a guilty man,* thought Callum. *That decision cost him his life.*

In early 1911, Otto Slade boarded the next boat for Scotland and, instead of clearing his name, he was found guilty as charged by a jury with a nine-to-six vote in favour of convicting him. Callum scowled. In Scotland, the jury is made up of 15 peers and only a majority is needed for a conviction, even if the majority is by only one vote. That system is still in place today. Callum preferred the American concept of 'reasonable doubt'.

In the transcript, after hearing the verdict, Otto Slade had implored the court:

"My Lord Gunter, may I be permitted to speak? I knew nothing about the crime until I was notified. You are convicting an innocent man. ... I returned from America to Scotland, willingly, to get a fair trial. To prove my innocence because I knew nothing about the horrid affair, absolutely nothing. I hadn't known the name of the victim. I had never met her. ... I cannot understand how I can be condemned."

Lord Gunter made no comment of any kind to the defendant's statement. He apparently placed the dreaded 'black cap' upon his own head and sentenced Otto Slade to be hanged on Thursday, 27th May, 1911. The execution was to take place within the old Duke Street Prison in Glasgow.

There was enough of a public outcry about the verdict that Otto Slade's sentence was postponed for nearly a year, and petitions were signed and presented to the Lord Advocate. But pleas fell upon deaf ears, and Otto Slade was hanged on Wednesday, 17th of April, 1912. His execution went mostly unnoticed by the public, as all news was eclipsed by the sinking of the *Titanic* a few days earlier.

It was a travesty of justice to say the least, thought Callum. He knew without a doubt that Otto Slade had been set up as a scapegoat. *Why?* How could his own grandfather have botched up an investigation so horribly? Moreover, how could a conviction and death sentence be handed down with such circumstantial evidence?

Callum knew he could only learn so much from the files Percy had given him. Now he needed to find what wasn't in the files. The truth. To that end he was going to Scotland, not sure of where to start. After almost 70 years would any of the witnesses still be alive? Would the flat where the murder took place still be there or would he find it demolished and a supermarket standing in its place?

Callum Toughill soon had his answer standing in front of him. It was a short walk from St. Georges Station. The corner where Molly Wheelman claimed to have last seen the victim alive now housed an Asian restaurant, but the rest of the street still looked much like the photo taken in 1909. Gone were the old flickering gas lamps and hitching posts for horses: modern streetlights and bike stands had taken their place. Asphalt had been paved over the cobblestones but the buildings themselves looked exactly the same. He counted his way to number 13 Queens Terrace, where the front steps were flanked by a low wrought iron fence on either side. The once elegant carved stone arches had eroded with age, and decades of rain had stained the columns. The photo in Callum's hand had a brass plaque with the word *thirteen* affixed upon it in a graceful script; whereas, today there was a weathered piece of wood with the number 13 painted upon it. *Odd,* he thought to himself, as most people thought the number thirteen to be unlucky. There was rarely a thirteenth floor in tall buildings and, as a child, he was often confused as to why the number 13 was never listed on the panels of any of the lifts he rode. Likewise on streets, the houses would skip from 11 to 15. It was an accepted superstition which he believed to be rubbish. It was, however, most certainly unlucky for Agatha Gilcrest.

Callum strode up the half-dozen steps to the front door. He raised his hand and was about to ring the buzzer, then paused. He hadn't considered what he would say. Would the new owners of the flat know a murder had taken place? *Good afternoon, I'm investigating a bloody murder that took place in your home seventy years ago. May I come in?*

They would think him a *nutter*. He sighed. He'd just spent five hours traveling to Scotland to look for clues on a very, very cold case. It was no longer about the brooch he had been initially hired to find but rather a personal mission... because of his grandfather. Callum shook his head. He *was* a nutter.

"How now," a shrill voice in a thick Glaswegian accent called out. "What do you want? State your business."

The voice had happened upon him so quickly it startled him. Callum saw that the front door had opened ever so slightly, and an old woman was peering out at him. The woman kept the safety chain secured, preventing the door from opening further. For a brief moment, he entertained the thought that it might be the ghost of Agatha Gilcrest, but upon closer inspection he saw it was not so. This woman's elderly face was longer and the eyes were very different, yet still full of life. "What do you want? You've been standing there, staring at my home for the past ten minutes. State your business before I summon the police."

"My apologies," stammered Callum, clearing his throat. "I'm an investigator and I'm investigating..."

He paused. The words wouldn't come out. He knew it would sound ludicrous to the old woman.

"Investigator investigating what?" asked the old woman.

"A murder," the words came out of Callum's mouth before he could stop them.

"A murder?" asked the old woman nervously. "Whose murder?"

"It was an old woman..." began Callum. He could see the look of fear being replaced with an odd wide-eyed expression on the old woman before him. "I'm sorry, it happened a long time ago. You couldn't..."

Embarrassed that he hadn't planned this better, Callum turned to leave without another word. As he started down the steps the old woman called out, "Toughill?"

Callum Toughill froze mid-step, then he slowly turned back to the old woman. The chain was off the front door and she stepped out towards him.

"Do I know you?" asked Callum.

"You look like Inspector John Toughill," muttered the old woman. "But that's impossible."

"Inspector John Toughill was my grandfather."

She stepped closer. "Your hair is lighter than his was. Shoulders are broader. And he had a moustache, but your eyes are the same... steel grey... and your profile."

It was true—Callum had seen photos of his grandfather when he was a younger man and many a relative had made the same comparisons. "You knew my grandfather?"

"Aye. He was a good man. I remember him standing where you're standing now, studying every detail with the same eyes."

Callum's mind was reeling. She remembered his grandfather? Who was she? Suddenly a million questions raced through his head. He opened his mouth but all that came out was, "When?"

"The night that still haunts my dreams. The night poor old Mrs. Gilcrest was murdered."

CHAPTER 11

Dr. Natalie Lindsay entered her new patient's room and was surprised to find her sitting up at the foot of the bed and looking at her reflection in the mirror. Natalie was impressed at the progress of her physical recovery. Earlier, the patient was so pasty, almost anemic-looking and physically weak. What a drastic change in just a few short hours.

"How are we today?" asked Natalie. Her patient slowly turned towards her. Natalie was once again taken aback by her intense blue eyes. The patient looked back at her reflection as she touched her own face.

"I don't know… I look at myself in the mirror but it's a stranger looking back at me. I don't know who I am," she said in a trembling voice.

"It's not uncommon with amnesia patients," replied Natalie. "I'm here to help you get your memory back… If you'll let me."

"But I know I'm sitting on a *bed*… I'm looking into a *mirror*. I know what things are called… I know how to talk and how to walk… how is it that I know that I'm feeling *cold* but I can't remember my own name?"

"Well," Natalie began as she sat in the chair next to the bed, "You could be suffering from either *post-traumatic amnesia*, which is usually a result from some sort of head injury. That is quite possible, since we have no idea how you got to where you were found. Unfortunately, I don't have your medical records so I haven't been able to determine if you suffered a concussion or anything like that. The other possibility is that you are suffering from *dissociative amnesia* caused by some recent traumatic event, or perhaps some repressed memory from childhood."

The patient looked at Natalie and said, "You sound like a psychiatrist."

"I am a psychiatrist."

The woman looked at Natalie so intently, it was as if those blue eyes were trying to see into her soul. Finally she whispered, "Can you help me?"

"I would like to try," replied Natalie.

They spoke for over an hour—time enough for Natalie to gain some of her trust and study her body language, getting to know her better. There was no doubt the patient was suffering from amnesia, but the doctor needed to know the extent of it.

After lunch, Natalie proposed subjecting her patient to hypnoanalysis.

"What is that?" asked the patient.

"It's a one-on-one hypnosis treatment."

"Hypnosis? I'm not sure about that."

"Contrary to popular belief, in a hypnotic state you are not asleep or unconscious," Natalie smiled. She was used to this kind of reaction due to all the films and stories of people being controlled through hypnosis to cluck like chickens or become hired assassins. She leaned closer to her patient and explained, "Hypnotic patients are completely awake and able to focus attention, with a corresponding decrease in their peripheral awareness. You cannot be made to do something against your will. You see, the goal of hypnoanalysis is to find the root cause of a problem or symptom through regression techniques."

"This is the best way to help?" blinked the patient nervously.

"Yes," Natalie replied calmly. "Hypnoanalysis deals with cause and effect."

Myra stared at her blankly, obviously not comprehending. Natalie continued, "Simply put, we think, behave, and feel emotions in certain ways because of happenings in our past experiences. This type of hypnosis can achieve results in dealing with emotions far more quickly and efficiently than psychotherapy or psychoanalysis, which could take years. I've seen breakthroughs in three or four sessions, sometimes less, but I don't want to get your hopes up."

"I want to remember," replied the patient. "I'm not sure why, but I have a strong feeling that I can trust you."

"I'm glad."

It took three attempts to get the patient into a relaxed-enough state to be able to commence. Natalie asked her to lift her arm. The manner in which the arm floated up confirmed that the patient was, in fact, in a hypnotic trance. In this disassociated state, the patient would be able to talk freely. Natalie grabbed her note pad and pen, and leaned over to make sure that the tape recorder was running so she could review the session later. Natalie started by asking some establishing questions that she already knew the answers to, in order to get the patient used to responding, and to read her responses. "What color are your eyes?"

"Blue."

"Are you warm or cold?"

"Cold. Very cold," replied the patient. Natalie already knew that because she could still see her shivering.

After three more such superficial questions Natalie quickly asked, "What is your name?"

"Myra," she replied without hesitation. Natalie wrote it on her note pad in short hand.

"Thank you, Myra. What is your last name?"

Natalie could see Myra struggle. Unable to answer, she began to show signs of agitation. Her breathing began to speed up.

"Relax, Myra. That's not important now," cooed the doctor. Normally Natalie asked her patients to imagine a tranquil lake or ocean setting to be their 'safety place' but given the circumstances of where Myra was found she chose not to suggest it. "Imagine sitting in front of a warm fire place. Feel the warmth embracing you, taking the cold and fear away from you. Let the crackling flames illuminate the darkness in your mind."

Myra smiled. She stopped shivering.

"Let's go back," continued Natalie. "Before you were found in the water, how did you get to the middle of the Atlantic Ocean?"

"I was on a boat," replied Myra.

Natalie was pleased they were making quick progress, "Can you describe it?"

"It's… big."

Hmm… Maybe not as quick. Natalie wondered if she was going to have enough cassette tapes. "Is it a yacht?"

"No… larger than a yacht."

"A cruise ship?" asked Natalie. Myra frowned as if not understanding the question. "Is it a passenger ship?"

"Oh, yes," smiled Myra.

"Are you traveling alone?"

Myra suddenly bemused, "No."

Natalie sat up. This was progress. "Who else is traveling with you?"

"My husband… my son." Myra smiled, "And…"

"And?"

"And someone else," Myra responded with agitation in her voice. She began tapping the arm of the chair with her finger. Natalie carefully moved the tape recorder to a safe distance where the tapping wouldn't drown out the voices.

She turned back to Myra and asked, "Can you see this other person's face?"

"Yes. It's a woman…" Myra's breathing became labored.

"What's wrong Myra?"

"I'm not feeling well. I haven't felt well for most of the trip. It's odd."

"Why is it odd?"

"I have traveled all my life and I have never experienced seasickness. Now I have a weak constitution. I am not capable of keeping any food down, and I've been burning up. I feel so dizzy."

"Did you fall overboard?" Natalie asked as calmly as she could.

"No..."

"Do you know how...?"

"Something's wrong!" Myra's voice started to grow louder. "The ship's engines have stopped. I've been asleep, where is my husband? Where is my son? I can't find them!"

"Myra, think of the fireplace," Natalie said soothingly trying to get Myra to calm down. "Feel the warmth..."

"The fireplace. Oh, I knocked the tea cart toward the fireplace."

"What tea cart?"

"My tea. I'm supposed to drink my tea to calm my nerves. My son's teddy bear was under the teacart. Where's my son?"

Myra started to breathe harder. "The state room...it's on an odd angle. The teacart is rolling past me... things are falling... I run into the adjoining cabin ... my son's teddy bear is floating by... Mr. Fluffy... he wouldn't leave Mr. Fluffy. Where's my son? I can't find my son!"

Natalie was torn. Should she calm her down? Or let this play out? It could lead to a mental breakthrough. Trying to sound calm and impassive, Natalie continued, "Use your other senses. Can you hear anyone?"

"I can hear people screaming... the ship is sinking?! It's not possible...!"

"Why is it not possible?" Natalie had the feeling she knew what Myra was going to say but she hoped she was wrong.

"The ship is *unsinkable*. We're on the *Titanic*!"

CHAPTER 12

"Would you like a biscuit, Mr. Toughill?" asked the old lady as she poured coffee from the glass hand-pumped cafetière into the glass mug. Callum was impressed by the traditional French press set. It certainly beat the brew he had back home.

"That would be nice," smiled Callum. "Thank you, Miss McArthur."

"Please call me Ruthie," the old lady smiled as she retreated to the kitchen.

"Are these pictures of your family?" asked Callum as he looked at the framed photos on the fireplace mantle. Most were black & white, some were faded and a few were in colour which was surprising for having been taken at the turn of the century.

"No," Ruthie called out from the kitchen. "Most of those pictures were taken by my father. He was a photographer. It was his life and joy. I've kept them because I look at them and I see what he saw. The people he knew or the ones he was proud of."

Callum looked at some of the photos that had colour tint to them. "Are these hand-coloured photos?"

"Oh no," Ruthie replied. "My father wouldn't have the patience for that. 'Twas why he took up photography. These were early colour photo experiments. In fact, the birth of colour photography was here in Scotland. A physicist named Maxwell, back in the mid-1800's."

Ruthie McArthur returned with a tin of sugar cookies. Callum had hoped for homemade. He took a cookie with a grateful smile. Still, it would satisfy the craving from last night. She pointed to one of the photos of a little girl. "That one was me, on my tenth birthday... he captured the colour of my dress and bows in my hair... I so loved that dress."

Just last night Callum had read about how Ruthie, only ten years old at the time, had implored her father to go back up and check on Miss Gilcrest. Here was that little girl as an old lady, still living in the same flat beneath the scene of the crime. Normally Callum didn't trust eyewitness memory but her description of his grandfather was dead accurate. Undoubtedly every detail of that fateful night in 1909 was forever burned into that girl's memory.

He took a sip of coffee to moisten the cookie, in order to be able to speak again. As he took out his notepad he asked, "Did you see the man that your father saw that night?"

"No I didn't, only Father saw him. 'Twasn't Mr. Otto Slade, he was very adamant about that, even to his dying day."

"Why didn't your father testify at the trial?"

She looked around nervously, then went and shut the drapes. *Why the paranoid behaviour?* He wondered.

Ruthie returned and in a low whispered voice began, "The police wanted my father to testify only if he would point the finger at Otto Slade, but my father knew it 'twasn't so."

"Did he tell them what he did see?"

"Aye. But the police continued to be… persuasive to get him to change his mind. But my father was a good God-fearing man and he told them that he would not break the ninth commandment."

"Thou shall not lie?" guessed Callum. She peered at him disapprovingly over her eyeglasses, with a stern schoolmarm glare.

"Thou shalt not bear false witness against thy neighbour," quoted Ruthie in an indignant tone.

"Right," replied Callum sheepishly. "Guess I'm not as well versed in the Bible as I used to be."

"You've lost your brogue and your Bible, Mr. Toughill," smirked Ruthie.

Callum smiled to himself. Sounded just like his mother. He looked down at what he had written and whispered; "In way were the police 'persuasive'?"

"Well, they were very, very cross. The authorities threatened my father with terrible things they would do if he ever made any public comments contradicting the findings of the law."

"They threatened to hurt your father?"

"They threatened to take me away. Can you imagine his fear?" she whispered. Her hand began to tremble. She set her coffee down. "He would get worked up into a frenzy any time I was late from school. He lived the rest of his life in fear. It took me a long time to realize he never blamed me."

"Why didn't you move away? Why stay right under the flat where the murder took place?"

"My father swore that he would never breathe a word of it and would take it to his grave, but, alas, he didn't want to forsake Miss Gilcrest. *To run away would be easy,* he would say, *with the truth at a distance it would be easy to forget.*"

Take it to his grave? The very same words Callum's own grandfather had used. *Ironic.* He wrote what she said, and then asked, "Why are you still here?"

"This was my father's home. It is all I have left of him," she said as she wiped her eye with a fingertip. "Besides I'd never find a flat this size at the rate I pay."

Callum chuckled. "Do you remember anything from that night?"

She nodded, closed her eyes for a moment and winced as if trying to stop the flood of memories. She opened her eyes but they were staring far away.

"After my father returned with Dr. Adams from across the street, I stole away upstairs. Father had told me to stay down here but I was far too curious," her voice drifted a little, as if to wait for her mental picture to play out. "I crept on my hands and knees to stay low. The door to Miss Gilcrest's flat was open. I could hear my father's voice as well as Miss Langlea's... she was Miss Gilcrest's new servant."

Callum scribbled along and circled the word 'new'.

"I sneaked in. I half expected to see Duff, Miss Gilcrest's dog, but then I remembered that she had been found dead a few weeks earlier. Miss Gilcrest was convinced someone had poisoned Duff and feared for her own life. She was certain someone meant to kill her, and Duff died by mistake. My father assumed that she was overreacting in grief but he decided to humor her. They devised this code that if Miss Gilcrest was in trouble she would knock three times on the floor," Ruthie pointed up to the ceiling above their heads.

Callum already knew the floor of Miss Gilcrest's sitting room was directly above, and barely looked up as he scribbled 'poison' in large letters and jotted a question mark above it.

"It was because of what had happened to the dog," continued Ruthie, "that I begged Pa to go back up that night."

"Did you see anything?"

"Aye. I noticed the loose papers all over room..."

Callum nodded. He remembered the photograph depicting as much. There was certainly nothing wrong with this woman's memory.

"I moved toward my Pa's voice, staying close to the carpet, then froze to the spot. There I saw her, near the fireplace..."

"Miss Gilcrest?"

Ruthie nodded, "There was blood everywhere. She was lying on her back... there was.... nothing left of her face... it had been smashed in."

Callum dropped his pen, "Her face?"

"The eyes were no longer in their sockets, her nose was shattered and dangling by her cheek... I will never forget the pitiful sound of her moaning."

"She was still alive?" Callum gasped. He didn't consider himself to be squeamish by any means but the thought that poor Agatha Gilcrest had sustained such injuries and was still alive, realizing what had happened and knowing that her life was slipping away, must have been terrifying for the poor old lady.

"Did she say anything?" Callum asked.

Ruthie shook her head as she replied, "She tried to… but her jaw was broken. I couldn't stop looking at her face."

Eyes gone? Nose shattered? Jaw broken? Callum was beside himself. He had read the preliminary medical report as well as the court testimony. It always listed the injuries as a blow to the head— nowhere did it say that her face had sustained any injury. To hit someone in the back of the head with a blunt instrument could be done out of desperation or fear, but to inflict such damage while looking at the victim… that was personal. That was an act of rage.

"I wanted to scream, I wanted to run away," whimpered Ruth, "But I couldn't stop staring at her. I watched as she gasped her final breath, then I nearly screamed as I felt a hand touch my shoulder. 'Twas my father. I was certain he was going to yell at me, but he simply turned my head away from the sight and walked me downstairs to here. I waited for him to get the wooden spoon to rap across my knuckles for my disobedience, but he never uttered a word about it… never. As I think about it now, I guess he knew I would never forget what I had seen… and that was the harshest of punishments."

"Would you know if Miss Gilcrest had any enemies? Anyone who would want to kill her?"

"No, she was the sweetest old lady you could ever meet. She always welcomed guests. More than I ever have I dare say," recalled Ruthie with a smirk as she sipped her coffee. "Even her former servant, Miss Fergraith, who left her employ when she got married… Oh, I can't remember the name of the man she married. Anyhow, she would be invited to bring her family to visit Miss Gilcrest for the holidays after she left. Miss Gilcrest had no children of her own, which I guess is why she spoiled Miss Fergraith's children with presents— treated them as if they were her own grandchildren. Did you ever hear of such a thing? A former employer. That's how sweet of a lady she was."

Callum nodded in agreement as he jotted down every word. Then he traced the tip of his pen to an earlier note, "You said 'new' servant. Did Miss Heather Langlea replace Miss Fergraith?"

"Yes," replied Ruth. "No, wait… there was another servant before Miss Langlea… oh, what was her name?"

Callum watched as Ruthie wrestled with herself, tapping her forehead with her hand as if trying to knock the memory forward.

"Cleaver!" exclaimed Ruthie finally, "How could I forget that name! 'Twas the first scandal I was ever aware of where I had known someone personally involved. I remember the day Miss Cleaver was sacked by Miss Gilcrest."

Sacked? Being terminated from a job could be a motive, Callum thought. "Why was she sacked?"

"Miss Gilcrest discovered that Alice Cleaver had murdered her own infant son. I think the child was also born out of wedlock. Still, it was a dreadful realization. What kind of mother would kill her own child?"

"Good question," Callum said as he scribbled the details as quickly as he could. *Once a killer,* Callum thought to himself. He then looked up at Ruth, "Would you happen to know whatever became of Miss Alice Cleaver?"

Ruthie cocked her head and said, "Last I recall, she had accompanied another family aboard the *Titanic.*"

CHAPTER 13

Natalie saw that Myra was under distress and snapped her out of the hypnotic state immediately. Myra began to hyperventilate.

"No! You have to help me get my memory back," implored Myra as she stood, putting her hand to her neck, her fingertips searching. "I need to find my husband and son. I need to find this ship... *Titanic*. Have you ever heard of it?"

Natalie's eyebrows raised in disbelief. *Was she for real?* Did this patient actually believe she had been a passenger aboard the most famous disaster of the 20th century? One thing was certain: the panic was real. She was afraid Myra was going to go into shock.

"Myra. I need you to calm down," replied Natalie as she put her hands on Myra's shoulders and guided her back down to the chair.

"Please, you have to help me!" Myra desperately pleaded. "Do you know where I could find the *Titanic*?"

At the bottom of the sea... Natalie thought to herself, then bit her tongue. That would not be the appropriate answer at this time. She took a deep breath and said aloud, "Let me look into that. But I need you to relax."

"But..."

"We'll continue the session tomorrow..."

Later, in her office, Natalie sank down into her chair behind her desk. She had thought the hypnosis session was going well until she realized that Myra seemed to have succumbed to delusional tendencies, perhaps even suspected borderline personality disorder. Myra's subconscious mind must have set up obstacles and had created this *Titanic* delusion in order to suppress some sort of traumatic experience. She suspected it had something to do with Myra's son. Natalie got up and paced about the room. There had to be some way to smash through this mental barrier.

Natalie picked up the old gray hardcover novel that was included with Myra's personal possessions. *Futility, by Morgan Robertson*. Her finger traced over the image of the ship sinking next to the iceberg. Was Myra reading this book? Was this the cause of her *Titanic* fantasy? She opened the front cover, where there was a child's pencil doodle of waves and an uneven rectangle above it… a boat perhaps? She put it back down and leaned on it for a moment.

Her eyes darted about the room as she tried to think what her professor and mentor would have said at this point. She could use a second opinion right about now. She was almost tempted to call him when something caught her eye on the front cover of the *USA Today* magazine she had put on her in-tray. She usually read this fresh, recently-launched newspaper on her commute to work, but today she had been preoccupied the Myra case. Now the headline struck an ironic chord:

TITANIC II LAUNCHES NEXT WEEK!
This Time It Really Is Unsinkable!

On the same page was a photograph of a very gnarled, wrinkled old man named Archibald Hoffman sitting next to his son, Edward. She had seen Edward Hoffman at many charity functions but never had the opportunity to meet him. Even though he was technically a senior citizen, his distinguished looks and youthful energy still made him 'an eligible bachelor' in some local New York magazines. Even in this newspaper photo his steel blue eyes radiated a sharp intelligence.

She picked up the paper and skimmed though the article. The reporter referred to Edward as a '*Titanic* Survivor, Author and Expert of the Original Doomed Ship.'

Interesting, Natalie thought to herself as an idea popped into her head. It would be a little unorthodox as far as psychiatric treatment, but what better second opinion than that of someone who was really there?

She skipped over all the pomp and details about the new ship and found a useful hint that the Hoffmans had their head office here in Manhattan. Natalie looked at her watch as she grabbed the phonebook, and hoped they weren't already closed for the weekend.

• • •

The first things Edward Hoffman noticed as he entered Dr. Natalie Lindsay's office were the diplomas that hung on the wall opposite the door. *Impressive for someone so young,* thought Edward. The room had the typical sterile feel of a hospital office, but there were also some obvious feminine touches — possibly an attempt to make it more comfortable. On the bookshelf behind the desk, he noticed a framed photograph of Dr. Lindsay, looking much younger. Next to her in the photo was another young girl with similar facial features. *A sister perhaps?* Unlike the diplomas and assorted knickknacks, this framed photo was dust-free and in a prominent eye-level space. *This photograph is special to the young psychologist.*

"Thank you for taking the time to come in on such short notice, Mr. Hoffman," said Dr. Lindsay as she gestured to the armchair in front of her desk. "It's a pity your father declined to join us."

"This sort of thing is not... his cup of tea," replied Edward as he gave his hat and coat to her outstretched hand. He made himself comfortable in the armchair as she placed the articles on the coat rack in the corner.

Since seeing the broadcast on television, Edward had suspected that he would end up becoming involved, somehow. He thought it interesting that this attractive young doctor was dressed so matronly, wearing an exceptionally long skirt. He was certain those had gone out of fashion a decade ago.

"Now, Mr. Hoffman," began Dr. Lindsay.

"May I interrupt you for a moment, Dr. Lindsay," interjected Edward. "*Mr. Hoffman* is my father, and as you have already experienced on the phone with him, he's a crotchety old goat. Please call me Edward."

"Very well, Edward. And you can call me Natalie," laughed Natalie. "I'm guessing you've come across... 'situations' like this before."

"Well it is safe to say that I've met my fair share of *Titanic*-nuts..." Edward paused and looked about. "I'm sorry, I shouldn't use phrases like that in here."

Dr. Lindsay smiled, "Many of our staff do. Just don't do it in front of the patients."

"Of course. As I was saying, I have met a great many *Titanic*-fanatics and most are quite harmless. Does your patient truly believe she was... aboard the *Titanic*?"

Dr. Lindsay stared at him for a moment, unable to answer. Edward smiled. He understood the ethical predicament Dr. Lindsay found herself in.

Edward leaned forward, "Would it help you to know that I have a PhD in psychology?"

"Really?" asked Natalie with a sigh of relief. "I wasn't aware of that."

"From NYU. Interned with Dr. David Wechsler at Bellevue Psychiatric Hospital. I originally wanted to help people after I returned from the war."

"Which war?" she asked.

"World War II," Edward said, trying to repress his memories.

"Had your own personal demons there?" asked Natalie. Then she caught herself. "I'm sorry I didn't mean to ask such a personal question. Occupational hazard, I guess."

"I understand. No offense taken. Let's just say I carry more than my fair share of survivor guilt from the first half of this century," Edward said with a smile. But he noticed Natalie's eyes flit over to the photo of her sister when he said 'survivor guilt'. He then added, "I guess we all have our own demons to battle."

Natalie looked over at him with a look of surprise.

"Forgive me. I didn't mean to pry," said Edward as he tried to think of a way of changing subjects. He spotted the rumpled copy of *Futility* that he saw on the news on the corner of Natalie's desk.

"It's okay," replied Natalie. "Most of the psychoanalysts that I know have their own issues to deal with."

"May I?" asked Edward, gesturing to the book.

"Go ahead," replied Dr. Lindsay.

Edward opened it up to see if there was a personalized inscription or name on the inside cover. The spine of the book crinkled and moaned as it was cracked open. He was surprised to see a child's drawing in pencil. *Waves? A boat?* He had an odd sensation of déjà vu. His fingers traced the waves for a moment.

"I tried reading it while I was waiting for you," Natalie said, bringing his thoughts back to the matter at hand. "It's not a very long book."

"What did you think of it?"

"It was okay, I stopped reading. It was getting too… anti-Semitic for my taste. The character of Meyer was so stereotypical— I have real issues with racial prejudice."

"Well, it was written in a different century," replied Edward as he flipped through the water-damaged pages, "Back in the late 1800's the Jews were being driven out of Russia with the *pogroms*. There was a huge immigration to Europe. They were a different culture, religion and appearance. Mankind has a habit of fearing and hating differences rather than embracing them."

Edward paused, he could see it was striking a chord with the good doctor. He decided to share a part of himself. "Near the end of the war, I witnessed first-hand the horror that mankind is capable of inflicting on another human being, when our company liberated one of the concentration camps in Poland. At the age of thirty-five, my own hair turned white when I saw what the Nazis had done to the Jews…"

Edward fell quiet. It was a tenacious image he had tried so hard to forget.

"I can't even begin to imagine," Natalie said after an awkward pause. "I've witnessed racial prejudice when I was a teenager. Not to the extent of near-genocide but… still brutal and unjust…"

Edward could see she wanted to continue but no words came out of her open mouth. Edward estimated the young doctor to be in her thirties. So when she was in her teens, it would have been during the late 1960's – when America was in turmoil over the civil rights movement. Another dark chapter in mankind's history. The racial prejudice she'd experienced must have been quite personal. He chose not to open up any further wounds.

"What did you think about the fact that this novel was written fourteen years before the *Titanic* sank?" asked Edward, pointing to the illustration of the sinking ship next to an iceberg on the cover.

"I thought it was interesting," replied Natalie, obviously relieved to be moving back to the case at hand.

"Just *interesting?*" prodded Edward, closing the book.

"It's merely synchronicity," replied Natalie.

"Synchronicity?"

"It's when a connection of two or more psychological or psychic phenomena occur without causation," explained Natalie.

"Yes, I'm familiar with Dr. Carl Jung's theory," interrupted Edward. "But do you believe it's simply a matter of experiencing two or more seemingly unlikely, unrelated events connecting together by chance?"

"Do you believe that cause and effect are held together by a higher power?" countered Natalie.

"Not every connection needs to have an explanation in terms of causation," replied Edward since neither of them were giving a straight answer. Turning his attention back to the book, he saw that aside from the water damage on the cover, the inside pages did not seem to have yellowed with age as did the copies he had under glass. "This would have been in remarkable condition before getting wet."

"I also thought it was very new-looking," added Natalie. "From what I read, the *Titanic* boarding pass she had in her possession was also in excellent condition."

"Where is that boarding pass now?"

"Still being authenticated as far as I know," replied Natalie. "What confuses me about this case, is that I'm sure this patient *truly believes* that she was on the *Titanic*...but would she go to the trouble of forging a fake *Titanic* boarding pass? At what point does awareness of her own actions end? She's either fully immersed in this fantasy, or she's a very good actress."

"I've dealt with good actresses before," replied Edward. "I once had dealings with a woman who claimed to be the only child that perished from First Class... and heir to a fortune, I might add."

"I take it she was a fake?"

"Completely," replied Edward shaking his head. "It was a terrible ordeal for the family as well to open up old wounds, but I was able to find the flaws in her 'story'. I expect to do the same with your patient."

"I read that you were two when the *Titanic* sank," began Natalie. "If you don't mind me asking, do you have cognitive memories from then?"

Edward paused before he replied, "There are some moments that are very clear from that night, but in all honesty, I've spoken to so many survivors over the years that there are times I'm not certain which are my memories, and which are theirs."

"I appreciate your honesty."

"Fear not, good doctor," Edward smiled. "I have enough knowledge and experience with real survivors that I can expose the truth. Once we prove she was not on the *Titanic*, you can proceed with her treatment."

"That was what I was hoping for," replied Natalie.

"Do you mind if I take this with me?" Edward asked holding up the book. "I'd like to have it examined."

"Go right ahead."

Edward placed it carefully in his briefcase. He then looked back at Natalie and said, "I'll assume that sitting in on a hypnotic session is out of the question."

Natalie grimaced, "I don't think she'll agree to it. It was hard enough to get her comfortable…"

Edward raised his hand as he nodded, "I understand, I expected as much. Besides, recalling a memory is never reliable. However, there are other senses that can tell us whether a memory is real or not. Can you answer me one question? What class did she say she was in?"

"Class?"

"First, second or third class passenger?'

"Actually she didn't say… wait…" Natalie opened her desk drawer and pulled out her notepad from the hypnoanalysis session. Her finger traced over the shorthand squiggles to the passage she was looking for and punched it with her fingertip. 'Here it is… she mentioned a stateroom, a fireplace, an adjoining cabin and a tea cart."

"Ah! First class!" For a moment Edward pictured the stateroom he and his family stayed in.

"What do you suggest?" asked Natalie, interrupting his thoughts.

"Dinner," replied Edward as he reached into his briefcase and pulled out a couple of books about the *Titanic*. He quickly flipped to a marked page and handed it to Dr. Lindsay. "This photo is of the dinner menu from April 14th, *Titanic*'s final meal."

Dr. Lindsay poured over the menu. Her brow folded into a frown. Then reading aloud, "Oysters a la Russe, Poached Salmon with Mousseline Sauce, Filet Mignon Lili, Páté d'foy grass…?"

"Páté de Foie Gras," Edward said, correcting her French.

"I don't even know what that is…" Natalie replied as she looked back at the menu in the book. Then she glanced up and remarked, "I don't think I can afford reading this menu let alone eating from it. It's an eleven course meal!"

"Cost is not a factor," Edward said without hesitation. "I will cover the expense. I know of a wonderful chef here in Manhattan who can prepare the whole meal."

"I can't authorize the patient leaving this clinic," interrupted Natalie.

"You won't have to. It will all be catered. As long as there's a room large enough to accommodate the three of us… and an eight-piece band."

"Eight-piece….well, er… I'm really looking forward to this," Natalie stammered as she handed the book back to Edward. "But don't you think our patient might have also read this book?"

Edward grinned, "That my dear Doctor, is what I'm counting on."

April 3, 1982

CHAPTER 14

The past whizzed by Callum's eyes as the microfilm scanner whirled through the thick spool of film. On each frame that spun by the illuminated screen was a page from a newspaper circa 1909. When Callum found a newspaper article pertaining to Alice Cleaver, he would deposit a 25p coin into the slot and make a photocopy of that page. Hopefully he'd find a clue to lead him to the murderer of Agatha Gilcrest or to the missing diamond brooch.

Callum had spent a better part of the morning feeding that machine in the bowels of the monolithic Mitchell Library. From the outside, the building looked like an imperial palace. Opened the year before *Titanic* had set sail, it had been expanded and renovated several times over the decades, now making it the largest resource library in the United Kingdom.

"How can anyone find anything in this massive building?" Callum had wondered aloud upon his arrival.

"Eventually computers will help index and store information," smiled the nearby clerk, her accent laced with a Northern Scottish lilt. "I'm experimenting with my BBC Micro at home."

It had been a rhetorical question but he supposed it was an occupational necessity for her to respond to any question regardless of how pointless. *Computers, ha! That'll be the day,* Callum thought to himself. Science fiction was once again a hot topic ever since that 'Star Wars' film came out a few years ago. Some colourful home computers were coming on the market but no one, except this clerk, seemed to be buying any except for their kids to play games. He had seen computers that could store small amounts of information. They were massive. They would need several extra buildings just to house those monsters. He glanced at his watch to check the time. Noticing the calculator on it, he imagined ten years ago this too would have been considered science fiction. He reconsidered the clerk's opinion and shrugged, *Who knows?*

Some hours later, Callum reached for the stack of articles he had printed and began to collate them as he tried to piece together what had happened. It was tedious but since most of the eyewitnesses were dead by now, it was the only way. Taking his red pen he underlined key points for reference later.

The way Callum could see it, on the cold morning of 21st of January 1909, laborers had made a gruesome discovery while laying plates on the North London Railway. Lying several yards from the railway tracks were the remains of a small baby boy. The foreman had told the press that he hoped it was a horrible accident, but as no-one had reported a child missing, the police treated the scene as suspicious from the start. Considering how far from the tracks the body of the infant had been, and where the impact on his tiny body was, the physician determined that the baby had been thrown violently from the train the night before.

Police began an extensive search of recent birth records in the area, while calling upon witnesses who may have seen a baby carried onto the train on the eve of January 20th. A few weeks later, police arrested Alice Cleaver for the murder of her own child.

Reading through the trial coverage, Callum surmised that Alice Cleaver had had a sad existence: she herself was the illegitimate daughter of an illegitimate daughter. There seemed to be no father figures in her family for a few generations. Alice Cleaver was unwed and distraught over the fact that the baby's father had abandoned her. Although not uncommon in today's world, back in 1909 being an unwed mother was like having the plague: such a girl was shunned and even ostracized by the general public. Alice Cleaver maintained her innocence throughout her arrest and trial. She claimed to have placed the baby in the care of a Mrs. Gray who ran an orphanage in Kilburn. Police tried to verify her story, but discovered that there was no such person or place.

The defense put forth a claim that Alice Cleaver was suffering some sort of depression from being abandoned by the man she thought loved her, just as men had abandoned her mother and her mother's mother.

Callum slumped back in his chair, remembering another case he had investigated five years ago. Weeks after giving birth, a well-to-do woman went crazy and took a knife to her husband's priceless artwork, and then drove herself and the baby into the family swimming pool in her husband's Jaguar. Both the baby and mother survived. Callum had been sent to investigate to see if it had been some sort of stunt to get the insurance money. He even spoke to a psychiatrist who insisted that the term 'baby blues' was an understatement. He stated an 'atypical postnatal depression' affected ten percent of women to varying degrees after delivery, and it was enough of a concern among the medical community to warrant further study. Callum believed the doctor, yet it perturbed him that the husband in question seemed more upset about his artwork than the condition of his wife and child.

Back in 1909, psychology was still a new science and not well accepted or understood. It was unlikely that the jury of Alice Cleaver's peers would have been forgiving.

As Callum flipped through the pages, he realized he didn't have a printout pertaining to the end of the trial or the verdict.

Upon turning back to the microfilm, he was taken aback by the following 1912 headline from an American newspaper: *Alice Cleaver Saves Child from Titanic Sinking!*

There was a blurry photo beneath the headline of a woman holding a small boy from first class. It was a far cry from the headlines printed three years earlier. The story went on to describe her heroism in the face of the disaster and how she kept a tight hold of the boy until both were safe in New York.

Unfortunately, in the following days the media turned on her once again. The truth began to emerge that she had been hired as a nurse by Hudson Allison, a wealthy investment broker from Montreal, and she was charged with looking after his two children: Trevor and Loraine. When the famous ship began to sink, Allison took the boy to the deck and was ushered into a lifeboat. The rest of the family did not know what had become of their son and refused to leave the ship without him. The little girl, Loraine, was the only child in First Class to perish.

Back to Titanic, Callum thought. He perused through the other pages hoping for a mention of the Gilcrest murder or the brooch.

"You were looking for articles on *Titanic* or Alice Cleaver?" The hushed voice yanked Callum back from 1912 into the present. He looked up to see the helpful clerk standing over him, holding a recent issue of a tabloid magazine. "There was also this article relating to the *Titanic*, since you made a comment about it."

"Thank you," replied Callum. He looked at the tabloid about a woman found in the North Atlantic in the same location where *Titanic* sank seventy years ago. *Bollocks*, thought Callum. He skeptically skimmed through the article, but looked at the picture of the lovely woman for a long moment. He had seen her face recently. *Likely some advert or on the Telly*. She had a movie star look to her. He shook his head as he reread the headline. The idea that she was somehow preserved alive in the freezing waters was sheer nonsense, perhaps some sort of publicity stunt or 'Candid Camera' style prank.

"Sorry, I couldn't help showing you that one," smirked the clerk. She then held up her other hand, which was holding a magazine. "However, I'm sure this article would be of more of interest to you. And far more recent than 1912."

Callum glanced at the page the clerk was holding open for him. He stood up with such excitement that his chair crashed backwards, shattering the sacred silence of the library. Ignoring the angry glares being hurled at him, he snatched the magazine from the clerk's hand and looked at the published date. It was indeed recent. Callum looked at his digital watch. He hoped he wasn't too late.

CHAPTER 15

"Will this other doctor be able to help me get my memory back?" asked Myra, wrapping the shawl around herself as Natalie escorted her from the room.

"I hope so. I also hope that you'll feel comfortable talking to him and answering any of his questions," Natalie replied as they headed to one of the lounges that had been booked for this occasion. As they drew near, Natalie was thrilled to hear music emanating from the room.

"Oh, how marvelous," exclaimed Myra. "Ragtime music!"

Natalie hardly recognized Ralph, one of the orderlies, dressed in a tuxedo. The doctor smiled, "You clean up really nicely, Ralph!"

Edward Hoffman seemed to be sparing no detail. With a small flourish, Ralph opened the door for the two women.

Inside the lounge, a small eight-piece band made up mostly of string instruments as well as the Clinic's piano, played jauntily. Natalie saw the familiar form of Edward Hoffman, who was lighting the candles on the table. Edward turned to meet them.

"Hello I'm...." He stopped suddenly and stared at Myra. The smile disappeared so quickly it was almost as if he had seen a ghost. Clearing his throat, he stammered, "Have we met before?"

"I don't believe so," Myra replied. "Although, there is something in your eyes that seems... familiar. Perhaps we have met someplace. I really cannot remember. I was hoping you might be able to help."

Natalie noted that for the first time since arriving here, Myra didn't seem to be shivering any more.

"Let's see what we can learn here first," Edward smiled. "Forgive me for staring. If I may be so bold, you have the most remarkable blue eyes I have ever seen."

"Thank you, Doctor...er..." smiled Myra.

"Please no titles here, please call me Edward."

"Very well... Edward." Myra replied, but his name seemed to drop off into a whisper. Natalie noticed an odd distant look in her eyes. Edward turned to Natalie expectantly, eyebrows raised.

"Oh, yes," said Natalie as she remembered her role in this scenario. "Edward, may I introduce: Myra."

Edward gently took Myra's hand and graciously kissed the back of it. Edward paused, then smiled. "What a coincidence. That's my mother's name."

"A noble woman, I hope."

Edward smiled again as he pulled the chairs out for both ladies and once they were both seated, he sat across from them.

"We'll be starting with Oysters à la Russe," Edward said to Myra. "Would you like White Bordeaux, White Burgundy or Chablis?"

"You're asking me?" Myra asked in a shocked tone.

"Is there something wrong with that?" asked Dr. Lindsay.

"It is not customary that a man would ask a woman to order."

"Ah, but you are the guest," replied Edward.

"Very well then. Chablis would be the best choice with oysters," replied Myra as she spread the cloth napkin across her lap. Natalie clumsily copied her.

Edward seemed suitably impressed. He nodded to the caterer standing nearby who looked to his assistant and proceeded to place the food in front of the ladies first.

Myra grimaced, then smiled "This was served the other night."

"Other night?" asked Dr. Lindsay.

"On board the *Titanic*," beamed Myra. "I remembered that."

"Excellent," smiled Edward. "I wanted you to feel comfortable. So I spared no expense in recreating the meal exactly as it was on board the ... *Titanic*." Edward then picked up his glass and held it to toast, "To recovering your memory."

"I'll drink to that," said Dr. Lindsay.

Edward savored the drink for a moment then turned to Myra. He waited for her to finish with the oyster she had consumed, then asked, "What do you remember about *Titanic*?"

"I recall images mostly. Very much like paintings," said Myra as she closed her eyes. "The smell of food and the music seems to help with the images. I can recall the Dining Lounge where this dinner was served."

"Can you describe it?" asked Edward.

"It was mostly white, which made the style Jacobean. I believe the furniture was oak, which matched the walls, and upholstered with green velvet. The dining room itself was very large, and the floors were tiled... not marble, but rather hundreds of soft tiles patterned to resemble a Persian carpet. On the high ceiling I recall a glass dome. Some lovely leaded windows and quaint alcoves. There were also recessed dining bays where families and other parties could dine with some privacy. I was in one of those bays."

"Really?" Edward asked leaning in. "Do you recall which one?"

Myra puckered her brow for a moment. Then she opened her eyes, looked at him for a moment, and then solemnly shook her head. "I'm sorry I cannot."

Natalie struggled through the rest of the first and second courses, watching Edward to see which utensil he picked up and how to handle it. Myra, on the other hand, seemed to have no difficulty. This made Natalie feel even more awkward and unsophisticated. However, Edward did not seem to notice. His sharp eyes were studying Myra's every move even while he smiled with a gentlemanly grin.

As the second course was cleared away, Myra stood up and Edward quickly also stood up at the same time. Natalie looked at them for a moment. She recalled seeing an old movie where gentlemen would rise to their feet when a woman got up from, or came back to the table.

"Will you excuse me?" Myra addressed Dr. Lindsay, "I need to visit the powder room."

"Of course."

An orderly escorted Myra out of the room. The moment she exited, Natalie turned to Edward. "This is all very nice. But have we learned anything?"

"Oh, yes. This woman is well bred."

Edward gestured to Myra's place setting. "She has done more than memorize the menu from a book. She has been educated in fine dining etiquette. And European etiquette to be exact."

"How do you know?" Natalie was curious, feeling like she was Watson to his Sherlock.

"From how she uses and places the cutlery," he smiled. Natalie almost expected him to say 'elementary.' Natalie hoped he didn't notice how she was faring with multiple utensils so she moved the discussion away from cutlery. She sighed, "So maybe she was schooled in Europe. That might also explain the slight accent — some kind of boarding school perhaps?"

"My thoughts exactly."

"So? How are we going to prove to her that she wasn't on *Titanic*?"

"She is about to fail the test," Edward smiled triumphantly. "Watch."

As the third course was placed on the table Natalie glanced at the clock on the wall, wondering where Myra had gone. Then she recalled the layers of undergarments that Myra was wearing and wondered how any woman could have managed.

Shortly thereafter, Myra was escorted back in. Natalie couldn't help but marvel at Myra's grace. She seemed to glide across the floor toward them, her feet invisible and silent beneath the billowing dress. Edward once again stood up and held the chair for her. As she sat, Myra glanced down and laughed.

"What's so funny?" asked Edward as he returned to his seat.

"Forgive me Edward. You have done a splendid recreation of the dinner from the *Titanic*. However, you have made a small error."

Natalie watched a bewildered, jaw-dropping expression form on Edward's face, as he hoarsely whispered, "Error?"

"Oh it's an honest mistake I'm sure. The dinner menu did state 'Poached Salmon with Mousseline Sauce'. We were, however, served 'Salmon Mayonnaise Potted Shrimps' instead."

Natalie could tell from Edward's fallen expression that this wasn't what he expected to hear.

"How did you know?" he stammered.

"I was there. I love poached salmon with Mousseline Sauce and was dreadfully disappointed when they didn't serve it. In addition, the music isn't quite right. Mr. Hartley's orchestra only played Ragtime during luncheons. In the evening he played more soothing pieces like the Merry Widow Waltz or the Blue Danube."

Without skipping a beat, the orchestra switched the music to what Natalie assumed was the 'Blue Danube'. The warm sound brought a smile to Myra's face. Natalie looked over at Edward, who had started rubbing his hands together and even heated them with his breath. Myra closed her eyes as she happily swayed to the music. Then her face suddenly contorted as she recalled an image.

"My son didn't like the potted shrimp. He dropped them on the floor and kicked them out of sight under the table. His father caught him in the act." Myra winced, "Without any warning he struck..."

"Stop!" Edward stood up from the table. The musicians stopped playing. Myra opened her eyes and looked at him with confusion. Edward, obviously embarrassed and confused, placed his napkin down on the plate. He looked down at Dr. Lindsay. "I've had enough of this charade. Please excuse me."

Without another word he shuffled out of the room without making any eye contact with Myra. She looked hurt and confused and then glanced back to Dr. Lindsay, her blue eyes searching for answers.

— — —

Out in the hall, Edward loosened his tie, his mind racing. Who could have coached her so well? He needed air, needed to clear his mind. He made his way towards the stairs. Suddenly he felt light headed. The stairwell seemed to collapse into a dark tunnel.

• • •

From inside the lounge Natalie heard a voice rising in panic from the hallway. A strange look fell across Myra's face. Before Natalie could say or do anything, Myra rose and dashed out of the room.

"Call 9-1-1!" a woman yelled as Natalie followed.

People were gathered and looking down the stairwell. Natalie saw Myra fight past them.

"Let me through," Natalie implored as she pushed through the current of onlookers. She spotted Edward collapsed on the stair landing. Myra flew down to him.

"Don't move him!" Natalie called after Myra, fearing a fall like that at his age could have caused internal trauma.

Natalie tried to descend the stairs. She glanced down to see Myra had already turned Edward over and was cradling his head in her arms, her hand tapping his shoulder in a rhythmic pattern.

— — —

Where am I? Edward wondered. It was dark and he ached all over. Someone was holding him. He could feel a gentle patting on his shoulder. There was something familiar and comforting about it. Edward slowly opened his eyes and looked up at the young woman… Myra. He blinked. There was a definite flash of recognition in her sky-blue eyes and the curve of her gentle smile. Tears started to stream down Edward's cheeks. With her other hand, Myra gently wiped the tears from his eyes.

The familiar touch simultaneously warmed and sent a shiver through him as he suddenly knew the truth. How many times had she wiped his tears?

Edward could not look away. He sobbed, "Mommy?"

CHAPTER 16

"You were on the *Titanic*? I must say, you look well for your age," remarked Callum Toughill as he sat across from the middle-aged looking woman.

"Well, I was only two when *Titanic* sank," she replied.

"Right then, for the record can I get your full name?" asked Callum.

"Certainly," she replied. "My identification states I'm Loraine Kramer but I was born Helen Loraine Allison. My parents were Hudson and Bessie Allison of Montreal, Canada. They both died when the *Titanic* sank and my brother was taken off the ship by our nurse, Alice Cleaver."

"Is that who took you off? Alice Cleaver?" asked Callum as he scribbled in his notebook. He saw from the magazine article that this woman who claimed to be Loraine Allison, the only child from First Class to perish on the *Titanic*, was now residing in a modest rooming house near the Balloch Castle grounds in West Dunbartonshire. After a quick ring to directory assistance he was able to call ahead to arrange this dubious meeting. Fortunately for Callum, the Charing Cross Rail Station was within spitting distance of the Mitchell Library and he was able to journey to West Dunbartonshire thanks to the new Argyle Line that opened a couple of years ago.

"No. Alice Cleaver was a wicked woman," muttered Loraine as she retrieved a bottle of Sherry from the small cupboard above the gas stove. Callum took note of the small room that housed her bed, living area and a small kitchenette, and as he waved his hand politely refusing a glass, he also observed how this woman was obviously bleaching her hair blonde. The real Loraine Allison was a blonde little girl. This Loraine was trying to hold onto a hairstyle that had gone out of fashion decades ago, and the shocking amount of blue eye shadow was distracting to look at when he needed to study her face. There was a hint of brogue that she must have picked up from living in Scotland but her accent was undoubtedly American. Southern States, he guessed. Loraine turned down the sound of some soap that was droning on the telly. She sat down as she continued, "Miss Cleaver hated me. Threatened to throw me off the ship."

"Why?"

"Because I knew the truth," replied Loraine as she tossed down the Sherry and poured herself another. "I knew she had killed her son the same way. Throwing him off a train."

"Extraordinary!"

"What is?"

"That at the tender age of two, you would understand the concept of homicide."

"Well..." replied Loraine with a scowl. "I overheard my parents talking about it."

"Really?" Callum exclaimed as he looked up from his notebook. "They knew of her sordid past and still hired her? I know Canadians have a reputation for being nice, but hiring a woman who committed *filicide* to look after their own children is a bit reckless, don't you think?"

Loraine shifted as she stammered, "They heard the gossip after the *Titanic* set sail."

"And yet they still entrusted you and your brother to her care? Curious," retorted Callum. He knew he was coming on strong but her story was dodgy from the start. Furthermore, after investigating several scam artists and fraudsters over the years, Callum had learned to detect the unconscious telltale signs of lying. The involuntary position of the eyes as a person tries to fabricate a story versus the exact opposite position of the eyes as they recall from memory, for example.

"Since you were only a toddler, how did you get off the sinking ship?" asked Callum. "Did Alice Cleaver take you off at the same time she took Trevor Allison?"

"No, I was taken off the ship by a Mr. Hyde," responded Loraine earnestly.

"That's H-I-D-E as in *hide and seek*?"

"No, Hyde, with a 'y' as in Hyde park!"

Or Dr. Jekyll & Mr. Hyde, Callum thought to himself. This was sounding as equally implausible as the fantasy tale. Or perhaps she was influenced by the outrageous storylines of the soaps she seemed fond of.

Loraine continued, "Of course, it wasn't until much later that I learned he was none other than Thomas Andrews, the architect who designed *Titanic*."

"Andrews?" interrupted Callum, trying not to betray his inner thoughts. "But if memory serves, Thomas Andrews went down with the ship."

"Oh no," Loraine said emphatically. "That's what Bruce Ismay, the owner of *Titanic* wanted everyone to believe. He paid Mr. Andrews to disappear, so that he would never testify at the inquiry."

Callum jotted her words in shorthand. Although he was not a *Titanic* aficionado, he had been, on many occasions, subjected to Percy's in-depth knowledge of the ill-fated ship. This included how several witnesses from the last lifeboat saw Thomas Andrews hurling deck chairs to the people in the water to use as floatation devices. All of them testified that, like the captain, Thomas Andrews went down with the ship he'd designed. There was an odd sense of chest-pounding pride whenever Percy recounted it, and Callum was often reminded that Mr. Andrews was from Percy's hometown of Comber, County Down, Ireland. Callum looked up at Loraine and asked, "What happened to him?"

"Mr. Andrews? He died. It was his death that motivated me to go public with my true identity."

Callum nodded, yet he couldn't help but notice that she always addressed her surrogate father by either Mr. Hyde or Mr. Andrews. Curious that she never used a less formal name or even a sense of affection in her voice. Wanting to explore this further he pressed, "So Mr. Andrews raised you all on his own?"

"Oh no," she replied shaking her head. "His sister, Mrs. Gray, ran an orphanage. She looked after me as well."

"Did you say Mrs. Gray?"

"Yes."

Callum flipped back in his notebook and found that the same name 'Mrs. Gray' was mentioned in the 1909 murder trial as the non-existent woman who was supposedly caring for Alice Cleaver's son. In Callum Toughill's line of work there was no such thing as coincidence. Turning his attention back to the woman in front of him, he asked, "What was the name of the orphanage, and where was it?"

"I don't recall the name. It was a long time ago but it was in the American Midwest," she replied in an over-rehearsed tone. "It burned down. There is nothing left of it."

"What state?"

"I beg your pardon?"

"You said the American Midwest. Which state was this orphanage?"

"Uh, Kansas."

Callum scribbled it down. Her accent was certainly not Midwestern American. He would look into it later but he was willing to bet that like the orphanage run by Mrs. Gray in Alice Cleaver's trial in 1909, this one didn't exist either. "Do you have any proof or evidence to back up your claim?"

"My attorney, Arthur Flynn, had Mr. Andrew's journal as well as my original birth certificate and other such documents."

Callum was shocked to hear this. *Why didn't she mention this before?* "Where might I find Mr. Flynn?"

"He died."

Of course he did. "So what happened to the documents?"

"They were destroyed in a fire in his office after his death."

Of course they were. He could tell she was making it all up.

"It was George Allison, my father's brother," continued Loraine. "He murdered my lawyer and destroyed the evidence. With my brother Trevor dead, he and his wife had inherited all of my father's fortune."

"I thought your brother survived the *Titanic*. Alice Cleaver rescued him?"

"But she done him in later," snarled Loraine. "He died of poisoning in 1929."

"Why would she do that? What would she stand to gain?"

"I told you she hated us children!"

"But that was seventeen years after the sinking of the *Titanic*. Trevor was no longer a child."

"He was murdered before his eighteenth birthday," interrupted Loraine. "That's when he would have inherited everything."

"Do you have anything that can back up what you've told me?"

"I have some of the jewelry that Mum brought on board the *Titanic*," replied Loraine, "I even have a letter from Alice Cleaver backing up my story and verifying that these were the jewels that we had on the *Titanic*."

"May I see them?" Callum asked, trying not to sound too eager.

She nodded as she set down her glass. "I'll have to ask you to shut your eyes. I keep them hidden in this room. I don't want anyone to know."

Callum complied. As he sat there with his eyes shut, he could hear her shuffle across the room and rummage around. His anticipation was growing. *Could I possibly be fortunate enough to find the diamond crescent brooch here? Did Alice Cleaver kill Agatha Gilcrest and bring the piece of evidence aboard the Titanic? Was she the mysterious person who filled out the claim form after the ship sank? Percy would be shocked if I came back to London with the brooch in hand.*

"You can open your eyes," said Loraine.

Callum opened his eyes, and he surveyed the small collection on the coffee table. His hopes sank with his smile. There was no crescent brooch among the half-dozen pieces. Still they were quite lovely at first glance. He looked up at Loraine. "May I?"

"Certainly, but do be careful," she whispered.

He picked up a diamond ring, and tilted it toward the setting sun seeping in through the window. There was no halo caused by refraction. He held it close and breathed on it. The condensation lingered. Diamonds conduct heat and no moisture should have been present. This was a fake. He examined the other pieces. From the way they were mounted – all were fakes. Not one piece of jewelry had any value to them.

"They're all I have left of my mother," said Loraine with an actual sound of remorse.

"They're lovely," said Callum softly. For a brief moment, Callum felt sorry for her. She must have known that these are not real or, she had told herself the story over and over again so many times that she now believed the lie as truth. Regardless, the trail of the lost brooch and the murder of Agatha Gilcrest ended here. There were no more clues.

As Loraine carefully gathered her precious jewels, Callum saw the newspaper on the coffee table for the first time. The headline read, '*Titanic II to set sail next week!*'

Beneath the headline was a photo of the Hoffman family. Callum recognized them as he had once investigated a 'break and enter' at their London estate. What disturbed Callum, at present, was the image of Edward Hoffman: It appeared that Loraine Kramer had taken a pen and angrily scratched out his eyes.

• • •

Natalie was not sure how to feel about the outcome of this evening — it had started out so well, then went so horribly wrong.

Myra had put up a struggle and insisted on accompanying Edward when he was placed in the ambulance, becoming hysterical and completely unmanageable when the ambulance wailed away without her. Fearing that she would hurt herself or someone else, Natalie had her sedated.

Even though her shift was long over, Natalie had stayed at the clinic to watch over Myra, wanting to be present when Myra regained consciousness.

Natalie began to question her judgment as she replayed the events over and over. Looking over at the picture of herself with her sister Loren, she realized that in a lot of ways, Myra reminded Natalie of Loren. Smart, elegant... vulnerable. Perhaps that was why Natalie's judgment felt clouded.

In her senior year of school, Natalie started dating a boy named Tyrell Lincoln —a young black man. Natalie had seen nothing wrong with him. He was very smart, fun to be with, could always make her laugh, and she liked that he had the same last name as the 16th President of the United States. However, her family was less than thrilled with her dating choice. Inter-racial relationships were taboo at the time. As a teenager, Natalie was appalled that they wouldn't trust her judgment.

"Why won't you defend me?" Natalie begged of her mother. But she knew her mother would never stand against her father.

"Honor thy father and thy mother," her mother would say, quoting the fifth commandment. Natalie subsequently rebelled against her whole family.

Even her little sister, Loren questioned her. "Why is it so important for you to always win? Can't you just make peace?"

Natalie refused to give in. She was angry at all of them. Her anger was the reason she hadn't gone with Loren that night... the night of the accident. It had been raining and Natalie and her sister were supposed to meet some friends at the movies, but Natalie refused to go out with a 'traitor'.

She wasn't with Loren when the drunk driver struck her car. She wasn't with her baby sister when her car was knocked into Skippack Creek. The heavy rains had caused flooding and her car was pulled under. Natalie wasn't with her baby sister when she was likely screaming, desperately trying to get out of a sinking car. Natalie wasn't with her baby sister when she drowned.

Angry at the whole world, she pushed against everyone: her teachers, her family and even Tyrell. He tried to help, even brought his minister for guidance. That was the end. What kind of god would punish an eighteen-year-old girl for dating a decent, honest young boy? What kind of god takes the life of a sixteen-year-old girl and lets the drunk driver live unscratched? Natalie was plagued with nightmares that she was standing at the bridge watching Loren's car sink - unable to help. She would see Loren's green eyes pleading for help before disappearing to the watery depth. Natalie wanted to go to the same spot where her sister died and throw herself into the river. She was suffering from typical 'survivor's guilt' and there was no one to help her.

Natalie went on a path of self-destruction and finally, after an attempted suicide, she received psychiatric care. She credited her therapist for saving her life, and he was her inspiration to follow in his footsteps, and help others.

Natalie had been thinking a lot of Loren since she began working with Myra. Was she somehow projecting her own survivor guilt onto Myra? Was she trying to save this woman… or was she still trying to save her sister? It was ridiculous. Her analytical mind knew that helping Myra with her demons wasn't going to bring Loren back. Natalie could save a thousand lost souls and that one fact would never change. She was not there when her sister needed her.

Although Natalie had left instructions to be notified when Myra came to, it proved to be unnecessary. She could hear Myra's awaking screams echoing down the hall.

"I need to see Edward again!" Myra exclaimed as she paced about her room like a caged animal. The grace and elegance that usually emanated from her seemed gone. Yet, the heavy skirts did not seem to hinder Myra's step as she seemed to gain speed in her stride.

Natalie sighed as she looked over at the orderly standing close by, ready to pounce should Myra become violent again. Natalie didn't feel it was necessary but it was standard procedure at this point.

"Please. Please! Let them take me to him!" implored Myra.

Natalie couldn't do that, even if she wanted to. The rules prevented Myra from being released in such a delicate state. Natalie knew that they were at a crucial moment in her treatment, and the wrong word now could forever halt any progress. Natalie gestured with her head toward the chair, as she poured water into a plastic cup. "I need you to calm down. Here drink some water..."

"I really don't care what you need!" Myra snapped as she smacked the cup out of Natalie's hand. The orderly took a foreboding step forward, but Natalie stopped him with a glare. Brute force wasn't the answer right now. Natalie needed to regain control of the situation. She turned back to Myra and in a chastising tone, "That was hardly the behavior of a lady."

Myra scowled at her, "There are times when niceties no longer prevail. This is such a time."

"Fair enough."

"What the blazes is happening here?" Myra wailed as she continued pacing about the tile floor. "I need some answers! Is that my son?"

"He's not your son," Natalie said slowly and carefully. "I want you to think about it. Edward is old enough to be your grandfather. Logically... it's not possible."

"Logic?" Myra laughed. Her voice trembled as she struggled to speak. "Nothing over the past few days has been what I would refer to as logical. All the people, your clothing, how you live, it's all changed. What happened to me?"

"I don't know. That's what I've been trying to find out," Natalie said in as calm of a voice as she could.

"What is Edward's family name?"

Family name? An old way of saying surname. Natalie had the feeling she was being baited. She studied Myra and replied cautiously, "I shouldn't tell you."

"You don't have to," countered Myra. She stood still for the first time, her blue eyes piercing and sure. "I already know. When I saw Eddie... in pain... my memory cleared."

Natalie couldn't suppress the surprise in her face. "Your memory cleared? Why didn't you say so before now?"

Myra made no reply. Was this some sort of deception? Was Myra trying to trick her into revealing personal information about Edward? Natalie wasn't going to fall for it, and asked as innocently as she could, "What name do you remember?"

"Hoffman," replied Myra calmly. "That is my name: Myra Amelia Sloan Hoffman. My husband is Archibald Hoffman and my son is Edward James Hoffman..."

"I'm sorry. I'm afraid that's not true," interrupted Natalie, shaking her head. *She must have read it somewhere.*

"Listen to me," interrupted Myra. "I know who I am. Why won't you believe me?"

"I believe that you believe in what you say," Natalie said honestly. She knew that Myra truly believed this 'reality' she created in her mind. Natalie did not doubt Myra's conviction. The *Titanic* manifestation and somehow her link or obsession with Edward was some sort of defense mechanism protecting her subconscious from the truth. Natalie also knew they could argue like this forever without either of them forfeiting. She was at a loss of how to proceed.

"What year is this?" Myra asked with an eerie calmness.

Natalie looked at her. There was a strong risk that she wouldn't be able to handle the truth. Her mind might not be able to accept that her *Titanic* experience was a fantasy. Natalie took a deep breath and cautiously said, "It's 1982. April 3rd, 1982 to be exact."

"Nineteen Eighty-Two?" Myra's eyes widened, her pupils tumbled around her eyes as her mind tried to grasp the concept that was thrown at it. Natalie studied her face carefully. There were no telltale signs of deception in her expression or body language. Myra sat down slowly in bewilderment, almost missing the chair. "Where have I been for seventy years?"

"Well… you were found floating in the North Atlantic but I can assure you that it is scientifically impossible for you to have been there for seventy years."

"Please. Can I see Eddie?" Myra looked at Natalie in earnest. The look of anguish in Myra's sapphire eyes was real. Tears cascaded down her cheeks. "Please, I need to know that he's all right."

"I'll see what I can do," Natalie whispered as she put her hand on top of Myra's, trying to comfort her. "But I can't make any promises."

April 4, 1982

CHAPTER 17

"Mrs. Myra Hoffman please," said Callum as he handed his business card to the butler at the front door. "She's expecting me."

"Wait here," replied the butler, and left Callum standing on the welcome mat while he went in to announce him. Callum would never understand the eccentricities of the rich, especially that of 'old money', clinging to a way of life and rules that were rapidly fading. He looked at the Rolls Royce, Bentley and Jaguar on display beneath the covered car park adjoining the estate. He had admired them five years ago when he wandered the grounds investigating the 'break and enter' case and now as he gazed at them, he realized that they were parked in the exact same position as if no time had passed. Callum couldn't help but wonder if the autos were ever enjoyed or if they were displayed there just for show.

"Mrs. Hoffman will see you now," announced the butler.

Upon entering the foyer, he handed his coat to the butler who, after hanging it on the iron coat rack, escorted Callum into the adjoining sitting room, which was filled with antiques. Every time he came to the Hoffman Estate it was like stepping into the past. Like at Ruthie's home, there were several framed photos that had been taken over the years. In a rare colour Kodachrome photo, Callum recognized the familiar features of Edward Hoffman looking very young and dashing in a military uniform. Time had been good to Edward. His parents stood proudly on either side. In the photo it was clear that Mrs. Hoffman had Heterochromia, a condition where each eye was a different colour. Since seeing the photographs on Ruthie's mantle, Callum had a new appreciation of colour photography. *Impressive for an early colour film to capture such detail*, he thought.

He heard the faint squeak of wheels as an elderly woman entered the room, pushed in a wheelchair by a private nurse of some sort. In one fluid motion, the nurse locked the wheels and adjusted the elderly woman's oxygen tank next to her, acting more like an extension of the old woman's consciousness than an individual person. In fact, the nurse gave no indication of being aware of Callum's presence in the room.

Callum was surprised to see how much the old woman had aged in the last five years. If memory served, she was a centenarian. Very few people lived as long as she, and she was using her wealth to sustain her life. Callum recalled that Mrs. Hoffman had undergone cosmetic surgery at some point, but it now seemed that time and gravity were fighting back, and the result was a ghastly, rubber-like grin that never seemed to fade. A thick pair of jewel-rimmed designer glasses confirmed and moreover, magnified her Heterochromia: her left eye was a deep brown and her right eye was a pale yellow-green hazel. Though grey roots were showing, the old woman had her hair dyed an unnatural shade of black, reminiscent of shoe polish. Her jewels and low décolletage did nothing but bring attention to her deeply wrinkled and age-spotted neck. Not at all flattering.

"Thank you for seeing me on such short notice, Mrs. Hoffman," said Callum as soon as the nurse took her position near the door. "It's good to see you again."

"You said it was urgent," puffed Mrs. Hoffman, gesturing for him to sit in the wood carved chair opposite her. "Would you care for some tea?"

"No, thank you. I won't be long," Callum replied with a smile as he took a seat. The chair was so old he was afraid that it wouldn't hold him. It creaked ominously, so he quickly focused his mind on the matter at hand. He had just flown back to London from Glasgow in haste, as he did not want to waste any time. *Not to mention the fact that this woman was old and might croak at any moment.* "Have you ever heard of a woman named Loraine Kramer?"

"Beastly woman!" replied Mrs. Hoffman without hesitation. She placed the oxygen mask over her face and stole a breath. "A charlatan who tried to pose as a child that was aboard the *Titanic*, saying that she had survived after all in order to claim some inheritance..."

"Yes I'm aware of all that," interrupted Callum as he pulled his notepad from his satchel. "Does she know your son, Edward? Or would she have any reason to have ill feelings toward him?"

"Why do you ask?"

Callum was not sure if he should burden her with what he had seen in Loraine Kramer's room, considering the old woman's health. He had tried to contact Edward in New York, but his office was closed for the weekend and he wasn't responding to his paging service. Callum responded cautiously, "I have reason to believe she wishes harm to come to Edward."

"Well that's nothing new," replied the old woman calmly. "My son Edward was the one who was able to disprove her claim. If it weren't for Edward that woman might have gotten away with her flim-flam. She vowed she would have her revenge on him — if it took her a lifetime she would find a way to ruin him the way he'd ruined her."

"When did she say this?"

"Let me think," Mrs. Hoffman paused for a moment. "Thirty years ago."

"Did you say 'thirty years'?"

"Aye, it was about 1950 or so," replied Mrs. Hoffman.

Callum was momentarily distracted as he noticed a hint of a Scottish brogue in her usual American accent. Something he hadn't noticed before. He looked at her intently and remarked, "You remind me of someone…. I can't place. You have a hint of brogue in your accent. Out of curiosity, what is your maiden name?"

"My maiden name?" she repeated, taken aback. "Why do you ask?"

"It's a hobby of mine. Dialects versus environment," replied Callum.

"A regular Henry Higgins," scoffed Mrs. Hoffman as she sipped her tea ever so carefully. Callum smiled, realizing she had still not responded to his question. Would a hundred year old woman forget her own maiden name? Still, if Callum lived to be a hundred, he could only hope he would have as good a grasp of his faculties as Mrs. Hoffman did now.

"Sloane," she finally said, breaking the silence.

"Sloane?" Callum repeated as he wrote it down in his book. "With an 'e' or without?"

"With," replied Mrs. Hoffman. "Now what does that have to do with Loraine Kramer?"

"Nothing," he replied and then added. "I'm afraid time has not healed her hatred toward your son, Edward. I was visiting her in Glasgow and saw something that made me concerned for your son's safety."

"Well, she is a devious woman," added Mrs. Hoffman. "There is no depth to which she would not sink with her lies and deception for her own personal gain."

"Do you know how I can get in touch with Edward?"

"I'm afraid I haven't heard from him," replied Mrs. Hoffman. "My husband is on his way back to England to oversee the final preparations of *Titanic*… The *Titan*'s maiden voyage… and it's our wedding anniversary. Neither of us have heard from Edward since yesterday. You don't suppose something could have happened to him?"

"I don't know. But, I wouldn't worry," said Callum in a reassuring voice. "Loraine Kramer was not living in luxury. I don't think she's in a position, financially, to orchestrate anything."

"Don't underestimate her, Mr. Toughill," Mrs. Hoffman interjected quickly. "She's the sort of woman who would sell everything she owns on a gamble."

"Noted. I shall look into her further," Callum was about to add her words into his notepad, when suddenly all the clock bells in the house started to chime. It startled him enough that he dropped his notepad. As he picked it up, he noticed his own shorthand notes from a few days prior. Reading them, he took a chance and asked, "Before I go, do you know whatever happened to Heather Langlea?"

The sound of breaking porcelain was the response. Callum looked up to see the old woman had dropped her teacup and the nurse flew to her to make sure she hadn't burned herself.

"Who?" replied Mrs. Hoffman as if unaware that she had dropped her tea.

"Heather Langlea," replied Callum. "I had read from the passenger list of the *Titanic* that she was your accompanying servant aboard the ship."

"Oh, her!" exclaimed Mrs. Hoffman as the name seemed to finally make sense. "Yes. That was such a long time ago."

"Do you know what happened to her?"

"I believe she married," replied Mrs. Hoffman in an annoyed tone. "She didn't give any notice, and I was forced to scramble to find a replacement. Needless to say, she didn't get a letter of reference from me, nor did I keep tabs on her."

Callum jotted this into his notepad.

Mrs. Hoffman then leaned forward in her wheelchair slightly, allowing the nurse to hold her hand forward as if to stay her. "If you don't mind. What is this all about?"

"Tying up loose ends so to speak," replied Callum. "Initially I was investigating a lost piece of jewelry and it's led me to an unsolved murder from almost a century ago."

"What does that have to do with Heather Langlea or myself?"

"Before working for you, Miss Langlea was employed by the owner of that jewel. That owner was murdered. Agatha Gilcrest. Did you ever know her?"

"No. But I remember the incident. That was so long ago, even before Edward was born. How do you come to be investigating it now?"

"We're investigating an insurance claim-slip for an item that may have been lost on the *Titanic*. That same piece of jewelry was taken the night Agatha Gilcrest was murdered."

"How is that possible?" asked Mrs. Hoffman. Callum looked at her and blinked. Spurred by his silence, she continued, "I mean, if a murderer stole a piece of jewelry from their victim, why would they file a claim in writing for it? Would that not connect them to the crime? Not very smart."

"Criminals aren't usually as smart as they believe themselves to be," laughed Callum. Still, she had a point. One that had crossed Callum's mind as well. Percy said the claim had turned up while Lloyd's was moving offices.

"It's an unlikely coincidence, if you ask me," huffed Mrs. Hoffman. Callum nodded, though there was something odd that he couldn't put his finger on. He flipped through his notes, "Another of Mrs. Gilcrest's servants was also aboard the *Titanic*. Did you know Alice Cleaver?"

Beep-beep-beep.

Callum's pager startled the old woman. He pulled it out and held it up for her to see. It was out of place in their current antiquated surroundings. "May I use your phone for a moment?"

She nodded and gestured to the phone on the nearby table. Even the telephone was an old fashioned Art Deco-style rotary phone with marble accents. He dialed the number. "Callum Toughill. Passcode..." Callum looked over at the old lady taking a breath from her oxygen mask. "Five-Zero-Five."

The operator for the pager company read a message to him, "From Ruthie McArthur: Information for you. Message from your grandfather. Come at once."

"From my grandfather?" Callum repeated into the phone receiver. Was his only living witness going bonkers? "Did Ruthie McArthur leave a contact number?"

"No she did not," replied the operator.

"Were there any other messages?" asked Callum. He had a very uneasy feeling about this call.

"No new ones, but Ruthie McArthur rang several times to see if you had received her message."

Callum looked at his wristwatch. He didn't know when the next flight to Glasgow would be — he would have to catch a cab to Heathrow and make travel plans from there. "Thanks, if she rings me again, get her number."

Callum hung up the phone and turned to Mrs. Hoffman as he gathered his notepad and stuffed it into his satchel case, "Thank you for your time. I have to go."

"Nothing serious I hope?" asked Mrs. Hoffman.

"I don't think it is," Callum said nonchalantly, more to reassure himself, but he had a terrible feeling in the pit of his stomach. What did she mean, 'a message from his grandfather'? Callum's grandfather had been dead for fifteen years.

CHAPTER 18

"Edward are you sure you're up to this?" asked Roger Zisholm, Edward's longtime personal attorney. "You should have let the hospital keep you for observation."

"I've had worse falls in my life," grumbled Edward as he pulled his jacket closer and stomped his feet to get the blood flowing. He felt very cold as he sat in Roger's law office. No matter what he did, he couldn't get warm. He assumed that the building kept the heat low over the weekend but it wasn't uncommon for his lawyer to be in his office on a Saturday. It was also possible that it was Roger's sterile, chromed furniture that gave the illusion of razor-edged strength, but lacked any warmth. The only specks of color were from the spines of the books on the nearby shelf.

Roger pressed the intercom button next to his phone and called out to his secretary, "Can you send the officer in?"

"Yes, sir," cackled the voice under static.

A young man in British Naval uniform entered the room sharply. Edward recognized from the crest on the white cap that this was an officer in the Ministry of Defence. He was impressed by the smart newer uniforms and realized he had been away from his Naval friends for a very long time. In his day, Edward had served with men from the Naval Intelligence Division, which was since absorbed into the Ministry of Defence. He felt suddenly old and out of touch.

"Good morning," said the young officer as he briskly shook the hands of the two men. Edward recalled that Roger had once served in the Navy Judge Advocate General's Corps, and seemed to still have connections there.

"'Morning," boomed Roger. "Would you tell Mr. Hoffman what you told me?"

The young officer nodded politely, placed his briefcase on the desk and snapped it open. Addressing Edward, he said: "Before Captain Sadler left for the Falkland Islands, he asked us to assist in the investigation of the woman found on April first."

From the briefcase he produced a green folder, from which he pulled a photo of a wooden deck chair. Edward knew the origin of the photo at first glance. It was one of the chairs from A-Deck of the *Titanic*. The White Star Line logo was indeed etched into the headboard, as it should be.

"The woman in question was found clinging to this chair."

Edward looked up from the picture. He knew that other survivors back in 1912 had been found afloat on these chairs, though not many.

The officer continued, "We were able to determine that the paint on it was not seventy years old, though the lead levels in the paint are high."

He handed Edward the typed report for him to read. Roger asked, "What else you got?"

The officer reached into his briefcase, "Secondly, we found this contract ticket in the book."

The moment he pulled it out, Edward knew it instantly. He turned the contract ticket over. Beneath the words: **'United States Immigration Act in Effect April 1, 1831'**, the names of the passengers should have been listed. Unfortunately, the ink had run from water damage, making the handwriting difficult to read. *How convenient,* Edward thought to himself.

"I have seen other contract tickets from *Titanic* survivors," remarked Edward as he continued to inspect it. He wished he still had his boarding pass, but it went down with the ship. Now he was holding a perfect replica. Flawless. Except...

"Those I have seen in the past are well preserved, but none were in as excellent condition as this one is. Time has not left its familiar amber mark on this one."

"Tests indicate that the ink is fairly fresh," continued the man. "It's certainly nowhere near 70 years old."

"Hardly a surprise," interjected Roger.

The officer ignored the interruption, "However, the paper stock doesn't have any watermark or date fibers, which are usually inserted into paper productions these days. Another interesting fact is that the ink used was manufactured in the style of the early 1900's as it does not have any of the present day quick-drying chemicals."

"What does that prove?" asked Roger.

"Someone has gone to great lengths to make us believe she's real," replied the officer.

"I can't imagine why," Roger blurted. "None of us are fooled."

Edward shrugged then looked up at the officer as he indicated to the reports on hand, "Can we make a copy of these?"

"Certainly," replied the officer as Roger buzzed his secretary.

"Was there anything else?" asked Edward. The secretary chose that moment to enter, interrupting the conversation.

"Make a copy of this for him," Roger barked to his secretary, who nodded as she took the papers and left without a word.

"Aside from that which you've seen," replied the officer, "the only other thing in her possession was a teddy bear."

"A teddy bear?" wondered Roger. "What teddy bear?"

"She was found clutching a teddy bear. I think it may have been returned to her."

Edward shivered involuntarily at the mention of teddy bear. *Someone has just walked over my grave,* thought Edward. He tried to focus back to his initial meeting with Dr. Natalie Lindsay. There was no mention of a teddy bear. Something so out of the ordinary would have been brought up. Teddy bear. The notion of it was giving him an odd foreboding sensation that he was unable to explain, as if he knew there had been a teddy bear, but that was completely absurd. Still…

"Edward?" Roger's voice was so loud that it derailed his train of thought. Edward glanced up and saw that Roger's secretary had returned with the photocopies. She and the two men were looking at him with concern. He seemed to have let his mind wander so far that he wondered if he had said anything aloud.

"Forgive me," Edward murmured as he shifted in his chair. "This has all been very overwhelming and disconcerting."

The man in uniform placed the original documents in the folder, straightened, and said plainly, "I understand. Is there anything else?"

"Not from me," sighed Edward. "I would say thank Captain… Sadler was it… for his time and attention."

"I would, sir," replied the officer, as he closed his briefcase. "But we are on different details, and he has his hands full with the Argentines."

"Right. The war."

"Thanks for your time," said Roger as he opened the door for the officer.

"Good day," snapped the officer as he turned and left.

As the door closed, Edward sighed. "You know for a moment last night, I almost believed her."

Edward was annoyed at himself for having given it a second of credence. He must have looked like a fool. His trick of recreating the last meal on the *Titanic* had worked to expose Loraine Kramer all those years ago, but somehow this woman had known about it and turned the tables on him. Of course, Edward thought to himself. He had unwittingly set himself up. The music, the food… it took him back to that fateful night in 1912. How could it not strike an emotional chord with him? And when he was most vulnerable, that's when she'd struck.

"Naturally you almost believed her," Roger repeated as he sat down. "Which is why I think you should press charges. That woman is a con artist, and she would stop at nothing to take advantage of a kind old man."

Edward felt very old indeed. More so now that he had to use a cane to get out of the chair, thanks to his tumble down the stairs. The phone rang as Edward gathered up his copies of the papers and put them into his jacket pocket.

"Yes. He's here," Roger said into the phone. "Thank you. I'll pass that along."

Roger hung up the phone and looked at his friend.

"What?" Edward asked.

"That was Dr. Lindsay from the clinic. 'Myra'… that woman wants to see you. Don't worry I'll handle it. I'll go see what she wants."

"I'll go with you," said Edward as he steadied himself with the cane.

"I don't think you should," replied Roger as he put on his coat. "You're in a vulnerable state. Go home and get some…"

"I'm going with you," Edward said sternly. He had to see her one last time. He had to see how she had been able to deceive him. Only then could he move on.

— — —

"Keep the change," mumbled Callum as he tossed some money to the cab driver, then bolted up the front steps of 13 Queens Terrace. The flight from Heathrow to Glasgow had been the longest hour and a half he had ever experienced. He'd tried to ring Ruthie McArthur from a payphone before boarding and tried again when he landed. Something was wrong. He could feel it in his gut.

His hand rapped on the door… and it creaked open under the impact of his knuckles. He saw the inside brass chain, from which had Ruthie first peered at him, dangling down, broken. *This is not good.* Slowly he reached into his shoulder holster and pulled out his Walther P38 pistol.

He started to push the door open as carefully as he could, keeping his finger on the trigger. He needed to keep his wits about him. As the sun was already setting, he needed his eyes to adjust to the dimming light. He continued pushing the door ever so slowly to give him a bit of extra time. *Don't want to shoot the sweet old lady by mistake.*

C-R-E-A-K!

Blast this old door! So much for the element of surprise.

Passing through the foyer, he debated whether he should call out for her. What if the intruder was still there? He paused as he approached the door to her living quarters, straining as he listened for any sound or movement.

Steeling his resolve, he burst into the room with his pistol held aloft in front of him. Nothing.

To be more accurate, there was no-one present. Callum's eyes quickly processed what lay before them: the room, which only recently had been tidy and orderly, was now in shambles. Papers were strewn about, knick-knacks broken. It was déjà vu, for this building. Callum recalled the crime photos of the flat upstairs, seventy years ago, after Ruthie's father had found Agatha Gilcrest's bloodied body. The similarities made Callum's heart skip a beat or two. It was unnerving. He opened his mouth to call out for Ruthie when he heard a *squish*.

The sound accompanied the sensation of having stepped into a puddle. Callum looked down and saw a river of blood swirling around his brown leather shoe. He followed the meandering crimson stream to the adjacent room, where he saw the body of Ruthie McArthur face-down on the floor.

CHAPTER 19

Callum was in shock. Stunned. Uncertain of what to do next. *Who could have done this? Why?* His eyes darted about the room looking for a phone to ring up 999 for an ambulance.

That's when he noticed it. Or to be more specific, noticed what wasn't there. Something was missing from the fireplace mantle. There had been several framed photos, and one of them had been taken. An obvious empty spot, next to Ruthie's tenth birthday —a faint imprint in the dust where the frame had been.

His thoughts of the missing frame were interrupted when he heard Ruthie moan. He flew to her and knelt down next to her. She struggled to turn over.

"Try not to move," he whispered softly.

"Detective Toughill?" she coughed. "Is that you?"

"I'm his grandson, remember?"

She struggled again to turn over, with more determination. Reluctantly, he helped her rather than try to fight her. Blood trickled from a gash on her head, and there was also blood seeping from a bullet wound in her abdomen.

"Who did this to you?" asked Callum.

"'Twas a man... he was..." whispered Ruthie through a mouthful of blood. "Like the men who threatened ...father... and your... grandfather."

"My grandfather?" Callum started.

"Hushhh," hacked Ruthie. "No time left... for me..."

"Save your strength. You're going to be all right."

"You're a... terrible liar..." she wheezed, using precious strength, struggling to talk. Callum was about to say something when she shushed him and continued, "Your grandfather... tried to prove Otto Slade's innocence and was... ruined for doing so."

Callum blinked, "He didn't botch it?"

Callum shook his head. Why didn't his grandfather say anything about it? As if reading his thoughts, Ruthie replied, "He continued in secret, but to protect his family, he swore an oath that he would take the secret to his grave."

He then noticed that Ruthie was grasping for her throat. He panicked. She couldn't breathe. He tried to reposition her. She struggled against him, her hand grasping a silver chain and tugging on it. But lacked the strength to pull it off.

"Help me," she whispered. Callum nodded as he lifted the chain gently. Her breathing was becoming more labored as she struggled to speak, "Take it."

He pulled it over her head and saw that a large ornate silver pendent was attached to it. It looked like a variation of St. George slaying the dragon. Not the usual one that was used on the United Kingdom's half-sovereign for over a century, as this one did not depict a knight on horseback, but rather the dragon under the knight's foot and his sword held aloft about to strike.

"Message... from grandfather..." She gasped for one last gulp of air, and with her last breath whispered, "dragonslayer..."

• • •

Natalie waited with Myra in her office, unable to take her eyes off her unusual patient. She saw Myra's eyes light up when she saw Edward enter, and watched as she sprinted out of her seat. Myra was obviously taken aback when Edward stepped away from her, raising his cane slightly for protection.

"Eddie? What is it?" inquired Myra, clearly hurt by his aloofness. "Are you all right? How is your leg?"

Edward's tone was cold, "I don't know who you are, but I must ask you not to call me that."

Natalie could see the anguish in Myra's face. Edward's words were like sharp icicles plunged into her heart.

"I'm Myra Hoffman..." insisted Myra. She again reached out for him and he physically pulled away, hobbling to the chair furthest away from her, as she continued, "I know I'm your mother. You knew it too. You called me *Mommy*."

"My client was in shock after falling down a flight of stairs. I don't think he was really aware of you," Roger retorted as he positioned his chair between Myra and his client.

"No, Sir!" cried Myra. Then, turning to face Natalie, she said, "Tell him. Tell him what happened. How I remembered what happened that night in the dining lounge!"

Natalie tried to speak, but Myra turned to Edward and continued to ramble, "I remember you woke up crying from a bad dream and I held you to calm you down. I remember our maid made me some tea to calm my nerves... then I felt... dizzy..."

"What was the name of the maid?" asked Roger with a curt tone.

"The name of the maid?" Myra repeated as she struggled to remember. "It's on the tip of my tongue. That's still fuzzy but... but... I remember how, Eddie, here, fell asleep in my arms and then... then... I woke up and everyone was gone. The room started to flood... I was locked in... I couldn't find the key."

Edward cut her off, "Myra Hoffman is my mother. She carried me off of the *Titanic*; she and my father are in England and will be celebrating their 75th wedding anniversary next week."

Natalie could see the enthusiasm drain from Myra's face, as she slowly sank into the nearby chair.

"No! It's not possible. I am Myra Hoffman. I..." Myra paused. Her brow furrowed, then she looked up at Edward, "Did you say 'next week'? No, Archie and I were married on Christmas Eve 1909. I have a locket with our pictures in it. Archie gave it to me for our second wedding anniversary. I had it with me in the hospital... before I was brought here."

Myra's hand flew to her bare neck as she looked over at Natalie, her eyes imploring. Natalie wished she could speak words of comfort to Myra but could only shake her head, "I'm sorry Myra. You didn't have any locket when you came to us."

Roger turned to Natalie. "Is there some kind of blood test we can do to prove to... this woman that she's not related to my client?"

"No. Blood type tests only narrow the paternal side. However..." She paused to gather her thoughts. "A colleague of mine, in England, can profile DNA..."

"DNA? What is that?" asked Roger.

"Deoxyribonucleic acid, it's the molecule that contains the genetic instructions used in the development and functioning of all known living organisms. It's apparently hereditary in humans, and my colleague is able to determine paternal and maternal relationships between parents and children."

"How so?" asked Edward.

"Well medically speaking we all have 23 pairs of chromosomes. Half come from the mother and half from the father. He will be publishing his findings very soon. I can ask him to run tests on both of you. It may be of value to his research."

"What would you need?" Roger asked.

"A sample of blood, I believe."

Roger looked over at Edward who nodded in agreement. Roger then reached into his coat pocket and pulled out a document, which he handed to Myra.

"We'll go along with the test but in the meantime, here is a written warning instructing you to never contact my client again. If you don't comply we will seek a restraining order."

Myra didn't take it. Roger set it on Natalie's desk. Myra reached out for Edward instead. He made no eye contact with her as he hobbled out of the room.

Natalie watched helplessly as Myra began to shiver. Even Natalie suddenly felt cold.

CHAPTER 20

Dragonslayer? Callum was numb. He had experienced the loss of friends and family through death but he had never witnessed it firsthand. He could still feel the weight of her in his arms, but she was gone. Her humor, her experiences, her memories — they were all gone. Who could do such a thing? Why? What did it have to do with his grandfather? Why now, after all these years? Who was still left?

Call the police, he told himself. Yet, it was the Glasgow police that had somehow been involved with the cover-up of Agatha Gilcrest's murder, seventy years ago. If Ruthie was telling the truth, that same police force turned on his grandfather and ruined him for investigating the truth. Would they betray him now?

Still he couldn't leave her body here like this. Placing the pendant in his pocket, he looked around in the darkness for his satchel case. Where was…?

C-R-E-A-K!

The familiar sound of the old door's rusty hinges alerted him that there was someone creeping into the front foyer.

Callum picked his gun up from where he had set it when he knelt down to Ruthie. He tried to stand, his leg buckled. His leg had fallen asleep from being crouched down on the floor. He squinted in the dim light as he peeked toward the adjacent room and saw the tip of a pistol emerge from behind the front door. Ruthie's killer had returned and Callum's leg was useless.

He fired toward the front door, and saw the other gun disappear for shelter. Callum had no extra magazine to reload his Walther P38. He wasn't going to be able to hold them off for long. He stumbled back toward the rear of the flat into the kitchen and limped to the kitchen table. He took a gamble and fired another shot in the darkness towards the front room. Then he pulled up the window and squeezed himself into the alleyway.

Once outside in the night air, he could hear the sounds of police sirens approaching. He had to get away. Stepping onto a rubbish bin and ignoring the pins-and-needles coursing through his feet, he leapt onto the fire escape and climbed up to the roof top for a better vantage point. He saw the familiar form of the white and orange police cars with blue flashing lights approaching. He thought about flagging one down, and then looked down at his blood-stained suit jacket. It would take some explaining...

BLAM!

A bullet ricocheted off the metal ladder next to him. The gunman had followed him out the window and was shooting at him!

Callum stole a glance at the husky man below before continuing across the townhouse rooftop. Now that his leg was getting back to normal, he made good ground, leaping from one end of each rooftop to the next, grateful that he was in decent physical condition for a man his age.

Of course, he couldn't keep this up forever. He needed to hide. He paused to get his bearings.

He checked his coat pocket with his left hand, keeping his right hand armed with the gun. The pendant was still there.

Dragonslayer! He could reach St. George's Cross Station — it was very close by. Just a few more rooftops and a dash across Great Western Road. When he toured the neighbourhood the other day, Callum had suspected that Agatha Gilcrest's murderer had made his escape to the St. George's Cross station seventy years ago. Perhaps there was a clue there? After all, it was St. George's image on the pendant.

— — —

Myra didn't eat or talk to anyone for the rest of the morning. She just sat in a chair and stared blankly into space. Still wearing the old-fashioned turn-of-the century dress, Myra looked like a pale, disheveled ghost.

Natalie felt horrible. She was the one who had contacted Edward in hopes of helping Myra and it had only made things worse. She had no words of wisdom to help. The best Natalie could do at this point was to simply be around when Myra started to talk.

At lunchtime, Natalie entered Myra's room with some take-out from McDonalds. It wasn't smoked salmon with some fancy sauce, but it was mildly better than the bland clinic food, and she hoped the smell might entice Myra to eat.

Natalie set two places at the table in Myra's room. Myra looked over at her, and without saying a word got up and shuffled over to sit next to her.

Natalie bit the inside of her cheek, as she struggled not to smile while she watched Myra trying to eat a Big Mac with a knife and fork.

After she was finished, Myra stared out the window for a spell.

Natalie took the time to reflect on the recent events, trying to find some glimmer of hope in the mess.

"I would like some clothing," Myra finally said. The words broke the long silence with a voice which still seemed hollow and distant.

"You're wearing clothes. That's a lovely dress you're wearing."

Myra shook her head and looked at Natalie, her sapphire blue eyes pleading, "No. I would like some garments similar to what you're wearing."

Natalie was delighted to hear this. *At last, a breakthrough.* "I'll make the arrangements."

Natalie hastened to tidy up the foam containers. With Myra's figure she'd look very stylish in modern fashions. After opening the door, Natalie leaned back into the room and said to Myra, "Congratulations. You have taken the first step towards recovery."

· · ·

It was visiting hours on a Sunday at the nuthouse. Nigel had to watch himself. He almost said that out loud once. He didn't want to lose his job at … the Clinic. Nigel, the doorman, stomped his feet and blew hot breath into his hands to keep his fingertips warm, something he wasn't allowed to do in front of the guests or their families. This was the main reason why he hated Sundays in wintertime. It was the most popular day for visitations.

He was about to light up a cigarette for added warmth when he saw a sleek woman about to exit the building. He quickly moved and held the door open for her. He wondered why she didn't have a coat. She was dressed in a trendy skirt and a warm-looking, green sweater. *Not hurting for cash.* Her piercing blue eyes looked about, trying to get her bearings.

Not a New Yorker, he thought. He was stunned by her beauty: the contrast of dark hair, blue eyes and pale skin made her absolutely striking.

"Would you like a taxi to take you to your hotel?" guessed Nigel.

The woman smiled, "Which way to Longacre… I mean, to Times Square?"

Definitely not a New Yorker. Nigel pointed westward. "Go that way and you'll see the lights. Can't miss it."

She started to walk in the direction he pointed. Nigel called out after her, "It's a bit of a hike. I can call a taxi for you!"

She turned, smiled, and politely responded, "Thank-you, no! I'll be fine."

Definitely not a New Yorker.

— — —

91

Callum flew down the stone steps from the street to the front door of the underground station. It had taken him longer than he had hoped to reach it, but he could only go so far by rooftop — he'd then meandered through the labyrinth of back alleys and side streets to avoid detection. His eyes were drawn to the glowing red letters *St. Georges Cross*. Even as a child he had wondered why there was no apostrophe on the sign when there was one on the subway map.

Stepping into the front door he could still hear several sirens wailing like a pack of wolves on the hunt. He hoped they scared the gunman away, but then saw the husky man huffing as he descended the stairs. Their eyes met. *Damn, he saw me!*

Callum turned and ran towards the fare box. Pushing past people with grocery bags, and without breaking a stride, he leapt over the turnstile. He could hear the muffled voice of the ticket-taker yelling at him.

The yellow-bricked island platform was dimly lit, looking very different from when Callum was a boy. The whole station had been recently renovated. Any clue that might have existed seventy years ago was long gone.

Callum spotted the gunman approaching from the far end. *He wouldn't shoot here. Not in front of all these witnesses.* The man raised his gun. Callum cursed that there were no pillars to hide behind. As he ran further down the platform, he prayed for a train to arrive. Either direction would be fine at this moment. None came.

He reached the end of the platform; there was no other exit. Just a metal door for the utility room or something, and for a brief moment he considered jumping onto the tracks. He turned back to see the gunman slowing down as he drew closer.

Then, over the man's humongous shoulders, Callum saw a handful of uniformed police officers with their black and white checkered caps approaching. Callum sighed in relief. The killer was now trapped.

"Put your hands in the air where I can see them," barked the husky gunman.

"What?" asked Callum incredulously, did the idiot not know he was about to be arrested by police?

The gunman kept his weapon trained on Callum as he reached into his coat pocket. Callum resisted the urge to raise his gun. The police would reach them soon. The man pulled out a black leather billfold with a blue metal insignia with gold accents on it. It was a Strathclyde Police Warrant card badge with the name: Detective Sergeant Milton.

"Police!" yelled Milton, the husky man. "Put your hands where I can see them! You're under arrest for murder."

Shite!

CHAPTER 21

"I just wanted you to know that Myra... escaped," Natalie said into the phone receiver.

"How the hell could you let that happen?" Roger bellowed so loudly that Natalie had to pull the phone receiver away from her ear. Natalie had asked herself the very same question, several times. *How could she have been so stupid? How could she have been so gullible?* She had so wanted Myra to make that first step towards reality that she had taken the desire for regular street clothes at face value. As they were approximately the same build she had gone out and purchased an outfit for Myra with her own money. Apparently no-one had recognized Myra when she left the building.

"I don't have time to get into the details," Natalie replied curtly. "We've sent someone to watch the Hoffman office building. She will likely go looking for Edward."

"She can look all she wants," grumbled Roger. "I'm personally driving Edward out to his family's lake house to get away from this madness."

"That's very kind of you," Natalie replied into the phone receiver. It was above and beyond the duty of an attorney. *Hope he isn't being paid by the hour for that.*

"Well, with all that's happened, Edward is in no condition to drive himself. Please call my pager when you learn anything new."

"I will," Natalie responded as she eyed his business card before placing it back in her Rolodex.

After hanging up, she put on her jacket. It was getting cold. As she turned up the thermostat, Natalie's anger melted into fear. The temperature outside was dropping rapidly. *It was as if Myra's presence in New York was bringing the Arctic temperatures with her,* Natalie thought to herself. Earlier, she had seen on

TV that some areas of the state were reporting 11°F. Natalie glanced out the window. Snow was starting to come down and there was no word on Myra. *How could she survive without a warm coat or food or money?*

Walking to the subway station, Natalie began to doubt everything. *Was Myra really alone? Was there someone else out there?* Natalie knew that the whole *Titanic* story was a fantasy but did Myra actually believe it or was there some ulterior motive?

Natalie hated herself for doubting her patient but she still knew nothing concrete about the person calling herself Myra. One thing was certain. There was no possible way she could be Edward's mother... so... who was she?

. . .

Officer Willowby was used to dealing with wackos. Manhattan was full of them. In his years with the NYPD he'd had to 'reason' with every kind. He still had a scar on his face from trying to subdue a teen that was high on PCP (also known as *'Angel dust'*), three years ago. Under the influence, the teen was unnaturally strong and lacked the capacity to reason, or feel pain. The youth was brandishing a broken bottle as a weapon, cutting his own fingers and not realizing it. Willowby had no choice but to break the teen's legs to immobilize him. Even then, the teen didn't feel his broken bones and continued to resist. In the struggle, Willowby's face was cut with the broken bottle.

Officer Greenwyn, his partner, once commented that Willowby would subconsciously run his finger over the scar whenever they were called out to a disturbance.

This case was very different right from the start. They arrived at the scene of Straus Park at 106th and Broadway around 5pm to find a young, attractive, brunette Caucasian woman gripping a newspaper and screaming like a hellcat.

She was smartly dressed so it was obvious that she wasn't a vagrant, but her demeanor showed that she still had to be handled with care.

"Ma'am..." said Willowby soothingly. "I need you to settle down."

The woman whirled around at the sound of his voice, her deep blue eyes blazing like a caged animal. Then those eyes focused on his uniform, and she became quiet. Unnervingly so.

It couldn't be this easy, Willowby thought cautiously. "Ma'am you need to take a ride with us."

She nodded quietly, still gripping the newspaper. Willowby noticed that she did not display any signs of intoxication, nor were there any of the familiar signs of narcotics present. Strange. He would remember this one for a long time to come.

April 5, 1982

CHAPTER 22

"I didn't kill her. How many ways can I say it?" Callum yelled, exasperated. It was very late at night and he was sleep deprived, but that's how they wanted it.

"Yet, her blood is on your clothes," said Detective Chief Inspector (DCI) Donald de Kirkhaugh, "You fired on my men. Do you have an FAC?"

"Yes, my Fire Arms Certificate is in my wallet. You have that."

DCI de Kirkhaugh picked up the wallet from the small plastic tray on the table and began to rummage through it. He pulled out Callum's business card.

"So, you're a freelance insurance investigator?" read de Kirkhaugh.

"Yes."

"Is business so slow that you turned to burglary?"

"I didn't burgl…!"

"Do you have a key?" interruped de Kirkhaugh.

"No," replied Callum.

"Then how did you get in?"

Callum knew there was no way he could answer that without incriminating himself. Under the eyes of English law, even if the door is unlocked, if not invited in, 'A person is guilty of burglary if, having entered a building or part of a building as a trespasser with the intent to steal or cause bodily harm.'

"She paged me several times," said Callum finally. "She said it was urgent. I flew in from London just to get there as fast as I could."

"Where's your flight ticket?" replied de Kirkhaugh. "We didn't see that with your personal belongings."

"I don't know," replied Callum. "It's probably in my satchel case. I left that either in Ruthies… Miss McArthur's flat or in the taxi I took from the airport."

"What taxi was it?"

"How the hell do I know? It was a taxi at the ground floor of the main terminal," sneered Callum. He was getting nowhere. They had been asking him the same questions for hours, ever since he had been brought to the interrogation room of the new Maryhill Office of the Strathclyde Police. Years ago, Callum had wanted to join the force when it was still the Glasgow Police, but around five or six years earlier, Glasgow amalgamated with almost a dozen neighbouring police districts to form the Strathclyde Police. Now he certainly had no wish to be a part of this group. He took this moment to really observe his interrogator. This fair-haired upstart looked too young to have earned the rank of DCI; his face even looked too boyish to be imposing. *Doesn't even look like he can grow facial hair,* Callum thought to himself. He supposed that's why the husky partner, who identified himself as Detective Sergeant Milton was standing close by — to make up for de Kirkhaugh's unimposing features.

Callum remembered, "The taxi was a Black Morris Oxford, 'bout 10 years old. White numbers painted on the doors."

"That narrows it down," de Kirkhaugh said sarcastically. "You still haven't answered why Miss McArthur wanted to see you so urgently."

Callum bit his tongue. He couldn't say he was investigating a 70-year-old murder case. Aside from it sounding absurd, it was the Glasgow police who had once threatened Ruthie's father and possibly ruined his own grandfather's reputation.

"Am I being charged?" Callum asked.

"Not yet," huffed de Kirkhaugh. "But you are under arrest."

"Then you can't detain me, without an arrest warrant."

"Nice try," replied de Kirkhaugh. "We have the power to arrest if one is *seen running away from the scene of a crime pursued by others.* And we can hold you in custody until we bring you before the district court. Don't worry tomorrow is Monday, we'll have you in front of the magistrate soon enough."

"Then if I'm officially under arrest," replied Callum. "I won't answer any further questions until I speak to a solicitor."

. . .

"Excuse me, Miss...?" stammered Willowby as he looked down at the paper where she had written her name in a style of penmanship so neat and precise that he hadn't seen in years. She did not have any identification to verify. "Myra, am I pronouncing that properly? Is there someone we can call?"

Willowby tried to smile as he placed a glass of water on the table of the interrogation room of the 27th Precinct in Manhattan. Myra delicately reached for the glass. Greenwyn's pen was poised above paper, waiting to take her statement.

"I tried to call..." said Myra, taking a moment to sip the water. As she carefully placed the glass back on the table, she quietly continued, "I finally found a telephone booth. I remember when they were introduced to New York in 1910."

Willowby and Greenwyn exchanged glances. Willowby glowered as Greenwyn shrugged.

Myra cleared her throat, "I picked up the receiver and dialed '0' for the operator and I asked for the number for Edward Hoffman... that's my son."

Greenwyn scrawled as she spoke and circled the word 'son'. Willowby squinted, as he tried to recall why that name was familiar to him. He asked, "You don't have your son's phone number?"

She paused, "It's complicated to explain."

The two officers exchanged knowing glances.

Myra continued, "The operator insisted that she had no listing for Edward Hoffman. Likewise, she had no listing for our residence on Bloomingdale Square..."

Willowby interrupted, "Where is Bloomingdale Square?"

Myra opened her mouth but a mere whisper came out.

"Where was that?" asked Greenwyn.

"Manhattan."

A look of confusion fell across Greenwyn's face as he jotted down her words. Willowby was equally perplexed. There was no such place as Bloomingdale Square. He asked, "As in the giant store Bloomingdale's?"

"Giant? Er..yes... named after the Bloomingdale Brothers. Bloomingdale Square used to be Schuyler Square."

"How do you spell that?" asked Greenwyn.

"Look ma'am," interjected Willowby. "I've lived in Manhattan all my life and walked most of the streets at some point and I've never heard of Bloomingdale Square or Shuler Square."

"Schuyler Square," corrected Myra.

"Whatever."

"Yes. The operator said the same as you. I understand why now, but didn't when I made the call."

"Okay, I don't follow."

"I'm getting ahead of myself," Myra continued. "The operator rudely disconnected the line and I made my way westward to Longacre Square... er... Times Square... you see, I had been... away... for some time but nothing could have prepared me for how much had changed."

"Changed?"

"The buildings are different, taller, colder. Photographs of women wearing hardly any clothes. Everyone is dressed so differently now... no one wears hats anymore."

Willowby opened his mouth to comment but then decided to let her ramble. Greenwyn tried desperately to take legible notes but she began to babble more quickly by the minute.

"I was in shock to see what had become of Times Square. You see, I remember when it was called Longacre Square..."

This caught Willowby off-guard. What kind of nut was she? It had always been Times Square. He found himself asking, "When was it called 'Longacre Square?'"

"Since the 1800's I believe. It was renamed 'Times Square' in 1905..."

"Nineteen-oh-five?" exclaimed Willowby. "But you said, 'I remember when it was Longacre Square.' Lady, that was long before any of us were born."

Myra looked at him for a moment. She seemed too much in control to be crazy. She had to be working some angle. He decided to play along to see if he could figure her out, and said, "Okay, for argument's sake, tell me more about these 'changes'."

"Well, The New York Times building was the tallest building in New York. It used to be the second tallest building in all the world, now it is overshadowed by buildings stretched to the heavens, and it's façade is covered with towers of giant square boxes and flashing adverts." She lowered her voice and spoke in confidence; "The word 'S...E...X' surrounded me on signs and storefronts."

Willowby nodded. He had seen firsthand how the sex shops had sprung up all over Times Square during the 70's, making the area cheap and a breeding ground for deviants.

"Of course, I shouldn't be surprised. I thought when they started showing Mutoscope "peepshow" flickers at the New York Theater it would be the end of Broadway."

"Sorry," interrupted Willowby. "Which New York theatre do you mean? There are tons of them."

"*The* New York Theatre," Myra replied incredulously. "That's its name. Just down from the Cadillac Hotel..."

Willowby was going to ask about where the hell the Cadillac Hotel was but the woman continued, "The glorious George M. Cohen shows..."

Who? wondered Willowby. But as he glanced down at Greenwyn's notes he knew he had seen the name written before.

"Then I saw him," Myra continued.

"Saw who?" asked Willowby.

"Georgie... George Cohen," she replied, her eyes focused a million miles away. "I knew his face instantly... But it was bronzed.... He's a statue, now.

With the inscription, *Give My Regards to Broadway*. Oh, I remember how proud he was of that song. Just last summer I was at a soiree... I guess it wasn't last summer... It was to me. The inscription listed Georgie's passing in 1942. They're all gone. All my friends are gone. What happened to them? What happened to my mother?"

Greenwyn wrote 'crazy' in the margin and circled it several times. Willowby nodded. He had been watching for the usual signs of lying to a police officer. She displayed none. She was either one hell of an actress or she really believed what she was saying.

Myra was now speaking more freely. "I made my way northward along Broadway towards my home... but home doesn't exist anymore. I understood why the operator couldn't find Bloomingdale Square..."

The two officers leaned forward waiting for the explanation.

"It was gone," she whispered. "It is now called Duke of... Something Street."

"Duke Ellington Boulevard," corrected Willowby. They had picked up Myra at the park right there at 106th and Broadway.

"My house is gone," Myra continued, only slightly agitated, "So is our neighbor's house... the Straus' home... gone... Even the Bloomingdale Reformed Church where Archie and I were married is gone. Gone. The life I knew is gone."

Greenwyn started to write in point form – no longer able to keep up in longhand.

"That's when I saw it," Myra prattled on.

"What?"

"A headline on a newspaper... fluttering on the park bench. I picked it up. There was an article about a *Titanic II*... "

Myra began to shiver. She rubbed her hands vigorously. Willowby wondered what one thing had to do with the other. How was the *Titanic II* of any importance?

"Then my hands began to shake as I saw the photo beneath the headline. The photo of the Hoffmans. I knew Edward, my son, and there was Archie! He had aged so much but it doesn't matter to me. My husband is still alive! I needed to see him, needed him to hold me... then I saw *her* picture."

"Who?" Willowby asked but she seemed glassy-eyed as she began to unfold the newspaper she had crumpled when they picked her up. Myra's finger stabbed at the image of an old woman in the photo between the two elderly men. "Her! Who is this woman?"

Willowby looked and recognized the image of Edward Hoffman: He was a respected business tycoon and wealthy philanthropist. She jabbed her finger again, losing her composure, "Who is the woman who dares call herself Myra Hoffman? Who is she? How could she steal my family? My life?"

Willowby watched as Myra started to tear up the newspaper as she screamed, "I want my family back! I want my life back!"

She sneered at the tattered remains, "*I am* Myra Hoffman! Why did she do this to me? How did she steal my life?!"

Officer Willowby ran his finger across his scar as he looked over at Greenwyn. He could tell by his expression that they were both thinking the same thing: She was nuts!

CHAPTER 23

Callum did not get much sleep in his holding cell. It certainly wasn't built for comfort. The white bricks had a yellowish tint to them, making the room feel more disgusting than it probably was. A battered cot sat in the corner and an old metal urinal on the wall completed the décor. It wasn't the inhospitable surroundings that were keeping him up all night, however—it was the string of incessant questions pounding in his head. All his life he was led to believe that his grandfather had made a mistake and was disgraced for it. Now with her last breaths, Ruthie revealed to him that his grandfather had tried to be honorable and was threatened for doing so. Who should he believe? Who could he trust, when his own beliefs were now in question?

Doubts began to flood over his mind. Why did his grandfather confide in Ruthie instead of his family? What if Ruthie was just saying that to make him feel better? *But who would do that when they realized they were dying?* He reviewed the case in his head. The eyewitness accounts of the man seen fleeing Agatha Gilcrest's murder did not match Otto Slade. Ruthie's father was not allowed to testify and his family was threatened if he spoke the truth. Somehow Otto Slade was the scapegoat. Callum's grandfather found out about it and was also threatened. Why? Who was the Glasgow Police protecting? Or was it all just jibberish rambling from an old woman as she lay bleeding to death?

Callum's thoughts were interrupted by the squeaking sound of a door opening down the hall. Footsteps on the tile floor echoed through the holding cells, and Detective Chief Inspector de Kirkhaugh's smug face appeared on the opposite side of the bars.

"Here to take me before the district court's office?" asked Callum without bothering to get up.

"No," replied de Kirkhaugh. "I'm here to ask why you're investigating a murder that took place almost a century ago."

Callum tried to keep a poker face, "What do you mean?"

"You can't deny it," de Kirkhaugh said with a definite tone. "I know you're investigating your grandfather's case. He was dishonorably discharged from the Glasgow Police for his incompetence."

"And how exactly do you know who my grandfather is?"

Through the bars de Kirkhaugh opened his fingers and the necklace given to him by Ruthie dropped and stopped at the end of the chain. "You were carrying your grandfather Inspector John Toughill's pendant. The inscription is on the back along with his police warrant number."

Callum hadn't the time to inspect the back of the pendant when Ruthie gave it to him, but at least now he knew she had told him the truth. The sight of de Kirkhaugh holding his grandfather's pendant infuriated him, but since it was the Glasgow Police that ruined his father he was not about to blurt out everything he knew. He simply gazed at the Detective Chief Inspector, who obviously couldn't stand the silence for long.

"So why are you investigating such an old case?"

"How is it any of your business?"

"It's my business when Ruth McArthur turns up dead and she was 'witness' in the murder case your grandfather investigated back in 1909."

"How is it that you're so familiar with the details of a murder case from 1909?" asked Callum.

"Well I could brag about my powers of deduction, or admit that I simply looked at the files and newspaper clippings in your satchel case. Your grandfather's name is all over it. By the by, you left it in the cab you took from the Glasgow airport to Ruth McArthur's flat."

"You had no right to go through my personal belongings," sneered Callum.

"You were a suspect in a murder case. That gave me every right to determine if I had a case against you."

"*Were* a suspect?"

"The bullet that killed Miss Ruth McArthur did not come from your gun."

"What caliber of bullet was it?" asked Callum. There was another moment of silence as de Kirkhaugh stared him down. He didn't answer. Callum added, "I'm just curious… in case I see something."

"I can't tell you," replied de Kirkhaugh.

"You don't trust me?"

"No, I don't," said de Kirkhaugh. "But even if I did, I still can't tell you. I know your gun wasn't modified to shoot £75 bullets."

"What?"

"You're free to go, Mr. Toughill," said de Kirkhaugh as he unlocked the door. Callum carefully stood up.

"That's it?"

"I know you weren't the assassin," replied de Kirkhaugh.

"Assassin?"

"The constable there will escort you to pick up your personal effects."

"Everything had better be back in my satchel," Callum said as he glanced over to where de Kirkhaugh was pointing and saw a uniformed officer standing by the door at the end of the hallway.

"A word of warning," de Kirkhaugh said as he held out the pendant for Callum to take. "Leave homicide investigation to the trained professionals. We're experts in what we do, and consider amateurs such as yourself to be obstructors of justice."

"Ha," snapped Callum as he snatched the pendant away. He'd had enough of this insolent twit. "It was your experts that botched up the case in the first place and sent an innocent man to the gallows. Then when my grandfather tried to prove his innocence, the 'professional' Glasgow police turned on him and disgraced him. So much for the brotherhood."

"Sod off," barked de Kirkhaugh. "You don't know what you're talking about."

Callum smiled. He finally got to him and left with a parting remark, "Prove me wrong. I dare you."

Callum was still feeling ebullient with his last word as the constable led him to the discharge area to pick up his personal belongings. His warm feelings of victory were short lived, however. They vanished when he saw the stern expression of Percy Winthrope from Lloyds of London.

CHAPTER 24

"What the blazes is going on with you?" demanded Percy before Callum could sit down with his cup at the Arcade Café, a centuries-old coffee house.

Callum took his time. He sat and stirred in some sugar as he gazed about at the ornate hand-carved wood décor on the walls. It was early enough in the day that the café wasn't too crowded, allowing them to speak freely. Where would he begin? He had hoped to have something more conclusive before presenting his findings to Percy. That way the end would have justified the means. However, at this point he was still essentially empty handed.

"I don't know what to tell you," Callum finally said as he took a sip. "I was just following the leads and they brought me to where you found me."

"Leads? What leads?" exclaimed Percy. "All you had to do was look at the evidence and declare it a hoax."

"Oh, now you're going to tell me what to declare?" Callum exploded. "Why bother having investigators then? Why not sit there in your tacky, stuffy office and rubberstamp your own verdict without any investigation?"

"I beg your pardon?"

"I meant no disrespect," continued Callum. "But I've been chasing leads all over the United Kingdom, I've hardly had any sleep, I've been shot at and accused of murdering someone I happened to like, and I don't appreciate an Irish bastard such as yourself telling me how to do my job."

"Are you quite finished?"

"For now. I reserve the right to call you a few more names after I've finished my coffee."

"I did not mean to suggest that you pass judgment without investigation," said Percy in a calm voice. "But I assumed that after seeing the scribbles on the back of that insurance claim, you would have come to the same conclusion and found the facts to back it up."

Callum's mind was reeling. *What scribble?* The claim had been taped to the file folder, and he never looked at the back of it. Not that he ever had a reason to do so. This was the second time he's neglected to look at the back of something that turned out to be important, but he didn't want to admit that now. He'd be sure to turn things over more often in the future.

"What was it about the scribble that made *you* jump to that conclusion?" asked Callum cautiously.

"The ink and handwriting didn't match what was written in the claim," said Percy as he seemed to be picturing it in his mind. "And the message itself: 'Evidence in the Agatha Gilcrest murder'. Did you ever? A little too on the nose, don't you think?"

"Not really," Callum replied, then leaned in to ask the question that had been plaguing him. "Where did it come from?"

"What?"

"The claim itself. It was for a brooch that was stolen from a high profile murder case. Who filed the claim?"

"I don't know. You saw the claim," replied Percy. "It was smudged when it was sent to us."

"Sent to you? By whom?"

Percy hesitated before responding, "It was sent anonymously. I was still a clerk at the time."

"When was this?"

"It was late 1963, I recall—it was around the time that President Kennedy was shot."

Callum remembered where he was when he heard that John F. Kennedy had been assassinated. He had just received his first investigative assignment for Lloyds. Almost twenty years had passed but he could remember it as if it were yesterday. He looked at Percy, "Anonymous, you say?"

"Precisely. You can see why I was skeptical."

"This information would have been useful to know before now." He studied Percy for a moment then added, "You thought because it was the case that destroyed my grandfather, that I would want to be done with it as quickly as possible? I would rule it a hoax, and if they ever found the wreck of the *Titanic*, you wouldn't have to worry about it. Didn't you?"

"Well... not in so many words..." stammered Percy. Then added, "but... yes. I expected that was what you were going to do. Instead you took off as if it were some bloody crusade and wound up in a jail in the highlands, and this 'Irish bastard' had to fly in from London to save your Scottish arse."

Callum smirked, "I was doing quite well without you."

"Oh, I can see that," replied Percy. Then he leaned in. "There's nothing to the case. It's as cold as..."

"An iceberg?" asked Callum. He used Percy's own metaphor against him. "You told me to look for icebergs... and I found several. It led me to re-open the case that destroyed my grandfather."

"To what end?" Percy asked. "It was so long ago, what does it matter now?"

"Ruthie McArthur died in my arms because she knew the truth. It matters to someone. Enough for them to silence her."

Percy stared at his tea for a moment. Then he asked, "What do you need?"

"Just a little more time," replied Callum.

"Very well," said Percy. "But I caution you. Our company has a reputation to maintain. If you get into a position where you compromise our integrity, I will disavow you and your behaviour."

"Understood."

April 6, 1982

CHAPTER 25

Callum's mind was back on *Titanic* as he traveled to Edinburgh. He had spent most of the previous day poring over his notes, trying to figure out where to proceed.

He decided he needed to find Alice Cleaver. Having worked for Agatha Gilcrest, murdered her own child, and taken another child off the *Titanic*, leaving the rest of the family to die, she seemed the best candidate as a suspect. Did she spend any time in jail for the murder of her infant son? And, what happened to her after the *Titanic* went down?

Callum made his way to the West Register House. It had at one time been St. George's church, but now it was the Scottish Record Office.

Finding the files he needed was not going to be an easy task, as all five floors of the renovated church were filled beyond capacity with file boxes. Having recently seen that American film, *Raiders of the Lost Ark*, he couldn't help but be reminded of its depiction of a massive storage facility.

It was going to be like looking for a specific snowflake on an iceberg.

• • •

Natalie sat behind her desk as an orderly brought Myra into her office. She had been returned to the clinic by two police officers in the middle of the night. Natalie had briefly glanced over their report as she waited for Myra to be brought in.

"Is there anything else?" asked the orderly.

"No, that will be all, Ralph. Please close the door behind you."

After the door closed, Natalie tried to maintain calmness as she spoke through gritted teeth, "I can't believe you betrayed my trust like that!"

Myra sat in the chair in front of Natalie's desk, staring into space.

RING

The phone interrupted the line of questioning. Natalie's reflexes reached for the phone, but she stopped herself. She was not going to let herself be distracted.

"Myra? Do you have anything to say for yourself?"

RING

Natalie ignored the phone as Myra continued to stare blankly. Natalie was about to say something else, when her answering machine clicked on. "You have reached Natalie…"

She paused as her own pre-recorded voice echoed from the machine in the outgoing message.

BEEP

A female voice could be heard being recorded onto the answering machine. "Hello, Dr. Lindsay? This is Denise Tosia calling again. Could you please call me as soon as you can? My number is 555-5904."

Natalie had no time to call her back now, and as soon as the answering machine stopped she turned her attention back to Myra. "Look, I'm here to help you but if you're not going to co-operate there is very little I can do."

Myra continued to stare and not say a word. A whole minute passed in the tense silence.

"Fine," sighed Natalie. "You leave me no alternative but to restrict…"

She was suddenly interrupted by a knock at the door, followed immediately by the swaggering entrance of a heavyset man with a ponytail and a long black leather jacket.

"May I help you!" snapped Natalie who was not impressed by the intrusion.

"Are you Doctor Lindsay?" asked the man as he fiddled with a gold chain around his neck. "I'm looking for…"

He then saw Myra.

"Mary!" he exclaimed. "Thank god I found you!"

Myra backed away as the man approached her. Natalie placed herself between them.

"You are?" challenged Natalie.

"Sorry, Doc." The man extended his hand to Natalie, "I'm Ian Kybartis. I'm Mary's husband."

CHAPTER 26

Natalie had reviewed all the paperwork that Ian Kybartis had given her. Everything seemed to be authentic.

"Here's her drivers' license," said Ian as he handed her the Canadian-issued identification. Natalie looked at the license. The name under the photo card was 'Mary Kybartis', and her date of birth was listed as 'October 31, 1957.' This was the definitive proof that this patient was not around in 1912 when the ill-fated ship had sank.

Myra, or Mary rather, sat staring at Ian. Natalie skimmed through the medical records that were enclosed in a manila envelope, as Mary kept tapping the arm of her chair with her fingernail. It was making it difficult for Natalie to concentrate. From what she could make out, it seemed that 'Mary' had been most recently a patient at a private clinic in Ontario, Canada.

"How long had she been there?" Natalie asked Ian.

"She's been in and out of clinics for the past five years," shrugged the young man, popping his gum. "She'd always go back to this weird *Titanic* fantasy. Even spent a bundle to buy this elaborate costume dress from that era."

Satisfied, Natalie picked up the phone and dialed. Then said into the receiver, "Could you have someone accompany Mary... Myra... to her room and help her pack up her belongings?"

• • •

Edward sat at his lake house, staring at one of the canvasses. Roger Zisholm sipped his wine as he surveyed Edward's work. "When did you paint these?"

Edward gestured generally in the direction of each painting, never taking his eyes off the canvas in front of him. "This one I've been working on since last week. That one I did during the Nixon administration. And that one over the fireplace I did when I came back from the war."

"Why didn't you tell me about these before?" Roger asked. He gestured too far and spilled some wine on the floor. He quickly set his glass down on the table and went back to the kitchen to grab a paper towel.

"I didn't think it was important. Until now..."

RING

Roger jumped as he was just passing the phone which sat on the pass-through window ledge, when it rang loudly. He stopped and reached his hand out toward it.

"Don't answer it," Edward said with an eerie calm as he continued to stare at the canvas.

"But what if it's important?"

RING

"Most people know not to disturb me while I'm here. There are only two people who ignore that request. One has just spilled wine on my floor. Serves him right for drinking this early in the day..."

Roger shifted uncomfortably, as he quickly grabbed the paper towel and began his task of mopping it up.

RING

The outgoing message of the answering machine started up as Edward continued. "And the other would be my father, who has no regard for anyone but himself."

Right on cue, the gruff voice of Edward's father, Archibald Hoffman snarled from the machine. "Edward are you there? Pick up the phone! Your mother and I haven't heard from you. Your mother wants to know what day you'll be arriving. Hopefully in time for the Anniversary dinner on *Titanic II*... er... I mean *Titan*... you know what I mean. Call us."

The call ended abruptly. The silence went on for a long time.

"Well, are you going?" Roger finally asked as he picked his glass up again.

"No."

"But, they're your parents. Besides, you're missing out on a historic event."

"I've had enough historical events in my life. I'm finished with *Titanic* ships."

— — —

Natalie waited as Ian Kybartis signed the release forms at the reception desk.

"Tell me," Natalie asked quietly. "Did she ever experience... losing a child? A miscarriage perhaps?"

"No, not quite," Ian replied as he signed the last form. "She found out that she was...she said 'barren'. You know, never going to be able to get knocked up."

Natalie nodded, "And that's when this *Titanic* fantasy started?"

He looked at her with amazement, "That's right. How'd you know?"

"That's my job."

At that moment, Mary returned with a few bags in her hands, escorted by Ralph.

Natalie forced her face into a smile. "Well Myra...I mean Mary. I wish you the best of luck and hope you recover fully soon."

"Thank you, doctor," whispered Mary. "I do appreciate everything you tried to do for me."

Natalie placed a business card in Mary's hand. "If you ever need anyone to talk to..."

She shook Mary's hand and was startled to find it ice cold. Almost like a corpse's hand. Ian's gum popping interrupted.

"Let's go Mary," snapped Ian. "We got a long drive ahead of us, eh."

Mary managed a smile to Natalie and left with Ian. Natalie stood there for a long time watching her disappear out the front door. *Something's wrong.* Natalie couldn't put her finger on it, but something wasn't right.

— — —

Something's wrong.

Detective Chief Inspector de Kirkhaugh had tried to get his mind on to other matters but something that blasted private investigator said kept nagging at him. *Prove me wrong!*

Naturally he had said it to bait him. To annoy him. It had worked. Callum Toughill was as crazy as those conspiracy nuts who think the Loch Ness Monster is a military weapon, hidden by the British Government. He wasn't going to buy into that rubbish.

On the other hand, he had determined that Ruth McArthur, an old lady who lived in the same house since the Agatha Gilcrest murder, was killed by a hitman. The bullets that were used were made up of an odd mixture of gallium, indium and gelatin coating. Upon impact, they would disintegrate from the body's temperature, making the bullets untraceable. The cost of a single 100-grain bullet was estimated to be £75. In addition, the gun used to fire such a bullet would have to be modified and the bullets transported in a cooler of some sort.

He had seen it before. This was the method of a hitman known only as 'Jack Frost'. But why? Why such a specialized and expensive assassin for a little old lady?

DCI de Kirkhaugh had hoped that Callum Toughill was 'Jack Frost' but he'd had no cooler for transporting such a bullet, and ballistics had determined that a modified weapon would be needed to fire that kind of bullet—the heat generated from the igniting gunpowder would melt the bullet before it left the chamber in a traditional firearm.

Callum's weapon was quite traditional—a Walther P38—and had no traces of gallium in it. Not to mention the fact that his pathetic story checked out.

Lost in thought, de Kirkhaugh found himself in the 'other morgue', known outside the department as the records file room. What was he doing here? It was ludicrous. He wasn't going to give Toughill that satisfaction. He was going to go back upstairs and forget he ever met Toughill or heard of Agatha Gilcrest...

"What can I do for you, sir?" asked the cheery voice of the records clerk.

De Kirkhaugh couldn't help himself, and found himself saying, "I would like to get the file on the Agatha Gilcrest murder."

· · ·

Ian's gold-colored sports car sped northward along Interstate 95, as Myra stared out the window at the world passing by. Nervously, she gripped onto the door handle for dear life. She was suddenly jolted by an odd ringing sound. Ian turned down the music from his 8-Track player and picked up the receiver of his car telephone.

"Yeah," Ian answered the phone ungraciously.

The voice on the end snarled, "Do you have her?"

He glanced over at her, "Yep. She's with me now."

"Can she hear me?" the voice asked.

Ian looked over at his passenger who continued to stare intently out the window, "No."

"Good. Do you have the directions?"

"Yup. We should be there soon," Ian replied.

"Remember, she can never be seen again."

Ian smiled, "Don't worry, I'll make sure of that."

CHAPTER 27

Natalie found it very difficult to concentrate for the rest of the day. By lunchtime she was ready to go home and decided to cancel the rest of her appointments and blame it on the impending storm. As she was on her way out, one of the nurses pointed her out to a woman at the front desk. As she approached, Natalie could see a hospital nurse's uniform peeking out from under her winter coat.

"Dr. Lindsay?" the woman asked. "I'm Denise Tosia. I've been trying to reach you all morning."

"Sorry, I didn't return your call," Natalie said bluntly. "I was busy."

"I see, but please understand that I have taken some professional risks to contact you."

"Look, I don't mean to be rude," Natalie interrupted, "But I'm not feeling well. Can I call you tomorrow?"

Before Denise could reply Natalie turned towards the front doors.

"It's about Myra!" Denise called after her. "It took some doing to track down that she had been brought here."

Natalie stopped and turned back towards her, "What about Myra?"

Denise pulled a hospital record file from her large shoulder bag. "I was her attending nurse at the hospital when she was brought in."

"Well, Miss Tosia. You're too late. I had been requesting her medical records for days and now Myra... or whatever her name is... is no longer a patient of mine," said Natalie. Then quickly added, "Or yours for that matter."

"I think someone's trying to kill her."

— — —

Ian is an idiot, Myra thought.

He obviously didn't know how loud his telephone receiver was. She could clearly hear the voice on the other end of the line. While he talked she turned her head and looked out the window at wind gusts blowing through the passing trees, pretending she couldn't hear. There was something familiar about the other voice but it was too tinny for her to identify it. One thing she knew for certain was that the man claiming to be her husband was going to kill her unless she thought of something quickly.

Myra had seen the pistol he was carrying as they got into the automobile. She decided, for her own safety, to act as if she hadn't.

She was suddenly jolted in her seat as Ian abruptly steered to the shoulder of the road, then slammed on the breaks. The automobile skidded to a stop.

Was this it? Was this the place where he was going to shoot her?

. . .

"We can speak freely here, Miss Tosia," said Natalie as she led her into the empty lounge. Most of the staff had gone home early to avoid the snow.

"Call me Denise."

"Ok, Denise," Natalie said as she set her purse down on the nearest table. She didn't bother taking off her coat, as she didn't plan on staying very long. "What can you tell me about Myra?"

"First of all, I'd like to mention that I've never taken a risk or followed up on a patient like this before, but this one's special," began Denise as she sat at the table. She took a moment to gather her thoughts. "I see death every night. I've often been the one to have to tell families that there is no medical miracle. I believed that… until Myra was brought in. By all rights she should have been dead twice over. I saw her come back to life… twice. She personifies medical miracle."

Natalie understood firsthand how Myra had a way of indelibly imprinting herself on someone, but was reluctant to believe that there was anything miraculous or supernatural about her. She decided to cut to the chase. "You said someone was trying to kill her. What makes you say that?"

"I wanted to go to the police but since Myra's identity was unknown, I tracked her down here," began Denise. Natalie nodded as Denise opened up the folder she had with her, "Myra's toxicology revealed traces of what appeared to be opium."

"Opium?" Natalie was confused. "The withdrawal symptoms of opium addiction are quite physical…sometimes violent. She didn't exhibit any of the signs. In fact our nurses here discovered she had low blood pressure."

"Our staff had the same findings," continued Denise. "Myra should have been having increased blood pressure from the withdrawals. So our on-call doctor ordered a new blood test to be run."

"And?"

Denise flipped the page in the folder, "They were able to determine that it was actually Laudanum in her system."

"Laudanum?" exclaimed Natalie. "I didn't know you could still get that."

"You can't. Well, there are variations of it known as Tincture of Opium for medicinal purposes. And from what the lab determined she's been ingesting it over a long period of time."

"After a long period of time, it would have the internal effects as opium: Dysphoria, respiratory depression, liver damage…" recited Natalie.

"The FDA deems it unproven treatment and potentially fatal after prolonged use. It's been tightly regulated since the 1971 Uniform Controlled Substances Act. Our hospital pharmacist tells me that because it's so regulated, it costs about $150 per ounce."

"There are cheaper ways of poisoning someone," remarked Natalie as she was trying to process it all.

"However, that's not the puzzling part," said Denise as she pointed to a section on the toxicology report. "The type found in Myra's blood stream had a higher percentage of the weight per volume of accepted levels of anhydrous morphine. And from what I'm told, that tincture of opium hasn't been available since the 1920's."

"Miss… Denise… I sincerely hope you aren't giving credence to Mary's delusion."

"Mary?"

"That's her real name. Her husband arrived this morning to take her home."

"To where?" asked Denise in surprise.

"It's in her file upstairs in my office… look, it doesn't matter. She created this *Titanic* fantasy as a coping mechanism after she discovered she could never have children."

"What?" Denise's one eyebrow arched. "Who said she could never have children?"

"Her husband."

Denise flipped some pages in the file, then handed her a photograph. Natalie looked at it for a moment, confused. *What am I supposed to be looking for?* Then, she saw it at the same time Denise said it aloud, "A Caesarian scar…a nasty one too. As a registered nurse who once worked in a maternity ward, I can say with certainty, she did bear a child!"

— — —

"Wait here, *dear!*" said Ian as he opened the car door. The way he said 'dear' made Myra's skin crawl, and she was hit with a wave of nausea.

She heard him undo the zipper on his pants, and then heard the stream of urine on the ground outside. *How vulgar!* She considered opening her car door and running, but there was nowhere to run… he would simply shoot her in the back. Then she noticed the automobile's phone between her and the driver's seat.

Myra pulled Natalie's card out of her pocket. She picked up the phone receiver and started to dial the number on the card. Nothing happened. Then she saw the 'send' button. She pressed it. The phone numbers beeped loudly as it dialed, and she quickly used her sleeve to muffle the sounds.

The driver's side door opened!

Myra quickly set the receiver down on the large phone base, somewhat askew in order to keep the line connected, as Ian let his rotund weight drop into the leather seat.

Ian started the car again and drove off. He frowned, "Looks like it's starting to snow."

Myra said nothing. She just started to nervously tap her finger against the phone receiver.

. . .

Natalie flipped through the file folder that Denise had brought. She felt like a fool. She was trained to watch for signs of lying and now in hindsight she could see that there were reasons to doubt Ian's credibility. Then something in the file folder caught her eye. Under personal effects she saw, hand written, *Gold Locket on a chain – with the inscription: To Myra, Happy Anniversary! Archie December 31.*

"Did you see this locket?" Natalie asked as she pointed to the description.

"Yes, there's a picture of it," said Denise as she reached for the folder.

"Where?"

Denise flipped to the pocket at the front of the folder and pulled out a Polaroid picture. "Here it is."

Natalie looked at the photo. There it was. Just as Myra had described it. Even the chain was distinctive with unusual Celtic-style ornate links. Suddenly Natalie felt the blood drain from her face. She had just seen that chain earlier today. It was around Ian Kybartis' neck when he first entered her office!

— — —

The visibility was starting to get worse, making the driving treacherous on the rural winding road. Suddenly, the car started to fishtail. As Ian tried to regain control, the phone receiver rolled onto his lap. The number pad was illuminated! There was a connection. He pressed 'End' and turned to Myra.

"Who did you call?" he yelled harshly.

"Watch out!" Myra screamed as she pointed ahead.

Too late! The road curved to the left. The sports car continued straight - and careened off the road.

CHAPTER 28

Light was dimming through the stained glass windows of the Scottish Record Office. Callum turned on the lamp on his table.

Something wasn't right. After a great deal of searching, Callum had been able to locate some files on the Alice Cleaver case. There was an arrest photo taken of her. Since none of the newspapers covering the 1909 murder trial used photographs, Callum had not seen her face before. Now here was a photo of her, taken at the Glasgow police station at that time.

She looked different from the photos in the American newspapers proclaiming her a heroine for saving the young boy, Trevor Allison. Rummaging through his satchel case he pulled out the copies he had made from the microfiche and compared photos. There was a noticeable difference in the shape of face and the bone structure around the eyes. It was only a three-year difference between photos, and no one's features change that quickly in just a few years.

He paused for a moment, looking about. There were staff members doing some filing, and a few other people seated at other tables. Everyone seemed busy, but Callum had the odd sensation that he was being watched. After a moment, he shook it off. He was just becoming paranoid since his incarceration.

Searching through some more files, he discovered the birth certificate for Alice Catherine Cleaver, born on 5 July 1889 in Kentish Town, St. Pancras, London. Her mother was Lavinia Alice Cleaver (née Thomas) and her father was listed as Joseph Cleaver, who was employed as a postman. This last point contradicted what Callum had read; that Alice Cleaver and her mother were each abandoned by their fathers before birth.

Flipping back through his notes, he found Alice Mary Cleaver born in Glasgow Scotland, Father: unknown. There was the difference: the middle names. Alice Catherine Cleaver worked for the Allison family and then returned to England, married a surgical appliance manufacturer and moved to Winchester, Hampshire.

By contrast, Alice Mary Cleaver, who worked for Agatha Gilcrest, had been sentenced to time in jail for the murder of her own child. She had just started her prison term when Agatha Gilcrest was murdered. She couldn't have killed her former employer. Alice Mary Cleaver did not have a happy ending to her miserable existence: she died at the young age of 26 of Tuberculosis while still in prison in 1915. Obviously, she was still in jail when the *Titanic* sank. Irrefutable evidence that she was not the same Alice Cleaver that had taken Trevor off the sinking ship. Yet so many newspaper articles and experts claimed they were one and the same. It was downright slanderous.

In a statement that Alice Catherine Cleaver made to the press regarding the death of the Allison family aboard the *Titanic*:

"I was serving as a nurse to Mr. and Mrs. Allison's two children, for two weeks prior to sailing on the *Titanic*. Loraine was three years old and Trevor was only 10 months old. After the crash, I had some difficulty in persuading Mr. Allison to get up and go to see what had happened. He did not hear at all and thought it was my imagination. Some long time after the engines had stopped he decided to go and make inquiries.

"While he was away, a steward warned us to leave the ship, so I helped prepare the children, but Mrs. Allison became hysterical and I was unable to calm her. About that time another officer came round to close the cabins and urged us to go on deck. That's when Mr. Allison returned and seemed too dazed to speak. I quickly handed him some brandy and asked him to look after Mrs. Allison and Loraine, and I would look after Trevor, the child I managed to get off the ship. There was confusion as to which deck we should go to and that is how we became separated. Later, I learned from one of the staff that Mrs. Allison became hysterical again and that Mr. Allison had difficulty calming her. I can only assume that is how they perished, as there was plenty of room in the lifeboats. It was surprising how many people refused to leave *Titanic*, believing it was safer to stay on the ship."

Callum dismissed the idea of contacting her. She had probably lived with the guilt that most of the Allison family had perished, complicated by the fact that her name was connected to a child murderer. Callum decided to leave the poor woman alone.

This revelation did prove one thing, though: Loraine Kramer, who claimed to be Loraine Allison, had lied to him. Callum looked over his notes, realizing that he was once again without either a suspect or a lead.

Beep, beep, beep

His pager went off, startling everyone in the records hall. He quickly hushed it. Taking his satchel case, he trudged down to the payphone at the base of the stairwell. As he descended the stairs, he heard solemn footsteps following him down. He thought nothing of it as there were others doing research. Each step echoed over the entire stairwell, bouncing off the walls. He paused to look at the time on his watch. The other set of footsteps stopped. *Odd,* he thought. Then when he started down again, the other set resumed. It was likely Callum's own footsteps that he was hearing echoing back to him. He stopped.

The other footsteps shuffled an extra step, then stopped as well. These were not his steps he heard. He looked up. And saw no one.

"Hello?" Callum called out. "Is anyone there?"

He heard the other steps shuffle and fade off on the floor above him. Callum continued down the steps and out the door. He dashed across the street to the cover of the wooded park of Charlotte Square. He watched the West Register House from behind a tree. A man stepped out and looked up and down the street. *Was he looking for me?* The man disappeared down the alley adjacent to the West Register House toward Queensferry Street.

Once the man was out of sight, Callum turned in the opposite direction and cut through the park, checking over his shoulder constantly and almost running straight into a statue of a man on a horse.

Callum felt relief as he entered the crowded Oxford Bar on Young Street. After ordering a pint, he recalled the page he'd received and found the phone box.

"Five-Zero-Five," Callum spoke his code into the phone.

The operator's voice crackled, "Message from Lumina. Urgent come quick!"

Lumina? He hadn't spoken to his sister in years. What could be so urgent?

. . .

DCI de Kirkhaugh sat at his electric typewriter, carefully using Liquid Paper to correct an error on his report, when his phone rang. Rolling his chair closer to the phone, he pressed the flashing 'line 3' and answered, "de Kirkhaugh!"

"This is Janna from the file room," the voice in the receiver whispered.

"Yes," de Kirkhaugh replied trying to hide his sudden enthusiasm. After all it isn't every day you get to look at the evidence of a 70-year-old murder.

"I had to go to the Scottish Criminal Record Office to retrieve file HH-13/31."

"If that's the Agatha Gilcrest file, that's the one. Did you find it?"

"Yes... and no."

"What do you mean, yes and no? You either did or didn't."

"I know where it is," replied Janna.

"Good. When can I get it?"

"You can't," she said softly. He would normally have thought she was fooling with him but there was something in her tone of voice that seemed odd.

De Kirkhaugh asked, "Is there a reason I can't get the file?"

"Yes, sir."

"Are you going to tell me?" de Kirkhaugh was trying to remain calm. "Or do I have to hire a detective?"

"You're a detective."

"I'm aware of that. And I'm going to be a very cross one if you don't quit beating around the proverbial bush."

"The file is sealed."

"Is that all?" laughed de Kirkhaugh. "Well, bring it up and I'll unseal it."

"No, you don't understand sir," continued Janna. "It has been sealed with an order that it not be opened until the year 2000."

"Two Thousand? That's..." de Kirkhaugh did the math quickly. "I'm not going to wait eighteen bloody years for it!"

"I'm sorry there is nothing I can do," said Janna in an apologetic voice. "I don't have the authority."

"Well I'm Detective Chief Inspector. I have the authority."

"No sir..." interrupted Janna.

"I beg your bloody pardon?" fumed de Kirkhaugh.

"I'm afraid you don't have authority here."

"Who sealed the file?" demanded de Kirkhaugh.

"The Lord Advocate."

De Kirkhaugh laughed, "I hardly think James Mackay would be interested in it. I can call..."

"Not that Lord Advocate," interjected Janna. "Alexander Ur."

"Who?"

"The Lord Advocate in 1909," she replied matter of factly.

"What if I get James?"

"There is also a royal seal," sighed Janna.

"What?"

"It cannot be opened until 2000."

He was about to say something but de Kirkhaugh knew that Janna was at the very bottom of the ladder. She had no authority to go against orders.

Even if the orders were absurd and given fifty years before she was born. "Thank you Janna. I'll make some inquiries."

"I'm sorry. Bye, sir," she whispered. Then he heard her hang up the phone.

De Kirkhaugh sighed as he replaced the receiver on his phone. The light on 'line 3' stayed illuminated for a moment longer, then went off. De Kirkhaugh stared at it for a moment. He picked up the phone receiver again and watched the light illuminate, then hung it up again. The light went out instantly… as it should. Which meant someone else in the department had been listening to the whole conversation.

CHAPTER 29

"Looks like we're getting a nasty blizzard. Mind if I stay the night here?" Roger asked.

"Not at all," replied Edward as he poured himself another drink. "We have plenty of spare guest rooms."

Numbly, Edward looked about. So many memories in this old lake house. It had been in the family for generations, but now Edward knew that the family line was going to die out soon.

Roger's nasal voice penetrated Edward's melancholy. "I wasn't going to tell you this, but that woman was arrested yesterday."

"Myra?" said Edward. He didn't know what else to call her.

"Yes, she was causing quite a scene in Straus Park."

Edward stopped in mid-pour, "Straus Park? You mean at 106th and Broadway?"

"Yes, according to my contact down at the 27th precinct," Roger took a gulp from his drink. "She was screaming and carrying on about some church, and that she was Myra Hoffman and her house used to be there. She's a dangerous woman, Edward. She needs serious help."

Edward had set his carafe onto the side table and sank down in the nearby overstuffed chair, his head spinning. He murmured softly, "Our house was there."

"What?"

"We used to live there," Edward said, his voice seemed distant as if pulled away with the memory. "When it was still Bloomingdale Square, we lived next door to the Strauses. Our houses were bought and torn down by that developer... what's his name?"

Edward snapped his fingers as he tried to recall the name. It seemed to snap him back to the present. "He did all that Upper East Side development in the 1920's."

Roger's face seemed to strain trying to recall, "Um... Ship... no, it was Schiff?"

"That's right!" Edward exclaimed. "Harry Schiff. He built the Cleburne Building where our houses had been. Both Isador and Ida went down with the *Titanic*, and that triangular park was renamed Straus Park in their memory. There was a church there, I was baptized there, but it closed down in 1913."

"You knew the Strauses?" asked Roger as he poured yet another drink. "You should write a book! Who else did you know?"

"Oh well... our family was well connected with the high society. Well, before *Titanic* at least." Edward sighed, staring at the model of the ship. "After the sinking, Mother became reclusive and we moved to California, then to England, but over the years I've met many people who had fond memories of my mother before *Titanic*. People like George M. Cohen, The Carnegie family, we even knew Guglielmo Marconi."

"Who?" asked Roger as he sat down in the opposite chair.

"He developed the wireless radio system," Edward said understatedly. "He told me that my mother had been a chief investor in the Marconi's Wireless Telegraph Company, and I was told that I learned Morse Code before ....I could speak..."

Tapping! Suddenly Edward's mind began to reel. It was there all along. Nagging at his subconscious mind. The tapping of her finger on the table... and the soothing rhythmic tapping on his shoulder. Just like when he was a baby.

— — —

Natalie hung up the phone with the clinic in Guelph, Ontario, Canada. They had never heard of Mary or Ian Kybartis. All the paperwork that Ian Kybartis had presented to her had been forged documents! *How could I have been so stupid?* In retrospect there were signs that something hadn't been right. Natalie's own gut instinct told her something was wrong at the time and she'd ignored it. Natalie felt awash in feelings of guilt. Did she ignore the signs because she was hoping to pass the problem off to someone else?

Natalie forced herself to refocus. Dwelling on her missed observations was not going to help the situation. The first priority was to get Myra back safe and sound.

Red-faced, she was about to call the police when she noticed the message light flashing on her answering machine. She was going to check it after she called the police but her gut instinct told her to check it now. She wasn't going to ignore her instinct again.

She pressed 'play' after the tape rewound. The machine clicked and from the tiny speaker she heard, "... Looks like it's starting to snow..."

Natalie recognized Ian's brash voice and pursed her lips in distaste.

Then she could hear a loud tapping. She knew that sound. It was that nervous habit of Myra's. *Why was she doing that now?* It would drown out their words.

Natalie jumped at the sound of her own phone ringing. She pressed 'stop' and answered the phone as the answering machine was no longer pre-set.

"Dr. Lindsay speaking."

"Dr. Lindsay, I'm glad you're still there," the familiar voice said from the receiver. "It's Edward. Edward Hoffman...."

"Yes, Edward, hello. I recognized your voice," she was surprised as he was the last person she expected to hear from today.

"Can I speak to Myra?" he implored. His voice sounded urgent.

"I'm afraid she's gone," said Natalie and with trepidation added, "Someone has taken her."

"Who?"

Natalie suddenly found herself rambling about Ian, the locket, the Laudanum poisoning and the scar. She must have sounded like a complete idiot to Edward.

"Dr. Lindsay," Edward interrupted. "We'll find her. I have friends in the Bureau. They won't get too far. Certainly not across any border."

"I hope not," Natalie said, "But I have my doubts that they're actually heading to the Canadian border."

"I have to ask something..." Edward's voice sounded hesitant. "It may sound crazy, but... did you ever notice Myra tapping her finger in a sort of rhythmic pattern?"

"Funny you should ask," replied Natalie as she glanced back to her machine. "She's just left me a phone message with nothing but that tapping."

"Let me hear it!" exclaimed Edward.

"Hold on, let me rewind," she said, then held the phone receiver to the answering machine speaker.

. . .

Edward quickly grabbed the notepad next to the phone, clicked the pen and started to write... or tried to write. The damn pen didn't work. He snapped his fingers at Roger. "I need a pen!"

Roger reached into his coat pocket and tossed Edward his pen. It worked!

Through the phone receiver Edward now heard the tape rewind, then a man's voice saying something about snow, then the tapping started. Very loud and very clear.

As he listened, Edward started to translate what he heard. He didn't seem to notice that he was speaking along with the taps. "Di-di di-dah dah-dah di-dit dah-dit dah-di-dit di-dah dah-dit dah-dah-di dit di-dah-dit."

Roger stared at Edward as if he had lost his mind. Then he glanced down at the paper his friend was writing on and read: *I am in danger.*

CHAPTER 30

Myra awoke to find that her head hurt. Had she hit her head on the dashboard?

She heard a low guttural moan. She looked over and saw Ian slumped over the steering wheel, starting to regain consciousness. This was her chance! She opened the car door and started running into the cold wilderness.

She shielded her face from the blowing snow as she tried to get her bearings. She knew this area. She hadn't realized where they were until about a mile ago, when they went into a tunnel built through the familiar reddish-blackish dolerite of West Rock. If she was right, her family owned a lake house nearby. Nothing else looked familiar. Each snow-covered tree looked like the next. Her grandfather used to take her and her cousins on sleigh rides through the woods, and during the summer she would climb *The Three Judges* cave, sit up top and see for miles. If only she could spot that cave to get her bearings, but at the moment she could not see anything. The blizzard was getting worse.

BLAM

A gunshot echoed through the trees. She glanced back to see Ian charging towards her. She continued to run towards the trees.

BLAM

Bloody hell! She should have taken the gun while he was still unconscious!

As she ran, she glanced back to see Ian struggling in the snow. It just occurred to her that, without a coat, she should be freezing, but oddly enough, it didn't seem that cold to her. This in itself could be a bad sign.

BLAM

The bark on the tree next to her head exploded. *Too close!*

Myra continued to scurry through the snow. Something looked familiar. *This rock formation... wasn't there a pond here?*

CRACK!

She felt the ice crack beneath her feet. Yes indeed, she had found the pond.

Another shot!

For a brief moment Myra considered which way she would rather die: by giving up and getting shot, or by making the effort to get away and risk falling through the ice. Icy waters were nothing new to her. She took a deep breath and started across the river.

CRACK!

Instinctively she slowed down to walk across the ice even though she knew Ian was getting closer.

C-R-R-A-A-A-C-K-K!

This one was different. She looked back to see Ian had reached the pond and had started across. Myra shuffled her feet as she tried to quicken her pace.

"Stop!"

Ian's voice echoed over to her. She paused and cautiously looked back at him.

"Let's go back to the car," Ian called out. "And I promise I won't hurt you."

Myra studied him for a moment. Not wanting to take her eyes off of him she started walking backwards, away from him.

Ian tried to shield his face from the snowy wind as he raised his gun and aimed directly at her. Myra prepared herself to drop, hopefully before the bullet hit her. As his finger moved to pull the trigger, the ice beneath his feet caved in.

His screams caused Myra to stop. She saw him struggling to pull himself out of the freezing water. The more he panicked the worse it got. The ice continued to break off around him.

Myra turned and started to shuffle away. She stopped.

She could hear his screams on the wind. *Why should she help him? He was going to kill her. Would he show any mercy if the roles were reversed? No, he wouldn't.* She continued to walk away. Suddenly a series of awful vernaculars that she had seen painted on the New York walls entered her mind.

She found herself crawling on her stomach, distributing her weight across the fragile ice, as she inched her way towards Ian. Myra knew it was insane but could never live with herself if she allowed a man to die like this. He continued to flail. She called out to him, "Stay calm. I'll be right there."

He paused for a moment, surprised to see her.

"Give me your hand," she shouted.

The arm holding the gun reached out towards her. She grabbed his arm and tried to pull him up.

CRACK!

Myra could feel the ice weakening all around her. She pivoted to give Ian the proper leverage. He pulled himself out of the icy water and without any warning, pulled her headfirst towards the hole!

She found her head submerged under the icy water. She struggled to pull herself up but his grip and his weight held her face beneath the surface. She couldn't hold her breath any longer.

In that instant, Myra realized she was still gripping on to his gun hand. She frantically twisted his arm and pulled the trigger.

BLAM!

Ian slumped forward, his blood swirling crimson in the icy water. Myra used his body to pull herself out and allowed him to fall back under the ice. He thrashed weakly as he reached out for her.

"Help me... please..."

Myra, lying as flat as she could to spread out her weight, looked at him suspiciously for a moment. *Once burned...*

Then she noticed something she hadn't seen before. She reached out, grabbed his hand, and pulled him towards her. Then she grabbed hold of the locket hanging from his neck. "I believe this is mine."

She yanked hard on the gold Celtic chain, snapping it, and then released her grip on his hand. She backed away and watched him slip beneath the surface.

She collapsed on the icy pond's edge and stared at the locket in her hand. As the blizzard raged on around her, she closed her eyes in exhaustion. *Edward. I've failed.*

CHAPTER 31

Callum had always hated his grandparents' century-old home in the outskirts of Glasgow. As he pulled his rental car into the long driveway, it was like stepping back twenty years, when he was last here. As a child he always thought this old house was haunted. The old grey stones always appeared to be weeping, and the ivy on the brick always seemed like an ominous green spider web consuming the house. Now as the sun was setting, the shadows from the jagged roof and stonework seemed to be reaching for him as he walked towards the front porch.

Bloody hell, he thought. Even the hideous gargoyle with the metal ring in its mouth that used to give him nightmares, was the same. As his hand reached for the odious ring, the door suddenly opened, startling his inner child.

"What took you so long?" Lumina hissed as she stepped out to greet him.

"Nice to see you too," grumbled Callum. He hadn't seen much of his sister over the last ten years, and each time they met he remembered why. "I was in Edinburgh when you called."

"Well, that's only an hour away," she said in her patented icy tone.

"An hour and a half..." contradicted Callum. "And only if the traffic is good. I still had to rent a car to get here. Normally, I live in London... so expecting me in less time is ludicrous."

"Why did I bother calling you?"

"I don't know but now that I'm here, what's the big emergency? Did Paul finally get a job?"

"Don't start," snapped Lumina. "Just get in here... And take off your filthy boots."

Callum nodded and entered. His sister waited impatiently as he unlaced his boots and dislodged the mud from the park. Like the house, his sister hadn't changed much. The years had been kind to her; she still looked tip-top — only her hands seemed to show any signs of aging. He considered making an attempt to say something complimentary or civil. He opened his mouth and asked, "So what the hell was so bloody urgent?"

She stepped aside, and he saw. The wardrobe doors were open, clothes strewn about, books thrown about the room, drawers open and overturned, and knickknacks broken.

"It's the same upstairs," Lumina said, her voice shaking. "All my personal belongings have been rifled through..."

"Is everyone ok? Where are Paul and the kids?"

"Paul is fishing with his mates... don't even start... I called his Mum to get the kids."

Callum bit his tongue. He didn't think much of Paul. They had two kids together but he'd never asked to marry her. Maybe Callum was old-fashioned but he found that shady. Still, it was his sister's life and he had no right to judge her. He simply asked, "Was anything stolen?"

"No, that's what frightens me. Nothing seems to be missing. All the jewelry is there, the stereo has been opened but it's still there, the telly is there... even Gran's silver is untouched. It's as if whoever burgled us was looking for something specific."

A fearful thought crawled under Callum's scalp as he dashed into his Grandfather's old study. He stopped in the doorway and surveyed the damage. Everything in the room was completely scattered and upturned. Even stones from the fireplace were removed and lay broken on the floor.

Lumina appeared behind him, "It's worse in here."

"Because they started here," Callum said. "They didn't find what they were looking for so they went through the rest of the house."

Lumina picked up one of the broken pieces of stone, "My god, why vandalize a fireplace?"

"To see if there was a hidden compartment or door," replied Callum.

"Why? What are they looking for?"

"Information pertaining to the Agatha Gilcrest murder."

"Don't be daft!" snapped Lumina. "That happened so long ago. Why would anyone care about that case?"

"Well, one of the witnesses was killed the other night," replied Callum. "She died in my arms..."

"Did you bring this about?" shrieked Lumina. "I should have known! My world's turned upside down because my good-for-nothing brother is in town."

Callum didn't blame his sister for being upset and chose to ignore her comment as he continued, "Did Granda have any notes or anything at all in regards to that case or the execution of Otto Slade?"

"What? No!" said Lumina shaking her head. "Have you been away that long? Don't you remember how bitter he was about that ordeal? How Mum tried to get him to talk about it and he always used to say he'd take the truth…"

"… to his grave." Callum finished the sentence in unison with his sister. "I remember. But there was something more…"

They were interrupted by a knock at the door. Callum peeked out the window and saw the familiar white and orange police car. "It's the police."

"'Bout time," said Lumina.

"You called the police?"

"What else do you do when you've been burglarized?" asked Lumina as she turned to leave. "Besides, you hadn't arrived yet."

Callum quickly looked about the room before Glasgow's *Glaekits* destroyed any evidence. There was nothing of any value or interest to anyone other than his late grandfather; some personal letters, postcards, books, and a stamp collection. Callum frowned. He didn't know his grandfather had been a stamp collector. Callum had become one, over the course of his travels.

He sighed. There was nothing official or law enforcement-related. He was surprised his sister kept all this stuff. He supposed she needed to keep something of the past. The rest of the house's décor had been updated and lived in, but this room was a shrine to her granda. She was always his favourite. Callum knew it as a child and always resented her for it. One of the reasons he never went to the funeral.

"Seems everywhere you go there's destruction in your wake," a familiar, nasal voice said behind him. Callum turned to see DCI de Kirkhaugh standing in the doorway.

"What the hell are you doing here?"

"A call came in about a burglary. Naturally I thought of you," replied de Kirkhaugh. "Then surprise, it's the old Toughill home. What are the odds?"

"Bit out of your jurisdiction, ain't it?"

"No, South Lanarkshire is part of the Strathclyde Police territory. As is Dunbartonshire."

"That's jolly."

"There is a Miss Loraine Kramer who has been reported as missing. Hasn't been seen in three days. Not since you paid a call to her. Any idea where she is?"

"No… How do you know all this?"

"We found your business card at her flat and an appointment written on her wall calendar," replied de Kirkhaugh.

"You think if I orchestrated some foul play I'd leave my card?"

"You'd be surprised what I've found left by killers before. Detective Sergeant Milton is investigating it further. You remember him."

How could Callum forget the husky gorilla-type officer? He sighed and replied, "When I left her she was busy watching her soaps."

"Like I said, you leave disaster in your wake."

"You two know each other?" asked Lumina as she led a uniformed constable into the study.

"Unfortunately," both men replied.

"Where were you when this happened?" de Kirkhaugh asked Callum.

"My brother would have nothing to do with this!"

"I'm just following procedure," de Kirkhaugh replied. "I have to rule out all possibilities."

"I was in Edinburgh at the time. I have a car rental receipt if you'd like."

"Yes, I would," said de Kirkhaugh.

"Where were *you* when this happened?" Callum asked de Kirkhaugh.

"Callum!" exclaimed his sister, in shock of his insolence.

"I have to rule out all possibilities," replied Callum. "Besides, I'm sure Granda is turning in his grave at the presence of the Glasgow police in his home."

De Kirkhaugh ignored Callum as he turned to Lumina. "Was there anything missing?"

"No, and I haven't been able to figure out how anyone got in here."

"Miss Toughill, would you be able to take the Constable here on a 'walkabout' of the entire property?"

"Certainly."

De Kirkhaugh then turned to the Constable and said, "See if you can ascertain how someone got in here if they didn't have a key. Check all windows, boarded up coal chutes, anything you can find."

The constable seemed pleased with the charge, "Yes sir."

The moment after everyone else had gone out the front door, Callum said, "They're not going to find anything."

"I already know how they got in," de Kirkhaugh replied. "Through the front door. There are fresh scratches from a lockpick. The lock is over fifty years old. She should have them updated."

Callum was a bit embarrassed about the fact that he'd been so fixated with the doorknocker that he'd never looked at the lock. But then he wasn't aware of the burglary until he was already inside. He turned to see de Kirkhaugh peering out the window. Callum began, "So... you never answered — where were you when that lock was picked?"

"At the Lord Advocate's office, seeing if I could get a file from a 70-year-old murder case unsealed," whispered de Kirkhaugh as he began to examine the fallen stones, purposefully making a noise as he spoke.

"Unsealed?"

"By the Lord Advocate at the time... and King Edward..." continued de Kirkhaugh.

"Are you mad?" Callum saw from de Kirkhaugh's expression that he was serious, then tried to look nonchalant. "Why would… never mind. Were you able to get them unsealed?"

"No…" de Kirkhaugh replied as he turned his attention to some papers, which he shuffled noisily.

Callum turned slowly toward him, "What were you doing trying to look into it?"

"You tasked me," answered de Kirkhaugh. "Mostly, I was intending to prove you wrong… and…"

"And what?"

"And now I'm being watched," said de Kirkhaugh. "I know I sound paranoid."

"Yeah… so am I..," added Callum cautiously. He was still uncertain that he could trust de Kirkhaugh. But if he was a part of it, he would already know this. "I was followed at the Scottish Records Hall today."

"Humph. Well, we've caught someone's attention…"

"Who?"

"Don't ask me! You're the one who's been investigating for days now. Don't you have any leads?"

"No," Callum replied solemnly. "All my leads are dead ends."

"To find out who," de Kirkhaugh looked at him earnestly, "you have to answer why? What was the motive?"

"Wish I knew."

"In most of the cases I've investigated," continued de Kirkhaugh, "the motive for murder is either passion or money."

"I don't think it was money," Callum replied. "From her vast collection of jewels, only one brooch was stolen. Some, which were worth far more, were left behind. The killer could have taken more in his pockets."

"There must have been something special about that brooch," de Kirkhaugh said thoughtfully.

"Her face was smashed in…" Callum added.

"What?"

Callum knew he was taking a risk confiding in de Kirkhaugh. But he could no longer think of a possible lead. He needed help now and de Kirkhaugh was very astute. He paused for a moment then continued, "Her face was smashed in…the fatal blows were caused by repeated strikes to the face with a blunt instrument."

Callum watched de Kirkhaugh process the information and the reaction was sincere. He hadn't known this information.

"That's more personal," de Kirkhaugh said, echoing Callum's initial summation. "I would say that's the reaction of a jilted lover."

"But she was an 80 year old spinster …"

"So... hardly..." de Kirkhaugh started pacing. "Did she have family? That's usually the next question I would ask..."

"No family," interrupted Callum. "She was an only child. Inherited her fortune from her father..."

Callum paused as he tried to remember something Ruthie had told him. Callum took his notebook from his pocket and began to flip back.

"What? What is it?" de Kirkhaugh asked nervously.

Found it! He read it aloud to de Kirkhaugh, "'Miss Gilcrest had no children of her own, which I guess is why she spoiled Miss Fergraith's children with presents. Treated them as if they were her own grandchildren. Did you ever hear of such a thing? A former employer. That's how sweet of a lady she was.'"

"Who's Miss Fergraith?" asked de Kirkhaugh.

"A former servant of hers," replied Callum.

"That's unusual."

"I don't believe she had done as much with any other former servant," Callum added.

"Is there anyone from that family still alive?" de Kirkhaugh pondered aloud.

CHAPTER 32

With a furrowed brow, Edward added another log to the well-used fireplace and pulled the protective metal screen shut. He turned to see the young woman who called herself Myra asleep on the couch in the main room of the lake house. She seemed so peaceful, under the circumstances.

He and Roger Zisholm had braved the harsh weather to find her. Through white-out conditions, he had tracked her down based on the encoded message left on Natalie's answering machine, and they had the license plate number from the parking permit at the clinic. The message had ended with 'West Rock Ri-', bringing the two men to West Rock State Park, where they found Ian Kybartis' yellow sports car.

Edward had followed the partially-covered footprints in the snow —it was obvious she had been running and Kybartis had given chase. With every step, he cursed his cane as it impeded his speed. The trail led them down to the pond's edge where the struggle had taken place. There they had found Myra unconscious in the snow: wet, freezing and clutching a gold locket.

Then they found Ian, dead, gun still in his hand, his eerie, bloated face staring blankly from under the slab of ice through which he had fallen. Though the chill of the cold night was slowly leaving Edward's old bones in the warmth of the fire, that ghastly image was something he'd never shake.

Edward's thoughts were interrupted by Myra's breathing becoming more erratic. Suddenly her eyes flew open. She let out a gasp and struggled to breathe.

"He tried to kill me…" she gasped, "I had to…"

Edward sat down next to her. He gently placed his wrinkled old hand atop her youthful ones and in a soothing voice said, "Shhh. It's alright. We found his… corpse floating in the water. One doesn't have to be Columbo to figure out it was self-defense."

"Who's Columbo?" she asked with a confused look on her face.

"Oh… he's like Sherlock Holmes. Well come to think of it, he's nothing like Sherlock Holmes, but a popular fictional detective nevertheless. The police had come to the same conclusion. My attorney has already filled out the preliminary reports. I persuaded him to go back and ensure our names are kept out of the press. The police will need to take a statement from you when you're up to it — they'll send someone here."

Myra nodded and sighed with great relief, "You found me."

"The directions you left with Natalie were excellent," smiled Edward. "It was a stroke of brilliance to leave a message by Morse Code."

"More like a gamble," she said with a shy smile, "I wasn't certain you would ever hear it. And even so, I didn't know if you would remember or even continued to learn it. You made up your own taps before you could talk."

"Truth be known I didn't remember that… until yesterday," Edward remarked. Then it occurred to him why his instructors were so impressed with his aptitude, as he recalled aloud: "I had received extensive Morse Code training during the Second World War."

"World War?" asked Myra.

He stopped, looked at her and said casually, "So much of the world has changed since 1912 and not for the better, I'm afraid."

Myra was visibly taken aback and looked at him for a moment, then smiled, "You no longer believe I'm a charlatan?"

Edward let out an exasperated sigh, "I'm not sure what I believe…"

He got up and walked over to the table as he continued to speak, "But something very strange has happened and I can't simply dismiss it."

He returned holding the locket that they had found clutched in her hand. He opened it and looked inside and pointed, "I recognize myself as a babe. I know that's my father in his youth, and that is you next to him."

He glanced back up at the painting he had been working on earlier, then back at her as he handed her the locket.

"You were so adorable in that outfit…" started Myra, then she noticed what Edward was looking at and exclaimed, "Oh my! That's me! Or, my eyes at the very least."

Edward turned to study her features again. It was undeniable. The same vibrant blue eyes he had painted so often. Myra's eyes then darted about the room looking at the other paintings he had made, all with the same theme.

"It's yet another reason why I can't dismiss you," sighed Edward, as he got up and walked over to the nearest one. "Some of these I painted decades ago…"

"I don't understand."

"I was seriously wounded during the war," began Edward, his voice began to shake as he allowed his mind to revisit that time. "At one point, I was delirious with a high fever, and then I saw those eyes in my dreams. They brought me comfort. Weeks later, when I recovered, I thought it had been a nurse tending to my wounds, but there was no nurse there who had those eyes. Over the decades those eyes... your eyes have stayed with me."

He had not noticed her get up and stride over to him while he spoke until she was suddenly there, gingerly wiping the tears from his eyes. Edward turned away, embarrassed. "Listen to me. I sound like a foolish old man. I'll make some tea."

As he hurried over to the kitchen, Myra wandered the main room. "That window wasn't so large before."

"No. They're patio doors. They allow for a lovely view of the lake in the summer. Not that you can see it now — there must be over two feet of snow out there. I've never seen a blizzard like this in April. On the radio they are calling this 'The Great Blizzard of '82'"

"The kitchen has moved. It was smaller and over on that side before."

Edward glanced up through the pass-thru window to see where she was pointing, "That's right. I had some renovations done many, many years ago."

"For me it feels like it was only a few months ago when we came up to visit Grand Papa. There used to be strong smell of his pipe here."

"Oh yes, I remember that! I had forgotten. Yes, it took me forever to get rid of that smell." He stopped and stared at Myra, "What's happening here?"

"I don't understand. Last thing I remember is looking for you on the ship," she paused for a moment as her eyes fell on the scale model of the infamous *Titanic* under glass. She suddenly shivered and began to rub her arms for warmth as she continued:

"I remember being dizzy, unable to walk very well... The ship was tilting. Teacart rolled by, the cups shattered. Cold water started pouring in from under the door... I saw your teddy bear... Mr. Fluffy..."

Edward smiled at the memory. He had forgotten it, until this moment. The image of a careworn teddy bear with mismatched eyes flashed through his mind.

Myra continued to speak, her voice cold and distant. "Mr. Fluffy floated out from under the red chaise... but I couldn't find you. My dress felt so heavy as I tried to get to the door to the hallway... It wouldn't open... it was locked... why was it locked? I had a key... I couldn't find it...Then I remembered I had set it on the book I was reading before bed... I grabbed Mr. Fluffy as it floated by... and found that book, but where was my key? I grabbed the book... then... "

Edward was drawn to her melodic voice, he found himself walking to her as she continued. "Then I awoke to a world that has completely passed me by. You've had a life that I was never a part of. You're the same age as my Grand Papa, but when I look into your eyes…"

She turned and looked into his eyes, his soul, with those soft blue eyes that he had searched for all these years. Myra softly continued, "When I look into your eyes… I can still see my little boy looking back at me."

Edward finally broke down into tears; his young mother took him in her arms to comfort him, tapping soothingly on his shoulder.

CHAPTER 33

Captain Sadler was making his way towards the ladder to his quarters, exhausted from the tense situation in the Falkland Islands. He tried to turn his mind to restful thoughts, but it kept going back to the conflict.

Today, U.S. Secretary of State Alexander Haig, on behalf of the Americans, tried to mediate in peace treaty negotiations, but Margaret Thatcher, the British Prime Minister, had demanded that Argentina withdraw its troops as a pre-condition for negotiations. Sadler had once met Argentina's new Naval Commander-in-Chief, Admiral Jorge Anaya, when he was Argentina's Naval Attaché in England, and had recognized the malevolence behind the Latin smile. Anaya had had a very colourful career fraught with previous military coups and would not be easily intimidated. As expected, he was as protective and dangerous as a scrap-yard dog. It came as no surprise to Sadler that Argentina refused Britain's demands and the negotiations fell apart.

Apparently, Haig was embarrassed by the whole mess and reports were circulating around that the Americans planned to boycott the Argentines and throw military support behind the British. Sadler knew that the British Empire would welcome the American support but it would only fuel the Argentines' fire.

The British Fleet was now ordered to regroup near Ascension Island. Sadler wagered this would now be their new base of operations. *This war isn't going to end any time soon,* he groaned to himself. His back ached. His feet felt like anchors, and he was looking forward to unlacing his boots and lying down for a few minutes of sleep.

He had almost reached his quarters when Lt. JG Westbourne intercepted him, "Captain, there is a shore-to-ship call for you."

The captain sighed as he turned towards the young officer, "Is it official?"

"No sir. Not exactly."

"Well it can wait, then…"

"But, sir…"

"No 'buts'… we're at war, son, and unofficial calls can wait 'til tomorrow," said the Captain as he started to walk away.

"Sir, you asked to be notified if anyone inquired about…" the officer paused to take a cautious look around before continuing, "…the old teddy bear."

The Captain stopped in mid step, turned sharply, and walked back to him. In a hushed tone he started, "Are you saying this shore-to-ship call, in the middle of a war, is inquiring about a *bloody teddy bear* we recovered last week from the North Atlantic?"

By the end of his tirade, Sadler's voice echoed along the metal passageways. Westbourne stammered, "Yes, sir."

Tired though he was, Sadler's mind slowly mulled over the ludicrousness of the situation. *Why?* Normally he would dismiss it, but he had a nagging feeling that there had to be something special about it. And Sadler always loved a good mystery.

"Sir?" asked Westbourne, who couldn't tell if the captain was annoyed or not.

Captain Sadler took a deep breath and straightened. Suddenly he no longer felt fatigue as he was once again drawn back into this mystery. With a new excitement in his eyes, he motioned to the young officer to lead on, and they both turned back toward the Bridge.

CHAPTER 34

All was quiet except the whistling wind. Edward limped into the main room, balancing a tray with a gorgeous old silver art nouveau tea set on it. He carefully set it down on the coffee table as Myra sat on the plushy upholstered couch, flipping through one of his many books about the *Titanic*.

"The iceberg struck the ship at 11:40pm on the night of April 14, and by 2:20 in the morning it was gone?" Myra exclaimed aloud. Her finger trembled as she traced the words, "Out of the 2,223 people aboard *Titanic* only 706 survived. A total of 1,517 perished."

"Two-thirds of the ship died." Edward said solemnly.

"I was supposed to be one of them," Myra said coldly. She snapped the book closed and looked up at Edward standing over her with a cup of tea. She sheepishly smiled at him, "Feeling any better?"

"Yes, I'm sorry. It's rather embarrassing."

"There's nothing embarrassing about crying on your mother's shoulder."

"You must admit that this is surreal. All my life there was this other woman who I always called 'mother' yet somehow... I think I knew different..."

"How so?" Myra asked.

"I don't know how to explain it. We were never close... at all. She was never affectionate... not towards me. I never knew why. Growing up I despised her, which became the subject of numerous arguments with Father."

"And she called herself Myra?"

"Well... yes," Edward replied. "Though in hindsight I think they purposely severed all social ties in New York and London with anyone who might have known you."

Myra nodded, as she seemed to try to comprehend how her life had been taken away from her. Then she looked at him with a troubled expression, "I can understand how you were misled. You were only two years old at the time. But how could she have fooled Archie? Surely, he would have known she was an imposter."

Edward set down his cup as he replied, "I can only suspect that he knew and covered it up."

"Oh no!" she exclaimed. "Not my Archie. He was such a sweet, loving man."

"Doesn't sound like the man I know," replied Edward.

"Eddie! He's your father!" Myra said in a stern voice.

"Precisely," replied Edward. "I don't know how sweet he was in 1909, but I can assure you that the man I argue with every time we talk is not sweet."

"Do you think it's possible that he's an impostor too?" Myra asked.

"So I was taken and raised by two strangers claiming to be my parents? Seems highly improbable."

"Yet, we can accept that I somehow traveled 70 years into the future?" asked Myra with a smile.

"I guess, if you put it that way... anything is possible." Edward chuckled.

"What other explanation could there be?"

"Well, he might simply just be a bastard," said Edward with a cocked eyebrow as he took a sip of his tea.

"Eddie, watch your language," Myra said with mock sternness. She shook her head, then paused as something occurred to her. "Does he know about me? Here and now?"

"Good Lord, no! It's not the sort of thing you tell someone by phone."

"Where is he now?"

"He returned to England two days ago to prepare for all the pomp and circumstance associated with the launch of the RMS *Titan*, a new ship he likes to call *Titanic II*. As a British ship, we feared that it would be called to the war in Argentina the way the largest luxury liner on the planet, the RMS *Queen Elizabeth 2* was now. Father has managed to secure *Titan's* safety for her maiden voyage, upon which Her Royal Majesty, Queen Elizabeth II will be traveling to New York."

"Queen Elizabeth? What happened to King George V? Oh, never mind... I have a lot of lost history to learn... A Queen. How exciting to have the monarchy aboard. However did you manage it?"

"It wasn't too difficult. She was already planning on coming to America on her way to Canada to sign their Constitution next week. We offered an exciting and highly secure means to travel."

"I've never met royalty before," lamented Myra.

"I could arrange it," Edward smiled. He wanted her to experience the life that had been robbed of her. "The *Titan* departs from South Hampton on the tenth of April."

"April tenth was the launch date of *Titanic*," she said, rising and putting down the book as if she no longer wanted to give it any further warmth.

"It's now a publicity stunt," sighed Edward. "Even charging extra for the maiden voyage."

"I would like to meet the Queen," Myra said as she went to the window and watched the cold flakes tossing about in the wind. "But moreover I would very much like to see Archie... I need to see him."

"Well, we're not going anywhere until the roads clear," Edward said, looking out at the continuing blizzard. "But I'll make the travel arrangements to take us to England."

Myra looked out the window and paced about, "If tomorrow is the seventh of April, we'll never get to England by the tenth. Unless ships are faster now."

"Certainly we will," smiled Edward. "We'll take my private jet. It'll get us there in eight hours."

"What is a jet?"

"That's right you wouldn't know," Edward laughed. "You're in for a treat."

It warmed Myra's heart to see him smiling. "I wish I could have seen how you grew into this fine man."

She stopped as she saw a framed photo of Edward as a young man, smiling, with a beautiful, young, red-haired woman showing off a diamond ring.

"Was this you?" She turned and looked at Edward, who nodded with embarrassment. "You look so young... and happy. Who's that lovely lady with you?"

"That was Dolanna. Dolanna Fergraith. We were engaged... but it wasn't to be."

"Why not? You looked so happy together," pouted Myra. "What happened?"

"I'll never know for certain, but I suspect Father had something to do with it."

"What?" Myra was aghast. "I can't believe that. I can't believe he's the monster you keep making him out to be."

"That's the problem," Edward lamented. "No one else did either, not without proof. And I have none. But in my heart of hearts, I've long suspected that he blackmailed her to leave me."

"But why? Why would he sacrifice your happiness? It doesn't make sense."

Edward looked at her as he spoke, "I had resigned from Arachson International, Father's company. Dolanna and I were to be married here in New York at the Waldorf and then I planned to move to Europe with her. Father was furious because he expected me to take over the company. He was deathly afraid of shareholders. He wanted to keep the business in the family."

"Obviously that's not what you wanted?"

"No, I wanted to become a psychiatrist. I wanted to help people, and perhaps try my hand at being a painter. Live in Paris. But Father wouldn't hear of it."

"I wish I could have been there for you, Eddie."

"No matter now. Old water under the bridge," Edward said with resignation. He walked over to her and together they watched the blustery snow in silence.

April 7, 1982

CHAPTER 35

66 Kelvindale Lane.

Callum looked at the address that de Kirkhaugh had given him this morning. He had been reluctant to help Callum, which was understandable. There was procedure and protocol that a police officer had to abide by, and this was the best he'd been able to do without jeopardizing his position.

Kelvindale Lane was located a few streets from where Agatha Gilcrest and Ruthie McArthur had been murdered. It was odd that Callum would keep coming back here. At the turn of the century, the area was known as "Square Mile of Murder" because all of Glasgow's most sensational killings had occurred within a few blocks of each other between 1857 and 1909. Callum hoped history wasn't repeating itself.

Callum walked up to the townhouse's front steps and pressed the door bell button. He paused. He had the same sensation of being watched as he did in the Records Office. Turning away from the door, he looked about. Across the narrow street was another row of townhouses. Small cars parked on the street. Callum craned his neck to see if there was anyone sitting in them.

He heard the front door open behind him. Callum turned back to the front door and froze.

"May I help you?" asked the elderly lady. Callum was speechless. He knew he shouldn't stare but her face was so strikingly familiar that everything he had practiced to say had vanished from his mind.

"Miss Fergraith?" stammered Callum as he regained his faculties. She nodded as he fumbled with his wallet, and pulled out his card. "My name is Callum Toughill…"

"Yes, the investigator who called this morning... come in..." Miss Fergraith said as she held the door open for him. "You have my curiosity piqued."

"Thank you, Miss Fergraith ..."

"Call me Dolanna."

"Thank you, Dolanna," Callum said as he took one last look to the streets. Nothing. He was getting paranoid.

As they walked to the living room, he noticed the décor was quite stylish and fairly modern, including a nice stereo system, telly, and video recorder. It wasn't filled with antiques as he had seen at Ruthie's or in the homes of most other people of that advancing age.

"Can I offer you a tea or coffee?" she asked as she straightened the magazines and pile of newspapers on the coffee table.

"Coffee please," Callum replied, he needed the caffeine. Or a way of getting it intravenously at this point. Someone really needed to figure out how to hold a drink on a car's dashboard.

"Make yourself comfortable," Dolanna said, pointing to the chairs. "I'll be right back."

As she started toward the kitchen, Callum looked about, and a framed photo on the nearby bookshelf caught his eye.

"Is that Edward Hoffman?" he asked, pointing to the young man in the photo.

She stopped by the kitchen door and looked over at it and sheepishly smiled. "Yes, that was taken many years ago. We were both very young."

"Is that you?" Callum asked as he studied the photo.

"Is it so hard to believe?" she asked, posing by the kitchen door. He turned to her. Though her hair was white, he could see hints of pale red scattered within.

"Not at all," he said. Then looked back at the photo. "It looks like an engagement photo."

"It was..." she said, walking slowly back toward it.

"But Mr. Hoffman never married," Callum added.

"I broke it off... for personal reasons," Dolanna stammered, her bottom lip quivering as she sat in the nearest chair.

Callum nodded. He took that last statement to mean she wasn't going to give him a reason. But he still blurted, "I can't help but notice you still wear the engagement ring on a chain around your neck."

He regretted saying it the moment it left his lips. Her hand touched the ring as if realizing for the first time that it was there.

"Sorry," Callum added quickly. "That's not what I came to discuss... So, Margaret Fergraith was your grandmother?"

The smile returned to her face, "No, she was my mother."

"I didn't think you were that old," he said as he took out his notebook and pen.

"Thank you, Mr. Toughill."

"Callum."

"Thank you, Callum," Dolanna continued. "Yes, Margaret was my mother."

"And she worked for Agatha Gilcrest," Callum stated as he made notes.

"Yes, that's right! What is this all about?"

"Did you ever meet Miss Gilcrest?" asked Callum, looking up from his notebook.

"Oh no, she… died a few years before I was born," Dolanna replied. "My older brothers had met her when they were little… and Mum would light a candle every 21st of December, the anniversary of her death. Every year for the rest of her life…. It used to dampen the Christmas spirit, I must say…"

Callum smiled as he wrote her comments. Normally he would find this annual memorial unusual for a servant to perform for her former employer, but a clearer picture was starting to form in Callum's mind.

"Oh, good gracious," Dolanna said as she rose. "I forgot to make the coffee. Wait here."

"Thank you, that would be wonderful," Callum said as he made some extra notes.

"You're in luck," Dolanna said as she started toward the kitchen. "The gasman was just here fixing the stove."

"Oh?" Callum said absent-mindedly.

"I didn't even know there was anything wrong with it!"

Panic then suddenly overtook Callum, "STOP!"

. . .

"I'm not asking for the sealed file," de Kirkhaugh whispered to Janna, the records clerk. She looked extremely nervous. It didn't help that he had chosen not to use the phone and had advised her to avoid doing so as well. "I'm just looking for any records that we have from that same year, specifically any unsolved crimes in Glasgow."

"From 1909?" she asked nervously.

"Precisely."

"What if they're sealed as well?"

"Just let me know…" de Kirkhaugh was distracted by a sudden swell of voices from upstairs. "Page me when you've found something."

De Kirkhaugh dashed up the stairs to the ground floor as some constables were scrambling out the door. He saw his husky colleague, Detective Sergeant Milton, putting on a coat that would have been more like a tent on most men.

"Milton? What the devil is going on?"

"Explosion, sir! Just came on the two-way!" Milton yelled.

"What?!" De Kirkhaugh exclaimed as he felt his breathing pause in anticipation. He dreaded asking the next question for fear of what the answer would be, "Where was the explosion?"

"Kelvindale Lane!"

CHAPTER 36

Natalie had hardly slept. She had been on pins and needles since the cryptic message from Myra yesterday. Edward had been able to decipher the taps and had hung up without giving her any details. She had left a message with the clinic to page her if he called her back.

When his call finally came in, Natalie had interrupted another session to take it, prattling off a dozen questions before Edward could even say 'hello'.

"Myra is fine. She's safe and sound. A far cry better than Mr. Kybartis I dare say."

"Where is he?" Natalie asked.

"He's dead," Edward said nonchalantly.

"What? How?"

"I won't bore you with the gory details. The police were here getting a statement this morning. They've ruled it as self-defense."

"My god," exclaimed Natalie. "Can I speak with her?"

"She's fallen asleep. The poor dear was half-frozen when we found her in the snow."

"Does she require medical attention?" Natalie asked.

"She'll be fine," Edward replied, then asked, "Could you fax me that information about Myra's Laudanum poisoning you were telling me about?"

"Yes, of course. Mr. Hoffman…," Natalie tried to sound professional again. "I would like Myra to return here for further examination. We still need to get to the bottom of who she really is, and why she's manifesting this delusional behavior."

"Yes… of course… but can it wait for a few days?" Edward asked. Even through the phone receiver, Natalie could hear the reluctance in his voice.

"I think the longer we put it off, the harder it will be to break down the mental barriers," she added.

"Of course," he replied after a moment. "I'll leave it up to Myra to decide when we return from England."

"England?"

"Yes, I think the key to solving this mystery lies there. If I'm wrong, we shall be back by April 15th and we'll connect again."

"But..."

"I'll talk to you then. Thank you for everything, Doctor. Bye."

Before Natalie could interject the line went dead. *Bye?* Perhaps she was overreacting but his voice sounded so final when he said that. She sat looking at the phone for a moment, wishing she had his phone number to call him back. England? Was there something in Myra's past there? She couldn't even hazard a guess as to what they could find. Natalie had the disturbing feeling that Edward wasn't being upfront with her.

Did he somehow believe the Titanic tale? Natalie wondered. It would seem unlikely that a man of his experience and intellect would become swept up in this preposterous fantasy. Perhaps there was some sort of codependent disorder at play. Was he somehow in need of a surrogate mother? It defied logic, yet Natalie was at a loss for any other explanation.

— — —

After hanging up the phone, Edward turned to see Myra still asleep on the large plush sofa, surrounded by encyclopedias. She had 70 years of history to catch up on, and more advancement had happened in this century than in the past thousand years.

He found it touching to see her reaction to the fact that a woman was the Prime Minister of the United Kingdom. When *Titanic* set sail in 1912, women were still not allowed to vote, and in spite of their academic achievements, were denied their PhD's because of their gender. Now she marveled that there were female psychiatrists, and other such professionals. She had seemed so pleased that he'd chosen not to dwell on the darker chapters of the 20th Century. Even with all the advancement in technology, this century had also seen the most violent and destructive side of humanity.

Edward's thoughts were interrupted as Myra groaned in her sleep. Gently grasping her hand, he was alarmed to feel how icy she still was. He had given her three blankets but she still had trouble warming up.

He limped over to the fireplace, added another log and stoked it, waiting for it to catch. Then he stood up and watched her as she slept. He couldn't stop looking at her. She was his mother. Her voice was the one he used to dream of as a child. The warm loving look in her eyes was what he had been longing for. He could feel in his heart that she was who she said she was. Yet, his mind had trouble grasping it. How was it even possible?

If she truly was his mother, who was the woman who claimed to be Myra all these years? *Why would someone take on an identity that wasn't theirs?*

Or, more logically, was he just wishing this young woman here was his mother because the one who had been in his life had always been cold and distant?

He had the sudden urge to call up the old woman in England whom he had always called 'Mother' to set the record straight. He marched over to the kitchen doorway and picked up the phone receiver and started to dial.

Then he hung up.

What was he going to say, *'Hello Mother, who are you really? What's your real name?'* No matter what scenario played through his mind, he would sound mentally unstable.

He looked back at Myra, asleep. Perhaps it would be better to see what the reaction would be if the two met face to face. Edward hoped the truth would reveal itself. He slipped his hand into his pocket and pulled out Myra's necklace. He opened the locket, looked at the photo of himself in the sailor suit, and smiled. He had a vague recollection of wearing that outfit long after it had gotten too small. Then, Edward studied the other sepia photo. It was unmistakably his father. He remembered when his father had still looked that way, and there was no denying the woman with him was the young woman asleep on his couch. *How?*

Edward turned the locket over and saw the engraving:

To Myra,
Happy Anniversary!
Archie
December 31.

Edward read the date again. It read 'December 31'. This made no sense. All his life, his parents celebrated their wedding anniversary on April 14… the same date that Titanic struck the iceberg.

He looked at his watch and calculated in his mind. The United Kingdom hasn't started Daylight savings time yet, so their clocks would be six hours ahead. It was still business hours there.

He picked up the phone and dialed '0'. Hopefully he could find some answers.

CHAPTER 37

Damn me for finding this address for Toughill! What have I gotten myself into, wondered de Kirkhaugh as he saw black smoke billowing from what was left of 66 Kelvindale Lane. Fire lorries and police cars surrounded the charred remains of the townhouse. Like vultures amassing around the carcass, the camera crews were already on the scene, vying to get the most spectacular and sought-after shot that would be played repeatedly on the news. The media and their thirst for sensationalism had been a bone of contention for most of de Kirkhaugh's career as a detective. As a reporter once said to him, *'Blood and Fire sells.'*

"Was this the work of radicals, or the Argentines retaliating?" a reporter screamed as they shoved a microphone into his face.

"It's too early to comment one way or the other before the investigation is complete," de Kirkhaugh said, and before they could ask another stupid question, he marched toward the charred townhouse.

The Fire & Rescue Brigade had doused the flames and the Fire Marshall was already inspecting the area. De Kirkhaugh and Detective Sergeant Milton showed their warrant IDs as they passed the yellow barrier tape.

"Was there anyone in there?" de Kirkhaugh asked one of the paramedics.

"No-one yet, but they haven't finished sifting through all the debris."

De Kirkhaugh turned to Detective Sergeant Milton, "If there were any witnesses, get whatever statements you can from them."

Milton nodded, then crossed to the crowd of onlookers as de Kirkhaugh continued into the house. He knew that Milton's intimidating build was an asset for encouraging people to tell the truth.

Strathclyde firemen were tossing smoldering cushions and anything else that could still re-ignite through the windows and onto the street. De

Kirkhaugh heard a crack under his foot, and looked down to see a broken picture frame. The photo had water damage from the fire brigade but the face within it was still recognizable. The unmistakable features of Edward Hoffman. De Kirkhaugh had seen his picture in the paper recently regarding a second *Titanic* or something like that. This photo was obviously taken long ago, as his hair was still dark, but the face was the same. De Kirkhaugh made a mental note.

Using a flashlight, the Fire Marshall traced the source of the fire. He was hovering around the gas stove.

"What do you think, Allan?" de Kirkhaugh asked as he approached.

The Fire Marshall turned and smiled, "*Awrite*, Don! What brings you here?"

"Seeing if this is connected to a case I'm working on," de Kirkhaugh lied.

"The fire originated here. No sign of accelerant. Old gas stove, no pilot or electric switch, so it still uses matches to light. My preliminary guess: simple gas leak."

"Was there anyone inside when it happened?"

"Not so far as we know," Allan replied, as he positioned himself in front of the stove. "They would have been standing here to light it. If the gas had been left on for whatever reason, or leaking, a simple spark could have caused the explosion. They would have been thrown against this opposite wall."

De Kirkhaugh looked over to where the Fire Marshall was pointing. Then he noticed the hallway next to the wall. He walked over to it.

The Fire Marshall, upon seeing him standing in the rear hall added, "The angle is off. Nobody would have been thrown that way."

De Kirkhaugh wasn't listening as he rounded the corner and saw the back door. He pushed it open to see it lead to the backyard. He had hoped to find Callum or the old lady but there was no way either of them would have reached this far if the gas explod…

He paused as something reflected the light into his eyes. Taking out his pen, he knelt down and pushed a 9mm casing that was resting near the doorframe. Callum Toughill's gun was a Walther P38 – a 9mm pistol. He turned and looked back toward the kitchen. He could still see a part of the stove, but the Fire Marshall was right. If it had been ignited by a match, they wouldn't have been thrown in this direction.

De Kirkhaugh raised his arm as if he was holding a gun and aimed toward the stove. A bullet could have started a spark. The explosion would have still thrown Callum backwards into the garden. Following the laws of physics, de Kirkhaugh calculated the direction he would have landed. *Grass. Soft landing. Smart.*

He looked about to see if there were any places he would likely be hiding. There were a few trees, and a fenced area where a garden would be started in a few weeks. De Kirkhaugh saw a run-down wooden structure with rusty-hinged door. *A tool shed?*

He walked up carefully. Callum might not be able to see and was likely undisciplined enough to have that 'shoot first and ask questions later' mentality. Crouching down to one side of the door, he reached out and pulled it open. He cringed, expecting a shot. Nothing.

He peered around the corner. His heart sank.

It was not just a tool shed but also a carpark. Another large set of double doors leading to the back laneway was open. De Kirkhaugh looked down and saw the fresh tire marks in the mud.

It was clear that Callum had escaped with the old woman. He was certain that the Fire Marshall would eventually find the 9mm slug, but for now, whoever had been following Callum might think he was dead.

CHAPTER 38

André Bossard, the Secretary General of Interpol, sat in his office comparing drafts. This latest version of the 'Headquarter Agreement' with the French Government had already been updated by his secretary but he had to double-check it against the mark-up before sending it back. His eyes were getting tired from staring at the pages. He realized he had read the same passage three times and he still wasn't sure he had compared it properly. The daunting task was mind-numbingly boring. He wanted to leave.

He looked at his wristwatch and frowned. There was no sense leaving work now—the traffic from Saint-Cloud, where the Interpol's head office was located, to downtown Paris would already be too thick. He would be sitting in his automobile for hours. Might as well stay and get some more work done. The sooner Interpol and the French Government could come to an agreement on jurisdiction the better.

A knock on the door jolted him in his chair. Although he was glad to have a break from the tediousness of the task at hand, he still managed to insert a level of impatience into his voice as he barked, *"Oui! Entrez!"*

A young clerk holding a piece of paper entered the room. From the way the page curled, André recognized it as thermal fax paper and surmised that it was important. He held his hand out and the clerk walked across the room to his desk to hand it to him.

As André suspected it was marked: *'confidentiel'*. André started to read the page. He stopped and re-read. He couldn't believe what he was reading.

"Quand est-ce que ceci s'est passé?" asked André. *When did this happen?*

"Aujourd'hui. Ce matin," responded the clerk.

André stroked his moustache as he contemplated his next move. He noticed the clerk still standing waiting for instructions, and hastily waved the man away as he reached for his Rolodex. He spun the dial until he found the index card with the United Kingdom's branch number on it. They needed to know about this. They could put someone into the fold promptly. He picked up the receiver of the large olive-green phone on his desk and dialed.

CHAPTER 39

"Wake up, Sleeping Beauty!"

The sudden voice startled Callum awake. He looked around the unfamiliar room to see where the voice came from, and through bleary eyes he recognized Pamela, in her military uniform, standing in the doorway. Callum looked down to see that he had fallen asleep in the chair he was in.

"How long has it been since you've had a decent night's sleep?" she asked. "Or a bath, for that matter?"

Callum ignored her as he looked about, "Where's Dolanna... Miss Fergraith?"

"She's resting. She's been sedated for the pain in her hip. I've assigned a nurse to her," Pamela replied. Then with a mischievous grin, "I must say Callum, she's not your usual type. A bit old for you, don't you think?"

"You're funny," replied Callum. He was too tired to think of something wittier than that. "Thanks for helping. I didn't know who else I could trust."

"That's a bit sad, " replied Pamela.

"You have no idea how much it depresses me."

"Oh, I do," she said with a grin. "Which makes this all the more pleasurable for me."

Callum rolled his eyes as he tried to stand up. His shoulder was aching from being thrown by the blast. "I need a coffee... and some painkillers."

"You still drink too much coffee," Pamela said, as she clipped the 'guest' pass onto his jacket. "Let me take you to the mess hall and get something nutritious into you and you can tell me what devil you've gotten yourself into."

To get to the cafeteria, Pamela escorted him through HMS *Neptune*, which was an understated misnomer. It was not a ship, as the initials HMS (Her Majesty's Ship) would suggest, but rather the name of the Naval Base located 25 miles from Glasgow on the shore of Gare Loch. This secret base was guarded by air defense Polaris missiles and four nuclear submarines, none of which were named Neptune. This location was used by the British Military as a strategic and launch site in both World Wars. The Naval Intelligence Division reactivated it in the 1960's when it became clear that the Cold War was not going to end.

Callum was so hungry that he devoured his food without taking stock in what he was consuming. Between large bites, he told Pamela everything about the brooch that was missing from the 1909 murder of Agatha Gilcrest, the recent murder of Ruthie McAdams, her cryptic message about 'Dragonslayer', the ransacking of his grandfather's study and the gas leak at Dolanna's townhome.

"Can I see the pendant?" Pamela asked.

"Certainly," Callum hesitated for a moment as he reached into his pocket. He loathed asking for her help. But she was good at her job. Always had been, which is why she was hand-picked from British Airports Police to join the new Ministry of Defence Police eight years ago. It was a great opportunity for her, a start of a new career, and the end of their marriage. How sad that the training she left him for is what he needed the most now. *What is a lowly, un-caffeinated guy to do?*

Callum handed the necklace to his ex-wife, who looked at it carefully, then said, "So you assumed that this was St. George but that Inspector... um..."

"De Kirkhaugh," said Callum. "He said it was St. Michael..."

"Of course he would. St. Michael is the patron saint of the police," she then looked up him as she added, "And lost causes."

"Which is it?"

"Well, given the knowledge that your grandfather was a police detective and a religious man, I'd say it could be either."

"Thanks. Do you have anything useful?"

"Don't get cheeky with me, or I'll have two hairy guards toss you out on your ear." She took a moment to study the pendant further, and continued, "Inspector John Toughill... Here is his rank and warrant number... so it looks like his retirement gift..."

Callum sat up, "But he was dishonorably discharged... "

"Okay, so if this isn't a cheap memento from the Glasgow Police, then it's a message for you."

"What message?"

"He was *your* grandfather... you would know better than I would," she said as she held it out for him.

"We hardly talked about his work. Don't you remember?" Callum said, grabbing it and looking at it carefully. "The only time we did was when he showed up one day in London…he wanted to take me out to celebrate. I had just started working as a investigator for Lloyds."

"Did he say anything interesting then?"

"No, well nothing obviously cryptic… just passing on some police advice … he told me: *Never jump to conclusions and always follow the evidence no matter how minute or insignificant.*"

"Good advice for police or investigator. So think back. He took you out to a pub for drinks. Was there anything in his demeanor…?"

"Pubs were closed for the day…" Callum interrupted as a memory stirred.

"What?"

"The pubs were closed out of respect… It was the day John F. Kennedy was assassinated…" Callum sat upright. He reached into his pocket and pulled out his notebook. "Percy Winthrope… you remember he's the man who sent me on this chase 'looking for icebergs'…"

"I know who Percy is, he and his wife were at our wedding… remember?" Pamela interrupted. "Go on, what about Percy?"

Callum found the page in his notebook, "He said the claim for the brooch was sent anonymously… scribbled on the back was the message: *'Evidence in the Agatha Gilcrest murder'*…"

"You told me that already."

"Wait a mo," Callum turned the page from his conversation with Percy, and traced along with his finger. "Percy said at the time he was working as a clerk for Lloyds when this claim, already smudged, was received anonymously… it was in 1963. He remembered because President Kennedy was assassinated."

"Aha! So, it was your grandfather who left it for you to find as a 'new job' present," Pamela said excitedly. "He was a man of his word and could never break his oath in order to investigate it… but he knew you weren't bound to that oath. He wanted you to take over after he died…"

"Why the hell didn't he just tell me?"

"Obviously the same person who had you followed, had *him* followed. He would have had to watch his every move… he couldn't just leave it all in his will for you. You would have been dead, too."

The realization of the extent of his grandfather's plan was slowly starting to dawn on Callum. He looked at his ex-wife and gestured to her military uniform, "Which is why he didn't want me to become a police officer…"

"You would have been restricted by the chain of command…"

"Ruddy hell," Callum exclaimed. "So what now? He didn't leave me any other clues."

"He must have... You just don't know it," Pamela said, in the sweetly condescending tone that he remembered so well. "Think. He must have said something about it..."

"No... he never did," Callum argued. "Anytime anyone brought it up, he simply said he was taking it to... his grave...oh, no... you don't suppose..."

"Where's his grave?"

"I didn't go to the funeral... but I recall... it was odd. He didn't want to be buried in Glasgow," the memory struck Callum. "He's buried in the graveyard of *The Church of St.George & St. Michael.*"

"No room for error there, Dragonslayer," Pamela grinned. His ex-wife left him feeling a bit inadequate as she so casually pointed out the whopper of icebergs.

April 8, 1982

CHAPTER 40

Callum peeked in on Dolanna before leaving. She was still sleeping in the infirmary.

"Don't worry. She's safe here," Pamela said reassuringly.

He turned and looked at her for a moment, thought about asking something and then thought the better of it.

"What do you want now?" she asked.

"What makes you think I want anything?" Callum asked defensively.

"I can see it in your face," Pamela replied. "You wanted to ask me something, then you changed your mind. Just ask me."

Callum sighed. She knew him too well. *Damn her*, he thought. "I was wondering if you had a chance to talk to Dolanna… if…"

"'If' what?"

"Can you find out why she broke off her engagement to Edward Hoffman?"

"Isn't that a little personal?"

"That's why I hesitated in asking…but…"

"But what?"

"But I think there's something there. Call it a gut feeling. She left him at the altar, yet she wears his engagement ring around her neck. I tell her there's a gas leak in the house and she tries to take her engagement photo with her…"

"Definitely doesn't add up," agreed Pamela. "Ok, I'll see what I can find out."

"Thanks," Callum smiled. "I really owe you for this."

"Believe me. I'll remember," she smirked.

A few hours later, Callum pulled up to the Church of St. George & St. Michael. High atop the monolithic structure, the statue of the Archangel Michael smiting Lucifer was silhouetted by the moonlight. Beneath it, the white flag with the red cross of St. George was snapping in the wind. *Did Granda take the secret to his grave... literally?* Callum did not relish the thought of a reunion by digging up his body.

Grabbing the electric torch from the passenger seat, Callum ventured toward the churchyard. The rusted gate clanged in the blustery weather. There was no lock on it. He gave it a push.

C-R-E-E-K-!!

The rusty hinges made such a loud grinding noise, they could have woken the proverbial dead. Callum looked about; there was no sign of life. Not a soul. Uncertain of which plot his grandfather lay under, he scampered as carefully as he could from tombstone to tombstone searching for the name: John Toughill.

After a long while, he paused to get his bearings, and realized that he wasn't even a third of the way done. However, he concluded that if he used the date of death as reference, he could narrow his search. He looked down at the one he was standing over. One name carved in the decaying stone: BLAKNEY. Died 1929.

Nowhere near the right area. Callum started forward and found his foot stuck. He pulled but it was firmly rooted to the grave, as if Blakney's hand had reached up from his coffin and grabbed his foot. His inner-child panicked and the pulled with all his might. His foot dislodged from the thick, viscous mud with a deep, retching sound.

With a soggy foot he continued hobbling through the graves like a hunchbacked gnome, which didn't make his sore shoulder very happy. Finally he came upon stones marked in the mid to late 60's. Now he was getting closer.

He aimed the beam of his torch at the next stone but the one at the other end of the row caught his attention. There was nothing distinctive about the stone itself but the earth had been recently disturbed. He moved closer to it. He glanced down at the stone he was passing: 1967. There shouldn't be any digging of new graves in this row.

He stood by the mound of fresh earth and illuminated the tombstone. His heart sank into his stomach as he saw the name: *John Toughill*. Callum looked down at the large hole where his grandfather should be buried. Either his grandfather had risen from the grave, or someone else had gotten here before him. Callum was enraged that someone had desecrated his grandfather's final resting place, and stormed about in frustration.

"You're trespassing on sacred land!" the voice behind him came upon him so suddenly, Callum nearly jumped out of his skin. He turned to see a blinding light, and in its beam, the end of shotgun barrel aimed at him.

Callum quickly raised his hands in stunned silence.

"What are ye doing here?" demanded the Scottish voice behind the torchlight. "Speak or I'll pepper your hide and make you truly holy."

"I'm here looking for something…"

"What would you be looking for in the dead of night in a graveyard? Did you do that?" the man said, gesturing at the upturned earth with the end of his gun.

"No, sir. It was like that when I arrived."

The man aimed his torchlight at Callum's face. "Wait, what is your name, lad?"

"Toughill. Callum Toughill," squinted Callum towards the light.

"So, are ye looking for answers, my lad?" the man said, lowering the torchlight.

"Yes, but none that you can help with," replied Callum. It was then that he noticed the white collar around the man's neck. "Are you a priest?"

The priest smiled, "Aye. Father Landon. And what business do you have with this grave?"

"It's my grandfather, but I may be too late. I believe he took what I'm looking for to his grave."

"What is the key?" Father Landon asked.

"What?" Callum looked at him with confusion. Then it occurred to him. "Uh... Dragonslayer?"

Father Landon lowered his weapon and extended his hand, "Welcome Callum, your grandfather told me you'd come and pick up the trail where he left off. That one day you would be investigating a murder… from long ago. Let justice be done."

"You've got to be fooling me!"

"I'm a man of God. I never fool… well except perhaps with this gun," said Father Landon as he held up the shotgun. Callum could now see that the trigger was missing.

"You were bluffing?" exclaimed Callum. "What if someone pulled a real loaded gun on you?"

"The Lord watches over me," replied Father Landon.

"I have a *real loaded gun* with me!"

"Did you draw your *real loaded gun*, my son?" replied Father Landon calmly.

"No…."

"The Lord watches over me."

. . .

De Kirkhaugh hadn't heard from Callum Toughill and a part of him was glad. Deep down, he regretted that man's intrusion into his life. However, de

Kirkhaugh hated unfinished business, and this case had been unfinished for almost a century.

Unable to sleep, de Kirkhaugh arrived early at the yellow-bricked Maryhill office of the Strathclyde Police. There were a few vagrants being processed at the front desk but it had been a relatively quiet night in comparison to yesterday when the press kept hounding him with calls. At least in the wee hours of the morning he was going to be able to get some work done.

He entered his office and hung his coat and scarf on the rack. He sat in his chair and was about to roll up to the desk, when something blocked the wheels from going further. He craned his neck to look under his desk and saw a stack of dusty, old file folders, with well-aged paper bursting between.

There was one of those new yellow 'Post-it' square papers with a handwritten note: *Here are the files from the SCRO you requested. L.*

It was odd that she put the old files from the 'Scottish Criminal Record Office' under the desk. But then again, perhaps paranoia was a virtue in this case. After closing the door and turning the blinds shut, he sat down and reached for the first folder. *Robert McLewlend – unsolved murder.*

— — —

In the rectory of the church, Callum sat at the old, early-70's chrome and laminex kitchen table with a shaded lamp on a chain overhead, while he waited for Father Landon to return to the modest room. The rectory was tastefully decorated with mismatched furniture; likely from the Salvation Army, but it all went together eclectically. Suddenly, Callum could hear the sound of wood cracking and splintering.

"Are you alright?" he called out to the priest.

"I'm fine," Father Landon's voice hollered from the other room. Within a few moments Callum heard him shuffling his feet along the plush green wall-to-wall carpet, and he reentered carrying a large iron box. Callum rose from his seat to help carry the weight to the table.

"What the Hhh… heck is it?" asked Callum.

"This is what your grandfather was to take to the grave with him," replied Father Landon. "In the end I convinced him it was better for me to keep it safe than to have someone desecrate his final resting place for it. Judging from the mess out there, I was right!"

"What would have happened if you had died before I came looking?" Callum asked.

"Are you always this optimistic?" Father Landon asked as he began to wipe the dust off the iron box.

"Only when I'm in a good mood," replied Callum.

"I had taken some necessary steps for someone else to inherit this duty should I become unable. But it would seem that responsibility will no longer be mine."

"How do I open it?"

"Use the key."

"What key?" Callum asked confused, "I don't have a key!"

Father Landon calmly said, "I asked you when we met by your grandfather's grave, what is the key?"

"I thought that was just a password."

"It is and more. What is the key?"

"Dragonsl-," replied Callum, then his mind wrapped itself around a possibility.

Father Landon said nothing as he watched Callum stand back up, and reach into his pocket to pull out the pendant. Callum looked at the iron box. It was dark and rusted, but images of St. George's cross and the knight slaying the dragon were carved elegantly into it. He then noticed the unusual, ornate indent. The shape and size matched the pendant. Taking it off the chain, Callum inserted the 'key' into the box, it turned, and he could hear mechanisms within grinding and snapping open.

"It was booby-trapped, should you have attempted to unlock it without the key."

"How cloak-and-dagger of Granda," Callum replied.

"He did not have the luxury of being careless. The risk was too great," Father Landon said, as Callum started to open the lid. "Wait."

Callum stopped as Father Landon started out the door toward the adjoining room.

"You're not staying?" Callum asked.

"Your grandfather said it was for your eyes only, and I shall continue to respect his wishes until you have seen it. You can stay here in privacy as long as you need to go through it. The others will likely continue looking elsewhere. Once you've seen it, you can decide who sees it and who doesn't."

"Thank you," Callum said quietly as he watched the old priest exit the room and close the door behind him.

Callum looked at the iron box. The last time it was open, his grandfather had put his secrets in it. Callum took a deep breath and ever so carefully, he opened the lid.

Inside he first saw a sleek, rounded blade, attached to the false latch by some kind of mechanism. Callum was very happy to have avoided that trap, as he enjoyed having all his fingers intact. He turned his attention to the other contents. There was a plethora of notes and photos stacked fairly neatly. On the very top was a legal document ambered with age, folded crisply. Callum carefully unfolded it. His eye was first drawn to a red inked stamp in the centre of the page with the word: DRAFT

On the very top, written in a calligraphy script:

Last Will and Testament
Agatha Marion Gilcrest

CHAPTER 41

"…Then this happened yesterday: a sleepy Glasgow neighbourhood was shaken to its core with a tremendous explosion…" said an overly dramatic reporter with a thick Scottish accent.

For years, Edward's lake house had been too remote for the TV antenna to pick up a decent reception: the picture was always snowy and the audio would crackle in and out. The C-Band satellite dish changed all that. Although it was, without a doubt, an eyesore on the picturesque waterfront, it was essential for knowing what was happening in the outside world. The blizzard had made reception sketchy but now, as it seemed to be subsiding, Edward weathered the elements, brushed the accumulated snow from the dish, and tuned into the news to catch up on current events.

"No word if any survivors have been recovered, but we have confirmed that it was the home of a local and well-loved resident named Dolanna Fergraith."

"What?" Edward wasn't certain he had heard correctly. He reached for the remote and turned the volume up, waking Myra from her slumber.

"What is it?" she asked blearily.

"It's Dolanna…" Edward muttered, not taking his eyes off the screen, as he sank into the chair. "Something's happened to her!"

"Oh my word!" exclaimed Myra as she sat bolt upright. "What happened?"

I've lost her forever, Edward thought. *I'll never get the chance to talk to her ever again. Or find out what truly happened.*

"I was doing some spring cleaning," a middle aged Scottish woman said as she was being interviewed on television. "That's when I thought I heard what sounded like a gunshot, then KER-BLEWY! The explosion knocked me knick-knacks on the floor."

"It knocked more than just the neighbour's knick-knacks," the reporter's voiceover said ominously. The footage on the screen cut to a townhouse with the windows smashed outward and black smoke billowing out.

"Is that Dolanna's home?" Myra asked. Edward, still shocked, nodded slowly.

The reporter's voice continued, "Everyone instantly assumed this was some sort of retaliation from Argentina, but the police were not so forthcoming."

A plain-clothes police officer appeared on the screen, trying to cross without being stopped, but to no avail.

"Was this the work of radicals, or the Argentines retaliating?" a reporter asked as they shoved the microphone into his face.

Looking very annoyed he simply said, "It's too early to comment one way or the other before the investigation is complete."

Edward shook his head. It made no sense. The Argentines, or any sort of fanatical group, for that matter, would not likely target a random suburban home. They would choose something larger or someone with a higher profile, like Buckingham Palace or the Queen. Not some poor woman from Glasgow, not Dolanna. He dropped the remote. He was shaking.

Myra gently put her cold hands upon his to calm him. He stared at his old engagement photo with a great sense of loss and regret. He looked into Myra's eyes.

"What if I've lost her forever?"

. . .

Commander Pamela Toughill entered Dolanna Fergraith's quarter of the Base's infirmary and saw the sweet old lady sitting up, bundled in military-issued blankets, reading a magazine from the stack next to her bedside.

"How are we doing today?" Pamela asked.

"Very well," Dolanna said. "Can you tell me what's going on?"

"What do you remember?"

"I remember your husband came to see me," replied Dolanna.

"My husband?"

"I assume he's your husband," she said as she pointed to the nametag on Pamela's uniform.

Pamela smiled and nodded, "Ex-husband."

"I see," Dolanna replied.

"What else do you remember?" Pamela asked as she pulled up a chair and sat down next to the bed.

"He said something about a gas leak," Dolanna continued. "Then he pushed me out the back door, and then there was the explosion… everything else is a bit foggy after that. Can you tell me what's going on?"

"In short, someone's trying to kill you."

"What? Why me?" Dolanna exclaimed. "I haven't done anything to anyone."

"No, not directly."

"I don't understand."

"Let me ask you some questions first," Pamela began. "Would you say your mother was wealthy?"

Dolanna laughed. "No, not by any means. She had been a servant girl. My father died in a pub brawl, and she had to work in a nail factory as well as take in extra laundry to feed me and my brothers."

"Yet you were engaged to someone wealthy. Why did you break it off?"

Dolanna looked at her for a moment, "What are you getting at?"

"It may indirectly be the reason someone's trying to kill you."

"You don't honestly think Edward would do anything so horrible," Dolanna said, fidgeting nervously. "He's not like that at all. There is goodness and an honesty in him that is not found in many men."

"What can you tell me about him?"

"Well, he's the CEO of…"

"No, I don't need his résumé," interrupted Pamela. "What can you tell me about him? As a person."

Dolanna softened, "He is a true gentleman. A philanthropist. A great conversationalist. Loves art and music. Knows everything there is to know about the *Titanic*. We both had an affinity for time travel stories…"

Her voice drifted as she seemed a hundred miles away.

"Yet you left him at the altar."

"We never got that far," replied Dolanna. "I left him at the blood bank… or whatever it was called then."

"I don't understand."

"In New York, at least back then, they insisted on blood tests before they could issue a marriage license. If I recall correctly it was to verify that the applicants were not carrying syphilis."

"Interesting. So, why did you break it off? Did you have syphilis or something?"

"Most certainly not!" Dolanna said in an indignant tone. "I know young folks today believe in free love but I was raised with 'no hanky-panky until after you were married.'"

Pamela couldn't help but smile.

"It's no laughing matter. In my day, a respectable lady did not go out on a date with a young man without wearing a pair of white gloves and having a chaperone along."

"So why did you break off the engagement?" asked Pamela, pointing to the engagement ring on the chain. "It's clear you still have feelings for him."

"Just like you still have feelings for your ex-husband?"

"We're not talking about me," interjected Pamela.

"Why not? Why did you divorce your husband?"

Pamela bit her bottom lip and said, "You're very good at changing subjects and being evasive but I'll tell you what. I'll tell you why I left and you have to come clean with why you left."

Dolanna said nothing.

"I'll take your silence as a lack of objection," Pamela said, then before Dolanna could interject, she added, "Callum and I were married to our work first. We never made time for each other... and I hate coffee."

Dolanna nodded.

"Your turn," Pamela said. Dolanna looked away. Softening a little, Pamela sat on the bed and said, "Please, what could be so horrible?"

"In short..." Dolanna spoke hesitantly. "Edward's father threatened me."

"Threatened you? In what way?"

"He had a dark secret about my mother and threatened to expose her if I didn't leave Edward."

"What secret?"

Dolanna's voice faltered, and then whispered, "That my mother had killed her former employer, Agatha Gilcrest."

CHAPTER 42

"So let me get this straight," de Kirkhaugh said into his phone. "Are you saying Dolanna Fergraith's mother killed Agatha Gilcrest?"

"No, I'm not saying that at all!" Callum yelled through the receiver.

De Kirkhaugh was certain everyone in the outer office could hear Callum through the phone. At first he found himself somewhat relieved that Callum had made it out alive as he suspected, but now that feeling was slipping away. "But you said the draft of the Last Will and Testament of Agatha Gilcrest was leaving her entire fortune to Margaret Fergraith and family. Why would a wealthy, eccentric spinster want to leave her entire fortune to a former maid? And why would that maid kill her before the paperwork was filed?"

"I also have a carbon copy of a letter from a solicitor dated 1889, for transfer of legal guardianship of Agatha Gilcrest's child… female child… to a Mr. Fergraith."

De Kirkhaugh paused and asked, "Did you say Agatha Gilcrest had a child?"

"Yes."

"So then she wasn't a spinster?"

"Apparently not. Think about that time period. A woman of her social stature having a child out of wedlock? She couldn't afford that scandal."

"So she gave the child up for adoption…" de Kirkhaugh said, slowly putting the pieces together. "And you think years later she hired that child to be her maid."

"Even after Margaret Fergraith left her employ, she and her family were invited over to Agatha Gilcrest's home for the holidays," Callum recounted. "And…when I first saw Dolanna, I was thrown by how much she resembled Agatha Gilcrest."

"Do you have any other evidence? An adoption form?"

"Just this letter and the Will," said Callum. "But that Will was never signed. Agatha Gilcrest was in the process of changing her Will to leave everything to Margaret, but it wasn't executed. The draft I have in my hands is dated 21st of December, 1909."

"That was the evening she was murdered, wasn't it?"

"Correct!" Callum exclaimed. "And Margaret Fergraith didn't get a shilling after Agatha Gilcrest's death."

"So I wager the killer was going to be cut out of the Will, making it personal enough to attack the old woman face-on."

"Precisely," Callum said excitedly through the phone. "And it would also explain why all her personal papers were strewn about the room."

"Looking for the Will," de Kirkhaugh said at the same time with Callum. He hated to admit it, but his theory seemed sound. "I don't suppose your grandfather left the name of who actually inherited Agatha Gilcrest's fortune?"

"Not that I've been able to find just yet," replied Callum with a sigh.

"No, of course not, that would have been too bloody easy."

"However, both of these documents have the name of the solicitor on them," Callum added.

"Perhaps the firm is still around. There's an outside chance they still have old records."

"Maybe I'll grow wings and fly," muttered de Kirkhaugh.

"What?"

"I said: 'it wouldn't hurt to try'. Go on, what's the name of the solicitor?"

"McLewlend," Callum read aloud, "Of McLewlend and Sons, Solicitors..."

"Did you say McLewlend?"

"Yes, Robert McLewlend was the..."

"He's dead," de Kirkhaugh said as his head sank forward.

"Well it doesn't surprise me, that was 1909..."

"No, I mean he died in *1909*. The 27th of December, 1909. A week after Agatha Gilcrest."

"And you know that off the top of your head?" Callum asked incredulously.

"On a hunch, I was looking into other unsolved murders from that year... murders that weren't sealed."

"How was he murdered?"

"Shot, and then his whole lawfirm went up in flames. His sons are all dead now, too." de Kirkhaugh said frankly, as he scanned through the older files dated the year *1905*."

"We have a strong case for motive," Callum added.

Suddenly a handwritten label caught de Kirkhaugh's eye: **Gilcrest, A. (arson)** *What are the odds?* De Kirkhaugh thought to himself. *What had happened in 1905?*

He opened it, expecting to see information pertaining to Agatha, but it wasn't her file. De Kirkhaugh asked into the phone, "Did Agatha Gilcrest have any other children or any other relatives with the same surname?"

"Why do you ask?"

"I have a file here on a male juvenile delinquent, who was seventeen in 1905, when he committed a series of arson attacks. His last name is Gilcrest."

BUZZ

Line 3 on de Kirkhaugh's phone buzzed and started to flash. De Kirkhaugh quickly said to Callum, "I have another call. I'll page you later with an address of where to meet."

"Cheers," Callum said.

De Kirkhaugh clicked off. *Did the light stay on?* He hadn't noticed. *Stupid Git!* He thought about what they had said and if a third-party had been eavesdropping… He had to be more careful.

BUZZ

"DCI de Kirkhaugh speaking," he said into the phone.

A man with an American accent spoke, "Are you the investigating officer of the explosion at the home of Dolanna Fergraith?"

De Kirkhaugh rolled his eyes. *More press.* He gritted his teeth and replied, "I'm sorry I have no information for the press."

"I'm not the press," the voice in the phone said politely. "My name is Edward Hoffman. I'm calling from America… Dolanna was… very close… to me."

De Kirkhaugh knew exactly who he was, and he had seen the charred remains of a photo in her house, "What can I do for you Mr. Hoffman?"

"Please," Edward pleaded over the phone. "Is she still alive?"

"I'm afraid I can't say," said de Kirkhaugh, still looking at the light on the phone.

"I know I'm not family but can you at least…"

"Sorry," de Kirkhaugh interrupted. Maybe he was paranoid but he had to be careful. "Can I get your number and I'll contact you later?"

— — —

After giving his pager number, Edward hung up the phone. He couldn't put his finger on it but something was not right with that police inspector in Glasgow. He sounded like he was hiding something. The uncertainty was killing him. He desperately wanted to get back to the city and jet over to the UK, but they were still snowed in. There simply weren't enough snow plows to dig everyone out, and this rural area would be on the bottom of the list of priorities. *Good thing the cabin was well-stocked.*

He turned on the TV to see if there was an update on the foreign news. The angular image of Alexander Haig appeared on the screen as he arrived in London, England. In an elegant British Manchester accent, the reporter announced, "The US Secretary of State Alexander Haig will meet with Prime Minister Margaret Thatcher to begin shuttle mediation."

The footage cut to war protesters, some with faces painted with the British and Argentine flag colors, marching through Trafalgar Square. Some were carrying homemade signs saying: *'Stop the War Negotiate Now'* and *'Reagan, Haig, CIA & Thatcher, How Many People Have You Killed Today?'*

Edward shook his head. All this turmoil for a few small islands. How many would die fighting for them? Would it be worth it? Edward had seen the price of war firsthand, which is why he had forbidden his branch of Hoffman International to be involved in any military contracts, despite the possible monetary gains. Another topic that had spawned many an argument with his father.

Edward was momentarily distracted by the name on the screen: *Loraine Kramer.*

He took a hard look at the photo of an old woman that appeared above the name. It had been decades since Edward had contact with that con artist but he remembered her eyes. *What was she up to now?*

"Loraine Kramer was last seen at her Glasgow home on the third of April. Anyone with information is asked to contact the Strathclyde Police."

What is going on in Glasgow? he wondered. It was too coincidental that two women from his past would appear on the news around the same time. Edward could vividly recall the venomous rage when he proved that Kramer was not Loraine Allison, the little girl from First Class who perished aboard the *Titanic.* He could still hear her mid-western accent screaming, *I'll get even with you one day. You'll pay for this! If it takes the rest of my life, I'll ruin you the way you ruined me!*

Thinking about what had happened at Dolanna's home, Edward couldn't help but wonder if Loraine Kramer had a hand in that misfortune. Was this somehow part of her revenge?

And then there was Myra…

Edward looked about the main room of the lake house. He hadn't seen her leave the room.

He called out, "Myra?"

No answer.

"Myra!" he called out again, even louder. *Where was she?*

CHAPTER 43

In the staff lounge, Natalie was watching the news about Ian Kybartis having been found dead in the freezing waters in West Rock State Park, New Haven. There was no mention of Myra at all. *This is all very strange,* she thought to herself.

"Coming up after the break," the reporter on the TV continued, "New Yorkers haven't finished digging themselves out of the snow, and there may be an encore from Mother Nature. We'll be right back…"

Natalie got up. This was a good excuse to leave early, especially since tomorrow was Good Friday and she was hoping to catch a flight home for Easter. She went to her office, and the moment she crossed the threshold, her office phone beeped.

"Dr. Lindsay?" the receptionist paged. "There is a call for you."

"Could you take a message?" Natalie said into the intercom.

"It's an overseas call from England."

"England?" Natalie repeated. Were Edward and Myra already in England? Curiosity got the better of her as she snatched up the phone, "Hello?"

"Hi Natalie, it's Jeff."

"Jeff?" asked Natalie, not recognizing the voice in the receiver. Then it hit her, her colleague conducting that new blood test. "Oh, Jeff! Yes, of course."

"I have your DNA results on your mystery woman."

"Excellent! What can you tell me?"

"Um... Do you have a fax number?" Jeff asked. "I'll need you to see this as I explain my findings."

"Yes, I do." Natalie looked over at the fax machine and read the number off to him.

"Great, I'll have to hang up to send it, but I'll call you right back."

176

"I can hardly wait," remarked Natalie. She sat there staring at the fax machine. It was like waiting for the proverbial pot to boil. The thought that an exact visual duplicate of a page was instantaneously being sent across the seas was mind-boggling.

RING

The fax machine sprang to life. After a couple more rings the 'machine' answered, and she winced at the terrible screeching of the two machines as they connected. She watched as the paper began to inch out and curl down. She grabbed the page and looked at it quizzically, not quite understanding what she was looking at. Then she made the connection. She couldn't believe it. She sat waiting for Jeff to call her back.

After ten minutes, she fished out her address book from her desk drawer and quickly looked up the number. She dialed.

She could hear the phone ringing but Jeff wasn't answering. He did say he would call right back. She hung up.

RING

She answered the phone, "Natalie speaking."

Click.

Whoever it was hung up.

She looked again at the page that Jeff sent her. DNA was a new science but she had read a few articles on it. She wasn't sure she was reading it correctly. If it was as she guessed, she had to tell Edward.

She grabbed Edward's lawyer's card from her Rolodex and punched in the numbers. After a few rings, the answer machine started up. As soon as she heard the beep, "Mr. Zisholm. This is Dr. Lindsay from the clinic. I have the DNA results from the blood work. I think Edward needs to see this… Can you get him to page me? Thanks."

. . .

Edward had searched the entire lake house. There was no sign of Myra. She wouldn't have been crazy enough to go out in the snow, would she?

Throwing on his coat and winter accoutrements, Edward ventured out into the harsh winter. It was April but it was clear that Old Man Winter was refusing to leave. The icy wind howled through the snow-covered skeletal trees, making them sway and crackle, then it turned to attack him, nipping at the exposed skin on his cheeks. Protecting his face as best as he could, Edward lumbered through the deepening snow, ignoring the sudden chill of snow slipping into his boots as he trudged up the laneway to where it connected with the road.

He squinted as he stared through the fury of flurries, looking for any sign of movement or life. There was none. Not even a rabbit or deer to be seen.

No animal was crazy enough to be out here in these harsh conditions, except him.

Edward was about to turn back when he noticed something on the road. Tracks. He moved closer to inspect. Snowmobile tracks. Considering how much snow was coming down, the tracks were fairly fresh. *Could Myra have gone with some stranger?* With the recent events in Glasgow still swirling in his mind, Edward couldn't ignore any possibility. His gloved hand reached into his pocket and found the keys to the Jeep.

His fingers felt numb and ached as he tried to turn the key in the ignition. The engine started with a reluctant roar. Even the Jeep didn't seem to want to move in this ungodly weather. Edward cranked up the heat and checked that it was still in 4X4. Then he started down the road after the tracks, before they were obliterated by the thick flakes.

— — —

Natalie couldn't wait any longer for Edward or Jeff to call her back. She needed to get back to her apartment and pack. Natalie bundled herself up in her coat and scarf, grabbed her attaché case, and plodded to the subway station.

She shielded her face from the winds. Despite the sub-arctic-like temperatures, the subway appeared to be running. Lucky for her. She had heard on the news that the snow in some areas had stranded people at their workplaces. President Reagan had called the National Guard to help clear out selected roads.

The shelter of the stairwell to the subway gave a slight respite from the biting winter winds. As she descended the stairs, a voice behind her said, "Dr. Lindsay?"

"Yes?" Natalie was surprised at the sound of her name. She turned and saw a familiar face. She pulled down her scarf as she smiled.

She never saw the gun.

BLAM!

The bang echoed so loudly that the metal gates around her rattled. She felt the heat of the bullet tear into her. She saw her assailant reach out to her, as if to help but instead grabbed her attaché case as she began to fall backwards. She felt every sharp corner of the steps as she tumbled down to the bottom.

Battered, broken and lying in a pool of her own blood, she tried to move. Her gaze drifted up the stairs. Her attacker had gone with her papers, and as she struggled to breathe she wondered: *why?*

CHAPTER 44

De Kirkhaugh wanted to cross-reference the Gilcrest arsonist with other possible arson cases in the 1909 timeline, considering that Agatha Gilcrest's solicitor had been killed in a fire that destroyed all of his papers. It put this boy as a prime suspect, and he might have continued his sizzling hobby over the years. *Boy?* De Kirkhaugh chuckled to himself. If the boy were still alive, he'd be an old man. A very old man.

Coming up to the desk of the 'other morgue', de Kirkhaugh looked about for Janna. The other records keeper, Collins, was atop a small stepladder fetching thick file folders from the top shelf.

"Can I help you, sir?" Collins asked as he started to descend the ladder.

"I was looking for Janna," de Kirkhaugh replied. "Have you seen her today?"

"No, she didn't come into work today. Left me short-handed. Is there something I can help you with?"

"No, that's ok," answered de Kirkhaugh. The fewer who knew about his 'research' the better. He started to walk away when he heard Collins mutter.

"This is the first time she's ever missed a shift."

"What was that?" de Kirkhaugh said as he turned back to him.

"Oh, nothing important... It's just that I've never known Janna to miss a shift. Even if she's not well, she still drags herself in here rather than deal with a pile up when she..."

De Kirkhaugh wasn't listening anymore. He had already turned and started down the hallway.

De Kirkhaugh dashed into his office and closed the door. He grabbed the files on the McLewlend murder and the arsonist. He knew what he had to do.

He stared at his phone. Taking Callum Toughill's business card out of his pocket, pressed 'line 2' to get a signal out, saw the light illuminate on 'line 2' as he pressed it. Then he dialed the phone number on the card. He got the answer service.

"The next time you go after a century old murderer," de Kirkhaugh yelled into the phone receiver. "Make sure you have all the facts!"

He slammed down the phone. The light on 'line 2' stayed on for a second longer than it should have. Now he knew for certain, someone in the department had been listening in on all his calls.

· · ·

Callum wasn't sure what was going on with de Kirkhaugh. First he called his answering service and told the operator to give him an overseas number of someone in America and now this odd message about having all the facts? What more did he bleeding want? He was trying the best he could.

"Didn't I give you this message before?" asked the message operator.

"No, this is my first time calling in today. Cheers!" Callum replied absent-mindedly as he hung up. He looked back at the priest's kitchen table. There, spread out in neat piles all over it were *all the facts* that his grandfather had hidden all these years. *I didn't have all the facts until now!* John Toughill had re-interviewed some witnesses like Ruthie's grandfather and Heather Langlea. Even a comment from Ruthie:

"I of'n saw a young man calling upon Miss Langlea when Miss Gilcrest wasn't home. I think it was Miss Gilcrest's nephew. Once they noticed me, and they made me promise not to tell Miss Gilcrest. They gave me chocolates. I hadn't had chocolates before."

Callum knew that as an only child, Agatha Gilcrest did not have a nephew. He wished Ruthie were still alive. He would have liked to talk to her about this arsonist named Gilcrest that de Kirkhaugh had told him about. The two might be one and the same.

He needed a break to gather his thoughts. Callum looked at his watch, calculated the time in New York and rang up the number. While the phone was ringing he surveyed his grandfather's work.

One pile held a photo taken at the Otto Slade trial in 1910; it was of Heather Langlea wearing a big flowered hat. Even in black and white there was something... odd about her eyes. Yes, there was a look of malevolence in them, but there was something else. Callum had the nagging feeling he had seen this face before, but that was quite impossible. There were no photos of Heather Langlea in Percy's files. He tried to think, but the more he tried the more frustrated he became...

click

Callum paused as he heard the ringing stop in the receiver. He was about to say 'hello', when a recording of an articulate man started to speak: "You have reached Edward Hoffman. I'm sorry to have missed your call…"

Callum hung up. It was good of de Kirkhaugh to get him this number. He would ring him up again later.

He looked again at the photo. Why wasn't he able to find anything further in regards to Heather Langlea's life? His grandfather had the same difficulties. In his notes, John Toughill had written: *No trace of Heather Langlea after boarding the Titanic.*

— — —

De Kirkhaugh had tried ringing up Janna's phone number several times but there was no answer. He even tried to get Detective Sergeant Milton to meet him at Janna's flat, but Milton had gone back out, following a lead on the missing Loraine Kramer case.

Out of sheer panic he needed to find out for sure if she was all right. Without 'just cause', he couldn't simply ring up '999' for emergency. Though it didn't stop him from running every red light on the way over to her flat. Thankfully, as a Detective Chief Inspector, personnel didn't question anything when asked for home address information.

As he neared the front door of Janna's flat, which was situated over a Chinese restaurant, de Kirkhaugh had a mixed feeling of untamed fear and the embarrassing thought that perhaps Janna decided to play hooky and he was about to find himself in an awkward situation.

After wrestling with his thoughts, he opted to find out once and for all. If she answered the door, he would make up some excuse for being overly protective. As the old adage: *Better to be safe, than sorry.*

He looked about for a doorbell, but it was obviously busted. His hand reached out and rapped the door. It creaked open from the slight impact of his first knock. This was not boding well. He cocked his head and listened for any sound of the telly or any other movement. Silence.

He was about to call out her name, when his paranoia crept back. *What if she is in danger? What if some assailant is still in there?* He withdrew his gun for added protection, and he was grateful that as a senior officer he was allowed to carry firearms.

Keeping his gun aimed inside, he pushed the door ever so gently with his other hand. There was a slight squeak from the hinges. De Kirkhaugh held his breath and he stepped in ever so carefully. The wooden parquet floor creaked loudly as he stepped into her flat. The element of surprise was gone.

"Janna?" de Kirkhaugh called out. "It's DCI de Kirkhaugh!"

He paused and waited for a response. Nothing.

He crept up the stairs to the first floor landing. With his gun held in front of him, he slunk around the corner as quietly as he could.

No one.

"Janna, are you home?" he called out again.

Still nothing.

Should he keep searching her flat? He didn't have a warrant to enter her premises. What if she's just stepped out to post a letter or something? How would he explain his presence in her home? Continuing to search would also mean looking into her bedroom and that would be a huge invasion of privacy should he be...

Wrong!

He felt the air drop out of his lungs as he spotted Janna's blonde hair, caked with blood. She was lying face-down in a crimson puddle in the middle of the hallway outside the loo.

De Kirkhaugh struggled to move toward her... to the final truth. He knelt down beside her and felt her wrist for a pulse, but she was already gone and going cold. There was no longer any denial. *This is my fault. I got her involved. She didn't deserve to...*

He noticed a metallic swirl in the pool of blood that had gathered on the wood-tiled floor. *Gallium!* It had melted from the heat of her blood. The bullet had oozed out of the wound. He had seen this before. Too many times. This was the M.O. of the assassin Jack Frost! *Bloody Hell! Why?*

Suddenly he heard the door creak open behind him. De Kirkhaugh spun around with his gun drawn. He could hear a heavy footfall on the downstairs landing. The footsteps were slow and deliberate. *Could it be Jack Frost? Why would he return?*

The footsteps were getting louder, nearing the top. In another second or two the intruder would be in full view. De Kirkhaugh held his breath so as not to make a sound as he positioned his finger directly over the trigger.

The mysterious figure appeared fearlessly around the corner and faced him straight on.

De Kirkhaugh let out a sigh of relief and lowered his weapon, "Oh, it's only you! Help me, Janna has been shot...!"

As he spoke, De Kirkhaugh turned back to Janna's body. *It's too late to call for help.*

"I know," the familiar voice replied softly. Then de Kirkhaugh heard the click of the chamber before he could turn back around.

BLAM!

CHAPTER 45

The snowmobile track had continued along the road for some time. If it had been someone's joy ride, there were numerous trails to be found in the area. On the other hand, even with a winter storm, traveling over the ice in April was not advisable as it was likely not thick enough to hold the weight of a snowmobile.

Edward followed until the tracks were too blanketed with snow to see anymore. Edward could only guess at its path for so long before a fork in the road made it impossible to proceed. It was likely an exercise in futility; he had no way of knowing with any certainly that Myra was on a snowmobile. He could have been chasing a teenager for all he knew.

WAK-WAK-WAK-WAK-WAK

Edward's thoughts were drowned out by the sound of a helicopter flying overhead. *That's dangerous,* Edward thought to himself. For many years, his company had been trying to perfect methods to provide an ice protection system for a helicopter's main rotor blade. Precisely because of an extreme cold, snowy weather situation like today, the rotor blades would be at risk of "over-torquing" the engine, if they froze up. This particular helicopter was taking a great risk in being out at all, and it was heading back in the direction of his lake house.

• • •

"You have reached Edward Hoffman. I'm sorry to have missed your call. Please leave your name and number and I will return your call at my earliest convenience. Thank you."

BEEP

"Hello Mr. Hoffman, this is Callum Toughill. We met a couple of years ago, I'm the investigator for Lloyds. Inspector de Kirkhaugh gave me your personal number to contact you directly. I have some information about Dolanna Fergraith. She's alive. Could you call me back as soon as you can?" Callum said into the phone after his third try to get through. He hated talking to answer-phone machines. He always felt like an idiot, talking to nobody. He hung up after leaving both his pager number and Pamela's direct line.

He had to remember to give Father Landon some extra money for ringing up long distance calls on his phone. Father Landon had shown such great generosity and patience by leaving him be while he took over the Rectory kitchen.

He had finally managed to go through all the little pieces of the puzzle left to him by his grandfather, though there were some that were perplexing items that had no explanation as to their importance. For example, an old invitation sent to Agatha Gilcrest for the wedding of Archibald Bartholomew Hoffman and Myra Amelia Sloan, which was to take place at the Bloomingdale Reformed Church in New York City.

Callum looked at the date on the wedding invitation. Agatha Gilcrest hadn't lived to see those nuptials. Why had his grandfather included this invitation with all the other clues? What relevance did it have to the case? It was another reason Callum hoped to speak to Edward Hoffman.

— — —

After Edward pulled the Jeep into the laneway, he started trudging toward the lake house when he spotted Myra sitting in the gazebo overlooking the frozen lake. Edward plodded through the deep snow past the cedar trees to reach her.

"Have you been here the entire time?" Edward asked as he stepped into the gazebo.

"No," she replied, still staring out into the lake. He noticed she wasn't wearing a hat or gloves, yet did not appear to be shivering. "I came out to find something familiar. Something untouched by time. There used to be a willow tree down there by the lake."

Edward looked over where she was pointing. He remembered it well. It had been damaged by lightning about twenty years ago and had to be cut down, for fear that it might topple onto the lake house.

"I had carved my initials into that tree…" Myra whispered. "When I was a young girl of twelve or thirteen."

Edward recalled the initials MS & WB having been carved on the tree and assumed MS was Myra Sloane. He had assumed that it was put there by the *mother* who raised him, but when he asked her about it once, she said she couldn't remember. Edward now sat beside Myra and tested, "What did you carve into the tree?"

"MS and… WB" she replied.

Edward blinked a couple of times, then asked, "Who was WB?"

"Walter Bertrum," she answered as she turned to look at him for the first time. Then she pointed to the west. "His family had a lake house down that way. And I was infatuated with him. He had red hair and freckles… and the sweetest smile. I used to dream that he would ask me to marry him… But I knew that could never happen."

"Why not?" Edward asked, bewildered.

"His family was of new money. His father was the tycoon of indoor commodes."

"Toilets?"

"His family was never invited to any social functions or soirées around here, and the way my family spoke about them made me want to be with him all the more."

Edward rubbed his hands and stomped his feet on the wooden planks for warmth as he continued to listen to Myra, who still seemed unaffected by the cold. "One day, just to be rebellious I invited Walter Bertrum to be my escort at a lunch social. It caused quite a stir. Mother was not pleased. When autumn came, I was sent to an all-girls finishing school in England. I never saw Walter again. Today I wandered by his lake house to see if it was still there."

"Was it?"

"No… it's gone. Now it's a part of a…. what's an 'R-V camp?'" Myra asked, the words sounding foreign on her tongue.

"Yes, the Bertrum family sold it decades ago. It's changed hands several times, and it's been a campground for about fifteen years."

"What ever happened to him? Did he ever marry? Have children? He's more than likely dead."

"Forgive me for being so bold," Edward began. "But what did you see in Father?"

Myra turned and looked at Edward again. After a long moment she took a deep breath and replied, "It was arranged by our families."

"What?"

"We were introduced at a social function. Archie was nice. He was also attending a boarding school, and while we were introduced, our fathers negotiated our marriage."

Edward found it astonishing that in the western world of the 20th century, arranged marriages still existed. "I find it difficult to imagine you went along with that."

"What could I do? Go against Father? The Hoffman family was of very, very old money, but the lineage had almost died out. Archibald was considered their 'miracle child'."

185

"How so?" asked Edward, never having heard any of this from his father.

"Francis and Elizabeth Hoffman had been unable to conceive a child for years and they were afraid of the Hoffman line dying out. Then along came their son Archie and subsequently, they needed him to have a son. Do you know what the first thing Mrs. Elizabeth Hoffman said to me?"

"I can't imagine."

"'You look fertile enough,'" replied Myra. "I felt like a mare brought to a stallion just to sire racehorses."

Edward watched as a tear streamed down her face, almost crystallizing in the cold. "They must have been relieved when I was born."

"Ecstatic," Myra answered. "…And I loved you the moment I first held you in my arms."

She turned and looked at Edward and placed her hand on his face. Edward gasped at how cold her hand was, but he found himself comforted by it.

He gazed into her eyes while she continued, "I was so afraid of the pressures they were going to put on you. I remember holding you in my arms the day you were born and I prayed to God that he would give me the strength to protect you. I made a promise to God that I would be there to keep them from controlling you…"

Edward took off his glove as he placed his wrinkled hand on her other icy hand. She didn't even react to the touch.

"Then I saw your face when you heard what had happened to Dolanna. I saw the same hollow look of regret that I've seen in the mirror — that you were also robbed of a chance for happiness… now you are the last Hoffman… so we both sacrificed happiness… and for what? Why did this happen?"

Edward put his arm around her and Myra broke down, sobbing uncontrollably. "I'm sorry Eddie… I'm sorry I broke my promise… I'm sorry I wasn't there to protect you."

"You're here now… Mother."

CHAPTER 46

After not having stepped out into the daylight for hours, Callum finally realized he needed food. Not wanting to carry the heavy iron box with him, Callum left it in the safety of Father Landon's rectory.

Stepping out, he realized that day had already turned into night. Callum took a deep breath of cool air and started to walk. A respectable stone's-throw from The Church of St. George & St. Michael was the Black Dragon Pub. *Ironic,* Callum thought.

Callum ordered a pint of ale from the attractive, young, green-eyed lady behind the bar. Then he pointed to the 'Specials Menu' and continued, "I'll also have the 'steak and ale pie with chips and peas.'"

The smell of food was driving him crazy. He was hungry now. Though he could have downed that pint in a single go, he thought it best not to drink on an empty stomach. He then added, "Could I also get an order of pickled eggs to start?"

"Right, luv," she smiled and nodded.

After he'd paid for his meal, he took his pickled eggs and ale and sat down at a table near the front where he could still see anyone that entered or left the pub. Callum savored the pickled egg, which went well with the nice pint of brown ale and a dusting of white pepper. He was also grateful that the pub had gone to the extra expense of obtaining padded seats. After sitting all day on a stark wooden chair in the rectory, he could feel every bone in his backside.

As he waited for his meal, Callum's eyes drifted up to the telly. A desk reporter was addressing the camera, and in a serious tone commented, "In response to the Hama uprising that began in February, Syria has closed its border with Iraq, shutting off the pipeline carrying Iraqi oil to the Mediterranean."

The door opened and a man in a dark coat entered. Callum set his ale down as he observed the man. The man's eyes darted about the pub, searching. Callum resisted the instinct to slink down or look away. The man's eyes lit up as he saw someone at the back of pub. With an energetic step he rushed towards an exotic looking young lady at a table in the corner. Callum watched as they kissed, and then as if aware of him, they glanced around warily. Callum's gaze moved quickly into his glass of ale. *Obvious,* he thought with a smirk. *A couple meeting clandestinely.*

"In local news," the reporter's voice droned on, "An officer with the Strathclyde Police was killed in the line of duty, today."

Callum's attention flew back to the telly.

"Detective Chief Inspector Donald de Kirkhaugh, a ten-year veteran and a familiar face here in Glasgow was gunned down during an on-going investigation. Unconfirmed reports state that he might have been killed by the assassin operating under the name of Jack Frost."

Callum dropped his glass, completely unaware of the river of ale cascading off the edge of his table. He had only taken a sip or two but could feel the room spin as the magnitude of the tragedy sunk in.

De Kirkhaugh was dead because of him. How many were now dead because of him?

Father Landon! Suddenly, his appetite was gone, and fear started to grip his mind and wouldn't let go. He needed to get back to the church, get the iron box of evidence and get Father Landon out of there. He stood up and grabbed his coat.

"I'll have to go," he said the barmaid behind the bar.

"But what about…"

"Here is a photo of the suspect believed to have killed DCI de Kirkhaugh in cold blood," the reporter's voice continued. "This photo was taken while being interrogated on another 'Jack Frost' murder."

Callum looked up to see a blurry black & white image of himself in the Strathclyde Police interrogation room.

"Bollocks!" he muttered under his breath. Then he turned to the inquisitive-looking barmaid and said quickly, "I think I know him!"

Then he dashed out the door.

Callum raced awkwardly from the Black Dragon Pub to the Church of St. George & St. Michael. He half expected to find Father Landon with his throat cut, his grandfather's iron box missing, and the church in flames.

When he arrived at the Rectory, he discovered Father Landon making sandwiches in his kitchen.

"I have to get you out of here," Callum said with urgency, peeking out the window through the orange curtains as a car drove by.

"I'm not going anywhere," Father Landon said as he sliced some cheddar cheese. "The Lord watches over me. Besides, tomorrow's Good Friday. I have a sermon to prepare. You need to sit for a moment and gather your wits."

"You don't understand," Callum interrupted. "Something terrible has happened... You're not going to believe what happened..."

"*Belief* is part of my job description," Father Landon said as he cut the sandwich.

"I don't even know where to begin!"

"Your ally in the police force was murdered and you've now been wrongfully accused of committing that crime."

"No... worse..." Callum began. "The Detective Chief Inspector who... what? How did you know?"

"I have a television in the other room."

"You watch the telly?"

"This is a Rectory, not a medieval monastery," smiled the priest.

Callum slumped down on the chair. Slowly it was beginning to sink in that he was out of options. "How did this get so insane? I have to get out of here. They're going to be looking for me."

"I know," replied Father Landon as he handed him a lunch bag with the sandwiches. "You'll need to eat while you drive."

"I wish there were more people like you," Callum smiled meekly at the generosity. "I don't even know where to go now. I'm ready to give up."

"Then they win," Father Landon replied.

"Who are *They*?"

"Whoever murdered Agatha Gilcrest, blamed an innocent man for that crime, ruined your grandfather's name and started the same cycle of blood all over again. History is repeating itself. It's time for you to stop it."

"How? This person seems to have unlimited resources and operates above the law. All of my allies are being killed off one by one. I'm alone now."

"You are never alone. And whoever this evil person is, they are not above all law."

Callum sighed. He knew this priest would dish out some sort of fortune cookie philosophy, but Callum was a realist. There was no room in his life or line of work for blind faith.

"Whoever this evil is," Father Landon began, "they're afraid of you."

"Afraid of me? I don't think so. Right now I'm scared shi...silly."

"Somewhere along the way, you have uncovered something — some dark secret that has made them come out of hiding after seventy years. Something that they're willing to kill for, to keep it in the dark. You must bring them into the light," said Father Landon, resting his hand on the old iron box. "The alternative is to spend the rest of your life running from this evil and the law, branded a murderer."

"I'm not a crusader. I'm an insurance investigator," Callum said dejectedly. "What you're asking is impossible."

"You are the grandson of Inspector John Toughill," Father Landon said with authority. "It's time to bring the justice he sacrificed for. Your job is to take care of what is possible, and trust God with the impossible..."

"I'm sorry, Father," Callum replied sheepishly. "I don't believe in miracles... certainly not after what has happened over the last few days."

"Because you've lost your faith."

"I don't think I ever had it," Callum mumbled. "What is faith, anyway?"

"For one who has no faith no explanation is possible. But if you have faith, no explanation is needed."

. . .

As Edward waited for the kettle to boil for some hot chocolate, he found his mind was in turmoil. His logical, analytical, common sense kept nagging at him, telling him this was all impossible. This young woman, who could pass for his granddaughter, could not possibly be his mother. It defied the laws of physics, time and sanity. Yet, she knew things that no one else could have known. And when he looked into her eyes, he felt like a lost little boy and found comfort knowing that she was now here. *Could he accept her on blind faith?*

He looked over at Myra, nestled on the sofa with one of his old photo albums sitting open on her lap. Her face bathed in a warm glow, she seemed mesmerized by the flickering flames in the fireplace that danced to the haunting melody from the stereo. This small section of the 25 minute opus *Rhapsody on a Theme of Paganini*, by Sergei Rachmaninoff was used in an inexplicable time travel movie two years ago: *Somewhere in Time*. Though not a commercial success, Edward loved the 1912 setting that the hero traveled back in time to visit. How ironic. In so many ways.

"A penny for your thoughts," Edward said, breaking the silence.

Myra looked up with a start and then smiled, "Is that expression still around?"

"Well it's been in our vocabulary for over four hundred years. Everything else has gone up with inflation but I suppose thoughts and opinions are still only worth a penny."

"I was still thinking about the world that has long gone," said Myra as she then looked down at the photo album and pointed to a picture of an elderly bespectacled woman standing next to Edward at a garden party. "Who is this other woman pretending to be me?"

Edward didn't know how to respond. The kettle whistled, drawing him away for a moment as he took it off the heat and poured it into two mugs with cocoa.

She continued, "Maybe you're right about Archie... or perhaps he was blackmailed... but what of my mother? How could she accept an imposter?" Edward paused from his task. How could he tell her? She had the right to know. He cleared his throat, "We never saw her again after *Titanic*."

"What do you mean? Why not? She lived here in New York with my sister, Maggie!"

Edward nodded, he remembered that detail, "They died in a fire."

"Fire?" Myra exclaimed. The photo album dropped to the floor. "Oh my god... that's horrible! When?"

"In 1912, the same year *Titanic* sank," Edward recounted, "Seventy years ago."

Myra seemed unaware as she spoke, "It was just as Mother feared."

"What do you mean?"

"She was paranoid of dying in a fire. Would get out of bed two or three times a night to make sure the fire was out in the wood stove. It was for that reason she never allowed smoking in the house."

"What did you say?" Edward asked coming out of the kitchen.

"She was paranoid of fire..."

"No, not that... your mother didn't allow smoking?"

"That's right," replied Myra. "Archie was quite annoyed with that the first time he came over to meet her..."

"That's how the fire was started," Edward interrupted. He strained to remember the earliest conversation he had with his father about the family tragedy. "I was told Grandma Sloane died in a fire caused by her smoking in bed and falling asleep. Your sister died from smoke inhalation."

"That's not possible! Mama didn't smoke!" Myra insisted.

"But Archie... did," Edward remembered how much his father used to smoke, before he had to get a new heart.

"Edward, what are you saying? You can't possibly think that your father is capable of murder? I can believe he could be manipulating and controlling... but not a murderer."

"Well, you were being poisoned."

"Poison?" Myra was shocked.

"Dr. Lindsay informed me that the hospital found Laudanum in your bloodstream. Judging by the amount in your system... you had been ingesting it over a long period of time."

"I don't remember ever having taken Laudanum," Myra absently picked up the photo album. Tears were welling up in her eyes, and she started to busy herself looking through older pictures of her family. "This is too much for me. To you they've been dead for seventy years. From my perspective, I only saw Mama and Maggie… a couple of months ago… and the idea that my husband could be responsible is unthinkable."

"I'm sorry," was all Edward could muster for comfort. The flashing light on his answering machine momentarily drew his attention. Sneaking a peek, he noticed that he had missed four calls while he was out looking for Myra.

"Is this you? Don't you look handsome!" Myra said.

Edward looked back to see Myra pointing at a photo, and strained his neck to see what it was. "Oh, yes, my high school graduation photo. I can't believe I was that boyish looking. Excuse the awful haircut."

"Oh no, I think you look handsome…" Myra stopped in mid-breath. Edward glanced over to see the color drain from her face as she stared at the photo. Her finger stabbed at the image of the woman standing next to young Edward and his father. "Who is that?"

"That's…motherrr…the other 'Myra'…."

Edward could see the rage swell in her eyes as she glared at the face of the woman who had taken over her life. Through gritted teeth Myra hissed, "I know her!"

April 9, 1982

CHAPTER 47

Callum had been driving aimlessly, trying to figure out what to do next. He knew he needed to dig up more evidence, but that would be difficult to do now that he was no longer able to show his face in public.

As he was approaching one of the few self-serve filling stations in the area, Callum looked down at the petrol gauge. The needle was at a quarter-tank. Better to top up Dolanna's automobile here. The fewer people he had to interact with, the better.

After doing so, he decided to check his home answer-phone to see if there were any messages or clues. After punching in his code, 505, he could hear the machine whirl as it rewound. First was a voice from the beyond as he heard de Kirkhaugh say, "The next time you go after a century old murderer, make sure you have all the facts!"

It was the same message he had left with his pager system. *What did he mean?* Now Callum couldn't help but wonder if there was some cryptic clue within it that he had to decipher. He pressed '4' to rewind again. *The next time you go after a century old murderer, make sure you have all the facts!* Callum wrote it verbatim in his note pad. What did it mean?

Click, Beep!

Then a male voice with an American accent said, "Mr. Toughill, this is Edward Hoffman. I'm sorry I missed your calls. Thank you for letting me know about Dolanna. I can be reached at the same number you called before. Tomorrow I'll be traveling but will be arriving there in London at Stansted airport on my private jet..."

Callum quickly jotted down the flight itinerary as Edward spoke. That settled it. Callum knew where he was going next: his flat in London to change his clothes, then to Stansted to find Edward Hoffman. But first one other call. *This is going to be unpleasant.*

. . .

"Commander Toughill, speaking," Pamela said into the receiver as she answered her office phone.

"Pamela... It's me."

"Are you mad?" Pamela whispered in a harsh tone, as her blood began to boil. "You can't ring me up here. I'm MOD Police... you are a wanted fugitive."

"I didn't kill anyone!" Callum exclaimed.

She could hear the frustration and desperation in his voice. "Don't you think I know that?"

"They're calling me Jack Frost. What does that mean?"

Pamela stole a glance to make sure there wasn't anyone within earshot.

"Jack Frost is the nickname of an assassin. Uses bullets made up of gallium and liquid nitrogen. In theory the bullet melts in the body... making it untraceable."

"It may be more than a theory. When I was released from Strathclyde Police holding, de Kirkhaugh mentioned a modified gun to shoot £75 bullets."

"Gallium is expensive. From what I recall, a private company made some prototypes and both MOD and our American counterparts were interested but the prototype didn't seem cost effective. Especially since the bullets needed to remain cool at all times, hence the modified gun...."

"Why?"

"The bullets would melt... you even need to wear gloves because body heat would compromise them."

Pamela stopped as she heard voices approaching.

"What about..." Callum started.

"Hold on a moment, sir, while I look that up," Pamela said into the phone, and started to rifle through some pages on her desk. As soon as the voice disappeared, she said back into the phone. "You can't stay on the line. However, you need to know that I read on the ARPANET..."

"The what?"

Pamela sighed. She didn't have time to explain how the *Advanced Research Projects Agency Network* was a global network of computers connected together for the sharing of science, medical and defense information for the last six years. Nor should she be overheard sharing that information. "... not important. Yesterday there were three shootings using gallium bullets, one in Glasgow, one in London and one in New York City. That's how we know it's not you."

"That means it's an international organization of assassins? Bloody Hell! What have I gotten myself into? "

"You're the one who always complained that your work was too dull."

"What about Dolanna?" Callum asked. "She's in danger too…"

Pamela was caught in a difficult position. She had to follow protocol. "I don't know if I can keep…"

"She's Agatha Gilcrest's granddaughter…"

"She didn't mention that when we spoke…"

"That's because I don't think she knows."

"Fantastic! That would explain a lot. How do *you* know she's related?"

"Gut feeling… I had hoped to get back to the Scottish Record Office, to confirm. But I can't go someplace so public."

"Well, I can assure you I can't get to Edinburgh right now… not without something more concrete."

"Pamela!"

"I'm sorry. My hands are tied. I will keep Dolanna here… for… um… medical observation."

"Oh, wait a mo… Could you get a blood sample from her?"

Pamela knew where he was going. It was at least something she could do without drawing attention. But she didn't want him to think that she would be on his beck-and-call. She needed to be careful. "I'll see what I can do… no promises."

"Thanks… I'm heading to…"

"I don't want to know," interrupted Pamela. "If someone asks me where you are, I won't have to lie."

CHAPTER 48

Emily Speck stood in front of a news camera, holding a microphone as she spoke in her friendly British manner, "Crowds have already gathered here on the docks of Southampton to marvel at the RMS *Titan*. Although named differently, it bears a striking resemblance to the infamous ship *Titanic*. Out of respect for fellow survivors, the *Hoffman* family has chosen not to name her *Titanic II* as originally planned."

Emily then motioned for a handsome man in a naval uniform to stand next to her, "I am speaking now with Captain Thomas Hastings, who will be in command of the RMS *Titan* on her maiden voyage. Captain, can you tell us about this new ship and how it compares to the original *Titanic*?"

"Certainly," Hastings said with a smile and gestured to the immense ship behind them. "The RMS *Titan* is even larger than the original *Titanic* which was 882 ft long, this one is over 1,300 ft long. Like the *Titanic* it is furnished with Art Nouveau décor, but with more modern amenities, like a five-star hotel, fit for a king."

"Or a Queen, as will be the case for the maiden voyage," Emily chimed in.

Captain Hastings nodded, "Quite right. Her Majesty The Queen and His Royal Highness the Duke of Edinburgh will be arriving tomorrow. For their safety, and the safety of all our passengers, the *Titan* boasts the latest in navigational systems. It's equipped with sonar and radar and is the first ship with the prototype Global Maritime Distress and Safety System developed by the International Maritime Organization as well as the NavStar Global Positioning Satellite."

"What does that mean exactly?"

"It's a satellite technology connected with the ship and ship-board radio systems. It provides faster tracking of the ship if in distress, provides the

Titan with any vital maritime information and can locate its position from space. Where the crow's nest used to be on the original *Titanic*, the *Titan* has aviation radar."

"History recalls that there weren't enough lifeboats for all the passengers aboard the *Titanic*," Emily recounted. "I wager that's not the case here."

"Quite right. Unlike its predecessor, the *Titan* has enough: 30 solid lifeboats and 26 self-inflatables to accommodate every passenger and all crew. Another safety improvement is a larger rudder to make it easier to turn, which was one of the many shortcomings of *Titanic*. Also, below the waterline on either side of the ship is a horizontal stabilizer."

"What happens if you run into icebergs?"

"Our sonar system will detect them and if that isn't enough, the *Titan* has a strengthened hull, an ice-breaking shaped bow and the power to plow through ice-covered waters."

"Smashing!" Emily said, pleased with her pun. "Have you any other tidbits of trivia for our viewers?"

"Well," Captain Hastings looked at the ship for a moment then pointed to the four smoke stacks. "The original *Titanic* had three working smoke stacks and the fourth was for decoration. If you take a look at this ship, all four provide air induction for the engines but are mostly for decoration since modern ocean liners are no longer steam-powered."

"But didn't I see photos of boilers in the brochure?"

"They're mainly as an attraction and picture opportunity but they do not burn coal for this ship. Ironically, they are filled with water as *ballast*, added extra weight, since without them and the added weight of the coal, the design of the ship would be top-heavy."

"Are those dogs I see leaving the ship?" asked Emily, pointing to the gangplank where uniformed constables were exiting with German Shepherds on leashes.

"Yes," said Captain Hastings. "Those are detection dogs and they just finished doing a sweep of the ship looking for explosives. They will be on hand tomorrow as passengers board the ship."

"I guess you can't be too careful."

Captain Hastings nodded, "It may seem like much but this time we can really say: it's unsinkable."

· · ·

A crew member with the name 'Smith' on his nametag ran his security pass through the laser scanner. The scanner recognized the bar code on his pass, the light 'beeped' green and the door to the forward hull was unlocked. Smith put his security pass in his pocket, picked up his tool box and strolled in, whistling.

Unrolling the detailed deck plans of the RMS *Titan*, Smith oriented himself with the layout of the drawings and moved forward, looking for a specific junction point below the water line.

Upon finding the exact section marked on the drawing, Smith set down the drawing, opened his toolbox and pulled out a spool of wire. Next he removed a large jug of ammonia. After unscrewing the top, he carefully pulled a clear plastic bag from the noxious liquid. Shaking off the excess, he then ripped the bag open and pulled out the dry C4 explosives. Using the drawing for reference, Smith went to work.

CHAPTER 49

"Sorry I'm late. The roads were hell," Roger Zisholm muttered as he dragged his leather luggage on a leash down the aisle of the Hoffman International private jet. The small wheels and poor balance made Roger's large case tip over repeatedly. "They should really figure out how to properly put wheels on luggage."

As Roger continued to fight valiantly with his carry-on, Jamie, the flight's stewardess, approached, "Can I get anyone some refreshments while we wait?"

"None for me," said Edward who always waited until they were airborne.

"No thank you," replied Myra.

"Brandy for me," grunted Roger as he stuffed his case in the overhead compartment across the aisle and threw his overcoat carelessly into the seat next to him.

"How does this machine work?" Myra asked as she reclined in the lavish seat. Edward smiled. In 1912, aviation was still in its infancy, something for daredevils rather than an accepted form of travel. He thought it would be best to let her experience it without any preconceived notions. He leaned over and whispered, "It's difficult to explain. Better that you see with your own eyes."

"It's larger than a yacht," Myra remarked.

"We'll be on our way soon," said Edward. *If we ever get off the ground, that is,* he thought. The flight was further delayed departing from the Bradley International Airport in Connecticut due to the weather. Edward set his copy of the *New York Times* on the table between his and Myra's seats and glanced out the window. It was no longer snowing, so that was a good sign. He could still see the scars of where the tornado had damaged the airport when it ripped through town a couple of years ago.

This airport had seen a lot of history over the years. The first time Edward had set foot here was the summer of 1941. It was a military airbase then, and Edward was a young officer flying to Canada for a covert training mission. He was here when the airport's namesake, Lt. Bradley, crashed his P40 during a training drill. The death of the young pilot was the first fatality of the new airbase. Edward still recalled the look of horror and shock on his fellow officers' faces — it was the same raw emotion he'd seen when everyone in his lifeboat had watched helplessly as the *Titanic* disappeared beneath the dark waters. No one could speak. No words could express the pain in their hearts, though he was far too young to completely understand it. In later years Edward was unable to attend live sporting events: the sudden cheer of a home run had the same volume and intensity as the last cries from the victims of the *Titanic*.

Then, finally, the plane jolted forward, breaking Edward free from the painful memories. He turned his attention back to Myra, as he was looking forward to witnessing her reaction.

"Here, trade places with me," Edward said as he offered his seat by the window. He looked over to where Roger was seated. Roger, now with a drink in hand, was struggling to keep his eyes open as he studied today's *Wall Street Journal*.

As Edward showed Myra how to buckle the seatbelt, the aircraft began to pick up speed. Myra looked out the window, and with some alarm, gripped the armrest tightly enough to turn her knuckles white. When the aircraft lurched upward, Myra started to scream, startling Roger who knocked over his drink and cursed loudly. Edward laughed but Myra was oblivious as she continued to scream. Edward couldn't tell if it was a scream of fear or exhilaration.

– – –

Callum's lower back ached after having driven for seven hours straight, except for two stops: one for refilling petrol again and another to visit the loo. Now he gave his wobbly legs a good stretch and stumbled up the stairs, carrying the iron box into his London flat. He looked at his watch to see if he had time for a shower. He unlocked the door. *Home sweet... Hell!*

Someone had been in his flat. Every door and drawer opened. He set the iron box down, took out his pistol, and carefully went from room to room. There was no one else there.

He returned to the main room and surveyed the damage. The whole flat had been angrily torn apart, likely because they didn't find what they were looking for. Only the extra files that Percy had given him were gone.

Callum knew they'd be back, but he needed a shower and a coffee. He walked by his phone: no new messages. Then he saw the red light flashing on his fax machine: *Out of paper.* Callum had some extra rolls of thermal fax paper but decided to hunt them down later. He needed coffee, now. Measuring out a strong batch, he poured the water and pressed the "on" button. The red light came on. *Why does everything have a red light?*

He stood there for a moment, swaying, trying to stay standing as he watched the coffee starting to drip… it wasn't fast enough, *damn it!*

Callum needed to occupy himself or he'd fall asleep standing up. Perhaps find the fax roll. A nice mindless task. Then he looked at the mess that was his apartment. *Sigh. Coffee first.* Then he would get to the fax… the fax… the fax…

The Fax!

Callum ran to the answering machine and pressed 'rewind' then 'play'. This time de Kirkhaugh's voice from beyond echoed through his flat. *"The next time you go after a century old murderer, make sure you have all the facts!"*

"Fax! Not Facts!" Callum yelled at himself, as he picked up an upturned drawer, searching. There he found a roll. He quickly unwrapped it and threw the wrapper on the floor as he popped open the fax machine and loaded the new roll in.

As soon as he closed it, it whirled to life. On the display screen he read: *Print from memory.*

Slowly a page began to emerge. Callum read the top: *Glasgow Police 1909*

"De Kirkhaugh, I underestimated you," Callum said as he watched the police files from the past start to spew out. "You knew your life was at risk… and you sent me the evidence before they could destroy it. You're bloody brilliant."

• • •

Later, the monotony of air travel had set in: nothing to see outside the window except the tops of the clouds. Finally able to release her grip from the armrest, Myra could take a sip of wine. Edward glanced over to Roger, who was fast asleep, snoring, with an empty brandy glass next to him. Edward gestured for Myra to follow him to another seat further down as to not disturb Roger's slumber. Edward leaned in and whispered, "Are you sure it's Miss Langlea?"

"Positive." Myra added, "I knew her face the moment I saw her…. Does she have different colored eyes?"

"How so?"

"Her right eye was ochre…" Myra closed her eyes as she spoke, "…or, yellow-green hazel might be more appropriate, and her left eye was a deep brown."

Edward nodded. She had it correct. The old graduation photograph that Myra had recognized was in black & white and in the other photos his 'mother' either had red-eye from the flash or a glare on her thick glasses. Myra couldn't have known this detail because of the pictures.

Edward looked over at Roger sleeping, then back to Myra, "So, how long had Miss Langlea been in your employ?"

"Not for very long. Since the summer of 1911. We were staying in London at the time. My previous Lady's Maid had to take a leave of absence when her mother fell ill, and Archie took care of finding a replacement. She had been a maid for another family member."

"How admirable of him."

"You still suspect your father?"

"Well it stands to reason. He was probably having an affair with her! You had already fulfilled your matrimonial duties and produced an heir, thereby guaranteeing Archie's claim to the family wealth. He couldn't divorce you, certainly not in 1912. The social scandal would have had him disinherited. So by disposing of you and having Heather Langlea take your identity, Father was allowed a new life, with no scandal, and all of your assets joined with his."

"But how could they have possibly known that the *Titanic* was going to sink?"

"Don't forget, you were being given Laudanum. You had told me that the night the ship sank, the maid fixed you some tea —Miss Langlea likely put the Laudanum in the teapot."

Myra seemed flustered and upset. Then she sat up and added, "But Archie had a cup of tea as well."

Edward sat back and thought for a moment. Then it hit him, "Most likely it was only your cup that was laced with Laudanum. In its day Laudanum was used as a sedative...produced sleep... probably to make sure you slept through the night, should they want some late-night tryst."

"Eddie!" Myra was shocked. Then as the truth sank in, "That would explain why I couldn't wake up fully when the cabin was filling up with ice-cold water."

"Exactly. The sinking of the *Titanic* presented a fortuitous circumstance to accelerate their plans for murder. You weren't meant to wake up at all."

"What do we do now? We have no proof."

"Even if we did, there would be nothing we could do. You're not dead so they can't be charged with murder."

"Surely we can argue that they tried," asked Myra.

"We would have to prove that you are the real Myra Sloane Hoffman. If we went to the authorities and told them that you've traveled forward through time they would have us committed."

"But what about...?"

Edward signaled Myra to be quiet as Jamie approached. She smiled at them both and asked, "Could I get either of you some more refreshments?"

. . .

Callum was reading the fax files excitedly, now fully awake. He was just starting to put the puzzle pieces together when he heard the door open behind him. He spun around and saw Milton, the familiar husky police detective from Glasgow, standing in his doorway. "Callum Toughill, you're under arrest for the murder of Donald de Kirkhaugh, Ruth McArthur and Janna...."

"Hold it! I didn't kill anyone," Callum said. "I have proof that I'm telling you the truth. Here's a fax from de Kirkhaugh."

"I'll take those," Milton said.

"Wait a minute," Callum said, withdrawing the papers, "You're Strathclyde Police. You have no jurisdiction outside of Scotland."

"Yes, I do," Milton said with a smile. "We're part of the United Kingdom... we can arrest where ever..."

"No," Callum interrupted. "I know Parliament is considering that move... but it's not the case... yet."

Milton pulled his gun and aimed it at Callum, "You're coming with me and you're bringing those papers... and that iron box you brought in. If you're telling me the truth, then you have nothing to worry about."

"How did you know about the iron..." Callum was suddenly distracted by the gun aimed at him, then looked down at the fax machine and said, "It's still printing. I'm going to have my coffee while it finishes."

Callum discretely pressed the large button on his answer-phone before he crossed into his kitchen.

"Just stay where you are!"

"I'm not going anywhere. But I've had a rough few days and I really need my coffee," Callum grabbed the pot. "Would you like a cup?"

"Put your hands up where I can see them!"

Callum turned back to Milton who had his finger on the trigger and a determined look in his eye. Callum casually asked, "Nice gun... so... how could you kill your partner?"

"What?"

"Modified weapon..." Callum said gesturing to the gun in Milton's hand. It had an extra attachment to the side and a cable or tube connected a battery pack attached to Milton's belt. "I wager that's the one that killed de Kirkhaugh... and Ruthie... and you were first officer on the scene. Isn't that convenient? Go in, kill as *Jack Frost* with an untraceable bullet, and then go back in as the investigating detective... to make sure you've covered your tracks... or add to them if you've left your fingerprints by mistake. Pretty smart."

"You're not," Milton sneered. "Because now that you know, I can't let you leave this room alive."

"Before you shoot me, I have to know: who hired you?" Callum asked.

Milton laughed, "What do you think this is, the bloody cinema? Must the villain tell the hero the whole diabolical plan?"

"Worth a chance," Callum said, still holding the coffee pot. "You tell me who hired you and I'll open the box."

Milton glanced down at the locked box. "I can shoot you now and open it myself."

"You can try. It's booby-trapped. Only I can open it," Callum said. Milton stole another glance at the locked iron box. Callum asked again, "Who hired you?"

"Couldn't even if I wanted to," Milton said. "Truth is… I'm given a name, address and when the job's done money goes into my account. Now where are your grandfather's notes?"

"Sorry, the deal was I would tell you if you told me who hired you," Callum said.

Milton aimed the gun at Callum's crotch, "I don't have to kill you quickly."

BEEP-BEEP

"End of tape," said the robotic voice from the answer-phone, which had recorded the whole conversation after Callum had hit the 'memo' button. Milton was distracted by the sudden beeps and voice. Callum took advantage of the situation and threw the coffee pot at Milton, who deflected it with his gun. The glass pot shattered, hot coffee burned his hand and Milton fumbled his gun.

Callum took this opportunity to unclip his gun from his shoulder holster and aim it at Milton, who had recovered. Now both men were aiming their guns at each other.

"Drop your weapon!" Milton demanded, his gun aimed at Callum's chest.

"No, you drop yours," Callum said with a grin. "I believe, in the cinema, this is what they call a Mexican Stand-off."

"I'm going to kill you," screamed Milton.

"Not if I kill you first."

Both men looked at each other. Jaws clenched. Fingers hovering over the trigger…

BLAM!

BLAM!

CHAPTER 50

Callum was flat on his back, staring up at his ceiling. His chest burning from the impact of the bullet, he struggled to breathe after having the air knocked out of him when he landed. He reached with his hand to feel the damage; his fingertips felt the thick liquid over his heart. Slowly, he brought that hand into the field of his vision, to see his fingertips covered in thick, metallic ooze.

He forced himself to sit up, and his ribs hurt. He reached under his shirt to feel his chest gingerly again. The bullet had not pierced the skin, but he felt a welt forming there.

Suddenly he heard Milton gasping. He looked over. Milton was not so lucky. Callum reached over to where his gun fell and grabbed it as he strained to get onto his feet. He hobbled over to where Milton was bleeding profusely from the wound in his chest.

As Callum neared him, he could see the look of confusion fall across Milton's face. Blood gurgled from his mouth as he spoke, "I shot you! I know I hit you!"

"Yeah, you did," Callum said. "And this is the part where the hero tells the villain how bloody stupid he is... I knew your expensive, untraceable bullets could be compromised if you weren't wearing gloves. Hot coffee really fucks them up!"

Of course it hadn't melted them as completely as Callum had hoped, and he was still in pain, but he wasn't going to give this sod the satisfaction of knowing that. Milton gasped trying to say something. When Callum bent down to listen, Milton grabbed him. Callum aimed his gun at Milton. It was too late. Milton was dead.

Callum released him and looked down at his broken carafe. So much for having a coffee. He could hear sirens in the distance. Someone had likely heard the gunshots and had rung the police. He looked about. Callum was still a fugitive, and now he had a dead Strathclyde Police Officer in his flat. Didn't look good. He hobbled over to his answer-phone and popped the cassette tape out of it. At least he had this recorded conversation on his side, but he wasn't going to trust this with just anyone, so he tucked it into his jacket pocket. The sirens seemed to be getting closer. He picked up the phone and dialed as he gathered up the faxes de Kirkhaugh had sent him and placed them in a large envelope from the floor.

"Commander Toughill, speaking," Pamela's voice said through the receiver.

"Pamela!" Callum exclaimed frantically into the phone. "I have a dead Jack Frost in my flat. The London coppers are on their way. Come and get him!"

"I'll send someone over," said Pamela.

"I won't be here," Callum said as he hung up the phone. Although the police in London did not carry guns, he didn't want a confrontation with them. He looked at the dead police officer on his floor. Obviously, whoever was behind this had money: not only did they buy military designed weapons with £75 bullets, but they were also powerful enough to buy police officials to form a network of assassins, and anonymously deposit money into their bank accounts.

Someone with a lot of money, who wanted to ensure that Dolanna's secret was never revealed. Callum looked at his watch. Edward Hoffman's private jet would be landing at the airport soon.

Callum placed the envelope on the iron box, to take with him. He checked how many bullets he still had in his Walther P-38, then looked down at Milton's corpse, "Sorry I can't wait for your friends —I have to go take care of Edward Hoffman once and for all."

– – –

For the in-flight entertainment, the flight attendant had chosen the movie *The Final Countdown*. It was a recent film and one that Edward enjoyed watching on a long flight to take his mind off other matters in the past. She had no idea that this time it would have the opposite effect, striking a familiar chord as Martin Sheen's character said on the screen, "All of us know, movement through time is possible. Einstein proved it…in theory."

The premise of the science fiction film surrounds a nuclear battle ship with 90 aircrafts and almost 6,000 men. They are inexplicably taken through a 'time storm' and find themselves back in time to the day before the attack on Pearl Harbor in 1941.

Do they sit idly by and watch the American fleet get butchered as history recorded it? Or do they interfere, thus changing the war and the course of history for the next 40 years?

Edward found himself having to explain to Myra the major events of World War II and the horrors of Hitler's Nazi Germany, D-Day and the conclusion with the devastating effects of the Atomic Bomb.

"So if it was such a terrible time," Myra pondered, "What is the harm in interfering?"

"Well, the ethical issue aside," Edward began, "They also create a paradox: Would altering history change their own existence?"

"I don't understand," Myra said.

"In time travel, there are many theories, but three that I subscribe to. First, that there is only one, single fixed history which cannot be changed no matter what we do. Even going back in time is already a part of that history. Here is an example: I go back in time to find out what happened to my mysterious ancestor who disappeared without a trace. In the process I end up meeting and falling in love with a woman. However, I return to the present to find that that woman was my great-great grandmother and I was the mysterious ancestor who disappeared without a trace... history is unchanged because it was always like that."

"So then whatever they choose to do, it wouldn't truly be interfering with the past if it was recorded as such?"

"In the case of this movie, we know that there was never a nuclear arsenal and fighter jets, so the second theory would apply: history is flexible and is subject to change. And now they can alter the history with advanced weapons."

"What is the harm in that?"

"Well let's say, I go back in time and accidentally kill my grandfather when he was a child. Therefore, he never had children and I suddenly cease to exist. And never existed."

"If you never existed, how did you go back in time?" asked Myra.

"There's the paradox," smiled Edward.

"I don't know what's so fascinating about time travel. I find it's giving me a headache."

Edward thought for a moment then said, "There is an inherent desire to conquer time, for in the end... it conquers us."

Myra studied him for a moment, then asked, "What is the third?"

"Third what?"

"You said there were three theories you subscribe to."

"Quite right," Edward said as he took a sip from his glass, "The third is the idea of an alternate timeline."

"What does that mean?"

"In that theory, there are multiple histories that coexist in alternate realities…" said Edward, but he could see the look of confusion in her face. "Ok, to simplify it, in that theory, there is a universe co-existing with ours where the *Titanic* never struck the iceberg at 11:40 pm and therefore never sank. Likewise, there is another universe where it did sink but you didn't drink the Laudanum-filled tea."

"And I got off the ship and lived a happy life raising you as my son."

"Precisely."

Myra sighed, "I wish I was in that universe instead of this one."

"So do I," said Edward as he raised his glass to her. "So do I."

CHAPTER 51

Out of habit, Callum started for Heathrow, then recalled that Edward had said he was arriving at the Stansted Airport, which was further north. Fortunately he realized it before leaving London, so it wasn't as much of a back-track to get onto the M11 motorway.

It was usually a good half-hour drive from Central London, but there was traffic queuing due to construction at one of the junction points. *Bloody Hell!* thought Callum.

He looked at the petrol gauge on the dashboard. It was uncomfortably low. *Bloody Hell, again!* Callum cursed to himself as he soon realized that the only service station anywhere on the M11 wasn't past the planning stages. To make matters more stressful, he found himself behind a police car that was patrolling the motorway. Callum was still a fugitive and was trying to drive inconspicuously, while feeling the urgency to reach Essex before he missed the plane or ran out of fuel.

He had to slam on the breaks suddenly as traffic came to a grinding halt, and nearly rear-ended the police car. *Too bloody close!* At this point it would be faster to walk. He was only inching now on the motorway. He glanced at the clock on the dashboard and frowned, *I'm barely moving but time is moving too fast!*

• • •

"How is time travel possible?" Myra asked after watching the film.

Edward looked at her and asked, "Are you asking how it was done in the movie or how you traveled through time?"

"Well, the fellow in the movie said it was possible," she remarked thoughtfully.

"The theoretical physicist, Albert Einstein, deduced that the faster you travel, the slower the time moves. If this jet could travel at the speed of light which is a little more than 299,000,000 miles per second, one minute to us in the plane would be one year to the people on the ground who are not traveling as quickly as we are. So if we traveled for two years, we would return to find two *hundred* earth years had gone by. So in a sense we would have traveled forward in time."

"But how could you get *back* in time?" Myra asked.

Edward shrugged, "You can't. Not according to Einstein's theory."

Myra pouted. Edward could see the frustration in her intelligent eyes as she asked, "Are there other theories?"

"Certainly," Edward loved discussing time travel possibilities. "There are beliefs in a celestial wormhole, a shortcut through space-time, but that's not proven. There were three fiction novels published within the last decade; one made into a film, where the protagonist traveled back in time through self-hypnosis, convincing themselves that they were back in time. Their thoughts simply became reality."

"But you said they were fiction," Myra added.

"Generally yes," Edward replied. "Time travel has always been a plot device used by authors but it has never been proven as possible… until you."

There was a moment of silence as Myra seemed to digest this information, then she asked, "What other theories are there for moving through time?"

"Countless," Edward said thoughtfully. "There was one horror novel that came out a couple of years ago in which the hero could see into the future of a person he touched. Though he was not physically moving through time, he knew what was going to happen unless he altered the flow of that timeline."

"Because it hadn't happened yet," Myra added.

"Correct," Edward smiled as she seemed to be grasping the concept. "The novel addressed the question that has been asked by many scientists and philosophers alike: If you could go back in time, would you kill Hitler before he became a dictator?"

"Is Hitler the one who ruled Germany, and invaded Europe…"

"That's right!"

"Would you kill him?" Myra asked.

"Hmmm," Edward pondered as he sat back in his chair. "Armed with the knowledge of the future, I would hesitate for a moment. After all, though his death might have prevented World War II from ever happening and would essentially create another timeline, or alternate universe, where six million innocent people might not have died in the Nazi death camps…. However, some believe there is no way to predict the outcome of a new timeline… and perhaps there's a worse dictator that would come to power… Then there's the grandfather paradox: Perhaps the chain of events in the new timeline will cause an early death in my own life and I cease to exist."

"So you wouldn't kill Hitler?" Myra surmised.

"I never said that... I said I'd hesitate for a moment. I would still kill him."

Myra looked at him in shock, "What about the uncertainty in the new timeline?"

Edward leaned in and said, "I've seen first-hand the horrors of his death camps and his attempt at genocide. I'd gladly sacrifice my own existence if there was a chance at saving innocent lives."

Edward signaled Myra to be quiet as Jamie approached. She nodded at Myra then addressed Edward, "There is a phone call for you, sir."

"Thank you. Wait here. I'll be right back." Edward followed the stewardess to the front.

— — —

"What do you mean 'delayed'?" Callum demanded of the clerk behind the desk.

"The Hoffman Private Jet was delayed in its take off due to poor weather conditions," replied the clerk. "It should be arriving shortly."

"Thanks," Callum grumbled. He had to get back to the car as he left it parked in the 'Short Stay' area. He noticed a security officer staring at him. He continued to walk casually as to not draw attention. He stole a glance to see the security officer talking to another airport officer while pointing in his direction.

Callum would not be able to sit around waiting for Edward. He looked at his watch. Now time was moving very slowly.

• • •

Moments later, Edward returned with a solemn look on his face. Myra tried to read his expression. He finally looked up at her and said, "Dr. Lindsay was mugged yesterday."

"Mugged? What does that mean?"

"She was shot and robbed as she was getting home, an all too familiar occurrence in large cities like New York."

"Is she all right?"

"The bullet has been removed but she's still in critical condition," Edward said. Then noticing the confusion in her brow added. "It's too early to tell whether she'll survive."

"Is there anything we can do?" Myra asked.

Edward shook his head, "I'm afraid not. Only time will tell."

Myra looked solemnly out the window. Edward could see the sadness well up in her eyes. His hand was reaching into his inside jacket pocket for his handkerchief when it felt the bulky folded paper.

"Oh, before I forget, you'll need this," said Edward as he handed it to Myra.

"What is it?" asked Myra as she took it.

"It's a security boarding pass," Edward said.

Jamie quickly came up the aisle toward them.

"The captain wanted me to let you know that we are starting our descent into London," Jamie said sweetly.

"Thank you, Jamie," Edward replied.

Myra looked at the sleek boarding pass with the embossed logo and asked as she ran her finger across the pattern of several vertical black lines, "What are these lines?"

"That is called a *barcode 39*," Edward said. "The system to read it was developed by the U.S. Department of Defense. With the Royal family on board the ship, the security is going to be tight, especially with the situation in the Falkland Islands. There has been an apparent death threat made on the Queen should the British troops not pull out by the end of the week."

"My word," remarked Myra. "Should the Queen be making the journey at all?"

"She's committed to being present at the transfer of the Canadian Constitution in Ottawa next week and she's a tough lady, not easily intimidated by radicals."

"But are you responsible for her safety? How safe can a ship be?"

"It's like a battleship. In fact, should it be called to war like the RMS *Queen Mary* was, it can be battle-ready. Complete with anti-aircraft guns and large sickbay for transporting wounded."

"They had nothing like that on the *Titanic*."

"No they didn't. It's a different world. A sad world where we have to anticipate every worse-case scenario, so that no tragedy can ever happen again."

– – –

Deep in the hull of the RMS *Titan*, Smith stood back to admire his work. No one would ever find it.

Smith looked at his watch and synchronized the clock on the bomb's timer with it. He smirked. *The maiden voyage of the RMS Titan will end with a bang.*

CHAPTER 52

Callum could see the small private jet with the Hoffman International logo painted on its side, as it was on its approach to the only runway at Stansted Airport. *It wouldn't be long, now!*

Sitting in Dolanna's car, parked in Rounded Coppice Road near a hotel, Callum patted his jacket and felt the Walther P-38 in his shoulder holster. He was going to get some answers from Edward Hoffman, one way or another.

"Sir, please step out of the car," said a male voice. With the deafening sounds of the airport, Callum did not even hear anyone approach the car. Callum looked to his right and saw an Airport Security Officer standing outside the driver's side of his vehicle. Callum looked into his rear-view mirror and saw another officer sitting in an airport security car. The officer repeated, "I said, step out of the car."

He looked ahead and saw the Hoffman Jet as it circled around again, preparing to come in for a landing. The wheels were already down.

Callum turned to his right, smiled and nodded at the officer. Then he tramped his right foot down on the accelerator as he popped it into gear, and the car shot forward.

He had only a few minutes of lead-time as the security car picked up the officer and burst in pursuit. Callum raced toward Long Boarder Road when he saw an Airport Security lorry racing toward him with its siren howling angrily at him.

When he could almost make out the colour of the oncoming officer's eyes, Callum spun the steering wheel hard and entered the second roundabout, turning his car back in the direction from which it originally came, narrowly missing the first security car as he came out of the circle.

Callum stole a glance in the rear-view mirror to see that the two security vehicles screeched as they skidded around each other, avoiding a collision. Callum laughed out loud as he dashed along the bend of Bury Lodge Lane.

Flashing blue lights atop a white car with black checks and a thick yellow strip caught his attention ahead. Since it had different colours than the Airport Security, Callum assumed it was the Essex Police. Its siren was also screaming as it charged toward him. Looking back, Callum could see the two security vehicles closing in. He was trapped between the two.

Callum screamed in frustration as he increased the acceleration and thundered toward the approaching police car. They must have thought he was bonkers when at the last moment he turned the wheel and flew over the kerb, onto the grass, ripping through Stansted Business Park. The other vehicles were in relentless pursuit.

Tearing past the flight hangers, sparks showered across the windows as Callum burst through the fence, tearing off his side mirror in the process. The car jerked and jolted before gripping the smooth surface of the runway tarmac. Callum's eyes darted around, *Where's the Hoffman Private Jet?* He had seen its wheels down, it should have been on the runway by now. A moment of eerie silence engulfed him, then:

WHOOOSH!!!

A deafening roar as the entire car shuddered and the windshield vibrated from the proximity of the jet's wheels, which were within arms' reach. Callum gripped the steering wheel with all his might as the plane's extreme velocity created a hurricane-like wind-tunnel causing the car to spin out of control. He stomped on the break with all his weight, whirling like a child's spinning-top while still being dragged by the wind suction.

Callum couldn't believe that the car hadn't completely rolled arse-over-teakettle as the car spun to a stop on two wheels and landed right-side-up. Feeling dizzy and fueled by adrenaline, he needed a moment to get his bearings. He spun the car 180 degrees and saw the Jet as it raced along the tarmac to where a set of stairs on wheels and a white stretch Bentley was waiting to take Edward Hoffman away.

"Oh no you don't!" Callum said aloud as he once again stomped down on the gas, blazing along the tarmac to reach the private jet as it was taxiing to its stop. The jet was growing larger and larger again as Callum sped closer and closer. Suddenly the car began to sputter and grind… then it started to slow down. Callum tramped on the gas with all his weight… and it continued to coast even slower. Callum looked down at the dials. *Out of fuel!*

"Bloody hell…!"

CRUNCH!

Callum was jostled in his seat as he felt an impact and the car spinning once again. He hadn't seen the security lorry approaching until it struck him on the left side. He skidded to a complete stop, then the other security car pulled up in front of him and the police car wailed its approach from the rear.

Callum was boxed in. He wanted to run but every muscle in his body ached and did not want to move. The airport security was outside his vehicle screaming at him but he couldn't hear them. His focus was on the Hoffman Jet as the staircase rolled up to meet its door.

They opened his door and he allowed himself to spill onto the runway.

"On your feet, mate! Hands where I can see them!" one of the voices yelled. "I said, 'on your…'"

His voice was cut off by the approach of two black Mercedes-Benzes with flashing lights on top, coming to a stop between them and the jet. *Now what?*

Several large men in suits emerged from the pair of vehicles.

The security officer barked at them, "You can't park…"

One of the men in a black uniform held up a billfold with identification as he said in a calm Italian accent, "Interpol! We're taking custody of Mr. Callum Toughill, here."

. . .

Edward could hear the chorus of sirens swarming around the jet as it was taxiing along the runway. He craned his neck to look out the window but the commotion was out of his field of vision.

Once the plane had come to a complete stop, Edward took his briefcase and coat and assisted Myra with her personal belongings as they made their way to the front. Roger struggled once again with his luggage, while the co-pilot opened the aircraft's door.

Edward had been in England a few months earlier, supervising the last stages of the *Titan*. It was a record cold winter for England but compared to the Great Blizzard that was dumping copious amounts of snow on the American east coast, he was glad that England was now practically balmy in comparison.

He held his arm out for Myra as they started to descend down the steps. Suddenly, two black cars sped across the tarmac to meet up with the cacophony of cars with flashing lights assembled ten feet from the tail fin. Men in suits and uniforms were moving towards him, dragging along a disheveled man being escorted between them.

The pilot had come out of the cabin and pushed his way in front of Edward to yell at the men below, "What the hell is going on here? Do you have any idea how dangerous that stunt…"

The nearest man in a suit interrupted by holding up his identification for them to see, as he hollered, "Mr. Edward Hoffman, I am Inspector Rait with Interpol. We have a warrant to arrest this woman, who calls herself 'Myra Hoffman.'"

Edward blinked, bewildered. Then he descended the stairs to look at the identification with the Interpol insignia. He cleared his throat and demanded, "On what charges?"

"For fraud, grand larceny and murder," replied Inspector Rait, holding out the warrant for Edward to see. "She is a con artist and has outstanding warrants all over the world: from Europe to Argentina."

Edward ignored the piece of paper flapping in the Inspector's hand. He could not believe what he was hearing. "That's not possible. Roger, do something."

"Sorry, Edward, I have no jurisdiction here," Roger replied as he took the warrant from the Inspector to inspect it anyway.

"I'm afraid it is possible sir. We have connected her to accomplices involved with several murders here in the United Kingdom, including a police officer and a DNA scientist, Dr. Jeff Alec, as well as the attempted murder of Dr. Natalie Lindsay in New York."

"That was a random mugging," said Edward cautiously.

"One of our agents from our New York Office got a statement from her as she was recovering from her surgery. She identified 'Myra' as her attacker."

"No!" cried Myra, "I would never hurt her. I was with Edward all this time. Tell them."

"It's true, Inspector, she was with me," Edward said. Then he thought of the brief time she was away and the helicopter that flew overhead. He chose not to mention that as he continued, "And in fact, her life was in danger – she was almost killed herself."

"By Agent Kybartis? He was one of ours sent to extradite her back to England."

An Interpol Agent? Edward's mind was reeling. *This wasn't possible.*

"No, he was going to kill me!" Myra exclaimed. "I heard him talking to someone on the telephone. He wanted to murder me!"

Another man in a dark suit handed Inspector Rait a file folder. Rait opened it and produced several pages. "Here is the original warrant for her arrest. Here is a document pertaining to her recent plastic surgery to pass herself off as Myra Hoffman."

"Plastic what?" cried Myra.

Roger took the entire file folder from Inspector Rait, and flipped through it as the agent spoke.

"As you can see there," Rait continued, "she's been casing you for the past two years. You are not the only one. Five years ago she conned a British couple that she was their long-lost daughter abducted from childhood."

This was a low blow to Edward. It wasn't possible! He needed to see it with his own eyes. He took the file folder from Roger and began to sift through its contents. Two Polaroid photos fell to the ground. Edward picked them up.

"We recovered those from one of her accomplices here in England," Rait said. "As you can see she had been studying you for some time."

Edward looked at the photos. One was of his *Titanic* model and the bookcase behind it; and the other was a close up photo of his video collection of time travel movies. Edward recognized the titles of his own collection: *World Without End, Final Countdown, Somewhere in Time, The Time Machine, Time After Time, Berkley Square, Brigadoon, Planet of the Apes,* and *...Time Bandits?* Edward raised an eyebrow... then glanced back down to the date scribbled on the white border, beneath the image: 10 May 1981, almost a year ago. He looked at the photo again. He was beginning to understand what was happening.

He continued to browse through the thick file folder that contained details of his life, his daily activities, and his education. Edward paused as he looked at the page detailing his Military record. He now knew the full extent of his betrayal and deception as he read the official document detailing his training in wireless decoding in World War II.

"I'm sorry Mr. Hoffman. She preys on lonely old men… she has no limits to how low she will stoop," said Rait who then turned to Myra, "May I have that locket?"

Her hand flew to touch it, "Whatever for?"

"Evidence, my dear," Rait said, "I have a warrant to seize a locket, an Edwardian dress, a deck chair and a replica of a 1910 Bing-Bear Teddy Bear."

Edward could feel 'Myra' looking to him for support. But he needed to distance himself emotionally. He purposely turned away. He couldn't look at her.

"Very well," replied Myra with a trembling, tearful voice. "I'll go with you, if for no other reason but to prove my innocence. My dress is in my bag, but I don't have any deck chair or teddy bear."

"Put her luggage in the boot," Rait called out. Another agent complied and took her bags and put them into the back of the stretch Mercedes-Benz Sedan.

Suddenly the disheveled man stumbled forward to Edward, "Mr. Hoffman. I'm Callum Toughill. We met once before…"

Edward looked at him. He remembered Mr. Toughill as always being impeccably groomed. He could hardly recognize him looking unkempt, unshaven and in rumpled clothing. He remembered they recently exchanged phone messages. With his mind still whirling, Edward muttered, "Dolanna?"

"My wife… er… ex-wife is looking after her," Callum Toughill said as he suddenly grasped Edward's hand, shaking it firmly. "I had hoped to discuss things with you."

Edward felt Toughill press a small rigid piece of paper into the palm of his hand. He nodded in understanding and said, "Thank you, Mr. Toughill."

He then pulled his hand back, fingers curling shut, hiding the exchange.

"We have to get going now," Inspector Rait said, interrupting as the other agent pulled Callum away from Edward. "Mr. Toughill, you'll be coming with us. The information you have will be invaluable against this woman."

"The information *I* have?" Toughill blinked as he was hauled towards one of the black cars. Another agent was carrying a black metal box from the nearby battered car.

"Eddie," Myra implored, "it's not true! You know in your heart that it isn't true!"

One of the other men grabbed her by the upper arm and escorted her to the same car. Edward could not watch. With his mind whirling, he turned and walked toward his car.

Edward didn't look back as he sank into the back seat of the Bentley, allowing the chauffeur to close the door, shutting Myra from his view. He looked down as both cars drove off. Then, while Roger went back to the jet to retrieve the overcoat he had left in his seat, Edward looked at his palm to see what Callum Toughill had given him. It was a small white business card with the logo of the British Military of Defense Police. Printed in black ink was the name: *Commander Pamela Toughill*

He needed to speak with her, but first he had to make one other urgent call. Edward picked up the heavy car phone and began to dial.

CHAPTER 53

Interpol does not conduct investigations, nor do they have the power to arrest anyone, Callum thought to himself as he sat in the Mercedes-Benz stretch sedan.

Interpol has been portrayed in the cinema as some international police force solving crimes and arresting spies and terrorists, but Callum knew that was just a myth. At best, Interpol could be described as glorified paper pushers who are good at cutting through international red tape but don't have their own officers. Instead, police forces from around the world loan their officers to Interpol.

So who are these blokes? Callum wondered. He knew he was out gunned by them, and they could have easily just shot him by now. And no one would think twice about it. There was obviously some careful planning and great expense to fool Edward with those documents and these cars. They wanted this woman, and an 'arrest' was easier than kidnapping. Callum decided to play along. He hoped Edward would call Pamela and tell her what happened. She would know what to do.

He looked at the beautiful young lady sitting across from him and asked, "Have we met before?"

She glared at him with her icy blue eyes and replied, "No, not likely."

Callum nodded. He looked over at the two 'agents' sitting next to them. Callum liked that this sedan was spacious and they were able to sit across from each other like on a train car. However, he hated having to sit backwards while the car was in motion, it made him slightly carsick. He decided to distract himself from it. He glanced up at Rait, sitting beside him, who was curiously eyeing the iron box between Callum's feet. *He's practically drooling,* Callum thought. The other agent, sitting next to the woman who called herself 'Myra' had his gun trained on her. Callum gestured to him, "Is that necessary?"

The agent said nothing, but just glared at Callum. *OK, fine.*

Callum fixed his thoughts back to the striking woman sitting in front of him. He recognized her raven black hair and piercing blue eyes from the tabloid magazine in the Mitchell Library with the story of her 'miraculous' recovery from the *Titanic*. But even when he saw her face on that magazine cover, he had sworn he had seen her before, but couldn't place where. It was driving him crazy now. He struggled for a moment to remember what name was used when they arrested her on the tarmac.

"So, let me get this straight," Callum said to her. "They say you think you're Myra Hoffman."

"I don't *think*. I *know* I'm Myra Hoffman," she replied. Her accent was American but Callum noticed a hint of the Queen's English. Perhaps went to school in London, he guessed.

"I have news for you, lass," Callum began. "I've met the real Myra Hoffman. You ain't her."

"She's not the real Myra Hoffman," said Myra.

"How is that even possible?" Callum asked. Rait chuckled. The young woman said nothing, but her eyes seemed to become a colder shade of blue, as she fixed her gaze in anger. *Hell of an actress,* Callum thought. *Actress?* He remembered thinking before that he had seen her picture somewhere, in a poster... advert... on display... He paused and looked about to see if there was a window open, as he suddenly found it drafty in the moving car. He saw the other sedan following close behind.

Rait cleared his throat before he spoke, "Is that your grandfather's legacy?"

He jabbed his chin towards the iron box.

Callum nodded, "Yes, what little there is."

"It will help us bring justice," Rait replied, then he tried to look nonchalant as he asked, "May I see it?"

Callum could see Rait was champing at the bit and took advantage.

"Only if you'll allow me a peek at her locket," Callum suggested. He guessed it was important when they took it on the runway. "Might give me a clue as to who she really is."

Rait thought for a moment, then nodded as he reached into his pocket. Callum picked up the box and traded it with him. Rait studied the markings on the box with great interest. "How do you open it? Is there a key?"

Callum looked over at him, and replied, "No, I've had to jimmy it open with a knife."

Rait reached into his jacket pocket and pulled out a switchblade. He pressed the button and the blade sprung open and locked in place. *Guess the 1959 switchblade ban doesn't apply to this wanker,* Callum thought to himself.

"May I?" Rait asked, but with a tone that did not really sound like a request for permission.

"Knock yourself out," replied Callum, as he turned his attention to the little gold locket in his hand. *Elegant gold chain, Celtic design. Pity it was broken and re-knotted.* He raised his eyes to see 'Myra' glaring at him with venom in her stare. It was as if he was a heathen defiling a religious relic. He popped the latch. He heard the sharp, hateful intake of air through her teeth. Ever so gently, he opened the locket. There were two photos. One of a boy in an old fashioned sailor suit. And the other was a picture of the young woman here in the car directly across from him, with - -

"Are you sure you don't have the key?" Rait asked as he was trying to pry the lock with the tip of his blade.

"Nah, it's been a pain," Callum replied. "The damn thing re-locks every time I close it. I keep telling myself to jab something in it next time I open it, to keep it from locking."

Callum looked back down at the locket and this time he decided to inspect the back of it. He turned it over, then squinted his eyes as he tried to read the engraving:

To Myra,
Happy Anniversary!
Archie
December 31.

Callum felt a shiver run up his spine as he read the inscription. He looked up at Myra again and asked, "What's your full name?"

"Myra Amelia Sloan Hoffman," she replied without any hesitation.

"Sloan? With an 'e' or without?"

"Without."

Callum suddenly sat up straight, as he opened up the locket again. He held it to the light from the window. It was her eyes. Myra's eyes. *Now I know where I've seen her before!* Callum thought to himself. He looked up at her, she was staring at him inquisitively as if sensing his sudden realization.

Callum's tired mind started to put the pieces together. *Of course!* It's a nutty conclusion, but now he knew who really killed Agatha Gilcrest in 1909!

SLICE!

His revelation was interrupted by the sudden sound of grinding metal, like a butcher sharpening his knife, then a spray of liquid on his rumpled suit.

An ear-piercing scream like a banshee being expelled from Hell rattled his eardrums. Then he saw Rait's hand still holding the switchblade next to his shoe, blood spurting from the bloody stump where the hand used to be.

CLICK

The other agent, horrified at what he had witnessed, now turned his gun from Myra and aimed it directly at Callum's face.

Myra suddenly grabbed his gun arm.
BLAM!

April 10, 1982

CHAPTER 54

Edward had arranged for the porter to take his luggage to his stateroom while he rushed to speak with Captain Hastings on the bridge of the RMS *Titan*. He was about to ascend the fore staircase when he suddenly stopped. It was as if he was transported back in time.

The pattern of black tiles inlayed on the white floor was exactly the same as the *Titanic*'s First Class entrance. Edward's hand rested on the bronze cherub holding the lamp at the base of the grand staircase. He had not been on the RMS *Titan* since the decorators had begun doing the finishing touches. He knew that they were going to be similar; he had no idea that it was going to be so exact. He remembered feeling so small, the stained-glass dome in the ceiling seeming so high and enveloping. He had been lost and found his way to the clock and waited... waited for ... *Mommy*...

Edward slowly walked up to the landing before the stairs split into two directions. His fingers touched the replica of the detailed oak carving entitled, *Honour and Glory Crowning Time*. For a moment he was a little boy again, staring, enchanted by the beautiful carved angels flanking the large wind-up clock face with Roman numerals.

Now, as an adult he could inspect it more closely. The angel on the right named Glory, is fanning a palm frond over the other angel's head. Honour, the angel on the left, is ignoring Glory. Instead she is concentrating as her foot rests on a globe... the world... she is busily inscribing on a tablet resting on the clock. *Is she recording history?* The wreath of Victory is at Glory's feet, resting against the pedestal that supports the clock... or time. *Was this glory of victory over time?*

"Edward! There you are!" a voice from the distance called out.

He turned, almost expecting to see someone else but his thoughts shattered back to the present as Roger's rotund form came barreling down the marble staircase.

"Yes Roger, what is it?" Edward asked, as he continued up the stairs to meet him.

"Have you seen this?" Roger huffed, out of breath. He then handed Edward a folded newspaper.

"No, what is it?" asked Edward as he unfolded the local *Saturday Comet*. A color photo answered his question. It showed two black Mercedez-Benz cars, overturned and battered, along the side of the road. The headline read: *Horrific Car Crash in Essex!*

"Are these the same…." Edward started to ask.

"Yes," Roger replied. "It says it happened yesterday. According to the estimated time, it happened not long after they left the airport."

Edward scanned the article but then realized nothing was sinking in. There was a long awkward moment of silence as he found himself staring at the photo of the wreckage.

"Edward? Are you alright? Everyone's been asking for you…"

"Were there any survivors?"

"The article doesn't say. But I called someone at the Essex Police. They haven't identified all the seven bodies pulled from the wreck yet."

"Seven?" Edward repeated. "How many agents were present yesterday?"

"I don't remember. But they did confirm that *none* of the dead bodies recovered were female."

"She survived," Edward said.

"It gets more interesting," Roger added. "It seems that the driver of the stretch sedan was shot in the back of the head."

"Is that what caused the crash?"

Roger replied, "That's their preliminary speculation but they won't make a definite ruling until they finish their investigation. But right now Myra… the con artist… is on the loose… and she may be armed. Should we warn your parents?"

"No," said Edward. "I don't think we should bother them with this."

"Under the circumstances maybe we should get them off of the boat. What about when we dock at Cobh tomorrow?"

"No, it's their anniversary cruise," replied Edward. "I won't allow that woman to ruin it for them. The security is clearly tight due to Their Royal Highnesses but they should be informed. I'll take that responsibility."

Roger grumbled in dissatisfaction, "Do you have one of your drawings or a photo of her? We can have her face plastered on every TV set on the planet. She'll be caught in no time then."

"No," Edward commanded. "We don't want that kind of publicity. Not with the Royal family aboard, and we certainly don't want her to upstage the anniversary dinner tomorrow night… I don't want to give her that satisfaction."

"But…"

"No buts," Edward interrupted. "Follow my instructions to the letter. I'll contact my associate in the British Intelligence. We'll make sure that there's extra security in all the nearby airports."

"Airports?"

"She's fixated with me," Edward replied. "She's going to try to get back to New York. An airline is the only way to get to me, unless she can make it to Cobh port in Ireland by tomorrow, which isn't likely without any money or resources."

"You sure?"

"Positive," Edward replied. "Right now she's going to lay low and try not to attract attention."

. . .

Debi loved working in London's oldest toy store. She was always a child at heart and enjoyed testing out the new toys. What she loved the most was seeing the look of complete joy in little kids' eyes: that expression when they found that 'perfect' toy, the one that was made for them.

The other perk Debi enjoyed was creating the window displays. She would put a lot of thought and planning into the themes that were given to her. Hours were spent on each one, but the end result was always worth it. She got a kick out of seeing some hard-hearted Londoners hurrying by the window, then stopping for a moment just to have a look. For a brief instant she could see the childlike twinkle in their eyes. Then it would vanish quickly as they dashed off to the Tube or to catch a taxi.

Debi was working on a special Easter display when she noticed a beautiful woman standing outside looking lost and bewildered. Since yesterday had been a holiday, most people were rushing about trying to get shopping done but this woman looked out of place. Although stylishly dressed, she didn't seem to be comfortable. Debi studied her for a moment as she read their sign: *Since 1760*. The woman had a porcelain doll's face with a gorgeous mane of hair that was darker than black licorice, and her eyes were deep blue. Debi was surprised to see her come in.

"May I help you?" Debi asked as she stepped down from the window display.

"Didn't you used to be on High Holborn?" the beautiful woman asked with a strong American accent.

"Yes," replied Debi. "But we moved to this bigger location last year. Is there something I can help you find?"

"Yes please," the woman answered as she pulled a photograph from her handbag. "Do you have something that looks like this?"

Debi took the photo from her and looked at it. She knew it immediately. "This looks like a replica Bing Teddy Bear... wait a minute."

She looked at the photograph more closely. The manufacturer's identification marker, a silver arrow with the initials GBN, for Germany Bing Werke, was visible on the right ear of the bear. This only existed pre-World War I. After 1919, the marker was changed to an orange circle with the black letter BBN, Bavaria Bing Werke, under the left arm or wrist. That meant the bear in the photo was an original vintage Bing Bear and would be worth almost £1000—if it were in mint condition. Pity the bear in the photo was weathered and worn.

Debi looked at the woman and said, "We do carry a line of replica Bing Bears but they don't have the mechanisms that they used to have inside. The ones we have are collectors' editions and come with a certificate of authenticity."

"Certificate of what?" she asked.

"A lot of people collect them, and display them in their unopened boxes."

"I just need one that looks like this one."

"Wait here," Debi said. "I'll be back in a tick."

A short while later, Debi returned carrying two boxes under her arm. She saw the striking woman watching a little boy sit on his mother's lap while she read him a storybook.

"Here you go, ma'am," Debi said as she approached the woman. "I have two 1910 replicas, they're both slightly different shades. Which would you like?"

"Oh, they're lovely," she took out her photo, compared it with both and picked the one on the left. "I'll take this one."

"That will be £125," Debi said. She saw the look of surprise flash across the woman's blue eyes. "The replica collectors' bears are far more expensive than the regular teddies. If you prefer something cheaper for a little boy to play with...."

"No, I'll take it."

"I'll take you over here to the cash register. Would you like it in a gift box?"

"No," replied the woman as she pulled out a thick handful of cash from her hand bag. "That won't be necessary."

The woman placed £140 on the counter, and while Debi counted out her change, the woman took the Bing bear out of the box.

"Thank you!" the woman said with a smile, and she walked out of the store leaving the box on the counter. Debi threw it in the rubbish bin and went back to the window to work on the display.

She was suddenly frozen to the spot with shock. Just outside the window, she could see the same beautiful woman grabbing the expensive replica bear by the feet and smashing it repeatedly against the brick wall, completely oblivious to the odd looks she was getting from other passersby.

Debi screamed when she saw the woman throw the bear down on the pavement, on the edge of the kerb and stomp on it with her high-heeled shoes. She hoped that there were no children watching.

CHAPTER 55

BLEEP   BLEEP   BLEEP

Over a week ago, Denise didn't believe in miracles or coincidences. Since then she had seen the most astonishing recovery she had ever witnessed, which changed her thinking forever. It was a cruel, bitter irony that Dr. Natalie Lindsay lay unconscious in the same bed that Myra had been in only one week earlier.

The heart-tracking ECG bleeped very slowly. It was still too early to tell if she was going to pull through. Dr. Rowland had said that it was "touch and go" during the surgery. Although there had been no exit wound, he apparently could not find the bullet—only traces of a liquid metal that he had sent to the lab for further analysis.

Denise sat with her for a moment and held her hand. She had just been to this woman's office only a few days ago. Denise was breaking the rules, but she had feared that someone was trying to kill 'Myra'. Were the same people responsible for Dr. Lindsay's condition? *Would they be coming back to finish the job?*

Denise never believed in miracles until she met Myra. Now Denise prayed for another.

• • •

Pamela Toughill entered the massive white building of The Royal Bank of Scotland Group Archives in Edinburgh. She had been reluctant to get involved but ever since learning of Callum's fate, she was determined to follow this through to the end.

She walked across the marble floor to the gentleman at the information desk. He looked at her and her uniform and immediately straightened his back and addressed her formally. "Yes… Ma'am. My name is Adrian. How may I help you?"

Pamela smiled to herself. Obviously Adrian had once served in a branch of the military. She asked politely, "Do you have bank records of the Drummonds Bank of London?"

Adrian nodded, "We have customer ledgers going as far back as the 1660's."

"Can you find these ones?" Pamela asked as she slipped him a piece of paper.

He took it and read it. "1910? I'll see what I can find. Have a seat and I'll have Bob bring you a tea or coffee while you wait."

For a moment, Pamela considered coffee, but still said, "Tea, please."

— — —

Darren cursed under his breath as he looked at the orange juice stain on a gorgeous Elizabethan costume. *Why can't actors learn not to eat in their costumes?* He wasn't sure that stain would come out! Especially around the hand beading and the embroidery.

RING-LING

Darren looked up at the sound of the front door of his store opening. A handsome woman with pale alabaster skin, sapphire eyes and raven black hair strolled into the costume shop. She was fabulously dressed. Her heels made her legs look nice and long with the perfect line. Too many actresses these days didn't know how to walk properly in heels.

"What can I do for you, miss...?" Darren asked.

"You can call me Myra," the woman replied in an American accent.

"I'm Darren. Are you an American actress?"

"I just flew in from New York," Myra replied.

"Oooh, Broadway or Off-Broadway?"

"Off Broadway. I'm looking for a dress… in the 1910 era."

"*Gigi* or *My Fair Lady*?" asked Darren.

"I beg your pardon?"

"Are you looking for 1910 France style or 1910 British style?" he asked. He knew there were subtle differences between the two. Especially in ladies' fashion.

"Oh, British," Myra nodded.

"Wait here, darling. I'll pull some stuff that'll make you look stunning."

"Thank you," Myra replied. Darren turned away from the counter. Then he heard her call after him. "Excuse me? You wouldn't happen to have any stray mismatched antique buttons I could buy from you?"

"Buttons?" he asked, perplexed. "How many do you need?"

"Just two."

Darren grabbed a pickle jar filled with buttons from under the counter. "Here darling, help yourself."

. . .

Edward sat in the smoking lounge, staring at the old painting of New York that was hung above the piano. The idea of a smoking room caused a heated debate among the board of directors. In the end, the point that solidified keeping the smoking lounge was the popularity of posh cigar bars in Manhattan that served expensive port and cigars. So it would be on the RMS *Titan*.

The space had been modeled after the smoking room on the original *Titanic*, complete with ornate wood carved walls and stained-glass partitions. Added features included HEPA (high efficiency particulate air) filters which were now used in hospitals to purify the air quality, and electric smokeless ashtrays. Both of the elder Hoffmans sat comfortably in their wheelchairs, enjoying a smoke and a drink. It was bordering on ridiculous since Mrs. Hoffman had a portable oxygen tank and a disapproving nurse close by.

"Sonnyboy, try the brandy. It's excellent!" Archibald Hoffman said to Edward.

"On the *Titanic*, women weren't allowed in the smoking lounge," remarked the elder Mrs. Hoffman. "This is very nice, at last…"

"This isn't the *Titanic*," grumbled Edward. "Can we go through this trip without mentioning that damned ship?"

"Are you going to sulk the whole time?" Archibald Hoffman asked.

"Forgive me, Father. I have been a little unsettled."

"I can't believe you thought that woman was me," wheezed Mrs. Hoffman. "I mean, really! That sounds like the plot of a Twilight Zone episode."

Edward glared at Roger, who took another sip from his brandy rather guiltily. "Roger, I didn't know you were back to being in-house council for Hoffman International."

"It's not like that, Edward," Roger replied, wiping his mouth. "I've been worried about you as a friend. And I felt, as your friend, that your parents needed to know what was going on… should anyone ask."

"Did you really think I wasn't your mother?" Mrs. Hoffman asked.

"I'm sorry but I don't want to talk about this anymore," Edward said curtly as he picked up the menu. *I need a drink to survive this trip*, he thought. Just then a steward came in, saw them sitting at the table and marched over to them.

"Mr. Hoffman?" asked the steward as he neared.

"Yes?" replied both Edward and Archibald at the same time.

"Mr. Edward Hoffman?" the Steward asked, embarrassed.

"Yes," Edward replied, holding up a finger.

"There is a telephone call for you," said the steward. "They said it was urgent."

"Thank you," Edward said as he rose, trying to hide his relief behind his linen napkin which he then placed on the table.

Archie Hoffman hurriedly remarked, "Don't forget we're having dinner at the Captain's table tonight."

"I know," replied Edward as he turned and followed the steward out of the lounge.

— — —

Deep down in the hull of the ship, a digital clock attached to an explosive detonator blinked to life: 24 H 00 M

23 H 59 M

. . .

Percy Winthrope was done for the day. As he crossed the marbled lobby of Lloyd's of London, he paused and looked back at the clock behind the front desk to check the time. It had been a long day. Not that it had been a productive day. He had found it difficult to concentrate since receiving the call about Callum Toughill. He was...

CLANG-CLANG!

His eyes drifted down from the clock to the Lutine Bell, which was suspended in the lobby from ornate wrought-iron, in front of the black marble wall. Recovered from the wreck of the *Lutine* which sank two hundred years ago, the bell was rung on eventful occasions only. It was struck once for good news, and twice for bad news, such as a ship in peril. It had been at least three years since it was last rung.

Percy blinked. And looked again. The bell could not possibly ring without someone on a stepladder next to it, pulling the chain. Percy looked about. Judging from the confused expressions on everyone else's face, he hadn't imagined it.

What did it mean?

April 11, 1982

CHAPTER 56

03 H 45 M

– – –

Commander Pamela Toughill and her team waited to board the first ferry boat to take them to the RMS *Titan*. Pamela had no wish to travel to New York and back but duty demanded her presence aboard the ship. While they waited, she couldn't help but overhear the nearby tour guide speaking through a loud hailer to the passengers that would be waiting a little longer for the second or third round of ferry boats to taxi them to the *Titan*.

"Welcome to Cobh, Ireland," said Jaclyn, the young Irish tour guide. "When the town was founded in 1750, it was called Cove… for obvious reasons."

The people listening chuckled as Jaclyn gestured to the large cove harbor that the town was built to overlook.

She continued, "Our forefathers may not have been original in their choice of name, nor were they in 1849 when it was renamed Queenstown in honour of Queen Victoria who visited our fair town that year. When Ireland became a free state we went back to the original name, but in Gaeilge tongue, so we are now Cobh… which is not actually a bloody word in any Irish language."

More laughter. Pamela glanced over to see the war protesters that had gathered and were being segregated by the police. They were the reason Her Majesty the Queen had cancelled her original plan to tour Cobh. It would have been the first visit of the Monarchy since Ireland became a free state. For safety reasons the security detail insisted that Their Royal Highnesses should remain aboard the *Titan*. *Just as well,* Pamela thought. At least the town wouldn't have to go through another name change.

"This was the final port of call for the *Titanic* before it sailed on her ill-fated maiden voyage," continued Jaclyn. Then she pointed out to the waters. There was an audible murmur of approval as the crowd marveled at the awe-inspiring sight of the RMS *Titan* as it sat anchored majestically in the cove.

"As it was in 1912, the waters next to the docks are too shallow for large cruise ships to dock. So the large vessels have to drop anchor in the cove and shuttle ferries are used to take passengers to and from the ships."

Three boats were en route to the shore as Jaclyn spoke, "The city is talking about a new 'cruise berth' to be used for docking large ships and we hope that one day it will get past the 'talking' stage. Look, we have a treat for all of you..."

Pamela followed Jaclyn's gesture and saw a group of actors in Edwardian costumes mingling along the queue and posing for pictures as the crowd waited to be tendered to the *Titan*.

One of the actresses caught Pamela's attention. She was an elegant lady with jet black hair, a very pale complexion and piercing blue eyes. She was the only one who seemed perfectly comfortable in the cumbersome dress.

• • •

Since Myra was blending in with the actors she had to wait for the important people to board first. *Class distinction still exists,* she thought to herself. She looked about and noticed a woman carrying a tabloid newspaper. The headline read,

"Titanic Survivor from 1912 found on an Iceberg!"

Myra shook her head, picked up a leather bag that she had purchased in London and walked towards the shuttle ferry.

All the actors boarded the ship as security checked their names off a list. "Name please?"

"Leonard Winslow," answered the performer in front of Myra. While the steward searched though the names on his clipboard, Myra glanced up and saw Roger pacing on the deck above. As he turned his head toward her direction, Myra turned away sharply. The momentum of the bag over her shoulder knocked Leonard Winslow off the platform and into the water.

"Man overboard!" a voice called out. The crowd happily applauded, assuming it was all part of the show.

During the sudden commotion, Myra moved ahead out of Roger's sight.

"Boarding pass?" asked a sailor in uniform. Myra handed over the boarding pass that Edward had given her on the plane. He scanned it. There was a moment of waiting.

"Is there something wrong?" a woman in a completely dark military uniform asked. Myra looked at her name badge: Toughill.

"The scanner seems to be having a problem with the boarding pass, Ma'am."

"Name please," asked the female officer named Toughill.

"Mary Sloan," answered Myra. "I'm on a list. Edward Hoffman hired me to be part of a special performance..."

"May I see your bag?"

Myra complied as Toughill opened the bag and rummaged through it. Myra's eyes watched closely as the female officer picked up the teddy bear, looked at it and placed it back. After a few more seconds of poking around, she closed the leather bag and handed it back to Myra.

"Here it is," the sailor read aloud from the list. "Mary Sloan, and her boarding pass has the VIP colour."

"Try the pass again," Toughill asked.

BEEP

The light over the scanner illuminated green. The sailor handed Myra back her boarding pass.

"Break a leg, Miss Sloan," Toughill said with a nod.

Myra nodded back, "Thank you."

A few minutes later, Myra made her way to the aft stairwell. She took the bag off of her shoulder and reached in. *Where was it? Ah there, under the false bottom.* Myra's hand grasped the gun.

"Can I help you?" asked a porter, approaching her from behind.

Myra quickly shoved the gun back into the bag, and then turned to the porter with sheepish eyes. "Yes, I'm one of the actors. I've been hired by Edward Hoffman to do an anniversary presentation for his parents, but I can't remember which cabin they're in."

"Actor?"

"Yes, you didn't think I'd dress in this tight corset and itchy knickers for fun did you?" Myra asked, smiling at him.

"Do you have a boarding pass?"

"Of course," replied Myra as she pulled the pass out of her bag and handed it to him. "Now can you tell me?"

"Um... I'm not sure if I'm supposed to tell you."

"I understand." Myra replied as her lip started to quiver and her eyes welled up. "I'll probably get sacked. I can never do anything right."

"Don't, don't cry. Um..." The porter checked his clipboard. "Here it is. They're in Cabins B-94 and 95. Adjoining suites."

"Now I remember. The largest suites," Myra smiled.

"Actually the second largest, the largest is on the other end of the deck being used by the Queen and..." The porter grew pale, with an expression that he may have said too much.

"Thank you so much." She smiled sweetly, then, as she continued up the stairs to "B" deck, her hand reached back into the bag for the gun.

– – –

01 H 00 M
00 H 59 M

• • •

Edward waited respectfully as Their Royal Highnesses left The Café Parisien where they had enjoyed a late breakfast on the RMS *Titan*. Protocol dictates that no one leaves before Her Majesty.

The Queen, Prince Philip, their security and their entourage, travelled up one level to the upper deck for a photo opportunity with the press before the ship left the Irish coast for New York.

The 'B' deck became much more quiet without the royal presence. Edward sighed as he walked toward his parents' suite. Back in 1912 the Hoffman family had stayed in three adjoining suites aboard the *Titanic*. Naturally, his father would insist on similar accommodations.

Suddenly, a pile of luggage on a dolly emerged from Cabin B-94, nearly running Edward down.

"Watch what you're doing!" barked Archibald from within the suite at the steward pushing the dolly. "And you too, *Sonnyboy!*"

"What is going on here?" Edward asked as he entered the spacious, luxurious executive suite, which was decorated in an Art Nouveau style with modern amenities including a King size bed, private balcony, a separate sitting area featuring a sofa bed and desk, television, refrigerator, mini-bar, a roll-in closet, and wheelchair-accessible bathrooms with spa tubs.

Mrs. Hoffman's magnified eyes looked up at Edward reprimandingly as she pulled off her oxygen mask and scolded, "I can't believe you wouldn't tell us that that horrid woman was on the loose!"

It all became clear as Edward turned to see Roger looking sheepish.

"They asked what the extra security was about," said Roger. "I couldn't lie."

"And you call yourself a lawyer?"

"Our bags are almost packed," snorted Archie. "We should get going."

The private nurse nodded as she wheeled some medical supplies out the door.

Edward closed the door behind her. "I disagree. I think you're safer here. Besides, what will Her Majesty say? You two have been planning this anniversary cruise for the past five years... the dinner is tonight. You're letting a con-artist spoil it."

From her wheelchair, Mrs. Hoffman smiled the most fake smile Edward had ever seen. He suddenly found her differently-colored eyes morbidly distracting. She continued to smile as she said, "I appreciate the thought. But the truth is I'm not up for ocean travel. I'm not twenty years old anymore, and I find it difficult to maneuver this chair while the ship is swaying."

"Likewise," Archibald said.

"Well it's a good thing I stopped by instead of waiting to give you this tonight." Edward said as he handed his mother a large, flat, brightly colored gift. "Happy Anniversary."

"Oh, how thoughtful," Mrs. Hoffman exclaimed as she took the present. Her trembling wrinkled hands ripped away the wrapping paper, to reveal an elegant frame. "I don't know what to make of it."

"It's your marriage certificate. I managed to track down a copy from the Manhattan archives."

"It's a lovely thought," remarked Mrs. Hoffman, as she replaced the oxygen mask over her face. "Isn't it lovely, Archie?"

"Yes, yes... quite lovely," he grumbled absently. "Come on, we have to get going before the last ferry departs for shore."

"I am confused about one thing," interrupted Edward. "It says on the document that you two were married on December 31st, yet you always celebrate on April 14th. Why is that?"

That caught Archibald's attention. His bushy eyebrows went up, and the elderly couple looked at each other as if to see who would answer.

"Because April 14th is the day they poisoned the real Myra Hoffman's tea...and left her to die..."

The familiar voice of Myra came from the adjoining cabin. She suddenly appeared in the doorway and continued, "Isn't that right, Archie?"

Roger stood up, but she aimed the gun at him.

"Be a dear, Mr. Zisholm, and step over there with the others," commanded Myra.

Roger complied quickly.

"What do you want with us?" demanded Edward with his hands up in the air.

Myra, still holding the gun, smiled at Edward, "I have something for you... Eddie."

CHAPTER 57

"What do you hope to gain?" Roger asked Myra.

Myra looked at him. "Revenge, plain and simple. These two people have committed a heinous crime and have gone to great lengths to cover it up."

"I didn't kill anyone!" cried Mrs. Hoffman, her voice muffled from behind the oxygen mask. "I'm the real Myra Hoffman!"

"Really?" Myra turned the gun at her. "You never did answer Eddie's question: Why do you celebrate on the wrong day?"

"That's the day we renewed our vows," snarled Archibald. "Plain and simple."

"That sounds reasonable," Roger added.

Myra, still holding the gun, glared at him which caused him to take a step back. She turned her attention back to Mrs. Hoffman. "What was your sister's name?"

"What?" Mrs. Hoffman looked at Myra with confusion.

"Your sister. You had a younger sister. What was her name?"

"It was…. umm… it's on the tip of my tongue…"

"Maggie," Archibald answered.

"The question was for her, not you!" Myra screamed. "What was the name of the church you were married in?

Mrs. Hoffman stammered for a moment before managing, "Bloomingdale… Reformed Church."

"What was your grandfather's name?" Now, Myra barely waited for the answer. "What was your mother's name? You take my life away and don't have the decency to remember the names of my family?"

"You're crazy!" replied Archie. "My wife's memory isn't what it used to be. You could ask her what she had for breakfast this morning and she'd likely not be able to answer you."

"Ok, Archie," Myra said pointing the gun at him. "This question is for you... how did my mother die?"

"I don't know who you *really* are, so how the hell should I know how your mother died…. and I don't care."

"How did Myra's mother die, then?" demanded Myra.

"I'm not going to sit here…"

CLICK

Myra cocked the gun, "Answer the question!"

"She died in a fire from smoking in bed," replied Archibald.

"She didn't even smoke," Myra said coldly.

"Oh yes, she did!"

"No, she didn't!"

Edward interrupted, "I think this could go on forever…"

"I remember you smoked, Archie," Myra said. "You would roll your own unfiltered cigarettes… you'd keep them in a silver cigarette case that your father gave you."

"You could have found that out somewhere," Archie snarled, unimpressed. Myra sighed. He was indeed a tough, bitter old man.

"How did your parents die?" Myra asked Archie.

He flummoxed and floundered, "I don't have to sit here and be interrogated by some crazy woman."

"This crazy woman has a gun," Myra reminded him. "Answer or else."

"Or else what? You'll kill me?" Archie challenged. "You don't have it in you."

"Father…" Edward spoke up, "are you sure that's a wise move?"

"I've been around long enough to know when someone's bluffing. She may be crazy… but she doesn't have what it takes to take someone's life."

"I would never kill anyone," Myra admitted.

"See! I was right!" He guffawed as he started to roll forward.

"Death would be too easy," Myra said as she lowered the aim of the gun. "You need to suffer in long, agonizing pain…. Just like my mother did when you burned her alive… Didn't your uncle die in a fire? Or what of Barry Mackenzie's store…?"

The old man fidgeted about and bristled, "I have no idea of what you're babbling about…"

"Your old school mate… in Glasgow…. His family lost everything in yet another mysterious fire… because he started flirting with…" Myra said as she slowly looked at Mrs. Hoffman, "Flirting with Heather Langlea… a lowly servant girl who used to work for Agatha Gilcrest before coming to work for us."

"Us?" Archie snarled. "You truly believe you're Myra?"

"I'm the real Myra Hoffman!" cried the old woman from her wheelchair.

"No you're not, you misanthropic old crone!" Myra hissed as she gestured with her gun. She continued calmly, "You're Heather Langlea. You had an illicit affair with Archie. Then after I gave him a son, the two of you conspired to kill me so you could be together with my money and…"

"Now listen here, you bitch…" snorted Archibald.

Myra aimed the gun at him, "Archie, that is no way to talk to your wife."

"You're a sad, pathetic lunatic!" Archie retorted.

Roger cleared his throat as he spoke carefully, "No one's going to believe a story like that! You have no proof: just wild conjectures."

"It doesn't matter what anyone else thinks. As long as Edward knows what these people did, how many lives they've ruined."

"What do you want me to do?" asked Edward who had been watching quietly from the corner.

"I want to give you a parting gift. Something that you can have and will prove that I'm telling you the truth and that I have always been honest with you."

With the gun still aimed at Archie, Myra reached her other hand into the bag and pulled out a tattered old teddy bear.

A look of wonder and awe fell across Edward's face and slowly expanded into a smile as he asked, "Mr. Fluffy?"

Myra noticed the look of surprise, shock and determination that crossed the older Mrs. Hoffman's face.

"Look," said Myra. "Here is where I stitched in your name on his foot. And here are the buttons I sewed on after you chewed his eyes off…"

She extended her arm to give it to Edward. She could see the look of confusion cross his brow. Slowly he came forward and started to reach for it.

Without warning, Mrs. Hoffman grabbed Mr. Fluffy by the head, "No! Leave him alone! I'm his real mother, not you!"

"Let go!" shrieked Myra as she pulled on Mr. Fluffy's legs, forgetting the gun. Mrs. Hoffman's grip remained surprisingly strong. Myra pulled so hard that she almost tugged the old woman out of her wheelchair. Archie reached over and also took hold of the bear's head…

RIPPP!

The bear's head tore off and stuffing exploded from its body. Myra released the bear as Mrs. Hoffman dove out of her chair to search through the stuffing.

"You tore Mr. Fluffy's head off," Edward moaned.

"Where is it?" Archie yelled from his wheelchair. "Find it!"

"I'm looking," yelled Mrs. Hoffman on her hands and knees, picking through clumps of plush and fur. The oxygen tank toppled over with her movements but the old woman didn't seem to care. "It's got to be here!"

"What are you looking for?" asked Myra.

"They're looking for this!"

The voice was behind them, emanating from within the adjoining suite. The elderly couple turned their heads toward the voice. There was a wide-eyed, stunned silence as they saw a figure emerge. It was Agatha Gilcrest, also in a wheelchair.... very much alive and holding the crescent moon-shaped brooch with twenty-two diamonds that had been stolen during her murder.

CHAPTER 58

"Well, what do you have to say for yourself, Archie?" Agatha Gilcrest said sternly, still holding the diamond brooch.

Archibald opened his mouth and his usual gruff voice was reduced to a whimper, "Mother?"

"What was that?" Edward was obviously flabbergasted. Edward looked about and the dumbfounded looks and dropped jaws told him everyone else had heard the same thing. There was a long silence. Edward finally cleared his throat and asked, "What did you say?"

Archibald shuddered in shock at the jarring sound of Edward's voice. The expression on Archibald's face was foreign to his features. He looked like a frightened child, caught with his hand in the cookie jar. Then in an instant, it was gone. The acidic old man returned.

"Bullshit!" Archibald roared, his bony finger stabbing toward Agatha. "This is a trick. There are no such things as ghosts… do you hear me? This is bullshit!"

"You said, 'mother'?" Myra asked.

Archibald now turned and screamed at Myra, "You're not my wife and she's not Agatha Gilcrest!"

"You recognize her, then?" asked Edward.

"Why was the brooch so important to you?" asked Myra, obviously trying to get another emotional reaction. "Surely a man of your wealth, you could buy a thousand of these without putting a dent into your wallet. What is it about *this* brooch?"

"It's because of the inscription on the back," replied Agatha Gilcrest. "Shall I read it, Archie?"

Archie started to roll his wheelchair aggressively toward Agatha Gilcrest, startling her enough to drop the diamond brooch.

Myra blocked his way and cocked the gun. Edward picked up the brooch as Myra said to Archibald with an eerie calmness, "Do you really think frightening an old woman is necessary, ... *Mo muirnín*?"

The Gaelic term of endearment struck a familiar chord with Edward. He could see by the way Archibald's eyes widened when she said it, that it was familiar to him as well.

Edward looked at the beautiful crescent moon brooch, encrusted with several sparkling diamonds of various sizes. He turned it over and saw an elegant inscription engraved into the silver.

"*'To my beloved Agatha. Love eternal, Francis Hoffman - 1889'*," Edward read aloud. He looked up at his father after recognizing his own grandfather's name. "1889 is around the time of your birth, isn't it?"

"Yes," replied Agatha. "He was born Archibald Gilcrest, and Francis formally adopted him. His wife Elizabeth was... barren."

"So you truly are a bastard!" said Myra. "And that's why the brooch was stolen... It was the only thing that could connect your father to Agatha Gilcrest. The only thing that could connect you to her murder."

"This is very entertaining but this proves nothing!" Archibald sneered. "What motive would I have to kill her?"

"Because you were a bad seed," replied Agatha. "Even as a child you stole what you wanted, and burned anything that got in your way. How embarrassing to learn that you called yourself Archie *Gilcrest* when you had run-ins with the law. You just *had* to protect your precious Hoffman name, didn't you? Tsk! I was right to cut you out of my will and give it all to the Fergraith family. At least Margaret Fergraith was a child a mother could be proud of..."

With surprising quickness, Archibald rolled his wheelchair over Myra's foot, and knocked the gun out of her hands. The old man grabbed it with his gnarled fingers and aimed it at Agatha Gilcrest.

"I was right to smash your face in!" he snarled. "This time I'll make sure you stay dead!"

CHAPTER 59

Callum Toughill, dressed as a ship's porter, limped in behind 'Agatha Gilcrest' and aimed his Walther P-38 at Archibald Hoffman.

"Drop the gun!" Callum growled, suppressing the pain in his leg from the second car crash the day before. The painkillers were wearing off and he was grumpy. "Believe me, I have what it takes to shoot. And the only reason I don't blast your ugly mug to kingdom come, is because my ex-wife won't let me. So I beg you... give me a reason to do it!"

Callum took great pleasure in seeing the look of shock in Archibald's face. The old man probably never expected to meet him face to face... especially not after the car crash. Archibald lowered the gun. Myra took it from him.

Edward reached over to the nearby table and picked up his portable cassette recorder and hit 'stop'. He pressed rewind and played: *I was right to smash your face in! This time I'll make sure you stay dead!*

"You were in on this?" Roger asked. "Why didn't you tell me? I nearly crapped myself."

"Sorry, old friend. But I knew that someone was going to great lengths to keep her away," Edward said as he gestured toward Myra. "And since there wasn't any real proof of her identity I couldn't figure out why such drastic and expensive measures were being taken."

Callum chimed in, "Likewise, when my investigation into this brooch started a whole new killing spree just after I met with you, Mrs. Hoffman. Just after I checked my messages in your presence. You heard my pass-code, didn't you? Someone was going to great expense to keep all of this a secret. Someone started killing everyone I had contact with, even overseas, so it was someone with power and connections...then I saw the photo in this young lady's locket with the same date of the wedding invitation Agatha Gilcrest had received. The *correct* date, I might add. This photo matched the one that was taken by Adam McArthur, who lived under Agatha Gilcrest's apartment. His daughter still had his copy sitting on her fireplace mantle: it was that same photo that was stolen from her flat when she was murdered last week. Only the one in Ruthie's flat was in colour — her father had experimented with colour photography. It was the only colour photo taken of the real Myra Sloan Hoffman… and she had dark hair and piercing blue eyes."

Everyone looked at Myra.

Callum was feeling very Sherlock Holmes at this point. His brain told him that he was being too dramatic but he couldn't help himself.

"I also found this," Callum continued as he showed the photo that was taken at the Otto Slade trial. He looked down at the old woman still on the floor amidst the teddy bear stuffing, "I believe this is you, Miss Heather Langlea. When you were younger."

"I can verify that," Edward added. "I have my graduation photo to match. She's wearing the same hat."

Callum added, "I even have a description from a local Glasgow reporter in 1910… describing your differently-coloured eyes."

"None of this proves I was involved with any sort of murder," the elder Mrs. Hoffman cried.

Edward then spoke up, "Well, the real Mr. Fluffy had my name stitched in the foot. So imagine my surprise when I received a call from the military, informing me that they had discovered this diamond brooch while X-raying my old childhood toy that they'd found in the Atlantic. I was appalled that my Mr. Fluffy was being used to cover up a crime. I agreed that the real teddy bear should be ripped open to retrieve what was inside. You gave yourselves away when you both dove for this bear that Myra had. You knew what was supposed to have been there."

"I'm an old woman. Have pity," wailed the elderly Mrs. Hoffman.

"Pity?" asked Myra. "Agatha Gilcrest was an old woman, and you two not only killed her but you testified against an innocent man who was executed for the crime you two committed."

"So, who is this?" Roger asked pointing to Agatha Gilcrest.

"May I introduce you to Dolanna Fergraith, my former fiancée, and sadly, as I have recently discovered through blood tests, my cousin."

Callum filled in the stunned silence with more police-show bravado.

"When I first met Dolanna," Callum added. "I saw her striking resemblance to Agatha Gilcrest. That's when I knew she was related to her. At first, Agatha had planned to leave her fortune to her illegitimate son, Archie. Then I saw my grandfather had found the draft of her last Will and Testament which decreed that all her money was to go to Margaret Fergraith instead: her *other* illegitimate child… the one she had hired to be with her and whom she always treated like family."

"Something she never did with me," Archibald growled.

"Because you were a self-centered arse... and an *ars*onist," Callum cheekily replied. "You killed your own mother to get all of her money. We have her bank records from 1910."

"Now I know why your father stopped us from getting that blood sample," Dolanna said to Edward.

Edward looked at his father, "You were afraid somehow we'd find out we were related by blood. I suppose that was one good thing."

"Now I know why we were so much alike," Dolanna said sadly.

Edward looked at Dolanna and softly said, "At least I know it wasn't something I'd said."

This touching moment was shattered quickly when Roger indelicately cleared his throat and asked, "So how did these two survive the crash and the Interpol agents didn't?"

"Simple," Callum replied to Roger. "Everyone in the car survived... even the fake Interpol agents, they're alive but in prison... well, except for the one who lost his hand but that's another story. We just made sure you thought I was dead so that you would tell Archie here."

"You mean... tell Edward," Roger laughed nervously.

"Sorry, old friend," Edward joined in. "I've known for some time that you were involved. When Natalie was shot, I knew you had betrayed me. You were the only other person who knew about the DNA test that she had received. Also, when the 'Interpol agents' showed me that Polaroid photo of my video collection taken 'last year'... *Time Bandits* had only recently been added to my collection. It couldn't have been photographed in May 1981, as the movie hadn't been in the theatres yet. You took that photo the other day, when even you started to believe Myra's story."

Roger smiled then suddenly grabbed Myra, took her gun and aimed it at her head. He yelled at Callum, "Drop the gun or I'll shoot her!"

"Go ahead, pull the trigger," Callum said as he aimed the gun at Roger. "And you'll be dead."

"So will she," Roger said... his voice was trembling.

"No I won't," Myra said calmly. "I was opposed to carrying a gun... until I was reassured that it would be empty."

Callum enjoyed the look of shock on Roger and Archibald's faces.

Roger said, "You're bluffing...I'll prove it. Say good-bye to Mommy, Edward."

Roger pulled the trigger.

CHAPTER 60

"Good-bye… *old friend*," Edward said solemnly. Roger pulled the trigger again. It just clicked.

Roger looked up at Myra, "Empty?"

"I said so!" she replied. A victorious smile formed on Myra's face.

Edward carefully took the gun out of Roger's hands, "Even though I knew you were involved, I knew you didn't have the means or resources to stage a fake arrest, complete with police cars. There had to be money and motive behind it. Though I suspected it was my father, I didn't have the proof until the fake Inspector gave me the file on the runway. You obviously told my father about the Morse code incident."

Edward turned to the others. "See, the files contained official documents of my training in Camp X in Canada, except there are *no* official documents of my training there. It was a secret base set up by Churchill, Roosevelt and a Canadian working for the British Security Coordination. The Canadian government didn't even have any knowledge or documentation. As an American, I wasn't supposed to be involved in the war effort before the US declared war. The only person who ever knew I was there was you… Father. I wondered why you needed to travel to London so early — to provide information? Make payments? This is why we went through such an elaborate charade to get a confession out of you. They're all yours, Commander!"

Pamela and two other Ministry of Defence Police Constables emerged from the adjoining cabin behind Callum.

Archibald roared, "This is entrapment! I'll make sure my lawyers suppress that tape. You have no jurisdiction here!"

Pamela smiled sweetly, "Actually MoD Police *do* have jurisdiction to arrest on a British vessel." She cocked her head in a slightly sarcastic way, "Oh look! The RMS *Titan* is a British vessel. How lucky."

Archibald opened his mouth but for the first time ever seemed at a loss for words.

Straightening, she added with seriousness, "For future reference, neither Interpol nor MI-5 have the power to arrest." She looked about the room, "Now, who has my sidearm?"

Edward stepped forward briskly and handed it to her in the way he had been trained to do for so many years. Pamela appreciated the formality and said, "Thank you very much, sir."

Archibald pointed to Myra, "Surely, you don't believe that this woman is the real Myra Hoffman, who somehow traveled in time?"

Roger quickly added, "You have no proof! Such wild conjectures from a fugitive..."

He jabbed his chin towards Callum, then pointed to Edward's recorder, "We can have that recording suppressed as entrapment and just wait until the public hears that you believe this young woman is your mother. They'll have you committed."

Edward gritted his teeth as he replied, "Not when I tell them that she was an actress... who I first saw in a production of..."

"My Fair Lady," Myra blurted. "Off-Broadway."

"Right," Edward said, "She was playing Eliza Doolittle with... oh I can't remember the name of the actor who played Henry Higgins."

"Leonard Winslow," interjected Myra.

"Right!" Edward pointed to Myra and continued, "As soon as I saw her I realized she was the spitting image of my real mother. You see, Dr. Ballard discovered Mr. Fluffy and the locket in his ongoing search for the wreck of the *Titanic*... you see, *Father*, I can play the art of war as well as you."

Pamela leaned in to Archibald, "With the assistance of André Bossard from the real Interpol, we have learned that there has been a global network of assassins using very expensive guns that shoot expensive, untraceable bullets. Thanks to my ex-husband here, one of the assassins was taken down and we have his weapon in our forensic lab... I'm sure we'll trace it to the owner soon enough."

Archibald grew increasingly pale, as he murmured, "No court in the world will convict two elderly people confined to wheelchairs."

ding, ding, ding!

The elegant Art Nouveau gilt-bronze and mahogany clock, which sat on the fireplace mantle, continued to chime its melody, bringing Archie's attention to it. He suddenly began to panic, "We have to get off this ship!"

"We will, when we reach New York," replied Pamela. "The authorities in America have been notified and they will be taking custody of Roger for the attempted murder of Dr. Lindsay."

"We have to get the last Ferry to Cobh!" Archibald roared.

"Ireland is long behind us!" Callum replied.

"We're moving?!"

"Couldn't you tell?" asked Edward.

Archibald was starting to hyperventilate, "This ship is never going to reach New York!"

"Are you planning to hit another iceberg?" Edward asked. Callum laughed.

Archie made no response. He looked like he was going to have a stroke. Callum stopped laughing. Edward looked at Roger, who stared blankly back. No one said a word.

"There's a bomb on the ship!" blurted the old woman.

"A what?" Myra asked.

"A time bomb!" replied Archibald looking at his old wind-up wristwatch.

"What did you do?!" Edward demanded as he roughly grabbed his father. "Why the hell would you do something like that?"

"Where is it?" Pamela demanded.

Archibald made no reply.

"Don't play games now," Edward demanded. "Please don't tell me you're sacrificing the lives of everyone on board for some insurance payout."

"Actually an insurance company won't pay out for sabotage..." began Callum.

Pamela looked at him incredulously.

"What? They wouldn't!" Callum said. He had enough experience at Lloyds to know that... hmm... he needed more painkillers. "I'll shut up now."

"It makes no sense... we've spent so much money... publicity... the Royal..." Edward paused. He looked at Myra, then at Archie. "Argentina!"

"What?" asked Pamela.

"There were supposedly threats against the Queen unless Britain withdrew its armada from Argentina." Edward turned to Archie, "Your phony inspector on the runway made a reference to a warrant in Argentina. You planned to make this look like a terrorist attack on the Queen..."

"The death of the Queen by radical terrorists would create a huge uproar," Pamela followed aloud. "That would put an end to the war protesters because the British citizens would demand retribution."

"That's why you gave in to the name change so easily. You needed Her Majesty to be on board. You were paid to kill her."

"I was not!"

"You would profit from the war if..."

"We don't have time for this," interrupted Pamela. "Where is the bomb?"

Archie shrugged, "Why should I help you? What kind of immunity can I get?"

"Where is the bomb?" Edward demanded as he yanked his old father completely out of the wheelchair and started shaking him violently.

"I don't know. I just hired someone…"

"Notify the captain and the Queen's security detail," ordered Pamela as her men dashed out the door, their voices barking into their two-way radios. "Get everyone to the lifeboats!"

Edward dropped Archie back into his wheelchair and then turned and dashed out of the room.

Pamela produced a few pairs of handcuffs and turned to Callum, "Could you give me a hand?"

Callum kept his gun aimed as Pamela started to handcuff all three of them to the wrought-iron décor around the fireplace, then brought the oxygen tank to the old woman.

"Wait," Archibald exclaimed. "You're not going to leave us here. We have to get off the ship!"

"Better pray your son finds the bomb," Pamela said. "If you have any idea, now's the time to speak up."

"I already said I don't know. Someone was hired to plant it!" exclaimed Archibald.

"You can't leave us here!" wailed the old woman as she took a breath from the tank.

"Watch me," Pamela replied as she clicked the old lady's handcuffs shut, "You left Myra to die in 1912. Call it poetic justice."

She then gave them a little smile, turned and quickly dashed from the stateroom.

Myra started after her, then stopped at the doorway and looked back at the two old wretched, withered trolls, "Oh, and Miss Langlea… remember on your 21st birthday when you said you told me you wished you had my life?"

Callum saw the look of shock in the old woman's eyes as her memory stirred.

"You had my life. I'm taking it back," Myra continued, and glanced at Archibald, "I was wrong about you two. You deserve each other. I sincerely hope you both rot in hell…"

CHAPTER 61

00 H 30 M

• • •

"…fasten lifejackets and proceed to the upper decks," a voice on the loudspeaker instructed. "Crew will assist in the orderly evacuation of the ship…"

Callum could hear Pamela approaching as she barked into her radio, "What is the status? Over."

A voice crackled in response, "All ships large enough to accommodate the *Titan*'s compliment have been deployed to Argentina, over."

"Lovely," Pamela growled sarcastically, then into the radio, "Copy. What about the *Britannia*… the Royal Yacht… I know it couldn't make the trip to Argentina. At least get it here for Her Majesty?! Over."

"Copy!"

She looked up to see Callum limping, using Dolanna's wheelchair for support, with Myra following close behind. "Why aren't you at the lifeboats yet?"

"The elevators stopped working when the alarm went off," Callum grumbled with annoyance.

"Let me help," Pamela said. They all struggled to carry Dolanna's wheelchair up the stairs to the upper level.

"You think a tycoon in a wheelchair would have made his ship more wheelchair friendly," huffed Callum. "If I get off this ship in one piece, I'll never complain that my life is boring again."

"I'll try to walk it," Dolanna said as she looked up the stairs.

"Are you sure?" Callum asked. "That was a nasty spill you took when your house blew up."

Dolanna nodded as she used the handrail to pull herself up, Callum helped to support her weight as Myra struggled to lift up the empty wheelchair.

"Here, like this," Pamela offered, and collapsed it like an accordion, making it only slightly less cumbersome to carry up the stairs.

Once up top, Pamela unfolded it and Myra held it steady as Callum helped Dolanna into it again. He took a moment to catch his breath; his leg was throbbing with pain.

"Your grandfather would be proud of you," Pamela smiled. "This plan that you and Edward cooked up was crazy."

"But brilliant!" Callum huffed. He was proud that his plan worked. "They had destroyed some of my evidence in my flat, so it was the only way to get Archibald to confess."

"Thank you for trusting me," Myra said.

"I thought he was crazy," Pamela added.

"But, as I said, brilliant!" Callum happily interjected. "I learned to trust my instincts... they served me well these last few days."

Callum then looked at Myra. "I had faith in you."

"Actress, huh?" Pamela said. "That'll look good in a report."

Myra smiled.

The harsh Atlantic wind hit them hard as they pushed open the door and stepped onto the outer deck. They looked about. Mayhem had begun to set in. People were crying, huddling together trying to stay warm. The davits' wheels were squeaking as they began to lower lifeboats into the ocean. A small five-piece orchestra was playing 'God Save the Queen.'

Pamela turned to Callum. "My first duty is to the Queen."

"I know," he smiled weakly. "I'll get them to the lifeboats. Cheers!"

Pamela smiled back, "I'll see you in New York. And we'll toast your 'brilliant' plan."

A moment passed, then a brisk handshake, and Pamela turned to walk sharply away.

Callum watched as Pamela left. Dolanna tugged his sleeve. "I can't be with the person I cared about... but it's not too late for you."

Callum nodded, understanding.

Myra knelt down next to Dolanna, who still had the brooch, and said to her, "My apologies for the pain and suffering you endured at Archie's hands — what he did to your family... and to Edward..."

"And to the countless other people he killed... and ruining my grandfather's career," Callum added. "Not to mention letting Otto Slade hang for their crimes. You can't carry that burden — you're too good for that."

"Thank you, Mr. Toughill."

"Can you take Dolanna over to the lifeboats?" Callum said, gesturing to the nearby boats being loaded with passengers. "I'll go help Edward find the bomb."

"You've been injured," Myra observed. "I'll go help Edward. Please, get Miss Fergraith to safety, take the brooch.... make sure the whole world finds out what atrocious people those two are."

Callum shook his head. Maybe it was macho bravado, but he couldn't allow her...

"I can't leave Edward," Myra said. Then added in a whisper, "Not again."

Callum looked at her for a moment. *For one who has no faith, no explanation is possible. But if you have faith, no explanation is needed.* Callum shook her hand, "It was a pleasure meeting you... Mrs. Myra Sloan Hoffman. Good luck!"

— — —

Since all security was now occupied with the safety and evacuation of the passengers, Edward took it upon himself to try to locate the bomb. He decided to concentrate his efforts closer to the engines. After all, that's where he would have planted a bomb for sabotage. He made his way down to the bowels of the ship, through crew catwalks and bulkheads. Then he heard Myra's familiar voice calling his name, "Edward?"

"Please Mother, go back above deck."

"Oh no. I lost you once before on a ship like this. Not again. This time I'm staying by your side."

Edward sighed with resignation, "Very well. You can help me find the bomb."

Myra nodded, "What are we looking for?"

"First and foremost: Wires. Or Dynamite."

"Wires like this?" she asked, pointing to a long cable that ran the length of the ceiling.

"No, those are communication cables. Look for something smaller and possibly more colorful."

"What about the boilers?" asked Myra.

"They're only for decoration. They're acting like ballasts... they're filled with water for weight." He opened one of the cubbyholes and peered in. "I must say, Mother, you missed your calling. You could have been an actress. You were quite convincing."

"I only followed the instructions you and Mr. Toughill gave me."

"Well," said Edward as he climbed a ladder to peer above some pipes. "No one would believe you were my mother from 1912. I had to come up with a plausible explanation. Saying I had hired an actress ensured you wouldn't go back to the funny farm."

"The what?"

"Euphemism for the clinic where you were kept. You played the part well. I almost believed you were an actress. Where ever did you come up with the name of the other actor?"

"He's actually an actor on this ship. I sort of had a run in with him as I boarded." Myra stood up from where she was looking, "What is *My Fair Lady*?"

"It's a musical based on a play written by George Bernard Shaw," chuckled Edward as he craned his neck to look through some nooks and pipes.

"Georgie. Brilliant, charming but abrasive. How is he?"

"Dead," replied Edward as overturned some crates. "He died thirty years ago."

"Oh dear, I keep forgetting," whispered Myra. "How?"

"I don't remember, but he wasn't young. Near a hundred. Like dear Archie upstairs."

"Last time I saw my husband he was a young man insisting that I drink my tea." Myra paused, "Now he has become this horrible, wretched old man, who's committed unspeakable crimes."

"He was always horrible," muttered Edward. "Don't forget, the tea was poisoned. It prevented you from leaving the *Titanic*. He left you there to die... while he safely got off the ship..."

"I know, and from what Mr. Toughill told me..." Myra said as she steadied herself on a metal stepladder, "...I can't believe I was so blind to the evil that he truly was."

"You're a good person," replied Edward. "I think that trying to see the good in others is a virtue. In his case..."

"What's that?" Myra asked, pointing to a red wire peeking out from behind the coaxial cable for the ship's video system. Edward followed the wire and found some dynamite set into a familiar gray clay-like substance: C4 explosive. He had first worked with it during his training in Camp X.

He noticed more cables attached to it. He followed them to another set of dynamite.

"This is not good."

"What's wrong?" Myra asked.

"There's enough explosive strategically set to ensure that no evidence would be found."

Edward continued to follow the cable to where a timer was running. Edward looked at the clock readout. Less than 30 minutes. They would never be able to evacuate the passengers and crew in time. It would take two hours to get everyone off the ship and they would all need to get away from the blast radius. *Would there be time to alert Pamela that he'd found it? What are the odds that someone on that detail could disarm a bomb?* Edward had the necessary training, and made a choice.

Edward frowned as he studied the bomb. It was a highly sophisticated IED which was constructed with components scavenged from conventional munitions.

"What are you going to do?" Myra asked.

"We don't have time to evacuate, so I'm going to try to disarm the bomb."

"Do you know how?"

Edward nodded, "Something else I was trained to do during the war."

"You were trained to disarm bombs?"

"Well... not exactly... I was trained to build bombs. They weren't quite as sophisticated as this one."

"That's doing very little to heighten my confidence."

Edward took out his pocketknife and used the screwdriver component to remove the casing. He then carefully avoided the detonator in order to access the wires connected to the trigger. Now, which wire to cut?

"It's always easier in the movies," mumbled Edward.

"I beg your pardon?" asked Myra.

"I have to decide which wire to cut. If I cut the wrong wire..."

"I understand."

Edward looked at her for a moment, and then smiled, "I don't know how or why you got here. Maybe it was to expose those two, or to save all these innocent people, or maybe just me."

"You?"

"I always knew that there was something important missing from my life. Now I know it was you. And I'm glad I got the chance to know you."

"And I'm proud of the man you have become," replied Myra. "It's what every mother hopes for. I'm sorry I wasn't there for you."

She tapped his shoulder gently. He chuckled.

Edward looked at her and sighed, "You know, when the ship hit the iceberg, you should have switched the teacups."

Myra looked shocked, then laughed, "Like the film you love so much, with that ethical choice whether to alter the past with the knowledge of the future?"

"Alternate timelines. Wish it were that simple."

She kissed him gently on the cheek, "If I knew then what I know now."

Edward turned back to the task on hand. He opened up the scissors component of his utility knife, studied the bomb for a moment then made his decision. He carefully placed the blades over the wire and took a deep breath, "God save the Queen."

"I love you," Myra said as she closed her eyes.

He stole one last moment to look at her, "I love you, too... Mother..."

...snip...

April 14, 1912

EPILOGUE

Myra's eyes were still closed. She still heard the rumbling of the ship's engines. She could still feel the momentum of the ship moving. She could smell salty air mixed with roses, and lemon-oil soaked into wood.

Very slowly, she opened her eyes. A look of confusion spread across her face. How did she get back into the ship's stately cabin? She heard voices in the adjoining room. She stumbled to the door and was surprised to see Archibald and Miss Langlea together. Not so much that they were together, but that neither of them was in a wheelchair. Archie was as she remembered him: a strapping young man, poised and polished. He was indeed very appealing, except for the cruelty she now could see in his eyes. And what a waistline Miss Langlea had. She tied her apron to show off her curves. Myra realized that something was different - she looked insincere somehow.

Was it all a dream? It was so real!

"You should be resting my dear," said Archie, walking up to her. "Miss Langlea, could you prepare some tea for us?"

Tea? Myra felt her heart skip a beat.

"Right away, sir." Langlea curtseyed in a cute manner before she turned to leave. Myra noticed a slight exchange in their eye contact. *No! I am overreacting!* It was a dream. A horrible nightmare. Yet, she had the overwhelming urge to run down the hall warning everyone that the ship was sinking and to get to the lifeboats.

Suddenly, the cries of Myra's young son snapped her back to the moment.

"Eddie?"

Little Eddie, her sweet little boy, came waddling to the doorway of his room, clutching Mr. Fluffy with one hand and rubbing his eyes with the other as he whimpered, "Mommy... I had night mirror."

Myra rushed over to him and scooped him up into her arms. She sat with him on the lush red chaise and then rocked him, while rhythmically tapping his shoulder. Soothed, the little boy stopped crying. The image of the older version of her son flashed through her mind.

"What's the date?" Myra asked as nonchalantly as she could.

Archie pointed to the elegant Art Nouveau gilt-bronze and mahogany clock on the fireplace mantle, "It's still Sunday…April 14th.'

"Nineteen Twelve?"

"Well of course nineteen twelve. How long did you think you slept?"

Myra studied the clock herself. Quarter-to-twelve. In the *future*, she recalled reading in one of the books that the *Titanic* struck the iceberg at Eleven-Forty. *That was five minutes ago.* She looked at her little boy in her arms. *Could this mean it never happened?* It was all a horrible nightmare. An uncharacteristically detailed nightmare, but a nightmare nevertheless.

Yet, this was also the week that Otto Slade would be executed. For an insane instant she thought of tearing open the Teddy Bear. If she found the brooch, there was still time to send a letter to Callum's grandfather, Detective Toughill, who was still a police... then she suppressed a laugh. *Are you listening to yourself?* She sounded like she had taken complete leave of her senses. She was still reacting to her horrendous nightmare.

The truth was: the *Titanic* did not strike an iceberg. It was still unsinkable. She paused as she looked at her husband, then at Miss Langlea. They were not killers. Her tea was not poisoned. And after the tea calmed her nerves the terrible and bizarre dream would fade away like a stain of breath on the window.

Myra glanced down and saw her little boy using her pencil to draw on the inside cover of her book, "No, Eddie. You don't draw in books."

Myra kindly took the book away from him and looked at his sketch of wavy lines and an oddly shaped rectangle. *Not bad for a two year old.* She looked down at Eddie, "This is nice, though. Is this a boat on the waves?"

Little Eddie smiled. She adored his smile. She closed the book and looked at the cover, *Futility.* The story was set in the month of April, aboard an enormous ocean liner named *Titan.* In the story, the ship is referred to as 'unsinkable'. The story goes on to tell how the ship was traveling too quickly, struck an iceberg in the north Atlantic and sank. More than half the passengers perished due to the lack of lifeboats.

Myra now recalled how she couldn't finish reading it. Though it had been printed fourteen years earlier, it was far too unsettling, given that she was traveling on a ship with a similar name. Some other names were also striking too familiar a chord with Myra. It was as if this book was a foretelling of the fate of the *Titanic.* She had put the book down with her room key and retired for the evening.

It was little wonder that in her sleep her imagination would run wild, creating her own prognostication of the future. And what a future it was! Not only did the *Titanic* sink but New York had become a towering, cold-hearted city. Two world wars, high-speeding automobiles with phones, aircrafts and worst of all: a future where her husband had murdered his mother, framed an innocent man, poisoned her tea and left her to die as he fled with their son and a mistress to become an industrial tyrant – ridiculous!

Miss Langlea re-entered the room, pushing the teacart with a pot and two cups already poured. Myra set Eddie down gently on the chaise chair and was about to reach for the closest teacup when Archibald studied his pocket watch and compared the time to the clock.

"I daresay that one of these timepieces is wrong," said Archie.

Myra's hand pulled away from the teacup as she felt warmth drain from her veins, "Wrong? In what way?"

"One of them is five minutes off."

In that instant, there was a sudden jolt beneath their feet along with a dull thud that echoed in the night. Mr. Fuffy fell from the chair and rolled under the chaise. The tea set on the cart rattled violently.

As everyone else was distracted by the large specter of the massive iceberg scraping by the starboard side of the *Titanic* past their porthole window, Myra simply stared at the two teacups.

• • • _ _ _ • • •

HISTORICAL NOTES

RMS *Titanic*

The characters of Myra and Edward are fictitious and not directly based on any *Titanic* survivors. Their names, however, were inspired by truth.

There was a Mary (or May) Sloan (or Sloane), aboard the RMS *Titanic*, who is credited with saving many lives due to the fact that she knocked on many doors, waking up a number of passengers and informing them that *Titanic* had collided with an iceberg. Many witnesses state that she pulled life jackets out of cargo bins and helped people board lifeboats. By all accounts, Mary/May Sloan(e) was the last person to board the last lifeboat before the ship sank into the ocean. What happened to her after the survivors arrived in New York in 1912 remains a mystery.

There were no real Hoffmans aboard the RMS *Titanic*, but the name was used as an alias by Mr. Michel Navartil, from France, who had kidnapped his two sons from his estranged wife. As the ship was sinking, only women and children were allowed to get onto the lifeboats, so the two boys survived but Michel Navartil aka 'Mr. Louis Hoffman' did not. The children were later reunited with their mother.

There actually was an Alice Cleaver on *Titanic* who served as a nanny to the Allison family. Due to an unfortunate miscommunication she had taken the boy, Trevor, up to the lifeboats to safety and assumed that Mr. Allison would follow with his wife and daughter. They perished looking for Trevor. There have been many non-fiction historic books and even a TV mini-series that stated that this Alice Cleaver was the same Alice Cleaver who murdered her infant son in 1909, but this information isn't correct. Callum's discovery that they are two separate people is historically accurate: Alice Mary Cleaver was in jail for murdering her son when Alice Catherine Cleaver was escaping *Titanic*.

In 1940, a woman called Loraine Kramer claimed to be Loraine Allison, the little girl from first class who perished on *Titanic*. The wild story described in this novel is based on her actual tale, including a "Mrs. Gray" as did Alice Mary Cleaver in 1909. After it was proven she was not the real Loraine Allison, Kramer disappeared.

Other details of *Titanic* such as the descriptions of the contract ticket, the stateroom, the dining area, the music and the flowers are as accurate as possible. (The menu is faithful but the change of meal is my fabrication.) Even the fact that the RMS *Titanic* was insured after it sank is true. (*Risky Business, An Insider's Account of the Disaster at Lloyd's of London*, by Elizabeth Luessenhop and Martin Mayer.)

Futility is a short novel written by Morgan Robertson. Its first edition with the cover illustration of a ship sinking next to an iceberg was first published in 1898 - fourteen years *before* the *Titanic* set sail. (A photo of the first edition and other details can be found on DepthOfDeception.com.) Our Edward points out several eerie similarities between *Futility*'s *Titan* and the real *Titanic*, all of which are authentic.

One of the characters in the novel, *Futility*, is a little girl named Myra.

Unsolved Glasgow Murder

The murder of Agatha Gilcrest is based on the true life case of Marion Gilchrist, who was brutally murdered in 1909. The only thing missing from her home was one piece of jewelry from her extensive collection. A man by the name of Oscar Slater was arrested, and despite having flimsy evidence against him, he was sentenced to hang. Lord Pentland, the Secretary for Scotland, received an anonymous letter from Marion Gilchrist's 'relative' who wrote: "I am so frightened you are going to hang Oscar Slater - He never committed the murder."

Oscar Slater was given a stay of execution from the King, but with a condition that he had to remain in prison for the rest of his life.

The author of Sherlock Holmes, Sir Arthur Conan Doyle eventually took up the cause and was able to prove Oscar Slater's innocence. After spending almost twenty years in prison, Oscar Slater was freed and was awarded six thousand pounds for wrongful conviction.

An early draft of *Depth of Deception* had incorporated Doyle's defense of Otto Slade, but the feedback was unanimous: it was too far-fetched to believe that the author and creator of Sherlock Holmes would come to the legal aid of an innocent man. After all, I was already asking my readers to believe so much.

For more information on the actual historic case, I recommend a wonderfully researched book: *Oscar Slater: The Immortal Case of Sir Arthur Conan Doyle* by Thomas Toughill. (A link to buy this book is available on my website.) The details of the web of conspiracy and cover-up are far more tangled with family and political connections than in my novel. Sometimes fact is stranger than fiction.

Thomas Toughill's book was dedicated to John Trench, the original investigating officer who tried to prove Oscar Slater's innocence; as well as to the 'anonymous lady' who sent the letter. Trench was dishonourably discharged from the Glasgow Police Force for doing what was right. Due to Thomas Toughill's research, Chief Constable John Orr of the Strathclyde Police paid tribute to the late Detective John Trench in 1999 by unveiling a small memorial plaque dedicated to Trench's integrity.

Locations

The descriptions of real locations such as Times Square, Straus Park, St. Georges Glasgow Station, the Mitchell Library (Glasgow), West Register House (Edinburgh), Cobh Cove (Ireland), etc., are accurately described as they were in 1982.

The offices of the Strathclyde Police, Lloyd`s of London and Interpol are, in this novel, in their actual 1982 locations. All three have moved since then.

For residential areas in Glasgow (ie. where Agatha was murdered or Dolanna's home) I used Victorian-era street names in order to respect the privacy of anyone who happens to live there now. Likewise, there is no Church of St. George & St. Michael in Scotland.

There has not been an HMS *McKinley* in the British navy since WWII. It had been reported destroyed by the Japanese, but its fate has remained a mystery.

The base used by the British Ministry of Defence now known as HMNB Clyde used to be the HMS *Neptune* but was expanded in 1982.

'Camp X' was a secret spy training facility in Ontario, Canada operated by American and British Intelligence and the Royal Canadian Mounted Police during World War II. The Canadian Government was unaware of its existence. (As an author, I found 'Camp X' particularly fascinating, and I do believe that Edward's adventure there will be expanded in a future novel.)

Other Details

In 1982, car phones were rare, very expensive and had to remain in the car. Computers were not common nor were they very powerful so electric typewriters were still widely used. Pay phones were everywhere and fax machines were the latest communications gadgets. Hospitals were using 3-

lead ECGs (electrocardiograms) and bellows-style ventilators. DNA was still a new and unproven science - it would be another five years before it was introduced as legal evidence.

Events described in this book, such as shows on Broadway, popular films, the Great Blizzard of April 1982, the Argentine invasion of the Falkland Islands, and Queen Elizabeth traveling to New York on her way to Canada to sign their Constitution, are historically accurate right down to the dates mentioned in the novel. Although there was no *Titan* or *Titanic II* in existence, there were plans for a *Titanic 2* to be built in South Africa, but it was going to cost $500,000,000 and the plans were postponed indefinitely.

In 1982, Dr. Robert Ballard received funding from the US Navy to find the wreck of the *Titanic* so long as he found two sunken submarines first. He did so, and *Titanic*'s awesome prow was seen for the first time in nearly 75 years on September 1, 1985.

There are more historical details and reference photos on the 'Bonus Features' page on the official website for *Depth of Deception*. You will be asked for a password. If you have read the novel, you will know the password when prompted.

http://www.DepthOfDeception.com

Preview

Alexander Galant's next historical thriller novel:
BLOODY MARY KELLY
To be published in 2013

PROLOGUE

Egypt - In the year 1323 BCE

"The Blade of Anubis will get the heart!"

The words growled and echoed through the dark, empty high ceilings of the palace of *Labushhkamaukkn* near Giza, Egypt. Horemheb, the young commander of the military and advisor to the Pharaoh, immediately recognized the voice and prayed to Ra, the Sun God, that he was wrong.

All the servants had been dismissed for the night but Horemheb continued his patrol of the royal grounds. Four other women had been found brutally murdered over the last four moons. It was his charge to keep the palace safe, especially since the Pharaoh's new queen could be a target. Horemheb drew his sword and crept ever so quietly, pressing himself around the wide column, avoiding the sharp precious stones embedded into the painted relief. He froze at the sight he beheld. In the flickering light from the torches that illuminated the hall, a woman lay dead. A stream of her blood cascaded down the marble steps that led to an altar for the god Anubis. Horemheb immediately recognized the victim, Sheriti, one of the ladies who tended the baths. Sheriti's killer stood above her, still holding her beating heart in one hand and the murder weapon in the other.

"Hold!" Horemheb commanded. The killer turned his face toward him. Horemheb's heart sank as he recognized the familiar angular features, confirming his worst fears. Suddenly Horemheb's sword became too heavy to hold, but it no longer mattered. He could not use it here. Certainly not against his own king. "Your Highness, how could you?"

"I'm dying," wheezed the deformed young Pharaoh, "This is the only way to preserve my life... allow me to reign... forever."

Horemheb looked at the weapon in the King's hand and immediately recognized the jagged, twisted crescent of gold and the head of the Jackal bedecking the hilt: The Blade of Anubis, from a forbidden dark sect of the God of the Underworld. On a cycle of the blood moon, the ritual calls for the extraction of certain internal organs from five different impure women. These organs are placed into *five* special canopic jars. Usually there are only four of these ritual jars to hold the organs of royalty for mummification, but these ones are different. Beautiful but corrupt, with one more than usual: with the snake head of Aapep, for storing the heart. In normal mummification, the heart is not preserved. It is set aside for the god Anubis to weigh against the feather of Ma'at to determine the fate of the soul in *Duat*, the Afterworld. Keeping the heart in a jar was a desecration of their beliefs and customs. A Pharaoh of Egypt should know better than to take the heart.

"You murdered all those women?" cried Horemheb.

"They gave their lives to save their King," smirked Pharaoh, his tar-dark eyes full of venom. "Just as you swore to sacrifice your life for me in battle."

"I am willing to lay down my life for the good of Egypt. But these women were innocents..."

"No! They were all impure and beyond redemption... just as I was instructed."

Horemheb cursed the foreign Magi that had corrupted the Pharaoh's mind with his wild tales of the forbidden occult. "You cannot believe that. There is no certainty that there is any truth to the Blade of Anubis."

"But what if there is?" rebuked Pharaoh. "What if my deformity will heal with tomorrow's sunrise? What if my bones finally harden? I am willing to sacrifice five good-for-nothing women to rule with strength. Is that not good for Egypt?"

"Do you really expect this sacrilege to give you everlasting life?"

"It is my only chance to preserve my lineage. I cannot sire children, so I shall rule forever."

"But what if it is not forever? Will you continue to kill women to save your own life?"

"If it must be," replied the Pharaoh as he placed the heart into the jar. It plopped to the bottom with a squelch. "It shall be done."

"I cannot allow this perversion to continue," Horemheb said as he finally raised his sword. "Give me those vile vessels."

"Are you really so high of morals? Or is it because my immortality would cost you the throne?"

"What? No!" Hormenheb desperately tried to reason with him. "By Ra, I swear I am trying to protect you from the wrath of the gods. Now give me the jar."

Horemheb briskly stepped forward and grasped the white snake-headed jar. The frail Pharaoh refused to surrender his prize but his grip was no match for Horemheb's strength. Horemheb nearly pulled the young king fully off the ground, but the Pharaoh's slim fingers lost their hold. The young Pharaoh cried, "You have no right! I command you to give it back or die!"

Horemheb looked upon his king with pity. He had no words left to say. He quietly turned to gather the other four canopic jars sitting upon the marble slab that held the stone statue of Anubis, with the body of a man and the head of a jackal.

"NO!" the Pharaoh screamed as he limped toward him. He then raised the Blade of Anubis to strike. Seeing the advancing shadow from behind him, Horemheb spun around and deflected the downward strike with his sword. Never having experienced battle, and hindered by a club foot and delicate back, the force of impact caused the Pharaoh to lose his balance. The young Pharaoh teetered as he tried to regain his footing but he slipped on his victim's blood on the top of the marble steps.

Horemheb dropped his sword as he desperately reached out to grab the Pharaoh's arm. It was as if Horemheb's feet were stuck in quicksand and time slowed against him. He watched in horror as the Pharaoh struck the back of his head on the sharp marble corner of the base of the pillar flanking one side of the steps.

Horemheb finally reached the Pharaoh but it was too late. The king was dead. He wept as he knelt over the lifeless body of the young Pharaoh in his arms, horrified and uncertain of what to do next.

"What have you done, Horemheb?" asked a voice. Horemheb looked up and saw only the frowning statue of Anubis holding the altar. *Is it possible that it had spoken?*

Suddenly a dark figure appeared from behind the statue. Horemheb recognized the feeble, withered features of Ay, the Pharaoh's vizier and Maya, Overseer of the Royal Treasury. *How long had the old man been lurking in the shadows?*

"It was an accident," stammered Horemheb, looking down at his dead king.

"Fear not," interrupted Ay. "I know your loyalty and I do believe you."

Horemheb sighed with relief. At least he had an ally.

"But," Ay continued, "There are others in the court who will not believe you and will call for your head."

"But you can tell them about the Blade of Anubis."

"It matters not," cackled Ay. "A scandal will always overshadow the truth."

"What scandal?"

"Were you not made the Pharaoh's *rpat*, his successor to the throne, even though he had recently taken a new young wife?"

"The king's illness prevented him from siring an heir," rebutted Horemheb.

"But since the king did not want to seem less than a man, that's not common knowledge." Ay argued. He gestured to the corpse of the king, and sneered. "How does it look that shortly after your appointment, the King is found dead at his successor's feet? The people will only see a young commander and advisor suddenly thirsting for power and killing his own king to seize the throne of Egypt."

Horemheb stared at him. The truth may be bursting through every thread of his being, but he knew that Ay was right. Perception would overshadow the truth. It did not look good for him. "What would you advise me to do?"

"Appoint me to the throne."

"What?"

"I'm an old man," replied Ay. "No one would suspect that I would be physically capable of murder. And by you appointing me as the new Pharaoh, it would take the motive away from you, and thus taking away all suspicion from you."

Horemheb knew Ay was stacking the odds in his favour, but it seemed like the best plan. Besides, Horemheb told himself, Ay was well over 70 years of age and would likely not sit on the throne for very long. Ay also had no heir, save for a boy who was also the son of a *courtesan*, a prostitute, and thus had no claim to the throne of Egypt. Horemheb could bide his time and regain the throne of Egypt once this old man died. For the good of Egypt, he relented.

Horemheb nodded, "So shall it be."

Ay's wrinkled lips cracked into a smile. "You are a good man. Now get rid of that abhorrent Blade of Anubis and destroy all those reviling reliquary jars. We will have all reference to them stricken from the temple. No one must ever know their dark, perverse secret. Now, if you will excuse me, I will attend to the funeral preparations of the boy king."

Horemheb looked solemnly down at the boy king's dead body, "Safe travels to the Afterworld, King Tutankhamun."

He watched as Ay hobbled out of the room. Gathering his strength, Horemheb took the knife out of the king's dead hand and looked at it. It was heavier than he expected. The jackal head was carved from black onyx, the eyes were rubies. Upon the gold blade was the forbidden mark of death. Their language did not allow for the symbol of death as they did not believe in death but rather *Duat*, a world in the afterlife. This blade had to be destroyed.

Deciding to have it melted in the ironmonger's fires, he placed it on the altar next to the other four traditional canopic jars, then looked back for the unholy fifth.

He walked over and scooped up the fallen jar, taking a moment to sneer at the carved serpent head of Aapep that sat upon it. A marking appeared upon the jar and then seemed to vanish. *What was that?* Horemheb wondered. He held it up to the torch light. From within the alabaster porcelain, the markings detailing the ritual appeared. As soon as he pulled the jar away from the light, the markings were imperceptible. He held it up again but this time not only did the writing appear but the sound of the sloshing heart from within the jar reminded him of the grim matter at hand.

He set the jar upon the altar, then turned and looked down at the body of his king. Horemheb had seen how years of deformity and growing illness had crippled the Pharaoh's spirit. He had seen the agony in the boy's eyes. This ritual must have been an act of desperation to end that pain. But future generations of Egypt would not be aware of that torment. History would not be kind. Horemheb couldn't stand the thought that the boy king would be remembered as some merciless killer. Then he turned to the body of the murdered woman. He would have to dispose of her body as well.

He paused. He thought he heard something.

"Ay?" he called out. He strained to listen. There was nothing. He decided that fear was causing him to hear things. He pulled the woven drapes down from the wall, brought them to the woman's corpse and carefully began the unpleasant task. Horemheb paused again and listened. He felt like he was being watched. There was still nothing. Where was Ay? It was likely that Ay was delivering the news to the late Pharaoh's young wife. As the new King, Ay would also inherit the young widow as his wife as well. He chuckled. She was lovely, and Ay was...

Horemheb stopped, listened. He was certain he heard some heavy breathing. He looked at the dead bodies. There was no one else. Likely the echo of his own breathing in the empty hall. He hoped Ay would return soon with the High Priest.

He needed to dispose of the Blade and jars next. He strolled to the altar and gasped. He clearly remembered having set the jars and the knife on the marble slab. They were gone. He looked about desperately. The two corpses lay covered on the floor. There was no one else to be seen. Now he was certain that someone else had been there. Someone else who had watched and waited, then left nothing but— *what was that in the flickering torch light?* Something small and flat sitting on the altar. A betting playing card made of papyrus. He turned it over – the Jackal of Swords.

He silently prayed to Ra that the dark magic within the Blade of Anubis was only a myth. *No one who could willingly kill in cold blood should have the power of immortality.*

JULY 10, 2010 - NEW YORK

A blanket of darkness shrouded Central Park. The general public didn't venture into the enormous urban wooded area in the center of Manhattan after the sun went down. Even fewer dared during a new moon, when the shadow of the Earth smothers its light. Tonight, leaves obstructed some of the strategically placed streetlamps, making the park far less inviting. Officer Holz hoped this was enough to keep trouble away. He wanted a quiet night before the expected stress of tomorrow, when he anticipated the freaks would flock to Central Park to celebrate the total solar eclipse. These sorts of things attracted not only the science geeks but also the weirdos, most of whom will be chanting about the end of the world, no doubt. *It happens every time and the world is still here.* He took comfort in knowing that he wouldn't be around for the aftermath. Tomorrow after his shift was over, he'd be off to the Adirondacks with his brother for a whole week of fishing.

Officer Holz and his partner had split up to patrol the wooded areas surrounding the park's baseball diamonds. Nothing but discarded newspapers and wrappers meandered through the grounds. On the southern end, close to East Drive, he spotted an LED light beam cutting through the trees. *So much for a quiet night.* Following the beacon, Holz could hear an odd scraping, scratching sound that grew louder as he drew nearer. From the protection of the surrounding evergreen trees he could see the clearing where the solitary Egyptian obelisk known as the 'Cleopatra Needle' stood erect before him. On the north side of the obelisk, beneath the plaque, a dark solitary figure was using tools to chisel away at the top 'step' of the white base of the monument. Careful not to cast a shadow, Holz leaned from the gnarled, twisted trees to see that only one of the lampposts positioned around the small octagonal courtyard was actually working. Was it fortuitous for him or for his suspect? Holz crept closer and crouched down at the edge of the treeline to watch quietly as the dark figure pried up some more bricks. From here, Holz could see that the access plate of the nearby lamppost was open and that the wires were pulled out. The darkness was deliberate.

When the dark figure jabbed the metal point of his tool into the hole, there was an odd thud, like metal hitting bone. Now that the suspect was no longer making any noise, Holz dared not move, even though Holz's leg started to shake from being cramped in one position, and his knee was digging into a manhole cover at the edge of the step. He held his breath as the dark figure withdrew a wooden box from the hole in the ground. Holz automatically placed his hand on his gun handle. The dark figure opened the box and held up a white porcelain jar with the head of a snake on it. Holz relaxed his hand. This was most likely stolen property. He guessed it might even be from the King Tut Exhibit on 44th Street. It was time to take this suspect in for questioning. The dark figure began to uncap the white jar. Holz forced himself to ignore the surge of pins and needles through his lower extremities as he rose, then paused at the sight before him. The dark figure now shone his LED beam into the jar, causing the porcelain to become translucent, revealing hieroglyphic symbols that seemed to magically appear from within. The figure turned the jar to inspect it closer, then in a low baritone voice translated aloud, 'The Blade of Anubis will get the heart."

What the hell did that mean? Holz was certain this guy was a nut-job. He wasn't going to wait any longer. Holz drew his gun as he called out, "Police! Keep your hands where I can see them!"

"This does not concern you. Please leave," said the male voice with an odd accent.

"You're under arrest!"

"On what charge?"

"Let's start with vandalism! Cleopatra's Needle is New York City property, and I'm sure that jar-thing was stolen from somewhere. I'm sure we can determine that once we examine it."

"You are gravely mistaken. This obelisk was carved a thousand years before Cleopatra was born and was actually stolen from the city of Heliopolis long ago. It and its twin stood in the desert, unmarred, for 3000 years. Taken from Alexandria, and after only a mere century of being here, exposed to your pollution and acid rain, the hieroglyphics have been eroded away. As for the 'canopic jar'… it belongs to me. So please leave."

Holz moved forward menacingly, "We'll see about…"

The dark figure casually tossed a small piece of paper into the air. Holz watched as it danced and fluttered in the breeze. It landed on the lock-bricks at his feet. He instantly recognized the familiar design of the face card: the Jack of Spades.

"What the…?" His words were interrupted by a sharp pain in his torso. Holz looked down to see a knife sticking out of his chest. *The Jack of Spades had been a distraction.* His hands moved instinctively to grab the knife, dropping his gun, which clanged on the pavement. Holz knew that pulling the knife out would cause the blood to flow faster. As his fingers resisted the urge to pull, Holz became suddenly aware that the knife handle had some pointy-eared dog on it.

"Sorry, Mate," whispered the dark figure. "I did not want to kill you. I even asked you to leave rather politely, but you left me no choice. There is a task I must perform, and no-one must bear witness to the act."

Holz reached down and grabbed his two-way radio. He was about to shout into it when the dark figure yanked the knife from his chest, and sliced his throat with one fluid motion. The radio clattered next to the gun as Holz tried futilely to hold back the flow of blood. He could hear his heartbeat pounding, each beat counting down the last seconds of his life. He could feel the life drain from his body. Holz stumbled forward. He needed to know who had ripped his life away from him. He needed to see the face of his killer. With the last of his strength, he grabbed the figure and spun him around. If Holz could have uttered a sound, he would have screamed. The face was not what he expected to see.

10 JULY, 1888 - LONDON

The streets were dark. There was no moon in the sky. The flicking flames from the nearby gas lamps did little to illuminate the cobblestone street blanketed by fog.

Inspector Fredrick George Abberline squinted tiredly as he stepped out of No. 4 Whitehall Place, the Central Office of Scotland Yard. It was one of many small buildings on Whitehall Place that made up the Metropolitan Police. The force had grown so large that they had to take over the neighbouring buildings, including the stable. Even then, they were practically bursting at the seams. *The new Scotland Yard building isn't being built swiftly enough,* Abberline sighed as he placed his bowler hat on his head. After spending his days behind a desk, his trousers were tighter— a walk to the Underground Station would do him good. He could not see the other end of the street but he could hear a cacophony of several horse-drawn carriages meandering through the adjoining roads.

The sudden ringing from Big Ben, just a few blocks south, echoed loudly through the night. Abberline pulled his pocket watch from his waistcoat and compared it to the chimes. *Hmmm. A little slow.* He adjusted the time and wound it all the way as he quickened his pace along the Victoria Embankment. He had been invited out for a pint at the Red Lion pub, but decided against it as it was late and he hoped to see his wife, Emma, before she retired to bed.

Foolishly he'd thought that being promoted to Inspector First Class and the transfer to the Central Office would end the long working hours into the night, but alas the criminals of London did not keep banker's hours. Still it was a welcome change from the fourteen years of patrolling the streets of 'H Division', the armpit of civilization known as London's East End. Overcrowded with immigrants trying to eke out a living with few jobs available and little room to breathe it was a breeding ground for crime and every form of depravity. He would die a happy man if he never had to set foot in 'H Division' ever again.

Abberline frowned as he huffed along the Victoria Embankment towards the Waterloo Bridge. He had hoped that the newly installed carbon arc lamps, part of a test of new electric lights employing alternating currents, would provide better illumination. Alas, some had already burned out and the others could not penetrate the thick fog.

Still, the soothing murmur of the Thames River reminded Abberline of the Stour River in his hometown of Blandford Forum, Dorset. He longed for the simpler days of fishing with his brother and two sisters.

Abberline's stroll through his memory was interrupted by a dark figure darting behind the Cleopatra Needle which stood at the river's edge on his right. Abberline felt concern, evidenced by his usual habit of running the fingers of his right hand along his moustache to where it joined his mutton-chops. His sense of duty compelled him to investigate. The giant stone obelisk was dangerously close to the water's edge. In this dense fog it could spell disaster. Abberline moved carefully but could see no one.

"'Allo?" he called out into the night. "I say, is there anyone there?"

Nothing. Were the shadows playing tricks with his eyes? He looked at the towering stone monument. He remembered attending the ceremony when it was presented to London as a gift from Egypt exactly 10 years ago. It was one of two obelisks; the other was given to the United States and was erected somewhere in New York City. This needle was flanked by two large Sphinxes that were carved here in London but it marked the start of England's fascination with Ancient Egypt. Over the years, lost treasures of Egypt were put on display in the British Museums. Its influence has begun to be seen in fashion, decor and also in architecture. Even the park benches nearby were adorned with an Egyptian motif, not that it could be seen on this foggy night.

Abberline paused. He called out again, "'Allo?"

No response. The fog was so dense that someone could very well be standing an arm's length in front of him and he would not be able to see them. Fine. If they wanted to play games, he was not about to join in. *Let them fall in the Thames for all I care,* thought Abberline.

He turned to resume his journey to the Waterloo Bridge when his foot hit something causing him to trip and fall outright. Annoyed, his hand felt back for the protrusion. It was a loose stone. He reached into his inside pocket and pulled out a matchbox. Taking out a wooden matchstick, he quickly dragged it on the cobblestone. A spark of flame shed some light on the situation. The loose stone was sitting atop another stone. Abberline held the match to the hole where the stone belonged. The hole gaped beneath the step next to the obelisk. Something had been buried there. Whoever that dark figure was, they must have been responsible. Something suddenly fluttered by his foot, but the flame of the match was burning close to his fingertips. He would have to extinguish it before examining it further. Just before shaking out the flame, his right foot stomped on the fluttering object and held it to the ground.

Darkness again. His eyes needed to adjust from the flaming light to the foggy darkness. Abberline was about to light another match when he heard the unmistakable sound of another breath. Someone else *was* there. If the years of policing the streets taught him anything, it was that unnecessary risks did not serve him well. Better to retreat and return in the morning. Even if the fog was thick, he was taking no chances. He made a mental note of everything as he crouched down as if to tie his shoe laces, then he set his hand on the object beneath his right foot. *A playing card?* Using the magician's technique of palming, he hid the card in his hand as he stood up. He then casually placed both hands in his pockets as he resumed walking along the Victoria Embankment. He could feel the hairs on the back of his neck standing at attention as he wondered if he was being watched. Or followed.

He strained to listen for that sound of breathing. The only thing he could hear was the approach of a horse and carriage. He turned to see the unmistakable form of a Hansom Cab. Abberline raised his hand to signal the driver. The driver pulled on the reins and brought the horse to a stop.

"Where to, Guv'nor?" asked the driver from atop the carriage.

"41 Mayflower Road, off Clapham," replied Abberline as he climbed in. Only after the carriage was well on its way, did Abberline risk taking the card out of his pocket. He recognized the pattern on the back as a common Hoyle deck. It may have already been there and had nothing to do with the hole that was dug beneath the Obelisk but as a detective he never ignored any detail. He turned the card over – the Jack of Spades.

Bloody Mary Kelly to be released in 2013.

Until then, please visit www.AlexanderGalant.com

ABOUT THE AUTHOR

Alexander Galant is a Canadian, residing in Toronto. He was the historical researcher for the novel *Dracula The Un-Dead*, which was on the *New York Times Bestsellers List* in October 2009. He adapted the novel into a dramatic stage reading for the Toronto book launch, which brought out the highest turnout for any event on the ...*Un-Dead* book tour.

Alexander has also written and directed several short films, including *The Missing Piece*, winner of the Silver Remi Award for Suspense Thriller at WorldFest Houston. His latest short, *Star Wars: Blasted Behavior*, is far more lighthearted, and was a finalist in the Atom/LucasFilm Star Wars Fan Movie Challenge in 2009 (George Lucas was one of the judges). It continues to make the festival circuit.

He is married and has two children.

www.ingramcontent.com/pod-product-compliance
Lightning Source LLC
Chambersburg PA
CBHW050717180626
46814CB00002B/480